CHOOSE YO

Fain looked at Dutch G... him was when his father had run the Dutchman... ranch.

"Don't want any trouble with you, Gruder. Never done anything to you, so leave me alone."

The brawny man threw back his head and laughed. There was no way Fain could avoid trouble . . .

Fain stared down at the brutally beaten man at his feet.

Someone from the crowd said, "Cowboy, you better start wearing a gun. Gruder ain't gonna forget this, an' if he's smart, which he ain't, he ain't never gonna fistfight you agin."

His face feeling like old dried leather, Fain looked at the man who'd given him the advice. The words had fallen between them like shards of broken glass, and Fain shook his head. "Tell 'im, when he wakes up, I'll be back through here in two or three days. If he wants to push his luck, I'll take 'im on with fists, guns, or knives—his choice."

Fain headed for the livery to collect his horses. He had miles to ride.

Titles by Jack Ballas

LAND GRAB
HANGING VALLEY
WEST OF THE RIVER
TRAIL BROTHERS
THE RUGGED TRAIL
GRANGER'S CLAIM
BANDIDO CABALLERO
THE HARD LAND
IRON HORSE WARRIOR
MONTANA BREED
MAVERICK GUNS
DURANGO GUNFIGHT
TOMAHAWK CANYON
ANGEL FIRE
POWDER RIVER
GUN BOSS
APACHE BLANCO

LAND GRAB

JACK BALLAS

BERKLEY BOOKS, NEW YORK

LAND GRAB

A Berkley Book / published by arrangement with the author

PRINTING HISTORY
Berkley edition / July 2003

ISBN: 0-425-19113-3

BERKLEY®
Berkley Books are published by The Berkley Publishing Group, a division of Penguin Group (USA) Inc., 375 Hudson Street, New York, New York 10014.
BERKLEY and the "B" design are trademarks belonging to Penguin Group (USA) Inc.

PRINTED IN THE UNITED STATES OF AMERICA

10 9 8 7 6 5 4 3 2

1

CORD FAIN LOOKED across the breakfast fire at the trail boss, Colonel Bane Taggart. Fain was surrounded by the trail crew. They would back Taggart. What Fain was about to say could get him killed . . . and he wore no gun.

"Taggart, I won't be a part of takin' land from those who fought Kiowa, Comanche, an' Apache; bled and sweat to make homes, ranches, an' raise families on that land. We been on the trail for over two months now. I want my pay."

Taggart stared at him a long moment. "You hired on to help drive these cattle to Montana. You ain't gettin' your pay till we get wherever we're goin'." As soon as he said the last word, he drew his six-shooter. "Now finish eatin' an' saddle up. We got work to do."

"If I thought you'd actually take these cattle to Montana, I'd stay; but you're not, so I won't."

Taggart lowered his massive head like an old bull buffalo ready to charge. "You will, or I'll kill you."

The soft sound of a horse's hooves in the dust outside the ring of firelight sounded about the same time a big Negro standing to the back of the crew drew his side gun. "Taggart, you can add my say to what Mistuh Fain done told you." His eyes swept the backs of the men surrounding the trail boss. "Reckon what I'm tellin' you is I want my pay too, an' you men figurin' to add yo guns to Taggart's bettuh think agin. I can drop six o' you 'fore you can git lead in me."

The hoofbeats of the approaching horse closed in. Into the firelight a tall, handsome man rode, then stepped from the saddle. "Well, looks like I rode into some sort of family fight." Without warning, his hand blurred to his side and he had his handgun pointed at the men backing Taggart. "Add my six shots to those the big Negro promised you."

The rider looked at Fain, "Howdy, Cord, you got a little trouble here?"

"Nothin' that you bein' here can't help. Howdy, Jack."

Blackjack Slade looked at each man there, then pinned the big Negro with his look. "Seems you were backin' my friend. Step over here where we can watch 'em all." His six-shooter waved carelessly toward the crew, but he had them all covered. "Gonna tell you folks right now, if you want to die right sudden, fifteen of my men are out there in the dark, an' every one of them has a long gun pointed at you."

Slade shifted his look to Fain. "You two men get your horses and bedrolls. Better take a packhorse too."

In only moments, Fain and the Negro led their horses to the side of Slade. "Let's get outta heah," said Slade. While he talked, the big black man swung into the saddle.

When out from the circle of firelight about seventy-five yards, Cord chuckled and looked across his shoulder at Slade. "Gotta tell you, Jack Slade, you're the lyin'est, gut-siest son of a gun I ever did see."

Slade laughed outright.

"What you all laughin' at?"

Fain looked at his newfound friend. "Matthew, meet Blackjack Slade. Slade, this here's Matthew Washington Black. Everybody calls him Wash." He again looked at Wash. "Now, gonna tell you what we're laughin' at." He chuckled again. "Wash, my friend Jack Slade here doesn't have even one man out here with a rifle. He just pulled one helluva bluff."

By now the sky's early light had strengthened such that Cord could see each of them plainly. Wash grinned. He shook his head. "Lordy, Mistuh Slade, you mighta got yo-self killed."

Slade nodded. "Mighta, but I didn't." He glanced at the big black man. "I threw both o' you in that pot too. C'mon, let's get on over to Cimarron. We'll eat breakfast and talk about how we're gonna collect your pay from that jackass."

Two hours later, they sat in Cimarron's only cafe. Eight of Slade's men sat at another table. A large plate of ham, eggs, biscuits, and gravy graced the table in front of each. While they'd been cooking, the smells from the kitchen had made Fain hungry enough he thought to eat his plate; he hadn't had ham and eggs in months. He frowned and looked at Slade. "What were you doin' out yonder alone that time of day?"

Slade shrugged. "My boys told me there was a large herd trailin' north an' I figured to see if I could buy fifteen or twenty head. We're tired of venison an' antelope over yonder in Red River an' Elizabeth Town." He raised his eyebrows. "When I got close enough I recognized you, an' it appeared you were in a heap o' trouble."

"I was, an' I sure as hell thank you." Fain grinned. "But if you figured to buy those cows, well, that sortta surprised me. Years past you'd of had your men just take 'em."

"Big herd, a lot o' drovers, I'd have lost some men. Didn't want to do that." Slade sliced a bite of ham, chewed a moment, then looked at Wash and Cord. "That brings me to how I figure to get your pay." He took another bite, frowned, then nodded. "I think it'll work an' if I work it right, we won't lose any men."

Cord scratched his head, then grinned. "Somehow I think I'm gonna hear a plan that tells me you haven't changed one whit."

Slade nodded. "Yeah, Cord, I'd say I've changed a little. I'm older, an' I believe I've softened some, but I still control my men with a tight rein." He shrugged. "I have to handle 'em that way; they're a wild an' mostly young bunch. I give 'em any slack an' they'd think they could run things as well as me."

Fain noticed Wash frown. "Wash, don't want you gettin' excited, but Blackjack Slade is boss over the Red River Gang, one of the wildest bunch of outlaws you can find west of the Mississippi." He shook his head. "Knowin' what I do about him, I've never heard of him takin' anything from the poor, or pushin' his will on those who couldn't defend themselves."

Wash pushed his hat to the back of his head. "Yes, suh, Mistuh Cord, I done heard 'bout Mistuh Slade evuh since I come to Texas aftuh the war." He shook his head. "What I was wonderin' 'bout wuz how you tie in with him. Wuz you a outlaw 'fore you went to cowboyin'?"

"Wash, I never figured that out for myself, but I'll tell you this. I'm not wanted by the law." He grinned. "I'll tell you the rest of the story some night while we sit by our supper fire."

"You mean we gonna be ridin' together when we leave here?"

Cord looked him in the eye, then nodded. "Yeah, Wash, reckon that's what I mean if you want it that way. You sided me when you could have gotten killed for doin' it." He gave a nod. "Yep, I reckon we're partners 'less you tell me different."

Wash showed all of his snow-white teeth. "I sho ain't gonna tell you no different." The smile disappeared, he frowned, and in a dead-serious voice said, "Mistuh Cord, I ain't nevuh had a partner befoe; always wanted one, but me bein' a nigra, an' pretty good with a gun, it jest seemed like most white folks shied 'way from me."

Slade cleared his throat, then chuckled. "All right, if y'all have that settled, let's talk 'bout how we gonna get you boys your pay." He looked at Fain. "How many riders has Taggart got ridin' with him?"

Fain studied the bottom of his empty cup a few moments, then nodded. "Countin' the cook, the wranglers, an' drovers, I reckon since Wash an' me quit he's got 'bout twenty-eight men left."

Slade looked across the room. "Slim, come over here a minute."

A tall thin man unfolded himself from his chair, and shuffled to stand beside Blackjack. "What you need, Boss?"

Slade tilted his head to look at the man. "You reckon we got thirty-five, maybe forty men here in town?"

"Got more'n that if you need 'em."

The outlaw boss frowned, then nodded. "All right. Have at least thirty-five of 'em saddled, sober, an' ready to ride at three o'clock in the mornin' here in front of the hotel." He grinned. "Tell the cook I want him here an hour before that. I want our men fed before we leave."

"Where we goin'?"

"Tell you in the morning; now round up the men. Oh, an' tell 'em to put extra shells in their saddlebags; we might need 'em.

By quarter of four the next morning everyone had eaten, and sat their horses waiting for Slade to tell them what they were gathered for.

"Men, we've all known 'bout that herd, maybe three thousand head, comin' this way. Well, at first I figured to buy us a few head for those of us at Red River an' Elizabeth Town." Slade shifted in his saddle, apparently to see all of them better. "I've changed my mind; we're gonna take sixty head for us and twenty each for Fain an' his partner. Would take the whole damned herd 'cept we'd have trouble gettin' that many cows through the canyon. Ya'll know Fain, an' that big man sittin' there grinnin' is Wash, Fain's partner."

Blackjack nodded. "Yeah, we gonna take about forty head for the two of them, then I'm gonna pay 'em for those cows, so we'll have a hundred head to drive through Cimarron Canyon. Gonna pay these two men for their cut 'cause that trail boss out yonder wouldn't pay 'em for the couple o' months they spent on the drive this far. I'll tell y'all how we gonna do it when we get outta town a ways. Let's go."

None of the men talked on their way out; the only sound was the soft clopping of horses' hooves, and the only smell was fine dust. When Slade reined in, they gathered around. "Slim, you take three men out to the herd and take care of the night riders. Don't hurt 'em 'less you have to. Bring 'em in to the fire."

He turned his eyes on the large cluster of riders showing ghostly in the predawn light. "The rest of you shuck your rifles, rest them across the pommel, and ride slow, quiet as possible. Don't fire unless we're fired upon. I don't believe we'll have any trouble. This time of day Taggart's crew'll be groggy, not fully awake till we're right in the middle of 'em."

The alkali dust under the horses' feet gave off only a muffled, muted sound, sort of like a man patting an over-stuffed mattress; less than the birds or night animals made while stirring around.

When still about a mile from the cattle, Slade told Cord and Wash to stay out of the firelight, but to keep their rifles trained on Taggart's crew. "Don't want Taggart goin' to the law in Raton or Trinidad, an' gettin' your picture plastered on a wanted notice." He looked at Fain and grinned. "Don't want your old man gettin' mad at me after all the trouble he's gone to to keep you outta all this."

Cord saw that Wash wanted to ask questions but held back; then finally Wash looked at the rifle Fain held across his pommel. "Notice you don't wear no side gun, but you hold that rifle like you ain't no stranger to it."

Slade chuckled. "Wash, when you get to know Fain better, you're gonna find out he's no stranger to all sorts of trouble." He shook his head. "I'll not tell you more, but wait; he'll tell you the whole story himself."

The big black man shook his head. "Don't make me no

difference, Mistuh Slade. I done got me a partner. I figger
to side 'im no mattuh what."

Blackjack and his men were well within rifle range,
maybe a 150 yards from the cookfire, before the cook, who
was always up and stirring around before the crew, cocked
his head and peered toward the large group of riders. He
stood there, squinting into the darkness, apparently trying
to figure out what he was seeing. By then Slade and his riders were within fifty yards. Slade had picked up the aroma
of coffee brewing when still a quarter of a mile out.

"Don't do anything foolish, Cookie, an' you'll live to
see a few more mornin' fires."

The cook stepped toward the wagon, stopped, and
turned back to look at the large group of riders, his hands
held shoulder-high. "Ain't gonna do nothin', Mr. Slade.
Gonna stand right here till you tell me what you're after."

"Wake Taggart. Tell 'im to keep his hands clear of
weapons. Tell 'im we got thirty-one rifles pointed at him
an' them who're in their blankets. Tell 'im this time he can
see the rifles pointed at him."

The cook shook Taggart. "Time to get up, Boss. We got
company. Don't reach for no gun; they got us all covered."

Taggart crawled from his blankets, put on his hat, then
shook out his boots and pulled them on. Not until then did
he look at Slade. "What the hell you want this time?"

"Well, Taggart, figure we'll set here an' drink some o'
your coffee till it gets good sunup; then we gonna cut 'bout
a hundred head o' your cows out an' drive 'em off." He
nodded. "Course we gonna relieve y'all o' your weapons
just so's don't none o' you decide to do somethin' dumb
like tryin' to stop us."

Slade looked at the cook. "That Arbuckle ready to
drink?"

The cook nodded, then grinned. "Yes, sir. Y'all break
out yore cups an' I'll bring the kettle around an' pour y'all
some." He took a rag from beside the cookfire, wrapped it
around the hot handle, and picked up the pot. While pour-

ing Slade's coffee, he looked him in the eye. "You got any use for a stove-up old cook in yore outfit? Woulda rode out with Fain, but I done been throwed off'n my hoss onto my haid too many times; takes me a while to make up my mind."

The outlaw leader chuckled. "Yeah, what you got in mind?"

The cook grinned. "Wuz jest wonderin' what this bunch would do if they had to cook fer themselves. An' like Wash, an' Fain, I don't like takin nobody's land from 'em."

Slade looked at the old man's skinny form, and he'd noticed him limping badly when he made the rounds with the coffee kettle. His chuckle became a wide grin. "If you don't mind ridin' the owlhoot, reckon you got yourself a job. Course they's always a bunch hangin' around Red River; they get hungry too. You might not have to ride with me."

"Ridin' the backtrails ain't somethin' I never done before. Reckon you done took on a pretty danged good cook."

"What name you usin'?"

"Y'all can call me Cookie, or Crip." He grimaced. "Reckon I done got used to answerin' to most anything."

Slade drank the rest of his coffee and glanced at the red orb to the east. "Sun's 'bout full up. Reckon we better get busy." He turned to one of his men. "Randy, take a couple o' men an' gather all the handguns and rifles you can find."

"Boss, they got some extras in the back o' the chuck wagon. Better git them too." Cookie looked at Slade. "Y'all got a extra horse I can ride outta here?"

Slade nodded; almost said the old man could ride one of Fain's packhorses, then remembered he didn't want Cord tied in with this job. "We'll get you a horse."

While they gathered the weapons, Taggart stood by the fire, his face flushed a deep red; veins stood out on his forehead and neck; his fists, hanging at his side, clenched. "Slade, if I live a hundred years, I'm gonna spend all that time figgerin' out how to get you."

Slade's face hardened. "You try it an' you won't live much past the thought you give it." He neck-reined his horse to ride away, then pulled him back. "Gonna tell you somethin' else. You ever figure to buck Cord Fain, you better check your hole card. That boy would chew you up, spit you out, an' never know he'd had any trouble."

Taggart laughed; no mirth in the sound. "Why, hell, that milksop don't even wear a gun; an' I'd tear 'im to pieces with my hands."

Slade shot him a cold smile. "Either way, Taggart, he'd take you." He glanced at his men. "All right, get rid of the rest of your coffee. We got cows to gather." He looked over his shoulder at Taggart. "I'll leave your weapons at the hotel in Cimarron. You can have someone ride in an' get them later."

The herd, already on their feet, had begun to graze. It took only a few, maybe twenty minutes to cut out the 120 or so head Slade wanted. He'd upped what he wanted when Cookie switched sides. He chose prime stock, and headed them toward Cimarron.

Back in the hotel, with his men driving the small herd through Cimarron Canyon, Slade ordered Fain, Wash, Cookie, and himself a drink. He glanced at them. "We took enough steers outta that herd for me to pay you for twenty head each. Now I'm not gonna give you what you mighta got in Denver, or even in Trinidad. Figure twenty dollars a head is fair, so I'm payin' each one o' you four hundred dollars." He counted out the double eagles into three stacks.

Cord stared at his old friend. "Jack, that's more'n we woulda got paid for those two months on the trail."

Slade smiled. "Reckon you gonna need eatin' money when you leave here, an' this decrepit old cook's gonna need a little extra, so take it an' head out."

Cord stared at the pile of gold coins. He still had what he'd left home with, plus money he'd earned since; money paid him for riding shotgun on stages, keeping the peace in trail towns, riding as top hand for different outfits. Hell, he didn't need the money, but he grinned and raked his share from the table. "Reckon I can use this good as you, Jack." He knocked back the drink Slade had ordered, and stood. "Well, Wash, reckon we better get goin'."

Wash stood, *and so did Cookie.* The gimpy old man shuffled his feet a moment, looked at Slade, then at Fain. "You reckon if you let me ride with you it'd slow you down too much?"

Cord stared at the cook a moment. "What about the job Jack gave you?"

"Aw, hell, Fain, you know danged well Mr. Slade don't need me. He took me on 'cause I'm so beat up he figgered I wouldn't make it anywhere else." He nodded. "Course if you don't want me ridin' with you, I'll head back to El Paso, maybe hook up with a outfit round there."

He looked at Slade. "Mr. Slade, reckon I thank you for bein' nice to me, but you don't want to be saddled with me, an' them cold nights, ridin' an' lookin' over my shoulder to see if the posse is catchin' up, ain't nothin' I want to go through agin."

Slade knocked back his drink, cleared his throat, and his face sober, nodded. "Don't blame you, old-timer. You do whatever you an' Cord decide on."

A few hours later, skirting where he thought the herd would be, Fain led Wash and Cookie toward Trinidad. They rode into rain, hard thunderstorms at the top of Raton Pass. He and his two companions huddled under an overhang at the side of the trail until the lightning let up, then headed down the steep grade toward the town at the bottom of the pass.

He looked at his two new friends. "Y'all go on to the hotel, get a room for tonight. I'm gonna see the law here an' tell him what kind o' crew'll be stoppin' in his town. I figure they're still two, maybe three days from gettin' here."

They rode down the main street of Trinidad until Fain spotted the courthouse. Thinking the law might have an office there, he reined to the side. "See you at the hotel. Get me a room while you're at it."

Cookie grinned. "Reckon I'm gonna git dried out; then I'm goin' to the closest saloon an' git warmed up from the inside."

Cord nodded. "I'll look for you there if you aren't in your rooms." He neck-reined his horse to the hitch rack in front of the courthouse, stepped from the saddle, and went inside. He could have walked in blindfolded and known he was in a courthouse. The musty smell of old paper, cigar smoke, and dust would have told him where he stood. Two doors adjacent to each other told him he'd found what he looked for; one sign read "Sheriff," the other read "U.S. Marshal." He figured the marshal would have a wider jurisdiction. He went in.

A weather-beaten man, about thirty-five years of age, looked up from a sheaf of papers. "Yes, sir, can I do anything for you?"

"I'm Cord Fain, Marshal, recently a drover on a trail herd that'll be comin' to your town in the next three or four days. Just wanted to let you know what you an' this town might be in for."

The marshal flicked his thumb toward a chair. "Sit an' let's hear it."

Fain told him what Taggart had said only a couple of days before. "Marshal, that's why I quit, me an' two others who rode in here with me." He grinned. "Reckon the three of us are now ridin' the grub line." He shrugged. "Not anything I worry about. I'd bet my saddle all three of us has found himself in the same situation before."

The marshal—he'd introduced himself as Tom Worley—frowned, looked at the sheaf of papers on his desk, then pinned Cord with a look. "They's a whole string o' ranches along the east side of the mountains all the way up to Montana. Reckon you ain't gonna go hungry; might even get one of 'em to take you on full-time."

"Tell you what, Worley. I figure to find out which one o'

those ranches Taggart figures to take over; then I'm gonna stick to the ranch owner like a south Texas tick; gonna help 'im fight Taggart."

The marshal raked Fain's side with a glance. "Mr. Fain, I notice you don't wear a side gun. A man who figures to back a rancher in trouble's gonna need to be right salty." He hurried to add, "Don't mean no disrespect, sir, but seems to me a man who cuts out the kind of job for himself such as you have will need to be able to defend himself."

Fain felt his face harden. "Worley, I promised my pa when I left home I'd leave my gun in my saddlebags. He told me it was one way to avoid trouble." He shrugged. "He's not my real pa, but he raised me." He glanced at his folded hands in his lap, then back to the marshal. "There were several on Pa's place who were right salty. They taught me how to handle guns, knives, an' scatterguns. Reckon when I need 'em I won't come up short."

He stood. "Better get goin'. Those two I rode in here with might drink all the whiskey in that saloon next door to the hotel."

Worley stood, held his hand out, and thanked Fain for the information. He smiled, a cold smile to Cord's thinking. "If I hear where Taggart is thinkin' to settle down, I'll ride out an' let the folks know."

Fain and his trail partners stayed the night, and were tempted to stay even longer, but didn't want to be in town when Taggart showed up with his trail crew.

The rain, unseasonal, continued. They saddled up and headed north. If Fain hadn't made up his mind to at least warn the ranchers along the way, he'd probably have headed for south Texas. He didn't relish having cold weather catch him as far north as he might have to go.

They made a cold and wet camp the first night north of Walsenburg. They rode all the next day, wet and cold, but Cord decided to keep riding on after dark, hopeful of finding a ranch at which to stay overnight.

About eight o'clock by his reckoning, they rode around the side of a hill and saw windows painted with lantern light a few hundred yards ahead. "Well, looks like we've found a small settlement, or a large ranch. Let's see which." He nudged his horse ahead.

It soon became obvious his last guess was correct. A large house sat out front, maybe fifty yards or so in front of what Fain guessed to be a stable, and to its left, closer to the foothills, a long low building looked to be the bunk-house and cookshack. "You men go on to the bunkhouse, see if we can stay in the stable. I'll check the ranch house."

At his knock, a tall, brown-haired, blue-eyed girl, maybe twenty years old, opened the door. From what he could see in the flickering lantern light, she was lovely; beautiful, in fact.

While he was still staring at her, the mouth-watering aroma from the kitchen almost caused him to push past her and seek the source of the wonderful smells. Instead, Cord jerked his dripping hat from his head. "Howdy, ma'am, just wanted to let you know a couple of my trail partners an' I would sure appreciate it if you'd let us sleep in your barn tonight. We been ridin' three days in this rain, ever since we topped out on Raton Pass. Sure would like to dry out a little."

She looked over her shoulder. "Pa, there's a man . . ."

"I see 'im, Ruth. You go sit. I'll handle it."

The man, obviously the girl's father, stepped out to the veranda. He held a lantern in his hand, and held it high enough to be able to study Cord. He looked him up and down, then returned his eyes to look into Fain's. "Damned if you don't look like a drowned pup. What is it you want, young man?"

"Just tellin' your daughter there's three of us, been ridin' in this rain three days, an' wondered if you'd mind us stayin' in your barn tonight."

"Plenty of room in the bunkhouse; y'all can stay there. Ain't started hirin' for roundup yet; every bunk would be full if I had."

Fain clamped his dripping hat back on his head. "Be-holden to you, sir. I'll put my horse away now."

"Feed 'im while you're at it."

Cord moved toward the steps, then turned back. "Sir, 'fore I leave in the mornin' I got somethin' to tell you. Know you're gonna want to listen."

The rancher nodded. "I'll hear you out. Come to the house after the cook feeds you."

When he led his horse into the stable, Wash and Cookie were there taking care of theirs. They'd already taken care of the packhorses.

Wash came over to help Cord. "Foreman said we could sleep in the bunkhouse."

Cord chuckled. "So did his boss." They finished with the horses; then Fain dug in his packsaddle and pulled out some jerky. "We better chew on some o' this till breakfast."

"Lordy, Mistuh Cord, I done missed more meals than you could count to in my lifetime. Jest bein' dry an' sleepin' dry's gonna be a real treat."

They went back to the bunkhouse, met the crew, most of them weatherworn, tough-looking men, all on the shady side of forty years old. Fain figured they'd all found the last job they ever wanted to work. When hired, the roundup crew would undoubtedly be a younger bunch.

Cord and his friends fit in with the Lazy T men right away. Cord found out Mr. Tuttle owned the ranch.

Wash sat in on a penny-ante poker game until they turned the lamps out and crawled into their bunks. He won twelve cents.

They ate breakfast before daylight; then Cord shaved, wet his hair, combed it with his fingers, washed up at the pump, put on a clean shirt, and went to the ranch house. It still rained.

The door swung open before he could knock, and holding the door open a pretty lady, maybe forty years old, smiled and told him to come on in, that Mr. Tuttle would be in in a moment.

She poured him a cup of coffee and told him to sit at the kitchen table. "We just about live in this kitchen, eat here, visit here, well, goodness gracious, we do just 'bout everything here 'cept sleep."

Cord chuckled. "Ma'am, reckon most families do it like that; know we did back home." Before sitting, he told her his name.

He pulled his chair out to sit when Tuttle came in. They exchanged names, then Tuttle told him to sit, poured himself a cup of coffee, and sat across the table. "All right, young man, you said I would want to listen to what you got to say, so let's hear it. I've already told you I'm not hirin' for roundup yet, so know you ain't gonna hit me up for a job."

Cord smiled. "If you had one, I'd take it, but no, sir, what I have to tell you might be trouble. You'll have to decide that for yourself."

"Trouble is somethin' I don't need."

"No, sir, few people do, but what I have to tell you might let you be prepared for it when it comes, an' from what I've seen of your ranch, it's comin'."

Tuttle's daughter came into the kitchen before he could go further. He found her name to be Ruth, and he introduced himself.

Her father told her Fain was about to tell them of trouble they had coming. She and Mrs. Tuttle pulled up chairs. Cord stood to seat them, but they shooed him away.

Fain looked from one to the other. "Well, reckon I might's well get on with it." He took a swallow of his coffee, put the cup back on the table, stared at the cup a moment, then looked up. "Gonna start back when we left Texas, not far outside o' El Paso.

"At first I signed on with a roundup crew to chouse longhorns outta the breaks down in the Big Bend of Texas; then that crew became the trail crew to drive about three thousand head o' mixed cattle to Montana; supposedly to start a ranch up yonder in that Lakota Sioux country. The herd b'longed to an Eastern cattle company. A man by the name o' Bane Taggart is the trail boss.

"Well, to make a long story short, after 'bout two months on the trail, Taggart told us 'fore breakfast one mornin' not far east of Cimarron, New Mexico Territory, that he didn't figure to take the herd all the way to Montana, figured to find land 'fore he got there an' just flat move the herd onto it regardless if somebody already had staked claim to it.

"I didn't see it that way, so I quit, an' 'bout the same time, the two men ridin' with me quit too. Taggart wouldn't pay us for the time we'd spent on the trail." Fain chuckled. "But we got our money anyway." He emptied his cup and Mrs. Tuttle stood, refilled it, and again sat.

"How'd you get your money?" Tuttle asked.

"Tell you that in a little while, but first, are those five men in the bunkhouse your full crew?"

Tuttle shook his head. "I got four more out in line shacks. Why?"

"Well, sir, Taggart has, by my best count, about twenty-eight tough fightin' men." Fain shook his head. "You don't have men enough to hold your ranch against that crew."

Tuttle's shoulders slumped. He sat there, obviously shaken, staring into his empty cup. He looked up. "I don't have enough hard cash to hire a fightin' crew an' pay 'em wages fer it. 'Sides that, I wouldn't know where to find that many men in the next few days."

Ruth stood, refilled all of their cups, then sat, her face somber. She looked at her father. "Pa, we've fought Injuns, gunmen, outlaws, we'll fight these." She brightened. "Besides that, this man Taggart might choose to take somebody else's land."

Fain nodded. "He might, but the way I got it figured, he's gonna take the first good range he can find, an' from what I saw while ridin' this way, yours is the best. You already got a nice ranch house, good stable, an' a bunkhouse to take care o' his crew." He shook his head. "Don't want to throw cold water on your hopes, ma'am, but to my way o' thinkin', you should be ready to fight."

She stared at him a moment. "No offense, Mr. Fain, but you ride in here after dark, in the rain, and tell us we're about to get attacked. Why shouldn't we think you've told us a wild story to get a job, or maybe some other reason?"

Cord's face stiffened. "Ma'am, don't reckon I've ever been called a liar. I told you what to expect." He put his hat on and stood. "We'll be ridin' out now. Thank y'all for your hospitality." He stepped toward the door, then looked at the tall, proud young woman. "'Sides that, ma'am, I don't need a job right now. I figured to let as many ranchers know what to expect as I could."

"Oh? Then do you consider yourself a modern Paul Revere?"

Fain's face turned hot with angry blood; then before he could snap back an answer, Tuttle put his cup an the table and stood. "Son, Ruth meant nothin' by what she said. It's still rainin', so why don't you an' your friends stay till the weather clears?"

"Thank you, sir, but reckon we better ride on. Thanks again."

"Fain, I know Ruth's done made you madder'n hell, but I seen one o' those men you rode in here with is old, stove-up; you ride in this rain, his bones're gonna be hurtin' somethin' awful. Think of him. Stay till the weather lets up a little."

Cord frowned. He'd let his anger take over without thinking of his two friends. He studied a crack between the boards in the floor, then gave a nod. "You're right, sir, I wasn't thinkin' of anybody but myself. We'll take you up on your offer." Then, without looking at Ruth, he nodded. "What I told you is the truth, sir. I was you, I'd start thinkin' 'bout where I could get me some riders who know how to use a gun, handgun an' rifle."

Ruth's acid voice cut in again. "I see you play it safe. You don't wear a handgun, so I suppose you wouldn't think of hiring on for a fight."

Fain flicked her with a glance, knowing his green eyes

spat fire. "Only if your father gave me a job, along with a promise you wouldn't be around to throw words at me, words that I wouldn't take from a man."

"No. I reckon you'd pick up your marbles and go home."

Fain clamped his hat down hard on his head, looked at Tuttle, and went out the back door.

2

As SOON AS Cord cleared the door, Ruth's father asked, "What in tarnation got into you, girl?"

She stared at him a moment. "I—I don't know. Reckon I just plain don't like him."

Eve, Ruth's mother, shook her head. "Well for heaven's sake. He's young, mannerly, talks like he mighta seen the inside of a schoolhouse, an' if I do say so, he's mighty handsome."

Ruth stared at her parents a moment. She couldn't imagine why she'd been so rude either. Maybe it was because her father seemed willing to accept what the man said without any proof. Too, they'd known some peaceful years, and now it seemed possible they would see some rough times again; she didn't want to face all that again.

"Well, being young an' all that other stuff doesn't mean anything. 'Fore we go out on a limb an' start movin' cattle, or gettin' ready to fight off an outfit we don't know nothin' about, I think we better find out more 'bout this man."

She shrugged. "Not sure why I acted like that. Don't know 'im well enough to say I do or don't like him; but right now I'm thinkin' I don't like 'im."

• • •

While walking toward the bunkhouse, there was no doubt in Cord's mind whether he liked Ruth. She was young, proud, mighty pretty; but headstrong and rude. He didn't like her. He was still angry and out of sorts when he went in the bunkhouse.

He looked for Wash, and found him sitting at the poker table. "Wash"—he glanced around the table to find the foreman, Jim Dealy—"an' Jim, Mr. Tuttle said we were welcome to stay till it quits rainin'. Reckon we'll stay 'nother day. See what the weather does."

He heard somebody behind him say, "Thanks, Lord," and figured it was Cookie. Knowing he'd done something nice for the old man wiped away some of his anger toward that snippy daughter of Bob Tuttle's. He'd heard Mrs. Tuttle call her husband "Bob."

Wash slid over on the bench, patted the space he'd left, and motioned Cord to sit. Fain shook his head. "Nope, saw a book back yonder on the shelf, figured to read a while."

Dealy nodded. "Good book. Done read ever' story in it five or six times. Feller by the name o' Twain writ it. Bunch o' short stories."

Fain read a couple of stories, dozed, read a couple more until his eyes got so heavy he couldn't stay awake, then went to sleep. The next thing he knew, Wash shook him and said grub was on the table.

Cord splashed water on his face and sat. Most everyone else had already helped their plates. As soon as he took his first bite, he figured Cookie had done the cooking: beef stew, with plenty of beef, carrots, potatoes, red-hot Mexican peppers, and other things he didn't bother to figure out. He slanted a look at the old man. "You cook this?"

Cookie grinned, then nodded. "Yep. Ted yonder said as how he'd been cookin' fer this here bunch; well, he stepped in an' done it when their last cook quit. Said as how ever' danged one o' 'em griped 'bout his cookin' all the time. Seemed as how he needed a day off, so I took over his job fer the day." He frowned, then looked at Jim Dealy. "Ted said he figgered to head for Texas 'fore snow come on y'all; woulda already took off, but didn't want to leave you hog-tied with nobody to cook fer you."

Then, his eyes wide, his mouth slightly open, his entire face showing hope, he said, "Jim, reckon you could let 'im head out soon's this here rain clears off? I'd shore be beholden to you if I could take over the cookin' chores."

Dealy pinned the old man with a steely look. "You cook like this all the time?"

Cookie stared into his plate a moment, then looked up. "Gotta tell you the truth; I fix some dishes better'n this, some 'bout the same"—he shrugged—"an' I reckon some ain't as good."

Cord swallowed the bite he'd taken only a few moments before. "Jim, I'll answer that. I've sat around a lot o' cook-fires here an' yonder, but I never ate chow anywhere as good as Cookie dishes up." He glanced at the old man. "Now don't you go gettin' all swelled up just 'cause I said somethin' nice 'bout you."

His smile trying to swallow his ears, Cookie shook his head. "Jest thinkin' how good it is to hear somebody say somethin' nice 'bout my cookin'. Most o' what I hear ain't nothin' but growlin' an' cussin'."

Dealy studied Cookie a moment. "Tell you what. I ain't got the last say in this, but I'll put it up to the boss. If he says yeah, then Ted can saddle up an' head for Texas. I'll ask Mr. Tuttle 'fore supper time. Let you know then."

For some reason, Cord felt warm inside, felt like he'd just gotten *himself* a new job; one that he'd wanted badly and didn't think he had a chance for. He looked at Wash. "Looks like we lost a partner 'fore we got a chance to know 'im very well."

Cookie still hadn't wiped the smile away. "Well, goshding it, you know danged well you an' Wash're glad to be rid of a stove-up old cowboy like me." The smile disappeared. "Why, hell, all I'd do is slow you down."

Fain shook his head slowly. "No. Way I got it figured, neither Wash nor me has very good sense. We were just gettin' to like you."

Wash, Cord, and the crew joshed each other for a while, like men everywhere who'd become friends are likely to do. Then Dealy looked from Wash to Cord. "What you men doin' ridin' north this time o' year? Most rannies I ever knowed would head south 'bout now."

Wash and Fain exchanged glances. Cord shrugged. "Might as well tell you. Trouble's headed your way. We figured to let folks in its path know what to expect."

Dealy frowned. "Trouble? Hell, most o' us sittin' here been with the outfit a number o' years. We seen trouble aplenty durin' that time."

Fain nodded. "Figured as much. You seem like a salty bunch who could handle most anything that came along, but this will be too much for the number o' men you got."

He then told Dealy and the crew what had happened along the trail, and why they were heading north. "I already told your boss, but it seemed like his daughter didn't want to accept anythin' I told 'em. Fact is, she just purely don't like me, an' she might make her pa think lightly of what I told 'im."

He pushed his hat to the back of his head, then frowned. "You'd be doin' Mr. Tuttle a favor if you say a few words to him, make sure he's ready for what might come."

Cord stood, poured them each a cup of coffee, passed his under his nose to catch the full aroma, then sat. He sipped the hot drink in front of him and shook his head. "Dealy, it'd be a terrible mistake if he doesn't get prepared." He gave a nod. "Course that bunch might bypass this ranch an' head for the next one—or one along the way somewhere."

He shrugged. "But knowin' Taggart, I figure he'll take a fancy to the first good-lookin' range he sees. This's a likely-lookin' place to push a big herd onto an' try to run you folks off of, an' I'll tell you like it is, I'd be ready."

Dealy, obviously worried, stood, then looked at Cookie. "C'mon, let's go see the boss." Then he glanced at Fain. "Gonna think 'bout what you done told me, then let the boss know what I figger." He shook his head. "Even if that bunch don't take a hankerin' fer this place, it shore as hell ain't gonna hurt to be ready."

Dealy motioned with his thumb for Cookie to follow him. They went to the kitchen door. Jim knocked. Tuttle pushed the door open and motioned the two men in. "What you need, Jim? Figured you an' the crew'd be takin' advantage of this weather to rest up."

Dealy nodded. "Were, but I needed to see you 'bout somethin'." He then explained about Ted wanting to head for Texas before cold weather set in, and that he'd found a man who could cook the best grub they'd had, maybe ever had. "What I'm askin' you for, Boss, is to take Cookie here on as the crew's new cook."

Tuttle nodded. "All right, but you didn't have to ask me; you know that."

"Yeah, I know, Bob, but figgered you should oughta know who wuz messin' round in the grub shack." Dealy made as though to leave, then turned back. "Got somethin' I want to think 'bout a while, then figger I need to talk 'bout it with you."

Ruth, standing beside the stove, had apparently been listening with interest to what the men said. She squared her shoulders, placed her hands on hips, and stared at the three of them. "That grub-line rider been feedin' you a bunch of stuff like he told Pa?"

Hot blood rushed to Dealy's face, but before he could say anything, Cookie stepped forward. "Ma'am, gonna say it like it is; I've knowed that boy long enough to know he don't lie, but even more, I was on that same trail drive an' watched 'im brace the trail boss for 'is money when he quit. That boy didn't even have a gun slung 'bout his waist.

"Took me till the next day to quit for the same reason

Cord Fain did. Don't know as how I'd a had the guts to quit if it wuzen't for him."

Cookie looked at his new boss. "Sir, reckon I done got off on the wrong foot with y'all. You don't want me workin' fer you, say so an' I'll ride on with my partners when thay leave."

Dealy had been listening all the while, and his building anger only got worse. Veins stuck out on his forehead, he knew they did because the pressure made his head hurt.

He'd helped raise Ruth, but had never seen her as unreasonable as now. "Young lady, yore mama, yore papa, nor me paddled your hind end enough when you wuz growin' up." He faced Cookie. "You ain't goin' nowhere. I ain't lettin' a good cook go. Now go stow yore gear in the bunkhouse. I'm gonna stay an' talk with the boss a little while."

As soon as Cookie closed the door behind him, Dealy looked at Tuttle. "Bob, don't care what Ruth thinks o' that boy; an' he ain't really a boy; 'bout thirty years old, I'd say; an' to top that off, he looks like he still has the bark on. Reckon he could be a mighty hard man if pushed. He's a cut above most punchers we see, an' you heard what my new cook said. I believe every word Fain told me. I think we better get ready for a fight."

Tuttle looked at his daughter. "We're gonna do like Dealy says. Ain't gonna cost us nothin' but some work to be ready. In the old days we wuz always lookin' for bad things to happen. We better clean our guns."

Ruth's shoulders slumped, and she nodded. "I just hate how Mr. Fain came in here an' turned our peaceful world upside down."

Bob Tuttle put his hand on her shoulder. "Know how you feel, young'un; makes me kinda upset to know we gotta go back to the old days."

Dealy studied them while apparently father and daughter settled in on the same thought. "Y'all talk 'bout the old days," said Dealy. "Why, hell, think back, it ain't been but two, maybe three years since our last Kiowa attack."

Ruth untied her apron and hung it over the towel rack.

She looked across her shoulder at Dealy. "When's Fain ridin' out?"

Dealy shook his head. "Don't know. Soon's the weather clears, I s'pose. Why?"

She shook her head. "I suppose I should say somethin' to him." She shrugged. "You know; tell 'im I'm sorry for the way I acted." She frowned, looked at her hands tightly clasped in front of her at her waist. "Where's he goin' from here?"

Dealy, sensing his answer would be important to her, thought a moment, then looked her in the eye. "He said somethin' 'bout ridin' on up the line; try to tell folks they should oughta be ready fer the worst." He shook his head. "Said somethin' 'bout tryin' to get them to agree to come to help them who'd had their land taken over by Taggart."

Her face took on a stubborn look, her jaw knotted at the back. "Seems to me he's right ready to get gun-totin' folks involved in this when he don't even wear a gun."

Dealy frowned. "Don't know 'bout that, young'un. Maybe he has a good reason for that, but I'll tell you like it is. He looks to me like the sort o' man who'd stand fast when trouble come along." He shrugged. "What I'm sayin' is this: I ain't gonna judge 'im without knowin' a lot more. He mighta had some bad happenin' in his past." He nodded. "Gonna wait'n see."

Ruth, her face set in stern lines, nodded. "That's what I'm gonna do too. I'll not tell 'im anything 'bout being sorry till I know if I really am sorry."

Dealy looked at his boss. "Well, I done told you. Now I'm gonna tell the crew to clean an' oil their weapons." He nodded and pushed back out the screen door.

He walked to the middle of the yard, stopped, frowned, and looked back at the house. Why had that young filly set her mind so solidly against Fain? Hell, to his thinking, the young rider was a right likable man. He shook his head, then headed for the bunkhouse. The rain had slacked off to a heavy drizzle.

• • •

The drizzle also fell on Bane Taggart. His temper rode a razor edge; it had been that way every since that damned milksop Fain had quit the drive and taken another rider with him.

He looked across the sputtering fire at Jed Mobley. He pointed a finger at him. "Come daylight, want you to ride out, stay close to the mountains, don't go no farther than Denver. Want you to check each ranch 'tween here an' there.

"Make like you're ridin' the grub line, but when you get back, I wanta know 'bout every ranch 'tween here an' Denver. Wanta know its size, ranch buildin's, how many cattle they're grazin' on how many acres—or square miles; an' I wanta know what brand each ranch is carryin'. Wanta know ever'thing you can find out 'bout each one o' them, then report back to me." He jerked his head in a nod. "Unnerstan' what I'm tellin' you?"

Mobley took a swallow of the cupful of coffee he'd only a moment ago poured, sniffed, apparently to get the strong smell of the smoldering fire from his nose, and nodded. "Gotcha, Boss. Want me to write down everything, an' identify it by brand, right?"

Taggart stared into the fire a moment. He didn't like Mobley, but the man was smart, had a better education than most, and was loyal. He rode for the brand.

Bane Taggart pulled his pipe from his pocket; a cigarette would get soggy in the drizzle. He took time to pack tobacco into the bowl, and lighted it before answering. "Yeah. You got a pencil an' paper in yore saddlebags. I seen you writin' stuff at night, so yeah, write down ever'thin' you find out."

He swung his gaze to take in the rest of the crew gathered about the fire, hunched under their oilskins to keep the rain off as much as possible. "Like I done told you; we ain't takin' these here cows to Montana. We gonna settle in on the best grass an' ranch buildin's we find." He puffed life back into the weakly burning fire in his pipe bowl, then took a swallow of coffee.

"Once we get settled in on the land we want, I'll let them who own this herd know where we are an' what kinda new ranch they got." He knocked the dottle from his pipe, stood, and went to his damp blankets. The crew, apparently knowing they could go to their blankets when they got ready, tossed dregs from their cups and turned in.

Taggart pulled his extra groundsheet over him, pulled his hat over his eyes, and stared into its darkness. Why the hell was he driving a herd of cattle north, branded only with a trail brand, for a bunch of Easterners who wouldn't know whether the horns fit on the butt-end of a cow, or on the front? He thought on the question long into the night.

The next morning, Mobley tied his bedroll behind his saddle and rode into the rain, which was still softly falling. He looked back at the breakfast fire, then rode past the cattle, mostly heifers or bulls, with a few steers mixed in. He rode on into the still-dark night.

While riding, he wondered at the depths to which a man could fall, born of a distinguished Southern family, educated in one of the best universities in the South, an honorable war record, then coming home after the war to find that everything he'd known was changed—lost.

And leaving the South, coming West, getting a reputation as a gunfighter, and now riding for white trash, a man he'd not have let come anywhere but to his back door before the war. He shook his head and muttered, "Mobley, you're not a damn bit better than Taggart; you've *become* white trash." At nightfall, he rode into Trinidad.

Taggart had given him a month's pay before leaving the herd, so Mobley, wanting to sleep dry for a change, rented a hotel room for the night, ate supper, then went to the closest saloon. Not wanting to live with himself, and seeing himself as he'd become, he drank, listened to good, hardworking folks talk about the weather, cattle, their families, their dreams, and not wanting to hear it, he figured to get drunk.

While he was sitting there, a tall, weather-beaten man pushed up to the bar at his side. Mobley felt the man's eyes

on him and twisted to look at him; then he saw the star on
his vest: a U.S. marshal.

"Howdy, stranger. You ridin' through, or figger to stay in
our town a while?"

Mobley stared at the lawman a moment. "Why?"

The marshal's face hardened. "Just tryin' to be friendly,
mister. You don't want it that way, fine." He turned his face
to the mirror behind the bar.

Mobley felt a rush of blood to his face. What the hell
had he become? "Sorry, Marshal. Reckon I been ridin' for
a man I don't respect, don't like, an' then too, I been ridin'
in rain for four days now. Didn't mean to be unfriendly."

Tom Worley chuckled. "Think nothin' of it. I been in the
same frame o' mind."

"Buy you a drink, Marshal?"

A thin smile broke the hard planes of the lawman's face,
and he nodded. "Yeah, if you'll let me buy you one too."

Mobley chuckled. "Oh, no, ain't gonna play that game,
Marshal. 'Fore you know it, we'd be standin' here half
drunk. I'll buy, then go to my room an' sleep dry for the
first time in a week."

While drinking, Mobley told the marshal that he was a
crew member of a large herd coming north, and the herd
was still south of Raton. "If Taggart's got any sense, he'll
take the herd around these mountains."

Worley nodded. "Yeah, it'll add only a few days to his
drive. Course he'll be deeper in Comanche country by
doin' that, but with a good-sized crew he should oughta be
able to fight 'em off."

The lawman frowned, nodded. "They wuz a young fella,
a big black man, an' a spindly old puncher come through
here a few days ago; said they had quit a outfit down the
trail a good ways." He cocked his head to stare at Mobley.
"They from that outfit you ride fer?"

Jed thought a moment, wondered how much Fain had
told the marshal about Taggart's outfit, then nodded.
"Yeah, they're from the same outfit." He took a swallow of
his drink. "They quit for the same reason I'm considering

leavin' that bunch." He pushed his still-dripping hat to the back of his head. "Haven't made up my mind yet, but I'm thinkin' about it." He knocked back the rest of his drink and stepped toward the door.

Worley chuckled. "You thinkin' 'bout it, son, an' almost said it. I reckon come daylight you'll be right close to makin' up yore mind."

A sharp nod and Mobley headed toward the door.

In his room, he took a hot bath. Later, lying in a dry bed, he stared at the ceiling. Was the marshal right? Was he close to deciding to leave Taggart? Besides, why would the trail boss ride roughshod over a lot of good, honest people to establish a new ranch—for an Eastern outfit?

He thought about the herd they were driving. To his knowledge, there were but few cattle in the herd that had a permanent brand; of course they all were trail-branded, but the hair would grow back after a while; then they would all again be as they were found down in the Big Bend—mavericks. He frowned into the dark. *Now that's something to think about.*

Too, there were few in the crew who were like Fain, men who didn't wear a side gun. All the rest were hard, gun-wise men. He thought about Fain a few moments. The man had been a puzzle to the crew. Somehow they'd decided that Cord Fain was not a man to cross, whether he wore a gun or not. And Fain had had the guts, the integrity, to quit as soon as he found out Taggart's intentions.

Mobley tossed and turned for hours, wrestling with his conscience. When day dawned, still dripping a light rain, he was as tired as he'd been when going to bed. He climbed to his feet, dressed, and went to the livery to get his horse.

On the third day, before Cord and Wash rode out, Dealy told Fain that there was a young woman, maybe in her late twenties, and her son, about eight years old, homesteading down along the creek.

"She doesn't have a husband?"

Dealy shook his head. "Did have, but the last time the Kiowa hit us he got killed."

"Why didn't she go back to wherever she came from, you know, back to family?"

"Her ma's dead, an' her brother and pa didn't come home from the war." Dealy shrugged. "Reckon she ain't got nobody left 'cept us. She sorta looks on us as family now, an' we gosh-ding sure are glad of it. She's a mighty nice girl."

Fain frowned, thought about a defenseless woman being alone down there, several miles from help. "Reckon you better tell her what might happen, an' get her somewhere safe."

Dealy nodded. "Wuz jest thinkin' that same thing. I'll tell the boss, then bring 'er up here to the ranch house—if she'll come."

"Make sure she comes, Jim. There're men in that crew comin' up the trail I don't trust; most of 'em, for that matter. Don't know what they'd do to a lone woman." Fain had been standing holding his horse's reins. He toed the stirrup, looked at Wash, nodded, then looked back to Dealy. "Gonna ride on up the trail, let those folks know what to expect"—he grinned—"but it might not be too long 'fore you see me again."

"You figger to come back then?"

Cord nodded. "Figure to do just that. If this is the place Taggart chooses to take over, you folks're gonna need all the help you can get. I'll try to bring back one or two men from each ranch." He smiled. "Men who, unlike me, pack a gun."

He looked at Wash. "Let's get along, partner."

Riding from the ranch yard, Cord felt Dealy's eyes on them until they had ridden several hundred yards. Too, Wash's eyes were on him.

"Why for you joinin' in this here fight, Mistuh Fain?"

"Gonna answer that, but first, I've told you to call me Cord. We gonna be partners, we sure as hell aren't gonna go round callin' each other mister."

A few long moments passed before Fain attempted to

answer Wash. He'd been wondering the same thing. Maybe if he explained it to his partner, his reasons would be clearer to him also.

Then, talking while they rode, he looked straight ahead. "Wash, I'm gonna tell you somethin' that might turn you against me, but reckon it needs to be said now, before we get too partnered up.

"You see, my pa was an outlaw—well, not my real pa, but he was the man who raised me, an' 'tween him an' his wife, a wonderful woman, they taught me what was right, and what was wrong. I promised both of 'em when I cut out on my own that I'd not ever do any man wrong. I been tryin' to keep my word to them."

"Well, now I swear. I done partnered up with a outlaw's boy." Wash said those words while grinning. He sobered. "Gonna tell you, Mistuh . . . uh, Cord, I ain't seed you do nothin' what'd make me 'shamed to be yo friend any time, any place."

Fain glanced at Black. "Thank you, Wash. There've been times I was mighty tempted to kick over the traces an' go to doin' things I know how to do only too well." He shrugged. "But so far, I've stayed on the side of the law."

"You gonna tell me moah 'bout you?"

Fain shook his head. "Not right now, partner, but soon."

They rode in silence for a while, then Fain realized he'd not answered Black's question. "I've told you how I was raised, an' I reckon that explains why I'm gonna side these ranchers against Taggart. What he has planned just plain isn't right, an' I reckon I'm gonna do whatever I can to stop 'im." Another quarter of a mile, and he said, "Don't want to rope you into any fight, Wash. It'll be a fight you might get hurt in, badly. So if you want to ride on after we tell the ranchers what to expect, I sure as the devil understand; won't hold it against you."

"Aw, now, Cord, I always figgered if a man's partner was gonna do somethin', if they was real partners then they done it togethuh. Reckon I'd do the same thing even if we wasn't gonna ride the same trail together."

A knot formed in Cord's throat. He didn't wonder that it did. This was the first time he'd ever felt close to anyone other than the dangerous man who raised him. He loved both him and his wife. He swallowed to rid himself of the feeling, but it did no good.

It took Fain and Wash a week to ride almost to Denver, warning ranchers along the way. But on asking for help, he came up dry. The only men still on the payroll with most ranches were year-around crew. They just flat didn't have anyone to send with him. He looked at Wash. "Reckon we better get on back to the Lazy T."

"You got it figgered that's the land Taggart's gonna try to take ovuh?"

"Yeah, an' if I got it figured right, it'll take him 'bout another two weeks to get that far. In the meantime I have an idea where I can get some men, fighting men, to help."

Wash grinned. "You gonna go ask yoah papa to lend you them men, ain't you?"

Cord slanted his partner a look he hoped portrayed his disgust. "You think you're so damned smart, don't you?" He nodded. "But, yeah, that's exactly what I figure on doin'."

Wash's grin turned into a belly laugh. "If we ride together much longer, Cord, reckon I'm gonna be able to read yoah mind."

Fain grimaced. "You damned near can do that right now. C'mon, let's head south. We don't have much time to waste." He frowned. "Been thinkin', if it's not the Lazy T Taggart figures to take, we can always follow the herd north till we see where he decides to roost; then we can help in some way."

Nodding, Wash said, "Reckon we can, Cord; reckon we can."

A couple of days after Mobley headed north, Taggart swung the herd to the northeast in order to skirt the more rugged mountains. The rain had stopped, but the day continued with leaden skies. He slanted a look at the clouds hanging heavy around the peaks ahead, and nodded his sat-isfaction. As long as the weather stayed like this, the parch-ing, baking sun would not dry the prairie. Dust would not be as burdensome, and he and the riders would sweat a lot less.

He dropped back from his lead position to ride along the side of the herd. He studied the lean, mean longhorns. If he could convince the Eastern owners to buy some good bulls, maybe Hereford, or Durham, these cattle in a couple of years would be carrying more weight, which meant a lot more money. He thought about that a while, then wondered why he should care what they did about upgrading their cattle.

Then he wondered how far Mobley had gotten on his ride north. He thought on the tall handsome Southerner a moment, wondered why he didn't like him, and wouldn't admit it was because the man had at some time been some-thing he himself could never be—a gentleman. Yeah, maybe it was because the man had obviously had a lot more in another day, another time, than *he* had: money, school-ing, maybe one of those Southern families that had every-thing and didn't work for it. Yeah. maybe that was it. Too, there wasn't a man in his crew who didn't think Mobley was a very dangerous man. Taggart envied the Southerner that quality of being able to throw what amounted to fear into a man without seeming to do anything to generate it.

His eyes swung the length of the strung-out herd again. Someday he'd have a bunch of cattle of his own.

Riding from Trinidad, Mobley swung in close to the moun-tains. He thought perhaps he'd find a line shack along the way to hole up in if it started to rain again. Too, he could check the probability of valleys branching off that might hold cattle for deep summer graze.

Late afternoon of the second day out of town, he rode along the banks of a shallow creek lined with cottonwoods; then he smelled woodsmoke. Maybe he'd lucked out. Maybe there was a ranch close by with a good cook.

Then he saw it, a snug little cabin, well built at first glance. Smoke streamed from the tin stack sticking from the stone chimney. A small barn stood close to the shoulder of the hill sloping in toward the cabin. He neck-reined his horse toward the cabin.

When he was still out about fifty yards a rifle, or shotgun, barrel poked between the closed shutters ahead of him. "Hello, sir. I mean you no harm. Just thought I might sleep in your barn tonight, an' if I may, I'd like to build a fire to prepare my supper."

"I'm not a 'sir,' an' yes, you can sleep in the barn, an' no, I'll not have you building a fire out there where you might catch something on fire. I'll feed you." It was a young voice, a woman's voice.

A deep-throated chuckle followed her words. "An' as for you causin' me harm, I reckon I'd a said the same thing if I was staring down the barrel of a Winchester. Ride on up. Let me take a look at you."

Mobley smiled to himself. That woman's voice, husky, and her chuckle showed she had a sense of humor. Lordy day, if she looked anything like she should with a voice like that, he might figure to hell with Taggart's orders. Then he frowned. Maybe he already looked on Bane Taggart's orders as something he might cast aside. He rode toward the voice. "All right, ma'am. Reckon I'm close enough for you to take a good look at me." He let a thin smile break the corners of his lips.

"Ride on down to the barn, strip your horse, wash up, then come on to the house; supper's almost ready. Bring your mess gear with you. You can help yourself, then go back outside to eat. Don't want to have to sit here an' hold this rifle on you while you're in the cabin. Hungry as I am, it'd just slow me down gettin' to the table."

Jed thought to tell her he'd accept her hospitality only as far as sleeping in the barn. He didn't want to cause her any anxiety. He cast that thought aside. He wanted to see what a woman with a voice like that looked like.

About twenty minutes later, his horse taken care of, and

his face and hands washed, he knocked on her kitchen door. He felt half naked. He'd left his gunbelt and Colt .44 hanging from a peg in the stable. Maybe it would make her feel a little safer when he came in the cabin.

She opened the door. She still held the rifle. "C'mon in. Food's on the stove. Help yourself."

He stared. Her voice had about halfway prepared him for what she was: auburn hair, brown eyes, flawless golden complexion, and she wore a gray chambray dress, tight bodice pinched in at a tiny waist.

He wanted to tell her she was the most beautiful woman he'd ever seen, but swallowed his words. He'd scare her if he complimented her. "Thank you, ma'am. I'll help my plate, then get outta your way."

While putting food on his plate—boiled potatoes, cabbage, venison, maybe, and small fluffy biscuits—he twisted to look at her. "Didn't see a man around, but your woodpile looked like he'd been busy. Looked like a couple cords of wood already split and stacked. I'll cut more before I leave in the mornin'."

"No need for that. My son Tommy likes helpin' me with things that need doin'."

Jed nodded. "Reckon you should know who you're feeding. My name's Jed Mobley, an' tell Tommy to come on out from wherever he's holdin' a gun on me. I have no intent to harm you, him, or anybody else."

The young woman looked him in the eye. "My name's Pamela Henders. Folks call me Pam." She smiled. "That is, when I see anybody to call me anything." She looked up toward the attic. "Come on down, Tommy. I don't figure this man's gonna harm us."

The boy came down, lugging a rifle that, if stood on its stock, would have been taller than the boy who climbed from the attic. He looked to be about eight years old. "Reckon I'll just sit over here in the corner, keep this Winchester handy, an' make sure he don't hurt nobody," Tommy said.

Jed stared at the little fellow a moment. "Son, you cut all that wood out there by yourself?"

"Yes, sir," he answered quietly, matter-of-factly. "Ma needs wood, or anything else, I try to get it for her. Since the Kiowa killed Pa, I'm all she's got. She needs me."

For the first time in years a lump formed in Mobley's throat. This young woman and her son loved each other, and were trying to make a go of it together, doing anything that needed to be done to help the other.

He looked at Pam. "Mrs. Henders, I'm mighty impressed. Know you don't know me well enough to trust me, but if you don't mind I'd like to sleep in your stable a couple of nights. During the day I'm sure Tommy an' I can find things to get repaired that takes two men. I have an idea he and I would work right well together."

She opened her mouth, obviously to accept or reject his offer, but Tommy cut in. "Don't need no help, mister. I make do."

Thinking maybe he'd hurt the boy's pride, Jed shook his head. "Aw, now, young man, I figure you could do most anything around here, but I'll bet there's work that *I'd* need help doin'. Maybe we could help each other."

Pam looked at her son, then to Jed. "Sir, if you're making that offer to try to repay me for feeding you, I didn't do it for pay." Her shoulders slumped. She looked at her tightly folded hands held in front of her. "But, Mr. Mobley, there are things that Tommy an' I've tried to do, working together." She shook her head. "We just didn't have the strength."

Suddenly aware that he stood with a full plate of food, and that it was getting cold, Jed glanced at his plate, then back to Pam. "Ma'am, reckon if I don't want to eat cold food, I better get on outside an' eat. We'll talk about things I might be able to get done in the mornin'."

She gasped. "Oh, my goodness, how thoughtless of me." She reached for his plate. "Here, I'll put it back on the stove. You'll eat in here with us, an' we can talk while we eat."

With Mobley's words that he would go back outside to eat, Pam had decided to trust him. She needed, desperately needed, to trust someone, and this man was clean-cut, not over two or three years older than she herself was, and yes, was a man who'd be considered handsome by any woman. She liked the direct way he looked into her eyes when he spoke, and the way he treated Tommy; he didn't talk down to him, he treated him as an equal.

While she put the food on the table, she studied him, trying not to show that she did. He was tall, black-haired, with hazel eyes, and he looked as though he tried to keep as clean as conditions would allow.

When Jed held her chair for her to be seated, she hesitated; she'd not had a man show her this courtesy in a long time. She liked being considered a lady, and shown the little things that said he considered her one and would treat her like one. She smiled and sat in the chair offered her. "Come on to the table, Tommy." She chuckled that deep-throated sound that came from her chest. "You can leave the rifle there. I think this man is a gentleman."

It had been a long time since anyone would have thought of Jed Mobley as a gentleman. Her words gave him hope that perhaps he could reclaim the ways he'd been taught by his mother and father. He knew then that he'd not go back to Taggart. The very thought of going back made him feel dirty.

When seated, with a cup of steaming coffee in front of him, and waiting for the food to reheat, he looked from Pam to Tommy. "Noticed the barn door needs to be rehung, an' your corral fence could stand a few new posts. If Tommy will agree, he and I can find other things to get back up to snuff."

Pam, about to put a bite of venison in her mouth, lowered her hand. She first stared into Mobley's eyes, then lowered her own to look at her plate.

She nodded and, in her low, husky voice, said, "Sir, I know things need a lot o' doin', an' like I told you, Tommy and I find some things too hard for either or both of us." She shook her head, then looked directly at him. "Mr. Mobley, I need help but I have no money to pay anyone."

She swallowed, and squelched her pride with the swallow. "We sell enough yearlings, enough to buy staples for the coming winter, and we have a pretty nice garden which keeps Tommy and me eatin' healthy through the winter."

She squared her shoulders and set her chin in a way she'd been told gave her a stubborn look. "We make do, Mr. Mobley, an' 'tween Tommy an' me, reckon we'll get through this. The longer Mr. Henders is gone, we find things comin' easier. We're learnin'."

3

TAGGART HAD MADE it through Comanche country without incident, and now bedded the herd down about a mile north of Trinidad. This was Kiowa land, but he thought they would not raid his cattle this close to a town. He left twelve men with the herd and led the rest of them to town.

When on the edge of where some Trinidad residents had built houses, he motioned the men around him. "Gonna pay y'all a month's wages, give you money to git drunk on, buy yoreself a woman for the night, then git back here by noon tomorrow. Them other men gotta git their ashes hauled too."

He doled out the money, and made a note of each man's name and how much he'd paid him, then led them on into town.

They stopped in the first saloon they came upon. It was the best watering hole in town, but had no women. The crew moved on to another saloon; Taggart stayed for a couple of drinks. He'd not stood at the bar but a few minutes when U.S. Marshal Tom Worley moved to his side.

He introduced himself, then said, "You the trail boss o' those men who just came into town?"

Taggart studied him a moment. "Yeah, somethin' wrong?"

Worley shook his head. "Nope, just don't want anythin' to go wrong. Thought if we had an understandin', it might avoid trouble."

Bane tightened inside. He didn't like the law, didn't like being around any lawdog. He stared at Worley a moment. "What you mean? We ain't started no trouble."

Worley nodded. "That's right, you haven't, an' to make myself clear, I don't want any. This is not a trail town. We don't cater to a lot o' hell-raisin'."

Angry bile pushed its way into Taggart's throat, and his face heated up. He swallowed, forced himself to relax. This might be the town closest to where he figured to settle in on some good range. He might need to be accepted as an upright citizen. He forced a smile. "If any o' my men get outta line, Marshal, I'll help you settle 'em down. I don't want no trouble either." Taggart took a swallow of his drink, and held it out toward Worley. "Buy you a drink?"

Worley shook his head. "On duty. Never drink till just before I go to bed." He wanted a drink, but didn't like Taggart, at first glance hadn't liked him, and besides, he was almost certain this was the man Fain had told him about. Some of the ranchers in his territory were sure to have trouble headed their way. He stood there a few moments, then turned and walked out.

After leaving Taggart, Worley went to the next saloon, and then the next, until he was sure he'd seen all the men who came in with the trail boss. Then he went to his office, opened his desk drawer, and pulled a sheaf of wanted posters from it. He remembered every face he'd looked on from Taggart's crew. He studied the posters for duplicates of those faces.

After checking every poster, he made another round of the watering holes, found them peaceful, went back to his office, opened his desk drawer again, and pulled a bottle of his own whiskey from it.

He poured a coffee cup full of the strong drink, and thought about what Fain had told him, and then Mobley too; he'd backed up all that Fain had told him.

Most of the ranchers along the eastern side of the mountains were people he liked. They ran good outfits, and several of the ranches had the type of land, homes, and outbuildings that would fit Taggart's scheme. After thinking on it a while, he had no doubt but what one of them would be the target of Taggart's greed. He wondered if there was anything he could do to help them.

The morning after offering to help get a few things repaired around the place, Mobley woke long before daylight and lay there a few moments staring at the ceiling of the barn's haymow. His decision to help Pam Henders and Tommy had marked the final split between him and Taggart's outfit.

He wondered if he should help Mrs. Henders a couple of days, then ride on north and get the information the trail boss had ordered him to get, give the information to Taggart, quit his job, collect his wages, and ride back to help the girl and her boy.

Mobley pondered that problem a while, gave a mental shrug, and figured to hell with Taggart and the rest of his wages; he had about a year's wages, top-hand wages, in his money belt, and he'd stay and help the girl.

He sniffed; bacon frying. He crawled from his blankets, washed up, and followed his nose to the source of the smell. The closer he got, the hungrier he got. At the back door, he knocked. Pam let him in.

She smiled. "Thought if I wasn't payin' you, the least I could do would be to fix you a good breakfast. Sit, I ain't fried the eggs yet, the biscuits are 'bout brown, an' the coffee's hot an' ready to drink. I'll get you a cup."

Mobley glanced about the room. "Where's Tommy? Figured he'd beat me out o' the blankets."

"I let 'im sleep in. We kept him up pretty late last night."

"Mrs. Henders, I know he has a lot of pride, wants to be your 'big man,' but before he went to sleep, did he seem to accept me helpin' do a few things around here?"

Pam frowned, stared at the egg she held in her hand, then cracked it over the hot grease and nodded. "I believe so; and yes, I think it's his pride more than anything else. Maybe by the time you've worked together about a half a day, he'll come around." She cracked another egg over the frying pan, looked over her shoulder, and smiled. "How many eggs you think you'll eat""

"Two if you've got 'em to spare."

When she had the eggs fried to her satisfaction, she dished up the biscuits, bacon, and eggs, then sat. They ate in silence for a few moments, and all the while Mobley studied on how much he should tell her of Taggart's plans. He didn't want to scare her, but she had to know what to expect; besides, if she had been through Kiowa attacks, he thought she had the stuff to take whatever he had to tell her.

He told her about the trail boss and his land-grab ideas. She listened to all he had to say. "So you see, Mrs. Henders, I'm not trying to scare you, but you will have to be ready. Is there a large ranch close by, one you could take shelter with?"

She nodded. "The Lazy T is 'bout five miles from here, good folks. Tommy, my husband, an' me, we stayed with them several times during Indian attacks.

"This ain't the time o' year they'll have many hands. They won't start hirin' for roundup for another couple months. They ain't gonna have enough hands to fight off as many riders as you say this man Taggart has."

Mobley thought about that a moment. He could stay on and help them fight—or he could keep riding and let his conscience eat his guts out. Why should he have guilt feelings for abandoning people he hardly knew? Why should he give a damn about anybody but himself? He couldn't answer that. Besides, what difference could one more gun mean in fighting off Taggart? He pondered that a moment. The only answer he came up with: self-respect. Somehow that had again become important to him.

"I think I'd better ride over there and tell them what I've told you."

She nodded. "Yes. They should know what's coming. I'll tell Tommy when he wakes that you've ridden on."

Mobley grinned. "No. He and I'll do our work today. I'll ride over there when we finish, and I'll be back in the mornin'."

"Now that *will* be an imposition, work all day, ride ten miles over and back, then again up early in the mornin'." She shook her head. "Mr. Mobley, I can't let you do that."

Feeling better than he had about anything in a long time, Jed grinned. "Ma'am, what if I just do the things that need doin' without you *lettin' me*." His grin widened. "You gonna sic Tommy on me; let him whip up on poor little me?"

She stared at him a moment, then smiled. "Mr. Mobley, you know I need the help, and that said, I'd like you to call me Pam, an' I'm gonna call you Jed. I feel like I've suddenly gotten a friend."

Jed sobered. "Ma'am, I haven't given it any thought, but I'd say you made a friend soon's I saw that rifle pointed at me, resting under one o' the prettiest cheeks I b'lieve I've ever seen."

Her face flamed.

Mobley knew he'd embarrassed her, and for reasons he couldn't explain, was sorry. "Aw, now, ma'am, I didn't mean to embarrass you. Those words just came out 'cause they needed sayin'. I'm sorry. Please forgive me."

Her throat bobbed; then she swallowed again. Her face faded from a flaming red to a pretty pink. "Jed, it's been so long since anyone said anything that nice to me, I . . . I guess it just surprised me. You don't owe me an apology."

Tommy saved them from any more explanation. He stuck his head through the door to the attic. "Gee, Mom, why'd you let me sleep so long? Got a lot o' work to do today."

She told him she knew he was tired and thought it might be good for him. He seemed to accept that, climbed down from the attic, went to the white porcelain wash-bowl, washed up, then went to the stove as though to prepare his breakfast. "Sit down, son," she said. "It'll take only a jiffy to fix your breakfast. Jed an' me, we've already eaten."

Tommy grasped the back of the chair across the table from Jed.

"Hey now," Jed said, "if we're gonna be work partners for a day or two, looks like we ought to sit next to each other; get better acquainted."

Tommy moved to Jed's side of the table and sat; he looked at the tall man a moment, stared him straight in the eye, then gave a jerky sort of nod. "Thought 'bout it long into the night, Mr. Mobley; decided I *did* need some help. Don't like my mom havin' to work so hard. She works round here like a man." He took a swallow of the milk Pam had put in front of him. "We ain't got many head o' cattle, but she an' me, we brand 'em, keep 'em close in to our homestead here, gather hay for 'em." He shook his head. "Why, heck, reckon 'tween us we do anything a top hand can do."

Mobley looked long at the little boy. "Tell you what, son, I think 'tween you an' me we can get things in pretty good shape around here before I ride on."

"Gosh, Mr. Mobley, you gonna ride away when we near 'bout git everything done?"

Those words hit right to the core of what Jed had been thinking. He looked across the table at Pam. "Well, I reckon you and I better see how the work comes. We'll talk about that later. Now eat your breakfast; we have a lot of work to do."

Cord Fain and Matthew Black rode into the Lazy T stable a couple hours after dark after four nights of being gone.

After taking care of their horses, they went to the bunk-house. Jim Dealy met them at the door. "See y'all come back. Figgered you'd be long gone by now; figgered you'd put some distance 'tween you an' that there trouble you told us 'bout."

Cord gave him a hard-eyed look. "Jim, you gonna learn I ain't made that way. I tell you somethin', then that's the way it is."

"Aw, now, Fain, I was only joshin' yuh. I knowed soon's I talked with you a while you was the kind who'd stick when the goin' got rough." He looked them over from head to foot. "Y'all et yet?"

Cord shook his head. "Not since breakfast. Reckon that old reprobate you got cookin' for you now would mind if we stirred somethin' up?"

"Well gosh-ding it," Cookie said, "knowed you didn't have no respect for me when we rode together. Dang tootin' I mind you stirrin' up somethin' in my cookshack." Cookie grinned around a huge chew of tobacco. "Gonna stir it up m'self. Ain't gonna have no tenderfoot tryin' to cook." He grabbed Wash by the arm. "C'mon, y'all don't know how much I been missin' you."

While eating, Fain told Jim the situation they were in. "All those ranchers north o' here are in the same boat you are. They've got only enough men left to do fence work, an' keep their cows on the same grass. Course they'll be hirin' in a month or so for roundup—but that's gonna be too late."

Dealy frowned, obviously thinking. He nodded. "Y'all go on an' eat, then come on up to the ranch house; boss'll wanta know what y'all told me. Then we better talk 'bout what we gonna do from here. Gonna be mighty tight fightin' off that bunch with the men we got."

Fain nodded. "Way I got it figured, but I also have some-thin' in the back o' my mind that might work. Tell you 'bout it when we talk to Tuttle."

Cookie put food on the table and motioned Fain and Wash to sit and eat. When they finished, he picked up their cups to refill them. Fain shook his head. "Figure Tuttle'll have coffee fixed when we get up there; maybe some o' the men'll drink what you got fixed."

"Reckon you're right, Cord. I'll jest let it set on the fire a while; now you git on up there. Mr. Tuttle's gonna want to hear what you got to say."

When Fain stepped out the door, he noticed that the kitchen had more than one lantern burning, judging by the brightness of the light coming from the windows. He headed for the back door; it swung open before he could reach for it. Tuttle pulled him on into the kitchen. "Come on in, we got a acquaintance o' yores in here. He done told us 'bout the same story you did."

As soon as he stood in the kitchen, Fain's look took in Jed Mobley. "Howdy, Mobley. Figured all along you were too decent a man to stick with Taggart." He stared at the tall man a moment, grimaced, then gave the gunfighter a cold smile. "You _have_ left him, haven't you?"

Mobley nodded slowly. "Howdy, Fain. Reckon you had me pegged before I knew myself that well."

"How far's Taggart behind you?"

"I'd guess it'll take 'im a week, maybe a week an' a half, to get this far. Depends on how long it'll take 'im to go round those mountains. Why?"

"Well, reckon I got a idea buzzin' round in my head; gonna think 'bout it overnight; see what I come up with."

"Hope it's got somethin' to do with helpin' these folks. Figure they're gonna need it."

The corners of Fain's lips creased into a cold smile. "If it works the way I got it figured, it'll help."

Fain then told Tuttle, his daughter, and Mrs. Tuttle the situation he and Wash had found on every ranch to the north. He shrugged. "Far as I can see, we won't get any help from any of them. They're as vulnerable on their ranches as we are."

Tuttle and his wife stared at him, their eyes showing fear, but also a stubborn determination to take what came.

Then he felt the hard, almost physical impact of Ruth's

eyes. "Mr. Fain, I hardly see that you can do anything. You don't even wear a gun. If what you say is true we need *fightin' men*."

Angry bile bubbled to the back of Fain's throat. His face burned with hot blood pumped to it. He wanted to give her an angry retort, but out of respect for her parents he choked back most of his words. "Ma'am, I've never been given to lying. But as to how I might help? Well, I been givin' it some thought, an' I figure maybe the dust my horse kicks up when I run from Taggart an' his bunch'll cause them to choke; might help y'all in a small measure that way."

He looked at Tuttle. "Sir, I'm gonna stay; see if there's any way I can help. Any further communication we have, I'll do it through Dealy. Your daughter's made it right clear I'm not welcome in your home." He shrugged. "But you see, sir, I can't ride away knowin' my help might make a difference. Dealy'll let you know what I'm gonna do." He clamped his hat onto his head, looked at the cup of coffee Mrs. Tuttle had put on the table in front of him, caught a little of its aroma, stood, and left.

As soon as the door closed behind him, Mobley stared at Ruth, then shook his head. "Ma'am, don't know what you have against that man, but I'll tell you this. I know he could never have done an un-gentlemanly thing in your presence. I happen to know of his family; they're mighty nice folk." Then he thought that now that he'd said this much, he might as well set her straight about Fain. "Gonna tell you somethin' else; I've never seen Fain pack a gun, but there wasn't a man in the crew who'd cross him. There's something about him that tells a *man* that he's one dangerous *hombre*." He stood.

"I came down here to see if Mrs. Henders and her son can stay here with you till we get Taggart straightened out. I figure to move her cows back into the hills till this is over."

He stepped toward the door and said over his shoulder,

"Thanks for the supper and coffee." He pushed through the screen door and before he left, Tuttle said to bring Pam and her son to the ranch.

Halfway across the yard, Mobley stopped, pushed his hat to the back of his head, and stared back at the golden hue of lantern light painting the windows. He wondered why he had defended Fain so strongly. They'd never been friendly during the drive up from Texas, but he'd somehow always known that a man in trouble—if his cause was an honest one—could depend on Cord Fain to side him. He stood there a moment, frowned, pulled his watch from his pocket, struck a lucifer to see by, and again frowned. It was nine-thirty; it would be after midnight when he got back to Pam's homestead.

While riding, he wondered what made him so certain that Taggart would pick Tuttle's ranch as the one he'd take over. He ran the things he knew for certain through his mind. Tuttle's ranch sprawled over several thousand acres according to Pam. It had good-flowing streams that never ran dry. It also had creases back into the mountains where the snow never got too deep for cattle to graze. Everything he ran through his mind further convinced him that this was the ranch the trail boss would steal.

He urged his horse into a lope. The barn and its warmth would feel good; the night had chilled.

He rode into the ranch yard an hour or so earlier than he'd guessed. Lantern light shone through the cabin window. Pam had waited up for him. For some reason that thought made him feel warm all over. He'd not had anyone wait up for him since he was a boy and had been in the woods all day hunting. It was a good feeling. He rode to the stable and took care of his horse.

Finished with his horse, he had placed a foot on the ladder to climb to the haymow when light spilled through the barn door. "Jed, I fixed us a pot of fresh coffee. Come up to the house; I'd like to know how the Tuttles took your message."

Mobley knew he had a hard day ahead of him on the

morrow, but a look at the woman holding the lantern high so he could see, tossed aside any thought he had of refusing the coffee. She was lovely. Her husband had been a lucky man to have had her as his wife, even if for a short few years. He removed his foot from the ladder and smiled. "Why, ma'am, even if I'd only this instant finished a cup, I don't think I could refuse your invitation." He nodded. "Yes'm, think I'd like a cup."

They sat long into the night talking, getting to know each other, Jed learning how the homestead was arranged along, and back from, the creek. He pulled the watch given to him by his father when he graduated from Virginia Military Institute. Two o'clock. "Lordy day, if I'm gonna get any work done tomorrow, I'd better get some sleep."

Pam's face flushed a delightful pink. "Oh, how thoughtless of me. I've kept you up, and you've already had a long hard day."

Jed smiled. "Ma'am, I'd do without sleep for a month to get to know you like I have tonight." He frowned. "You care if Tommy an' I round up your cattle and push them back into one of those valleys? We can leave them there till we see how this Taggart problem shapes up."

"If you think it's best to have them there. Then we can make things safe around here and go to the Lazy T."

Mobley had a puzzled expression when he left Pam. He wondered why he'd stepped into her life. He'd not done anything for anyone since the war. He'd vowed to himself not to let anyone get close enough to hurt him.

Pam had the same expression. Late though it was, she poured another cup of coffee and sat at the kitchen table to drink and think. She took a sip of her coffee and stared at the door through which Jed had only moments before left. How had that man walked into her life and taken over? Why did he have any reason to care what happened to her and Tommy? And why was she letting him do the things he'd offered to do?

In such a short while, only a little over a day, she was

letting him do the things her husband had done. Why? She thought about that a while, and decided that she had nowhere else to turn. She had to have help from somewhere, someone, and that someone had to be a man, for only a man could do the things that needed doing. But the fact remained that she had no money to pay him, and she'd not let him do the things he was proposing with only a meal as payment. She'd have to tell him on the morrow that he must ride on.

While Fain walked to the bunkhouse, he had trouble swallowing; his head ached from the pounding, angry blood pulsing through it. Why the hell was he staying, subjecting himself to Tuttle's daughter's rudeness? He didn't owe these people anything.

But his parents had taught him to never walk away from good, honest people in distress, and the outlaw and his wife who'd raised him had taught him the same lessons. He wouldn't quit on them now.

Then his thoughts fell on Mobley. His emotions calmed. Again he'd been right about a man. Mobley stayed for the same reasons he himself did. Then he wondered about the widow trying to run her homestead along with her young son. He nodded, even though no one could see him. Yep, Mobley would stick, and tomorrow Fain would have to figure things out as to what action he should take.

The next morning, after Dealy had assigned the few remaining punchers left on the ranch to their daily chores, Fain asked him to sit a while, said he needed to talk to him.

They each drew a cup of coffee. Fain called for Wash to join them; then they pulled chairs to the table and sat.

Fain looked at Wash. "Partner, I'm gonna leave you here in case anything happens they need you." He turned his look on Dealy. "Gonna tell you enough for you to know I've not deserted you and the fight you'll have to make."

He took a swallow of the steaming liquid in front of him. "Not gonna tell you any details 'cept I'm gonna go find some men to help us." He packed his pipe, lit it, and frowned into the billowing smoke. "Thought 'bout it long into the night, an' figure I can make it to where I gotta go an' back by the time Taggart gets his herd this far."

He gave both men a cold smile. "I'll bring back at least fifteen or more men, an' I guaran-damn-tee you those fifteen men'll be worth any fifty men Taggart'll have gathered round 'im."

Dealy frowned, rolled a quirly, put fire to it, then looked into Fain's eyes. "Where you gonna get men like that? Ain't nowhere close by I can think of where they's that many fightin' men."

"Dealy," Wash cut in, "I was you, I wouldn't ask that there question." He chuckled. "Don't think Cord would tell you noways. But let me tell you right now, he say he gonna git those men, then he gonna do it."

Dealy nodded. "All right, reckon I gotta b'lieve the both o' you. Reckon I better go tell Mr. Tuttle what you done told me."

Fain shook his head, and at the same time clamped his jaws tight. Then he forced himself to relax. "Don't want you to tell Tuttle anything. Tell him only that when you looked for me you found me gone. I know that spoiled daughter o' his will believe whatever you tell them 'bout me long's it's all bad."

Dealy leaned back in his chair, reached for his cup, and took a swallow. He frowned. "Cord, don't judge that young woman too hard. She done seen men die, men who helped raise 'er. She's been through more Injun attacks than most men out here in this country has."

He stood, walked around the table a couple of times, poured each of them another cup of coffee, then grabbed the back of his chair, twisted it, and straddled it. "You see, Ruth's been raised almost as a boy; she can ride, rope, brand; well, hell, she can do might nigh anything a man can do on a ranch. She done got used to a few months of peace, then you ride in here an' turn her world upside down."

Dealy rolled another cigarette, lighted it, and frowned through the smoke. He stared into Fain's eyes. "You see, boy, most people, when delivered bad news, tie those happenings to the one what brung it. Put some slack in yore rope, boy. She ain't near'bout as bad as she seems." He shrugged. "Know she done give you more bad mouth than any man ought to take from any woman, but b'lieve me, she ain't near as bad as she's been soundin' to be."

Fain stared into his cup, then pinned Dealy with a hard look. "Regardless what her life's been like, don't want you tellin' any of 'em what I'm doin'. I'll be back when I get done what I'm tryin' to do." He forced a hard smile. "'Sides that, that young woman's gonna b'lieve I cut out on y'all; she's gonna b'lieve I ran like a scared rabbit." He shook his head. "Let her b'lieve, an' say, whatever she wants."

Dealy took a drag from his cigarette. "She's gonna know better when you come back."

Fain nodded. "Yep, she will, but I reckon I'm gonna be as hard on her as she's been on me. If she's the kind o' woman you say she is, she'll apologize. I want to see her eat crow."

Dealy shook his head. "You're a hard man, Fain." He shrugged. "But reckon I'll let the hand play out the way you want. When you leavin'?"

"Soon's I drink the rest o' this coffee." He frowned. "You reckon you could spare me trail provisions for as much as four, maybe five days?"

"Yep, I'll have Cookie pack a tow sack while you get your bedroll."

Wash stood.

"Where you goin', Wash? I said these folks gonna need you here."

"Well, partner, I figgered you was gonna need a extra horse if you gonna make fast time. Was gonna go rope my horse for you."

Fain nodded. "I was gonna ask Dealy to loan me one o'

the horses b'longin' to the ranch, but that horse o' yours is a stayer, got a lot o' bottom. I'll take 'im."

Ruth pulled the curtains back to see better. Cord Fain rode past the wide veranda at the front of the house, bedroll and tow sack tied behind his saddle, rifle in the saddle scabbard, and leading the horse his partner had ridden to the ranch. He looked to be leaving—for good, leaving his partner when there might be a fight in the offing. Her shoulders slumped, a lump filled her throat, her chest muscles tightened. Even though she'd treated him in an awful fashion, and was secretly ashamed of it, she had hoped he was the man Jed Mobley had described to her and her family. Now he was leaving, seemed to be running, and she felt as though she had caused him to go.

Her first impulse was to rush out the front door and call to him, run to him and apologize. She shook her head. If he was going to run, he wasn't worth a second thought. She let the curtain fall back into place, and turned her steps toward the kitchen. Her mother was there.

"Mama, Cord Fain just rode out; looked like he was leavin' for good." She shrugged. "Reckon I've been right all along. Seems like he's ready to get other people into a fight, but when it comes right down to it, he don't figure to take any part in it."

"You sound like you're disappointed, Ruth. Why?"

She shook her head. "I purely don't know, Mama. Reckon I wanted him to be different, don't know why. I s'pose lookin' at him, well, you know, he's tall, well-built, good-lookin', an' at first glance seems like the kind o' man who'd stick by you." She shrugged. "Like they say, 'Looks can be deceivin'.'"

Her mother stared at her a moment. "Daughter, if a man ever treated me the way you treated that young man, I'd leave too."

Ruth nodded. "Yeah, I would too. Don't know why, but I wanted him to stay."

"You sure as the dickens didn't show it in any way. The fact is, you gave him every reason to leave long before now."

Again Ruth's throat tightened, and afraid she was about to cry, although she didn't know why, she shook her head and went to her room.

4

FAIN RODE SOUTH, paid Uncle Dick Wootten toll for using the Raton Pass road, bypassed the town of Raton, and headed for Cimarron.

In Cimarron, he looked for Blackjack Slade, and heard that he was in Eagle Nest. It was almost nightfall, and he wanted to make as many miles as possible, but gave in to his fatigue. He took a room at the hotel, then went to the saloon; tired though he was, he thought a drink would relax him.

He stood sipping his drink when he felt someone shoulder up to his side. He glanced at the man, squinted, studying him. The man kept looking at him as though waiting for Fain to recognize him. Finally, Fain grinned. "Frog Ballew." Frog got his nickname from the way he hopped along after a horse threw him. "What you doin' so far from El Paso?"

"Jest driftin' round, Cord. Ain't got no job, so decided to see a little o' the country."

"You ridin' with Slade?"

Frog shook his head. "Naw, but thought he might let me

hang around through the winter; be a place to eat till spring."

"You ridin' the owlhoot?"

Again Frog shook his head.

Fain thought on that a moment. Ballew's legs might be crippled up, but there was nothing wrong with his gun hand. Frog could handle a rifle or six-gun with the best. "Tell you where you can settle in for the winter, an' eat some o' the best grub you ever put in your mouth. The old man can't pay you fightin' wages, maybe no wages, but he needs help—gun help. You interested?"

Frog grinned. "Hell, Fain, I ain't never dodged a fight. Tell me 'bout it."

Cord told him about Taggart, and what he'd gotten from the trail boss's own mouth. He told him the whole story, including Taggart figuring to beat him out of two months' wages. He took another swig of his drink and looked over the rim at the gimpy puncher. "Still interested?"

Ballew nodded. "Yeah, but I got a question. Why ain't you up yonder helpin' this fella Tuttle?"

"Frog, I'm gonna get back there soon's I can, but right now I'm tryin' to find men who'll fight. Here it is a couple months shy of roundup time, an' he just flat don't have many men." He sniffed the smell of a cheap cigar from his nostrils. "Know where I might be able to get all the men I need. There's a man over yonder, in Coyote, who raised me. He keeps a bunch of fightin' men around. I figure he'll loan me all the men I need."

Ballew frowned. "Coyote. Ain't that the town where the sheriff don't look at a man's past too close?"

Fain nodded. "That's the town."

"You goin' in there wearin' no gun? Hell, man, you gonna get yoreself killed."

Cord grinned and shook his head. "Nope. Most o' those folks over that way know me. They'll leave me alone."

Ballew squinted at Fain. "Now it's my turn to ask; you ever ride the owlhoot?"

Fain stared into his now-empty glass, then slowly shook

his head. "No, Frog, but I came mighty close; probably
would have, but Pa kept a tight rein on me; so did Ma." He
smiled, a smile he knew showed not much humor. "But I
learned everything it took to *be* a bad man, even though I
wasn't allowed to use the things I knew."

"Tell me how to find this Lazy T ranch."

Fain gave him directions, told him to stay close to the
mountains when he got past Trinidad, and to tell the foreman, Jim Dealy, he'd sent him. "Tell Wash an' Cookie
howdy for me."

He looked at his empty glass, wondered if he wanted another drink, and decided to go to bed. He figured to be on
the trail before daylight.

He felt all right about not wearing a gun in Eagle Nest,
Slade would have passed the word to leave him alone, but
Taos, the next town he'd pass through after Eagle Nest,
was a different story. Taos was one of the roughest towns
he'd ever been in, and he'd not been in it long.

He made it to Eagle Nest the next night. Slade was there.
He told the outlaw leader where he was headed, and why.
"Hell, Fain, I'll send some men over there to help. No need
for you to ride all the way to Coyote." He grinned. "I didn't
like that bastard Taggart any way. Figure I'd enjoy takin'
'im down a notch or two."

Cord shook his head. "Jack, I already owe you more
than I can ever repay. Don't want any o' your men gettin'
shot on my behalf."

"Let me worry 'bout that, Cord. An' don't you ever
think you owe me anything. Your pa has done a lot o' fa-
vors for me."

Fain had another drink with Slade, then went to his
blankets.

In Taos, he stayed in the livery stable with his horses, the
only night he spent there. He figured if he stayed out of the
saloons, there would be little chance that anyone looking
for trouble would cross his path. He was wrong.

The next morning, when he stepped out the door of the
cafe, a big man, tall, wide of shoulder, and built like a

blacksmith, stopped in front of him. "Well, well, look what we have here?" He took a step toward Fain, then stopped. "You got any o' yore old man's men around to take care of you, sissy boy?"

Fain looked at Dutch Gruder. The last time he'd seen him was when his father had run the Dutchman off his ranch. "Don't want any trouble with you, Gruder. Never done anything to you, so leave me alone."

The brawny man threw back his head and laughed. There was no way Fain could avoid trouble.

In the middle of the Dutchman's laugh, Fain stepped into him, swung from the waist, and caught Gruder alongside the neck with a right. The Dutchman staggered to the side, choked, caught his balance, and charged.

He swung a roundhouse left that connected with the side of the slim puncher's head. Lights exploded behind Fain's eyes, he staggered, landed hard on his right foot, pushed back from Gruder, dodged a right fist that whistled past his ear, then stepped inside another right and landed a right to the Dutchman's stomach.

Gruder sucked for air. Fain followed up his advantage and threw three rapid punches to Dutch's gut. Gruder backed up a couple of steps, then stepped inside a right Fain threw at his head. That brutal left he'd used for his first punch came at Fain's chin.

Fain tucked his jaw behind his shoulder, took the punch on it, and stepped back. With the Dutchman outweighing him by at least fifty pounds, Cord knew he'd better stay out of his reach as much as possible. He'd have to do the things one of the men working for his Pa had shown him time and again. Boxing, the man had called it; said a fighter in New York had taught him.

Now Fain stayed on his toes, faded in, punched, and stepped back. Gruder now breathed hard. Too much time in saloons, Cord figured. He concentrated his attack on the Dutchman's stomach. He slipped inside another of Gruder's roundhouse lefts, pumped a left, a right, a left to

Dutch's stomach. Gruder's face flushed a bright red; he sucked for air.

Fain stepped in and swung at the Dutchman's face; his nose spewed blood, and as soon as his nose flattened, Cord swung a right to Gruder's cheek, cut it, and white bone pushed through the cut below his eye. Sharp punches above the Dutchman's eyes opened both eyebrows. Blood flowed into his eyes.

Fain stopped trying to knock Gruder out. Now determined to cut the man's face to ribbons, he dodged in and out of the blinded man's reach, punching with razor-sharp punches at his face, ears, and mouth. Gruder's left ear split. Fain took another swing at the gory ear, and tore it loose from the big man's head.

Gruder stood there, blinded, gasping for breath, his arms hanging loosely at his sides. Fain measured him for a last punch, and brought his right up from his knees. It landed full on the side of the Dutchman's head, right on the temple. The punch knocked the huge man to the side. He caught his balance.

Gruder took two, rubber-legged steps toward Fain, and like trees Cord had seen toppled, the Dutchman fell forward on his face, off the boardwalk, into the inches-thick dust of the street.

In the back of his mind while the fight went on, Fain had been aware that a crowd gathered; now the roar of it dinned in his ears. He stepped from the boardwalk to the street and stared down at the brutally beaten man at his feet.

Someone from the crowd said, "Cowboy, you better start wearing a gun. Gruder ain't gonna forget this, an' if he's smart, which he ain't, he ain't never gonna fistfight you agin."

His face feeling like old dried leather, Fain looked at the man who'd given him the advice. His words had fallen between them like shards of broken glass, and Fain shook his head. "Tell 'im when he wakes up, I'll be back through here in two or three days. If he wants to push his luck, I'll take 'im on with fists, guns, or knives—his choice." He spun and walked to the board-well, ducked his head under the ever-flowing artesian well water, and washed the blood from his face. He'd taken some punches too.

When Fain pulled his head from under the stream of water, a slim, tanned man with a star pinned to his shirt stared at him, a hard smile breaking the corners of his mouth. "C'mon, young'un, I'll buy you a drink. Ain't nobody gonna push a fight on you long's I'm around."

Cord stared at him a moment, glanced at the sun to set the time, then shook his head. " 'Preciate it, Marshal, but I got some ridin' to do, figured to be long gone by now, would've been too 'cept for the Dutchman forcing a fight on me that I wasn't lookin' for."

He shook the town marshal's hand and stepped away, then turned back. "Marshal, when I come back through here, he might want to take this up again. I don't want it, ain't lookin' for it, but whatever happens, want you to know I'm not gonna push for another fight."

The marshal again gave him that hard smile. "Don't figger if he's got any sense he's gonna push another fight on you neither. Take care, young'un." He stepped to the boardwalk and left.

Fain headed for the livery to collect his horses. He had miles to ride.

Ruth pulled the door closed behind her, pulled the chair away from the small table she had in her room, and sat. Then she looked out the window.

She squelched the tight feeling in her chest. If Fain was the kind of man who'd run from a fight, why did she sit here wishing he had stayed, wishing he had turned out to be the kind of man she could respect? She admitted to herself that she'd treated him badly, and if he'd intended to leave, why hadn't his partner gone with him? Maybe they'd split because Matthew Washington Black had more

backbone than his partner. She'd ask Dealy what he knew
of their split the next time she saw him.

She picked up the book from her bedside table. She'd
been reading it up until Fain had ridden in with his news
that had upset everyone on the ranch. She opened it, sat
staring at the page a few moments, slapped it shut, and decided to ask the foreman now what he knew of Fain's departure. She headed for the bunkhouse, thinking to find
Dealy there.

Jim Dealy looked up from the desk he'd had built in
front of the window by the door. Ruth was heading toward
the bunkhouse, and from her determined long-legged
stride, he guessed she had her dander up for some reason;
of course that had been her frame of mind ever since Fain
and Wash had ridden in.

She knocked on the door. Dealy looked around the room
to see if anyone might be there in some degree of undress,
although he knew every man on the ranch had already been
assigned his chores for the day and should be hard at them.
He answered the door.

She stood there, her shoulders square, breath coming in
short gasps. "Need to talk to you, Jim. Can I come in, or
will it be better to talk out here?"

He studied her a moment. "None of the men in here this
time o' day, come on in. Looks like you got a bee in yore
bonnet. What's got you so upset?"

"I saw Cord Fain ride out a little while ago. Wanta know
why. Even though he didn't wear a gun, I thought maybe
he had more guts than to ride off an' leave a bunch of people needin' help. He could have used his rifle if shootin'
started."

Dealy thought to tell her the tall young man would be
back, that he'd gone for help. Instead he clamped his jaws
together, clenched them, and decided to keep his word.
"Don't know why he left, prob'ly 'cause you treated him
like a bag o' garbage. If I'd been him, I'd a left 'fore
now."

She sucked in a deep breath, pushed it out between clenched teeth; then, it seemed to Dealy, the anger left her. Her shoulders slumped, her eyes shifted from his to the ground, then back to him. "Reckon I did treat him like a pile o' dirt, Jim." She shook her head. "Don't know why. Never had a man around who seemed like he could take care of anything, or knew what to do 'bout everything. He just rubbed me the wrong way." Her eyes again fell before his stare. "'Specially since when I first saw 'im I thought how handsome he was, and wanted to know him better." Her last words came out so softly, Dealy had to strain to hear them.

"You shore as hell didn't show that sentiment, young lady." He looked past her toward the house. "Yore pa up at the house?"

She nodded. "He's in his office shufflin' papers, doesn't seem to get his mind on business since Fain rode in with his wild yarn."

Dealy pinned her with a look. "You got anything else you want to talk to me 'bout?"

To Dealy's thinking, her face looked as though it might crumple, looked as though she might cry. She shook her head, spun, and headed back to the house. Now, if she thought so little of Cord Fain, why would she care where he'd gone—or why? Dealy glanced at his desk, shrugged, and stepped toward the ranch house. He might as well let the boss know why Fain had left if he'd keep it under his hat. No point in getting all their hopes up.

Tuttle called, "Come on in," and Dealy walked to a chair, twisted it around, and straddled it. "Gotta talk, Boss. We gotta make plans what to do if Taggart decides this here ranch is the one he's gonna take over."

"Well, hell, man, you know what we're gonna do. We're gonna fight; always have, always will."

Dealy nodded. "Yeah, I know that, but how we gonna fight 'im? Go to one o' the line shacks back in the hills, or stay here?

"Way I got it figgered everything's in his favor to pick this ranch as the one he'll try for." He stood, went to the window, pulled a chew from his mouth, threw it out the window, and bit off another large chunk of Brown Mule Chewing Tobacco. He got it settled between his cheek and gums, then went back to the chair and again straddled it.

"Got to thinkin', Bob, yore Lazy T brand fits too good into his plans for him to ride on an' select another ranch. You know, that T in yore brand'll fit Taggart as well as Tuttle." He nodded. "Yep, I figger this here's the ranch he's gonna try to take." He gave a nod. "Now what we gonna do 'bout it?"

Tuttle, his face looking as though carved from granite, frowned. "Jim, I wish I knew where to get some more men. We just flat out don't have enough men to fight the size crew that Fain, an' then Mobley, said Taggart's got."

Dealy jerked upright from leaning on the back of his chair. "Well, damn, Boss, that's what I come up here to talk 'bout." He shook his head. "Don't want you to say nothin' 'bout what I'm gonna tell you to the womenfolk; it'll jest git their hopes up."

"If there's a ray o' sunshine in this situation, let's hear it."

Dealy wondered how much to tell Tuttle. "Reckon you don't know it yet, but Fain rode outta here 'bout an hour ago. He's gone lookin' for men, says he knows where he might git maybe ten, fifteen salty gunhands to help us. Only thing wrong with that is that he don't know for sure they'll be where he thinks they might be, an' the other thing is, he might be too late gittin' back here with 'em."

His face still looking like sun-dried leather, Tuttle gazed at Dealy. "How long he figger to git there and back?"

"'Bout a week an' a half. He took Wash's hoss; said he figgered to swap hosses off an' on. Said he figgered to ride like hell, git there, an' git back soon's he could." Dealy chomped down on his chew, then chewed furiously for a moment. "Told you, you ain't to say nothin' 'bout this to nobody. Now we gonna fort up here, or go to the hills?"

"Here."

"How we fixed for provisions?"

Tuttle frowned, then nodded. "Figger we got enough to stand 'em off for 'bout two weeks. I brought in a wagon load o' grub a couple weeks ago; 'nuff to feed the roundup crew 'bout that long when we start the fall hirin'."

Dealy stood. "Think I better go down to the widder's cabin, git her, her boy, an' Mobley moved up here till this here little scroody-woody's over. I'll have 'em pack what provisions they got and bring 'em along. No point in leavin' stuff there for Taggart's crew."

"Good, was jest gonna suggest that."

"Boss, like I told you, don't say nothin' 'bout what Fain's doin' to nobody. They gonna all have to figger we gotta defend the ranch alone—make 'em fight harder. I'll git the boys to come help git the shutters put back on the windows 'fore I leave for the widder woman's place."

As soon as Dealy left Tuttle, Tuttle's mind went into double time worrying. They'd always been able to stand the Kiowa, or Comanche, off with whatever number of men they had on the ranch, but the Indians had not been as well equipped with weapons as Taggart's crew would be. Bows and arrows just plain couldn't stack up against Winchesters, Henry rifles, and Colt or Smith & Wesson handguns. He shrugged. They had it to do.

His thoughts turned to Fain. He liked the boy—no, not a boy, a man in anybody's book. He had the quiet confidence a fighting man always seemed to have; confidence that whatever came along, he could handle it.

He'd always wanted a son, and Ruth had settled into trying to fit the role of a boy. He loved her more than life, wished she had not tried so hard to *be* a boy. She was a lovely young woman, and he wished she was in an environment where she could act like one, and at the same time, he wished there had been a school close by, but there hadn't been. He nodded to himself. Yes, he loved Ruth as a daughter, and if he'd had a son, he thought he'd like one much like Cord Fain. He wished his daughter had treated the boy better.

5

FAIN LEFT TAOS and rode till long after dark pushed light from every crevice. Finally, thinking the horses must be as tired as him, he made camp in the barren mountains to the west.

In his blankets, tired though he was, his mind turned to his boyhood and the man and woman who'd raised him, and how they'd taken him in as a boy of fourteen.

Soon after his thirteenth birthday, his mother and father died of smallpox. He tried for over a year to run the Kansas farm. There was no one to help. The neighbors offered to help when they had time, but they were kept too busy running their own land.

The owner of the closest farm offered him twenty-five cents an acre. He rejected the man's offer for almost a year, before realizing there was no way he could handle the job. He sold the homestead for 125 dollars, then gathered up the mules, oxen, and horses, and took them into Abilene. He sold all of the livestock for 1438 dollars, kept the best two saddle horses for himself, and headed West.

Riding late one night, north of Dodge City, he came on

a fork in the trail; the left fork would take him into town, the other one west. As he sat there trying to make up his mind whether to go into town and sleep in a hotel, or head on toward the mountains, his mind got made up for him. Gunfire sounded, not too distant, coming from toward Dodge.

Out of the darkness a band of riders rode toward him, and about a hundred yards behind them another bunch rode their horses belly to the ground. All of them looked to be firing weapons at the bunch closest to him—about ten men, he figured.

That made up his mind. If he waited for the second bunch to come closer, he'd take lead from one of them, judging from the way they seemed to be firing at any and everything.

The group of riders being fired at swung their horses to cut across the V in the trail. Cord put spurs to his horse and fell in at their rear. Every muscle in his body tightened to ward off the pain of a bullet hitting him. It didn't happen.

After about another mile of hard riding, he looked over his shoulder. The posse chasing them slacked their pace, and finally pulled rein and turned back toward town. As soon as the leader of the riders with whom he'd joined looked back, he slowed his horse and held up his hand signaling his men to slow their pace. Then they pulled rein and stopped, gathered around him. He glanced at each of his men. "Any of you hit?"

"All okay, Ben," one of the riders said.

Their leader scanned them; then his eyes came to rest on Cord. "Where'd you come from, boy?"

"Well, mister, I was sittin' there at the forks when I seen y'all comin' at me, an' that other bunch followin' you shootin' at anything that got in the way." He shook his head. "Didn't figure to be something that got in the way." He shrugged. "So I just fell in an' rode with y'all."

The leader chuckled. "Well, boy, don't know as how you did yourself a favor. That was the law chasin' us." He reined his horse toward the west, then motioned with his head for Cord to come alongside, ride with him.

When Fain pulled alongside, the man looked at him, raked his overalls with a glance. "You a farmer, boy?"

He hadn't said "farmer" with any suggestion that it was anything other than all right. Cord shook his head. "Was till my folks died. Tried runnin' the farm by myself, but couldn't handle it alone, so I sold out; figgered to get somebody to teach me to cowboy. My name's Cord Fain, mister."

"And my name's Ben Markum, son. Come along, ride with us till we see what you want to do; then you can cut out on your own, or stay with us. My wife would be glad to have a boy round the house."

Mr. Markum didn't offer an explanation as to why those men had been firing at them, and although he wanted to, Cord didn't ask. He had a warm feeling in his chest being with people after the long, lonely days on the trail.

Besides, it seemed to Cord that the kindly-looking man had left it up to him as to what he wanted to do. Mentally, he shrugged. If that was the case, and Mr. Markum had a wife who'd like to have him around the house, he'd make darn sure he earned his keep.

They rode for four days, most of it in the New Mexico Territory. Mr. Markum had kept him apprised of where they were most of the time, and what Cord liked most, the tall quiet man treated him as a grown-up.

Markum pulled his horse over close to Fain and pointed a little to the northwest. "Over yonder's the town of Coyote." He swung his finger to the left. "An' there, 'bout ten miles south of town, is my ranch. We'll be there in a couple o' hours."

In a little less than two hours they topped a hill, and at the bottom, close to a stream, a group of buildings huddled. From where they sat their horses, it looked to be a pretty good-sized ranch judging by the number of outbuildings, the size of two buildings Cord took to be stables, and a long bunkhouse with what looked to be a cookshack attached. Cord figured he'd got lucky; found a place he wanted to call home. Mr. Markum still hadn't said why those men outside of Dodge City had been shooting at them. Now that he'd taken Cord home with him, Cord thought to wait; someone at the ranch would tell him sooner or later.

When they rode into the ranch yard, several men ran out to take the horses and shoo the riders to the bunkhouse. According to their words, they were all concerned that those who'd come in with Markum needed rest.

Their leader didn't show any signs of tiredness. He hustled Cord to the house with him. There, to Fain's thinking, one of the prettiest ladies he'd seen ran to the man who'd taken him into his group of riders, put her arms around him, and gave him a lingering kiss. That greeting made Cord homesick for one of the few times since his parents died. That was the way his mother always greeted his father.

Markum stepped back from his wife and motioned Cord to his side. "Mary, this's Cord Fain. I brought 'im home to live with us." He nodded. "Course, if he doesn't like it here, he knows he can go his own way." He grinned. "Told 'im I thought you'd be pleased to have a boy round the house to boss around; told 'im that'd probably get you off of my back."

Mary Markum placed her hands on hips and stared at her husband. "Oh, you did, did you? Well, what would you say if he and I ganged up on you?" Her smile told Cord she was only joshing.

She pulled Cord to her side. "Come, son, you look like you could use a nice slice of apple pie. Supper won't be ready for a couple of hours yet." While she walked him to the kitchen she told him to call her "Ma," if he didn't mind. "And you can call Mr. Markum 'Pa.' I think he'd like that."

Cord thought on that a moment, wondered if he'd be showing an attitude of not caring toward his own folks. He decided that he wouldn't be showing any disrespect toward them in that he'd called them Mama and Papa.

He looked at Mrs. Markum and smiled. "Ma'am, I reckon I'd like that pretty much. My mama and papa both died from the smallpox back in Kansas last year. I been pretty much on my own since then." He shuffled his feet a moment, looked at the floor to hide tears that threatened to embarrass him, swallowed at the lump in his throat a couple of times, then got his feelings under control. "Want you to know, ma'am, I figure to earn my keep, ain't gonna be a burden on nobody."

Mary Markum pulled him to her breast and hugged him, just about caused him to want to go through the floor. He hadn't been hugged by such a pretty lady since his ma died.

"Cord, I'll make a bargain with you. Let me teach you proper grammar, and we'll count that as part of your chores."

"Ma'am, I wouldn't count that as no chore. I always wanted more schoolin', but never had the chance. Schoolhouse was a mighty long way from the farm, an' they always seemed to be work to be done that kept me from makin' the trip to school." He nodded. "Yes'm, reckon I'd like to get more book learnin'."

She led him to the table and served him a huge slice of apple pie, then poured him a glass of frothy milk. "Just came from the cow this morning. Now you eat. It won't spoil your appetite—I promise."

Lying there under the stars, on the way home for the first time since he'd ridden out seven years ago, with a promise to Pa that he wouldn't wear a handgun, and promising Ma that he'd never do anything to make them ashamed of him, he wondered at the ease with which he'd slipped into being their only son.

He'd found, over time, that the punchers on the ranch, all young, except for the grizzled old-timer who did odd jobs that no one else seemed to want, had all ridden behind Pa, who'd been a major in the Confederate Army, and the old man had been his top sergeant. They came West determined to recoup what they'd lost in the war, and they didn't care how they got it as long as the property they stole belonged to a Yankee.

Ma and Pa were married before the war, and she came West with them. Over the years, most of them years during which Cord grew up within the family, Ma had gradually weened Pa and the boys away from lawless ways. When Fain left them, they had been law-abiding ranchers for some time. And Ma had kept him at the books until she said he talked, and acted, like a gentleman. Her smile told him she was proud of him.

While he was growing up, the ranch hands had taught Fain everything they knew about guns, knives, fistfighting, and how to survive in the wilderness. They'd also taught him all they knew about cows, horses, weather, water, and good grass. They now called him a top hand, and he was proud to wear the name.

Since leaving home he'd never worn a gun—but he had made it a habit to go off alone and practice with his handgun. Draw, shoot, always aware of what might be to the side, or behind him. The day he left, Pa pulled him aside and looked him in the eye. "Cord, your ma has taught you to read, write, and speak well. The boys have taught you everything you'll need to know to protect yourself, or others who might merit your protection. Now I'm gonna ask something of you, a promise, your word, that you'll never wear a gun unless it becomes absolutely necessary to save your life or to protect others. I'd come close to askin' you to get my approval before you strap on a handgun rig, but that wouldn't be fair.

"You're a grown man, got a good head on your shoulders, capable of knowing right from wrong. I trust you.

Gonna leave it up to you whether a gun is needed to settle your differences. Now you go on out in the world an' see what makes the wolf howl."

His pa swallowed twice, then swallowed again. "Hate to see you go, boy. When you get enough of the world, come back home. Ma and I'll be waitin' here for you." His pa turned away, but Fain had already seen the tears in his eyes.

After a moment Markum turned back, apparently having gotten his emotions under control. "Now you go on up yonder to the house, see your ma. She's waitin' there to tell you good-bye." He coughed, cleared his throat, then nodded. "Watchin' her say good-bye to you isn't something I believe I could take." He put his hand on Cord's shoulder and gave him a gentle shove. "Go on up there, boy. I'll wait till you ride out before I go to the house. That's when she's gonna need me."

That was the last time he'd seen his "family." He'd grown, both physically and as a man. He was now twenty-eight years old. He'd seen what he'd set out to see; and done the things all men do while becoming a man. Now he was going home, only to ask some of those men who'd taught him all he knew to side him in someone else's fight.

He rolled to his side and felt the heavy money belt full of what he'd earned topping broncs, branding cattle, and riding as a drover on trail drives. He'd left all but a hundred dollars with Pa when he left the ranch, asking him to take care of it for him. Now he had more to leave with him; he rarely drank more then two drinks, and he didn't mess around with loose women.

He remembered grinning when he said that if nothing else, leaving his money with Pa would cause him to come back. Too, Pa had always insisted on paying him after he learned to "cowboy," as he thought of it. Thinking on it, he realized he wasn't a poor man; many would think of him as a man of means.

Maybe after they took care of Taggart he'd come back,

get his money, and see if there was some land he could buy close to Ma and Pa. He'd like that.

Then his thoughts turned to the man he hoped to help, and to his rude, strong-willed daughter.

He wondered why he gave her a second thought. Hell, he'd never met a woman who could instantly raise his hackles just by his being in the same room with her. But he sensed there was more to her than what he'd seen, and for some reason he'd never understand, he wanted to know what that *more* was. Yeah, she was one good-looking woman, and yeah, she knew what she was doing around a ranch, and yeah, all the ranch hands seemed to like her, but damned if he could see why.

He tried to picture her as a rancher's wife, then mentally shook his head. *That* was one way he couldn't picture her. She'd deal some poor soul a lifetime of misery. He'd damn sure never put himself in that position.

But he had to admit to himself that when he thought about finding a ranch for himself, in that thinking he'd included a wife to come home to, a wife like Ma, a woman who'd stick by her man come hell or high water. He mentally nodded. Yep, that was the kind of woman he wanted. He turned on his back, stared at the stars a moment, and went to sleep.

Mary Markum stood at her big slab cutting table mixing bread dough. She'd only a moment ago picked up a huge handful of it and kneaded it, then moved it from one hand to the other. Abruptly she stopped, leaned to get her face closer to the window, stared a minute, dropped the dough she'd been kneading, and ran out the back door. "Ben— Ben, Cord's come home! He's out yonder at the top of the hill ridin' in!"

Her husband dropped the ax with which he'd been chopping stove wood and grabbed her by the shoulders. "Oh, Mary, you've been thinkin' every rider who topped that hill for the past five years was Cord. Now settle down." He wrapped her in his arms, held her close a moment, then smiled. "But if it'll make you feel better, we'll take a look an' see who it might be."

He took her elbow and turned her toward the front of the house. As soon as they could see around the corner, Ben turned loose of her and ran toward the rider. Cord Fain, his son, had come home.

Tears flooded the rancher's eyes. He didn't give a damn. His boy was home. "Get down, boy, get down; come on in the house." He reached up and practically pulled Cord from the saddle. Ben bear-hugged Cord, then stepped back.

Mary stood there, tears streaming down her cheeks, her arms bent at the elbow, reaching barely beyond her waist. Cord held out his arms. "Come here, Ma. Don't know when I've ever been more glad to see anyone."

She came into his arms; kissed his cheek, neck, missed trying to kiss his other cheek and kissed his nose, laughed, and ran her fingers through his coarse black hair. Ben came back in for another hug. The three of them stood there, their arms around one another.

Finally Ben threw his head back and laughed. Mary hadn't heard him laugh like this since her boy left home. "Well, gracious sakes alive, let's go in the house," she said. "Can't stand out here the rest of the day." She placed one hand in the crook of her husband's elbow, and the other on Cord's forearm.

Inside, at the kitchen table, Mary poured them all a cup of coffee. "Made it only an hour ago, son. It's fresh." She looked at her husband. "Ben, this is a special time. Why don't you freshen our coffee with some of that good bourbon you brought home from Santa Fe last time you were there?"

While Ben spiked their coffee, Mary asked a string of questions it would have taken Cord a month to answer. He sat there between the two of them basking in the glow and warmth of their love. This was even better than he'd ever dreamed it would be. He should've come home sooner, but his plans had been to have enough money to buy himself a place close to them. He thought that now he had enough.

"You home to stay, son?"

He thought on that a moment, wondered how to answer the man he thought more of than any other. He frowned. "Pa, I've got something I have to finish first, don't think it's gonna take more than a month or two." He nodded. "Then I reckon I might come over here, buy me some land close to you an' Ma, an' raise me some cows, an' if I can find a woman who'll have me, reckon we could even raise some babies."

Ma stood and poured them another cup of coffee. "You mean you're gonna leave again soon?"

"Ma, this's something I have to do."

Most of the joy left her face; her cheeks crumpled as though she might cry again. "It's been almost a year since we had a letter from you. Tell us where you've been, what you've been doing, an' what this is you think you have to do."

Ben picked up the bottle to pour more whiskey into their coffee. Cord shook his head. "Gonna tell you all that, then ask you for a special favor."

His father shook his head. "Can't think of anything you'd ask for that I wouldn't try to give you."

Cord nodded. "Yeah, I know, Pa, but listen to what I have to say first." He took a swallow of his coffee, then told them that he'd spent some time in Mexico, made four trail drives, on two of which he was a drover, and on the other two was the trail boss. He'd worked for a couple of ranches drawing top-hand wages, and then he told them about Taggart.

"Pa, I kept my promise to you. I've never worn a gun since I left here." He nodded. "Course, when I was out alone I've practiced my draw, an' popped a cap on a many a pistol cartridge. I still hit what I'm shootin' at, but I never drew on a human being, an' never shot one unless you want to count Indians, but then they were shootin' at me. I used a rifle then."

He toyed with his cup a moment, rolled it around on its base, staring at it all the while. After a few moments he looked across the table into his pa's eyes. "Pa, I'm askin' you now to release me from the promise I made you. I need to wear a gun. I won't be wearin' it in any saloons lookin' for a fight. I'll wear it, but I'll keep it in my holster unless I'm forced to do otherwise."

Ben frowned. "You figurin' to have gun trouble with this man Taggart?"

He nodded. "Pa, if he tries to carry out what he told the crew, I don't only figure, I *know* we're gonna have shootin'. I have every intention to stop him."

"How you think you're gonna stop him all by your lonesome?"

Cord locked eyes with his best friend. "That brings me to the favor I want of you. Pa, I need to borrow 'bout ten, maybe fifteen men, salty men who know how to fight dirty, or any other way it's gonna take to win."

"Son, for my say-so, I'm sayin' yes, but I wouldn't ask any man to do what you're askin'. If any o' the boys want to volunteer"—he nodded—"then you can take those who do. Take 'em all if they want to go with you."

Cord took a swallow of coffee, stared at the table a moment, then frowned. "I wouldn't have it any other way. How *are* the boys anyway?"

Ben grinned. "All o' them're a few years older; still wild as one o' those old mossy-horn steers down yonder in the Texas Big Bend country." He grinned. "But I keep a tight rein on 'em. Slater broke 'is leg a few months ago. Horse fell on 'im; rest are all fine. I'll keep Slater here at headquarters till his leg stops hurtin'."

"Pa, I won't take over fifteen men with me." He smiled. "If I remember them correctly, there won't be a single one who won't want part o' this. You wouldn't have enough left here to keep the ranch runnin' smooth." He nodded. "Fifteen'll be all I need."

Ben stood, frowned, then again sat. "Was gonna say let's

go to the bunkhouse an' let 'em know you're home"—he shook his head—"but they won't have come in for supper yet. We'll wait'll after Ma feeds us, then we'll go down there."

Ma stood and went to the heavy cutting board where she did most of her kitchen work. She picked up the wad of dough she'd been kneading when she saw Cord through the window. "Reckon I'd better get started on supper." She looked over her shoulder at her boy. "Son, you think there's a real chance you'll come home to settle down?"

He grinned. "Unless you've forgotten how to cook, I'll guarantee you I'll be comin' back."

After supper, Ben took Fain down to the bunkhouse. The boys pounded, hugged, shook Cord's hand until he thought if he survived their onslaught, he could survive any number of Taggarts.

Ben's foreman, Nolan Baty, stood back and measured Cord with a look. "Damned if the young sprout ain't done growed up." He cocked an eye at him. "Reckon you done forgot ever'thin' we taught you 'bout guns, fightin', cows, an' such?"

Cord grinned. "Let's pull the lead outta our shells an' see what I mighta forgot."

Nolan grinned. "Naw, don't reckon we need to do that. Yore look tells me you can do it all." The foreman studied him a moment. "You left here a twenty-one-year-old boy that needed some seasonin'. See you done seasoned right well. Too, you've growed some. What you weigh now?"

Cord chuckled, then shrugged. "Yeah, reckon I've seasoned right well. Seen the elephant an' heard the owl since I left here." He shook his head. "But I'm here to tell you I never killed a man; never felt the need to—till now. That's why I'm home."

Nolan squinted at him. "Tell me 'bout it."

The crew gathered closer around him. It was obvious none of them wanted to miss a word.

He told them pretty much what he'd told his pa, especially about Taggart. He glanced at the faces of each of
them. "Know you an' Pa did a lot o' things the law would
frown on, but you had reasons an honest man would understand." He spread his hands, palms upward, then shook his
head. "But none o' you ever took anything from an honest
hardworking family, a family who together had put together a life of toil so they'd have somethin' in their old
age." He pinned them with a hard look. "Now I've come to
where y'all enter my needs." He let the total silence drag
on a few moments, then nodded. "I'm askin' y'all for 'bout
fifteen men to ride with me; ride with me to stop Taggart.
Pa said I could ask you."

As far as Fain could tell, there wasn't a one of them who
didn't yell that he wanted to go. He grinned. "Tell you
what, there's no way I'm gonna strip Pa of his entire crew."
He shrugged. "I'd take all of you if it was right. There's not
a one of you who wouldn't stack up with the best fightin'
men anywhere."

He looked at Baty. "You're out. Pa needs you around
here to keep things goin' smooth." He shifted his look to
Slater. "Not gonna be party to you gettin' your leg hurt
worse. You stay with Nolan." He swept the rest of them
with a glance. "The rest o' you will draw for the chance to
go with me. I'll see Ma an' get some paper. I'll make slips
that say go or stay. The fifteen that draw a go will ride with
me; rest stay here with Pa. He needs you."

Nolan nodded, then smiled. "Sounds fair for all 'cept me
an' Slater. You know we want to go with you, don't you?"

"Never had a doubt, old friend." He stood. "Gonna go
write up those slips o' paper; be back down here in a few
minutes."

Thirty minutes later, he came back to the bunkhouse
with a fistful of paper. He'd used Ma's scissors to cut them
into exact sizes such that when folded, there was no telling
from looking at them whether they said go or stay. Ma had
made it a point to tell him that cutting paper with her

"good" scissors would dull them. He'd told her he would have them sharpened, or buy her a new pair.

Another half hour and the men knew who would ride with him. Those who drew the slips telling them they had to stay grumbled and growled that they hadn't had any "fun" in years.

Fain drew those who would go with him aside and told them to pack plenty of ammunition, pack like they were going on a trail drive, blankets, groundsheets, tobacco—everything they'd need to live in the outdoors. Then he told them that Ma wanted them all to come up to the house for breakfast the next morning.

At breakfast, Ma had fixed biscuits, eggs, ham, bacon, and grits. Cord knew none of them had ever given up grits for fried potatoes. They topped it off with gallons of hot coffee.

When they'd finished eating, and were ready to saddle up and leave, Ma stood at the head of the table. "Boys, I want every one of you to know you're as much my son as Cord. I just raised him from a tadpole; most of you were already war-hardened, young, but you'd been through what the major would have called hell." She seemed to Cord to try to push more words from her mouth, but they wouldn't come. Instead, she choked, covered her eyes, and tears slipped from under her hand. "Just want every danged one o' you back here safe and sound so I can nag you into doin' things for me." She stepped toward the front room. The boys stood and left to gather their horses.

Fain had told them to bring an extra horse each, that he figured to ride hard in case Taggart made his move before they could get back. Before leaving, he buckled his gunbelt, checked his Colt .44 for cleanliness, shoved six cartridges in the chamber, looked at the men, and grinned. "You won't believe how many times I've been shook right down to my toes because I didn't have a gun strapped to my side. Now that Pa released me from my promise, reckon if it comes to that, I can take lead without bein' shook."

One of the men, Gene Shelton, only five years older than Cord, gave him a hard stare. "Gonna tell you somethin', Cord, ain't nobody ever took lead without gittin' shook." He swept his hand to include every man there. "Ain't nobody in this bunch what ain't took lead in a gunfight. Yore Pa led us on some rough trails durin' the war. He took his share o' hurtin' right along with the rest o' us." He looked down at his hands stuffing shells into his gunbelt, then backup to lock his eyes on Fain's. "Reckon what I'm sayin' is that we gonna be lookin' to you to lead us like yore pa did."

Cord thought on Shelton's words a moment. He'd figured he was a grown man, and had seen it all . . . until now. Abruptly, the weight of leadership climbed aboard his shoulders. Without lowering his gaze from Shelton's, he nodded. "Tell you how it is, men. I've fought Indians with them using rifles, and bows and arrows. Had two arrows stuck in me, three rifle slugs, an' been cut with a bowie knife." He shook his head. "Tell you for a fact, I won't ever ask you to do anythin' I won't do myself. Now, I reckon we better get ridin'. Don't want Taggart to get the idea he's gettin' off free." He toed the stirrup and swung aboard. "Let's ride, men."

Around the campfire that night, Fain told his men that he'd had a little trouble in Taos. He told them about the fight. "Don't know whether he's gonna try to take it up where we left off or not. Kinda figure he will. If he does, I don't know how fast he is, or how accurate with his shots, but I damn sure don't want any o' you to join in unless someone tries to get at my back."

Buck Nelson grinned. "Hell, Cord, 'less'n you done forgot ever'thin' we taught you, you ain't got nothin' to worry 'bout."

"Didn't say I was worried."

Nelson shook his head. "Maybe I shoulda said *we* ain't got nothin' to worry 'bout. We'll leave it up to you, 'cept if somebody tries a backshot at you. That's a salty bunch in that there town, an' some of 'em ain't got no idea 'bout what's fair."

"All right, men, let's finish our coffee and get some sleep. We got a long ride ahead o' us tomorrow."

The next afternoon, outside of Taos, Fain circled his men around him. "We'll get hotel rooms when we get there. You fellas wet your whistle, do whatever you want, but come sunup we gonna be on these broncs headed for Raton. You drink too much o' that crack-skull whiskey, these horses gonna seem like they step in a hole with every step. Let your conscience be your guide."

It seemed to Fain that every step toward Taos brought more aromas of cooking food to his nose. He got hungrier and hungrier. Finally, about a quarter of a mile from the fringes of town, he urged his horse to a lope. "C'mon, men, I'm hungry enough to eat the south end of a northbound skunk."

"Ain't warm food I want. I'll settle for a good hot *señorita* an' a glass o' good bourbon."

Fain looked across his shoulder and grinned. "To each his own, Gene, to each his own. Gonna laugh like hell in the mornin' when you groan an' moan with every step your horse takes."

Shelton eased his horse over close to Fain. "You want I should stay close to you for a while, you know, till you see what this fella Gruder might do if he sees you?"

"No. Reckon no matter how hard a bunch this town holds, I don't figure they'll stand still for anything but a fair fight. Go on, see if you can find that *señorita* you been lookin' forward to."

They rode to the hitch rack in front of the hotel, went in, and all got rooms; then they took care of their horses.

Before they left the livery stable, Fain again pulled his Colt from its holster, checked it, then eased it gently back into the leather sheath that held it to his body. He didn't slip the thong over the hammer. "You men go ahead, get a few drinks under your belt, but remember we gonna get an early start in the mornin'." He grinned. "As to what I'm gonna do, well, I'm headin' for that cafe I smelled those good smells comin' outta."

In the cafe, Fain chewed the last bite of steak, pushed back from the table, and signaled for a coffee refill. That steak he'd only now finished was good, but not nearly as good as Ma fixed. He packed his pipe, thought about home, Ma, Pa, the boys he'd been raised with, and decided that was the place he most wanted to be. He nodded to himself. Yep, when he finished with Taggart, he'd head back to Coyote.

He'd been holding his unlit pipe in his hand while he daydreamed. He put fire to it, got it going good, and sat back to enjoy it and his coffee.

"Well, well, the yeller-belly done come back. Reckon this time you ain't gonna leave, 'cept to that there hill out yonder where they bury saddle tramps like you."

Fain went still inside. His shoulder muscles pulled tight on his neck. His head ached. He sat facing away from the bully, a solid disadvantage. He didn't dare turn to face him; he'd be too close and Gruder could sneak-punch him. "What's the matter, Gruder? That whippin' I gave you still botherin' you? You come lookin' for more?"

"We ain't gonna fight with no fists, mama's boy. This time I'm gonna blow yore brains out, if you got guts enough to strap on a gun."

Fain tried to judge where the bully stood, then thought he had it figured. If Gruder couldn't see that he wore a gun, neither could he see his gun hand, and he had to be standing behind and to the left. Fain eased his hand to his side, and gripped the handle of his Colt. It slipped into his hand. Not until then did he twist to look over his shoulder at the big man, still wearing the yellowish hue around his eyes where only a few days ago they'd been black and blue. The cuts on his face hadn't healed.

"If you'll look down at my left elbow, you'll see that I *am* wearing a gun an' I got it pointed straight at your gut."

Gruder glanced where Fain told him. His face turned the

color of dried putty. He stepped back. "You didn't give me no chance."

Fain nodded. "Yeah, I'm givin' you a chance, but not in here where there're decent people tryin' to enjoy their supper." He twisted further around to face the bully. He waved his handgun to point toward the door. "Turn your back to me; walk out that door and stop about ten feet out on the boardwalk. Don't turn to face me till I tell you."

Fain waited for Gruder to clear the door and turn it loose before he walked out behind him. He didn't take the chance that the Dutchman would slam it into his face. "Now stand there with your back to me until I tell you to face me."

Gruder's neck pulled down into his shoulders, his right arm crooked and tensed.

"Don't try it, Dutch. You do an' I'll bust your spine slam in two 'fore you can get turned around."

The bully's arm relaxed to hang at his side. Fain studied his back. If, like most, Gruder let his hammer ride on an empty cylinder, Cord figured to get off a couple of shots before Dutch managed to fire; Gruder would have to thumb back and pull the trigger twice in order to bring a shell under the hammer.

"Now stand there a minute; want us to be shootin' such that no bystanders get hit. I gotta figure what way to do that."

"What's yore name, mama's boy? Wanta know what name to put on yore marker."

"You never heard of me, Dutchman. I never shot a man before, but Cord Fain's my name." He figured if he told Gruder that, it would help make him overconfident.

He walked to the side such that they'd be shooting up and down the street, rather than point-blank into the restaurant. "All right, turn toward me and I'll holster my Colt. You can draw anytime suits you." He smiled a cold smile, without much humor in it, to his thinking. "Before you make me kill you, I'll give you a chance to walk away. My havin' whipped your ass isn't any reason to lose your life."

"Turnin' yeller, mama's boy?"

"If you really think that—try me. My handgun's in its holster."

The Dutchman, obviously wary, turned slowly, his right arm slightly crooked at his side.

Fain looked into the man's eyes. Fear rode in bitter bile at the back of Fain's throat. This wasn't like he'd practiced. That thick-shouldered man standing there would shoot at him, try to kill him. Fain swallowed—hard. The bitter taste still sat there, causing his throat to swell, causing him to want to vomit.

He heard himself say, in what sounded like a frog's croak to him, "Anytime, Dutchman."

Gruder apparently heard the nervousness in Fain's voice. He grinned, took a step toward Cord, and his hand swept toward his gun.

Fain watched the Dutchman's lightning motion bring his gun half out of the holster. Then Fain flicked his hand in the motion he'd practiced ever since he counted only fourteen summers. His body took over. His thumb worked automatically. Three shots rolled out of the barrel of his Colt sounding as one.

The shots knocked Gruder back a step, all hitting him as fast as they'd sounded coming from Fain's six-shooter. Then Gruder caught his balance with his right foot and pushed forward. Flame blossomed from his six-gun. He sprayed shots everywhere but where Fain stood; then he bent at the waist, and with each step sank closer to the ground. Then he fell off the boardwalk, his face hitting the deep dust of the street. He lay still.

His Colt streaming smoke from the end of its barrel, Cord's senses slowly tuned into the street and any people on it. There were no crowds close by cheering the fighters on as there had been during his and the Dutchman's fist-fight. Today, the street stood empty, silent. He twisted to look down the dusty street, then looked in the other direction. No one. Not one person stood on the boardwalks or on the street. Then his brain fed him the picture slowly. People pushed through the doorways. With them came noise. They talked and yelled at once. His Colt still in hand, he walked toward the nearest saloon.

6

JED MOBLEY WAKENED to the smells and feel of the hay he'd raked into a pile on which to sleep the night before. He glanced toward the barn wall. The cracks between the rough boards showed only darkness. He hadn't overslept, which he'd been fearful of doing after the work he and Tommy had put in the day before, and then the long ride over to Tuttle's ranch and back.

He and Tommy again had a long day ahead of them. He rolled over, clamped his hat on, pulled up his boots, climbed down the ladder, and went to the pump to wash up and shave. Lantern light painted the kitchen window a golden hue. He headed toward the cabin.

"Heard you workin' that squeaky old pump handle. Breakfast'll be ready right soon; sit."

Mobley smiled to himself. Pam wasn't one to waste words. While he pondered the kind of woman he'd chosen to help, Tommy came from the attic, went outside to the outhouse, and then to the pump. He came back in and seated himself next to Jed.

While eating, Mobley told them what he thought to do about the cattle. He looked at Tommy. "You reckon your herd is close by so we can gather 'em and push them back in the hills without havin' to search the place over?"

Tommy nodded. "I try to keep 'em on the same pasture; makes it easier to keep a check on them, know when new calves get dropped. Figger we can get 'em outta sight by sundown."

Mobley studied the little boy. He was going to make one helluva man in a couple more years. Mobley frowned. "I b'lieve we have ample time before Taggart shows up to do that and tend to a few things that need doin' around here.

"We'll figure today for movin' your cattle; tomorrow we'll fix that corral fence. I noticed a few broken poles in it." He glanced at Pam. "Noticed a couple ponies in the corral; they been broke yet?"

She shook her head. "I never thought I was good enough to stay on them. Tommy's too young. I won't let him on a green stud." She lowered her eyes, then murmured, "Couldn't stand to have him get hurt."

Jed smiled. "By the time I get through with 'em, Tommy'll have a couple ponies he can ride, even on a cold mornin' after taking the kinks outta 'em. Don't worry, I'll have 'em gentled down for a boy his age." He took a swallow of the coffee Pam had only then poured. He pursed his lips and blew. "Boy, that's hot." He shook his head. "Pam, I don't want him gettin' hurt either. Don't worry, I'll make sure he's safe."

Safe. For some reason she couldn't figure, she had felt safe since the tall, gentlemanly man had ridden into her life. She wished she had the money to pay him wages; keep him around for as long as the money lasted.

How long had Jed Mobley been with her and Tommy? Only two days, and she'd come to depend on him taking care of her and her son. And she admitted to herself that it was more than only a feeling of being safe. Her face warmed. She tried to squelch the feeling, knowing she must be blushing furiously—and she was.

Jed looked at her and frowned. "Pam, did I say or do anything to upset you? Your face is flushed."

She shook her head. "No. No, Jed; it's that the cabin has warmed an' I've been standing by the stove. Reckon I always do this when I've stood at the stove."

Mobley drank the last swallow of his coffee, pushed back from the table, and stood. "C'mon, Tommy, we better get with it or we'll be workin' till long after dark." He placed his big hand on Tommy's shoulder while they left the kitchen.

She stared at the door long after the two had gone through it heading for the stable. *Pam Henders, you got no right to feel the way you're feelin' 'bout a man who only two days ago rode in here. What would your poor departed husband say?*

She thought on the question she'd asked herself, then nodded. He'd say, "It's time you let me go, girl. Time you got on with your life. Be certain that you give your thoughts to a man deserving of you. Don't care if he's got a dime long's he's a hard worker an' will take care o' our son an' you."

Her face heated again. Her husband would have also said to make sure the man loved her, *and that she loved him. There* was the problem; she couldn't imagine loving a man after knowing him only two days. She shook her head. Maybe not, but she surely felt something more than just safety when he was around.

Tears welled up and ran down her cheeks. The picture of him walking out the door, his hand on Tommy's shoulder, squeezed her heart tighter. She'd better be careful. Security could never take the place of love. She'd made up her mind soon after Tommy Senior had been killed that if she did ever remarry, it would be for love; she'd had that in her marriage, and she wouldn't settle for anything less—but maybe, just maybe . . .

Dealy got the men busy closing and bolting the rifle-slotted thick oak shutters tight to the windows. The adobe walls, two feet thick from the outside to the inside of the house, had withstood attack before; they'd do it now. But he was worried.

The Kiowa had had ancient, rusty old rifles and bows and arrows. Those who would attack them this time would have modern weapons, weapons fully capable of penetrating the shutters. He shrugged. Hell, if they'd wanted to remain safe, they should all have stayed east of the Mississippi.

From where he worked on the shutters, he looked over his shoulder at Wash. "Have the men take four barrels into the kitchen, then have them start fillin' 'em with water. We might need every drop of it 'fore we git rid o' them varmints, or 'fore Fain gits back with whatever he manages to git from wherever he figgers to git it."

Wash grinned. "Done got it done, Dealy, only I had 'em fill five barrels." He frowned. "Jim, how much ammunition we got?" He shook his head. "Know I ain't got 'nuff to last through any long fight, 'specially since we don't know how long's gonna take Mistuh Fain to get back heah with them men."

Dealy stepped from the ladder. He frowned. "Been worryin' 'bout that, Wash. We better have the men bring all they got, keep all calibers separate, put it in piles and see what we think. This ain't gonna be like we're used to fightin' Injuns. *They* hit us once, twice, then gather up their dead an' them what're hurt, then leave.

"I figger these here men gonna stay till they kick our butts, or we kill 'em to the last man. While I finish up with these here shutters, you round up the men an' have 'em bring their shells up to the house. Use the kitchen table to pile it on."

"We don't have 'nuff o' what we figguh's gonna be 'nuff, ah'll take a packhorse, go into Trinidad, an' load 'em up."

"If Taggart's done got this side o' Trinidad, you reckon you can git round 'im?"

Wash showed every tooth in his head. "Jim, if I cain't, I don't figguh they's any o' that there white trash can take

me in a straight-up gunfight." His grin widened. "Fact is,
Mistuh Dealy, I got it figuhed they's only one man round
heah who can beat me with any kind o' weapon you want
to name."

"Yeah? Who's that?"

Wash stood there a moment staring into Dealy's eyes.
His teeth stopped showing, his face sobered. "Jim, I done
got it figuhed Mistuh Fain's maybe the most dangerous
man in this heah country. Don't know why—but that's the
way I got 'im figuhed."

"Fain? Why, hell, man, he don't even pack a gun."

Wash shook his head. "Know all that, Dealy. Don't
know why, but you wait n' see."

Dealy frowned, then nodded. "Hope you're right, Wash,
an' it's kinda strange, but reckon I find it easy to believe.
So far, he's been a man of his word, an' that's good enough
for me." He picked up a handful of bolts and stepped to the
ladder. "Go tell Bob Tuttle I said for him to give you about
twenty dollars, that you're goin' to Trinidad for more
ammo."

Fain looked back at the man he'd only moments ago put
three .44 slugs into. Gruder lay still. Cord sniffed gun
smoke from his nostrils, only then aware that he still held
his smoking gun in his hand. He opened the loading gate,
removed the spent cartridges, punched new ones into the
cylinder, slipped the big Colt into his holster, and pushed
through the saloon batwings.

He'd always heard that when a man killed his first vic-
tim he'd feel sick to his stomach, want to vomit. He didn't
feel that way at all. He'd done his best to keep Gruder from
pushing him into a fight, but the Dutchman had insisted—
and paid the price. Fain shrugged; if he hadn't taken
Gruder out, someone else would have.

When he walked to the bar, those standing there parted
and gave him more than enough room. Several of his men
stood farther down the bar. A man several steps from him
turned to one of the punchers Cord's father had loaned

him. "You know that man who just walked in here?" Cord could hear him plainly.

The cowboy, Pablo Menendez, nodded. "Yeah, I know 'im. Why?"

The man stared at his drink, then shook his head. "Reckon I only want to know who he is. I b'lieve I done seen most o' the real fast ones, or heard 'bout them"—he shook his head again—"but way I got it figgered, I ain't seen nobody fast as him. He's one o' them what gits talked about?"

Pablo smiled. "Not yet, *Señor*, not yet. But way I got it figgered, soon's people find out his name they'll start talkin'. I will not be the one to tell you his name. Don't think he wants to be known."

With Pablo's words, Cord sighed, thankful that the slim Mexican had not given him away. Pablo was right; he didn't want to get a reputation.

About that time, the marshal Cord met when riding through the last time pushed up to Fain's side. "Buy you a drink, son?"

"Howdy, Marshal. No, thanks, this one's enough. I'll buy you one, though."

The marshal shook his head. "Can't, I'm on duty." He chuckled. "Just goes to show you how wrong a man can be."

Cord frowned. "Don't follow you, Marshal. What shows you that?"

The lawman stared at Fain's image in the mirror behind the bar. "When you come through here before, I worried that Gruder would probably kill you when you come back, an' that there wouldn't be a thing I could do 'bout it." He laughed. "I never thought to worry 'bout *you* killin' the Dutchman." He sobered. "Why wuzn't you wearin' yore gun last time?"

Fain knocked his drink back, changed his mind about having another, and held his glass out for the bartender to refill, then looked at the marshal. "Still won't have one with me?"

"Yeah, reckon I will if you'll answer my question."

"Marshal, would you b'lieve me if I told you flat out that this is the first time I ever wore a gun in town?"

"Way you handle a gun makes it hard to b'lieve, son."

"Tell you how it is; I know I can outdraw an' outshoot most men. Pa knows it too, so he asked me a long time ago, years ago, to not wear a gun. Said it would keep me outta most trouble. I promised him I wouldn't till he told me otherwise. He's been right up till now."

He pulled his pipe from his vest pocket, motioned the bartender to bring a drink for the marshal, then packed his pipe and lit it. "I knew from the way Gruder kept pushin' for a fight last time I came through that I couldn't avoid another fight with him. An' after the whippin' I gave 'im, I knew he'd not fight me with fists again." He shrugged. "That left guns or knives. Turned out he wasn't any good with guns either."

Cord rolled his glass around on its base, saw the wet area he made, and stopped. "Soon's I get back to my saddlebags, I figure to again put my gun an' holster in them an' leave it there." He shook his head. "I just flat couldn't avoid this fight."

"You take my advice on somethin', boy?"

Fain grinned. "Don't know till I hear what it is."

The marshal shrugged. "Okay, here it is. This time when you rode into town, they wuz a whole bunch o' salty men with you. Know from that you ain't goin' to no Sunday school picnic. You got trouble on the end o' this ride, I wuz you I'd keep that there .44 you're wearin' right where it is. They's men who won't give a damn whether you're carryin' or not; they'll jest flat out shoot you."

Fain mulled the marshal's words over for a moment, then pinned the marshal with a look that would pierce an anvil. "Know you're right. I'll wear it till things get back to normal. I got plans, want to own me a ranch one o' these days." He knocked back the rest of his drink. "You got anything against me?"

The lawdog shook his head, then chuckled. "Nope. You

done me a favor when you killed Gruder. Don't b'lieve in punishin' a man who done me a good turn." He stepped toward the door, then turned back. "Somethin' else, son. Good luck." With those words, he left.

Cord stood there a moment longer, flipped a coin to the bar top, and headed for the livery. He needed sleep.

The next morning Fain and his fighting men left. The next night in Eagle's Nest, Blackjack Slade told Cord he might try to recruit his men, but knew they'd stay with Ben Markum. "You need more men for this fandango you're headed for, Cord?"

Amused at Slade's question, Fain let his humor show by letting his eyes crinkle at the corners. "Jack, if you had these men ridin' behind you, would you figure to need more?"

Slade slowly shook his head from side to side. "Not by a damn sight, old friend. Just thought I'd offer."

"Thanks anyway. I'm gonna have a drink and head for the livery. Gonna get some sleep. Figure to make Trinidad tomorrow night."

The next night, true to Cord's estimate, he and his men pulled rein about a half mile out of Trinidad. "There's a U.S. deputy marshal in that town, so any o' you men figure there's still a wanted notice out on you, go ahead an' make camp out here. I'll bring a couple o' bottles out to you. The rest of you come on in town with me; I want to see that marshal, let 'im know what we're up to."

No one stepped from the saddle. Fain grinned. "Okay, so all o' you figure you've outlived your past. Come on, let's see if those saloons still have good whiskey."

As soon as they got in town, Cord went to Marshal Worley's office. He wasn't there. Remembering which saloon he'd met him in before, Fain walked two doors up the street to that place of business and found him.

"Howdy, Marshal. Rode in to tell you what to expect up range a ways."

"Yeah, bet I can guess what it is. Saw you ride in with a pretty salty-lookin' crew. You figure to start a war?"

Cord shook his head. "Not 'less someone brings it to me."

Worley told the bartender to bring two drinks, then looked at Fain. "You got it figured who Taggart's gonna home in on?"

"Think so." He shrugged. "Won't know for sure till he starts spreadin' that herd out on land that doesn't b'long to 'im. Right now, I have a hunch it's gonna be Bob Tuttle's outfit."

"What makes you think that?"

Fain frowned. "Nothin' real solid, but it's well located to town; got good range, good outbuildin's, an' the thing that makes it a real probability is that Tuttle's Lazy T brand would be mighty invitin' to Taggart. That 'T' could stand for Tuttle *or Taggart*; it'd fit right in with his plans."

Worley knocked back his drink, looked thoughtfully into the empty glass, nodded, and murmured, "Well, I'll be forever damned if I don't b'lieve you've hit the nail on the head." He slanted a look at Cord. "What you figure to do?"

"You gonna let me handle it, Worley?"

"Don't see that helpin' a man protect his property is beyond the law." He nodded, then gave a smile, at least what he'd consider a smile. "Yeah, you handle it." Then he chuckled. "An' lookin' at that outfit you brought in here, I figure Taggart's in a world o' hurt."

"Hope you're right, Marshal." He gave Worley a straight-on stare. "Gonna tell you, I figured to let you know what we were gonna do. Didn't want any o' my men in trouble, *I* didn't want any trouble, an' I can tell you right now—I don't know how we're gonna handle it, 'cept I know damned well we're gonna fight for that man an' his family."

"That salty-lookin' bunch you brought in here—you know of any notices out on 'em?"

Fain pinned Worley with a look that would penetrate an anvil. "Gonna tell you straight. You don't look back further than ten years, you won't find anythin' on a single one of 'em; you take it back further than that, an' I expect you might."

Worley's eyes crinkled at the corners, which was usually as close as he came to an outright smile. "Know what, Fain? I only last night cleaned out my files; don't b'lieve I kept any paper over seven years old." He frowned as though giving his words some thought, then nodded. "Yep, damned if I didn't get rid o' all that old, browned paper that was practically fallin' apart from old age."

"Thanks, Marshal. Reckon I'll head for my blankets." He knocked back the rest of his drink, frowned, stepped toward the batwings, then turned back. "Taggart moved the herd yet?"

The marshal nodded. "Yeah, 'bout two days ago. Ain't had time to get more'n maybe twenty miles. You ain't even gonna have to ride hard to get to the Lazy T 'fore he gets there."

"Good. Gonna need time to find out how Tuttle figures to handle it."

"Fain, I know for a fact that man, his crew, an' his family's fought off many a Kiowa attack. Figure he's gonna have a good plan."

"The Kiowa are not Taggart. Might have to see can I influence him to fight the way it'll have to be done. That might be easy, but that hardheaded daughter o' his might buck me on it."

"Sounds like you an' Ruth didn't hit it off very well."

Cord grunted and said, "Yeah, reckon you could say that." He twisted to look about the room, then looked back. "Thanks, Worley, maybe I can do somethin' for you someday. Gonna get some sleep now."

He'd taken enough rooms at the hotel for him and his men, but before heading for his room, he thought to check the saloons to see if his crew were getting too much to drink; they had a long ride on the morrow.

The third saloon he went in, he came face-to-face with Taggart. The trail boss squinted at him a moment.

"Thought you'd be way up the trail by now, or all the way back in south Texas."

"Yeah? Well I sort o' figured you'd be with the herd figurin' to take somebody's land."

"Somebody might hear you say that an' git the wrong idea, milksop. Jest keep yore damned mouth shut, 'sides that, I figured to come back to town for a few drinks— wasn't long on horseback."

"Taggart, I don't ride for you, so I sort o' figure I can do, an' say, anything I damned well please. Now stand aside, I was headed for the bar."

The trail boss seemed to sense something different about his former drover. He stepped back and scanned Fain from head to foot. His eyes stopped a moment when they reached Cord's side gun. "You think you done growed up now, so you bought yourself a six-shooter?"

Fain thought he'd toy with the bully. "Nope, don't reckon I'm old enough to pack a gun yet, but sort o' figured to start learnin' somethin' 'bout 'em."

Taggart leered at him, a smirk showing his disdain for the man he'd treated badly. "Then I'd say it's my lucky day. Ain't nobody gonna fault me for shootin' a man with a gun, 'specially when I tell 'em you threatened me."

A man standing behind Taggart spoke up. "I'd fault you, mister. I heard the young'un tell you he wuz jest gonna learn 'bout weepons. Now gonna tell ya, I got a gun held right nigh against yore back. You make a move for a gun an' I'll separate that thing you call a backbone into two parts."

Fain looked over Taggart's shoulder, then grinned into the face of the man behind Taggart. "Howdy, Uncle Dick. Reckon you only this minute kept that big bad man from killin' me. Sure do appreciate you savin' my life."

Dick Wootton reached down and pulled Taggart's weapon from its holster; then, ignoring Fain's words, he told the trail boss to get out, not just out of the saloon, but out of town.

Taggart looked over his shoulder at the old man. "Wootton, huh? Well, I'm saying right now, I'll be in an' outta this here town in the comin' years. We'll see each other agin."

"Don't bet on it. You keep on actin' like yuh jest done, an' somebody'll blow yore damned brains out. Now git outta here."

As soon as the trail boss cleared the batwings, Wootton stared at Fain a moment. "Figgered to learn 'bout weepons, huh? What you tryin' to do, set 'im up real gentle to kill 'im?"

"Uncle Dick, you know from a long time ago I never shot a man. Fact is, never wore a gun till now." He glanced toward the bar. "C'mon, I'll buy you a drink. I already had two, so don't figure I need another."

While they stood at the bar, Fain told Wootton what had happened between him and Taggart, and what the trail boss, in his own words, said he was going to do.

The old man frowned. "I ain't fergot how to shoot a rifle since I got tame an' built that there pass over the mountain; then I built the hotel. I figger to join ya."

Cord raised his eyebrows and pulled his mouth to the side. "Way I got it figured, Uncle Dick, you could live to be a hundred an' you'd still know how to shoot." He glanced around the room, then back to the old frontiersman. He nodded. "All right, glad to have you." He smiled. "'Sides that, if I said no, reckon I'd be cuttin' you outta a bunch o' fun." He shook his head, his face somber. "Couldn't sleep at night if I thought for a minute that I'd hurt you like that."

Wootton chuckled. "Like hell you couldn't. 'Bout what time you cuttin' outta here in the mornin'?"

"'Bout an hour 'fore sunup. Meet you in front of the hotel." Fain left. Before turning in, he checked the saloons to make sure his men were all right.

Tuttle finished tightening a bolt on the last shutter, looked over his shoulder at Dealy, and nodded. "Reckon that does it, Jim. All we gotta do now is fight that land-grabbin' bastard off, then get on with livin' a peaceful life."

Dealy stared at his boss. "Hell, ain't it, old friend?

Seems like we been fightin' somebody off ever since we settled here."

"Yeah, but this's the first time we gonna be fightin' our own kind."

"Boss, look at it like this. We ain't fightin' our own kind; we'll be fightin' pure-dee white trash. From what Mobley an' Fain done told me, we wouldn't have a man like him in our bunkhouse—ever."

Tuttle stared at Dealy. "Ever since them two men, really three men, rode in here, I got the idea you put right smart stock in what they tell ya." He gave a nod. "Yep, I'd say you trust 'em to be the kinda men we'd like in this country."

"Well, Bob, you're right. I do trust 'em." He moved his eyes to take in the distant prairie, and a slight frown creased his brow. "Shore do wish Cord would get here with them men he went after." He shrugged. "But he told me it'd be right tight gittin' back here 'fore Taggart." His face brightened. "Reckon even if he is a mite late, we can hold them land-stealers off with what men we got."

Tuttle thought about Dealy's words a moment, and he had to admit to himself he wasn't really sure he could put any faith in what Fain had set out to do. He glanced at his foreman, then settled his look on the hills in back of the headquarters buildings. "You really b'lieve Fain'll be back with men?"

Dealy nodded. "If that's what he said he'd do, he'll be here."

"Well, Jim, if you b'lieve, reckon I do too." He pulled his pipe from his vest pocket, looked at it a moment, put it back in his pocket, and pulled a plug of chewing tobacco from the pocket on the other side. He offered it to Dealy, who shook his head.

He bit off a large chew. If he was going to enjoy having it tucked between his cheek and gums, he'd better do it while outside. His wife would raise hell with him if he came inside with it.

"Jim, I never knew you to be wrong about a man; hope you ain't this time. Maybe this whole ranch depends on it."

He frowned. "Wonder why Ruth took such a dislike to the man. He never done a damned thing to set 'er off. Hell, she acted like he said somethin' wrong to 'er, or done somethin' that wasn't proper."

"Didn't none o' that happen, Bob. She never wuz alone with 'im for it to happen." Dealy gathered a handful of bolts, stuck them in his pocket, then looked at the rancher. "Know what I b'lieve? I figger she caught herself to likin' that young feller too much, too sudden-like, an' fought it like a she-tiger. Figger she 'spected a man she'd like would be a fighter, an' somehow she tied bein' a fighter with wearin' a gun. She's gonna have to learn they's a lot o' men who don't wear guns're damn good men, men to ride the river with. You notice she's been mopin' round like a sick calf since he rode outta here?"

Tuttle nodded. "Seen somethin' like that. Figgered she was just worried 'bout havin' to fight that there Taggart."

"Naw, it's more'n that. She's done stood at our shoulders an' loaded rifles for us in at least six Indian attacks." He shook his head. "Reckon I'd say she's got worser troubles than a little ole gun fight."

Tuttle only shook his head, and wondered if raising a boy wouldn't have been a whole lot simpler. Of course he was proud of Ruth, always had been, and loved her right down to his toes, but, hell, he just flat didn't understand her—didn't understand any woman, for that matter. He thought about that for a few moments, and decided that there wasn't a man on earth who understood women. He felt a little better about his shortcomings after that. "Let's walk round the house, an' see if everything looks like we got done what we figured to do."

Dealy kept the crew close to headquarters. The days, hot and dry, passed. Dealy, always the optimist, thought that something good came of everything. Keeping the men close to the house had allowed them to spend time repairing things around headquarters, things he'd let slide for chores with a higher priority farther out on the ranch.

After a few days, with everything in good repair, he rode

out from the bunkhouse, away from the mountains three or four miles. The Lazy T branded cattle he encountered looked sleek and fat. It had been a good year; plenty of rain, plush grass, and a good calf crop. His boss would be happy with the way things stacked up.

In the midst of his feeling of well-being, he saw them, only three or four at first, then more and more longhorn cattle, pure longhorns. All the Lazy T cattle were cross-breed Herefords or Durhams, bred to longhorns.

His chest tightened. He swallowed hard. He swept the range with a long, searching look. There were no men on horseback in his sight, but that didn't mean anything; they could be in a ravine, a deep swale, anywhere. He reined his horse toward headquarters and urged him to a gallop, keeping his eyes busy searching every inch of the surrounding countryside.

As far as he could see, he was the only human on earth. But he'd seen Apache, Kiowa, or Cheyenne that seemed to appear right out of the ground.

A slight tug on his vest. He looked to see what might have caused it; saw a hole, then heard the sound of a rifle shot. He put spurs to his horse.

He looked over his shoulder. Two men, riding bent over the saddlehorn, topped a hill. From what he could see, they held their rifles in one hand, firing them pistol-fashion. None of the bullets came close enough for him to hear their whir.

A buffalo wallow ahead of him was the only depression he could see in which he might take cover; and with only two men chasing him, he was damned if he'd run.

His horse reached the deep wallow. He dragged his horse to a stop, slipped from the saddle, drew his Winchester from its scabbard, pulled his horse down beside him, jacked a shell into the chamber, and sighted on the lead rider. He took a deep breath, slowly squeezed the trigger, felt the recoil, heard the sharp crack of the shell, and a moment later the rider at whom he'd fired jerked back over the cantle, bounced when he hit the ground, and lay still.

Dealy swung his rifle to center on the second rider. The man pulled rein, slipped from his saddle, and stooped by the side of his saddle mate. Dealy lay there a moment. His finger tightened on the trigger twice before he relaxed it. Damned if he'd fire at a man trying to take care of a fallen partner.

He climbed aboard his horse and headed home. The news he had for Tuttle was not good.

7

FAIN HEARD THE two shots, and it appeared the sixteen riders behind him did also. Rifle fire.

Fain reined his horse toward the sounds; his men followed. They topped a ridge. Stretched out on his stomach in a buffalo wallow lay a man, and farther out a man squatted by a downed rider. Fain watched a moment. The man in the wallow stood, pulled his horse up, shoved his rifle into the saddle scabbard, climbed aboard, and spurred his horse into an all-out run. Fain recognized Dealy after squinting toward him a moment.

His course would cross Fain's line of travel. He held up his hand for the men to sit still, then rode ahead into the direct line of the man's flight. He held his hands over his head.

Dealy had been looking over his shoulder; now he turned his head to look in the direction where Fain sat his horse. He apparently recognized either Fain or his horse, because he slowed, then drew rein. "Knowed damn well you'd come back. Howdy, Fain. Shore good to see ya."

Cord raised his right arm above his head and waved it to him. His riders appeared from behind a rise and headed his way. "Brought some fightin' men. Looks like I'm a little late."

Dealy shook his head. "Naw, I'd say you done timed it right down to a cat's whisker." He flipped a thumb toward the rider who only then managed to get his partner across his saddle. "Them two are the first I seen what wuz strangers around here. Gotta say they didn't act like they wanted to be friendly."

He glanced toward the approaching men. "How many you bring?"

"Fifteen from home, an' when I came through Trinidad, Uncle Dick Wootton wouldn't hear of us havin' a gun fight without him, so he came along for the fun."

"Man by the name o' Frog Ballew showed up while you wuz gone; said you figgered I'd give 'im a job."

Cord nodded. "Yeah, I told 'im that. Glad he showed up, he's a good man."

The men gathered around Cord and Dealy. Fain introduced them, then Tuttle's foreman glanced at Fain's waist. "See you done strapped on a handgun. Don't know as how we gonna get in that close a range, but I gotta ask, you know much about usin' one o' them short guns?"

Before Fain could answer, Pablo Menendez cut in. "*Señor*, if Cord Fain don't know what to do with a *peestola*, there ain't a *vaquero* in this here country what does."

Dealy only studied the tall young man in whom no one but him had believed. He smiled quietly, then motioned toward the ranch headquarters. "Come. We better talk with the boss, see how we all think to fight this war." He chuckled. "I know one person there who's gonna be mighty surprised, an' from what I been seein', she's gonna be right happy she was wrong."

"What you mean, she'll be happy she was wrong?"

"Hell, Fain, she's been mopin' round here like a cow what's lost her calf." He smiled. "Yep, I b'lieve she's gonna be right happy she wuz wrong."

Fain puzzled over Dealy's statement a moment, then

thought of the man he'd sent to see Dealy. "Frog's gonna make you a gunhand or a cowhand, whichever's needed."

Dealy nodded. "I reckon. First thing he did after takin' care o' his horse wuz lay his weepons out on my desk an' begin cleanin' 'em while he talked to me." He nodded. "Yeah, I figger you sent me a fightin' man."

Cord let a slight, cold smile break the corners of his lips. "What Frog doesn't know 'bout fightin' ain't worth knowin'." He nodded. "Yeah, I sent you a man who knows all about trouble."

They had ridden another mile or so when Fain thought about Jed Mobley. "Better send someone to tell Mobley to bring the widow woman an' her son to the ranch, if that's where we decide to fight 'em."

A worried frown creased Dealy's forehead. "Been thinkin' 'bout 'em. Been worried since I seen that first longhorn back yonder; Taggart mighta already got to 'em. He has, an' Mobley's in a heap o' trouble."

"Soon's we get to the ranch, point me in the right direction an' I'll head out for the widow's cabin. I'll either be able to help fight 'em off, or help 'em get up here."

"Why don't you come in an' tell Tuttle what you brung. Then y'all can see if you agree on the way he plans to fight."

Fain shook his head. "No. I figure time is pretty important as far as makin' sure Mobley an' the widow woman're safe. Gonna get on over there first." Dealy nodded.

Pam stood to red-up the dishes. She'd fed Tommy and Jed. Two days ago they'd pushed her slim herd back onto mountain pasture; then they'd repaired the corral, and Jed had gentled the two ponies he'd promised to Tommy. The homestead hadn't been in as good a shape since before her husband died.

The tall Southerner just had a way about him. If he was anywhere around, she was certain people would look to him to take the lead. With her and Tommy, he'd not been blustery, demanding, bossy, none of that. He had only suggested that this, or that, needed doing, and had set about getting it done. She picked up a dish, dunked it in the warm soapy suds, washed it, then put it under the pump and rinsed it. She wasn't ready to think about loving him, wouldn't admit it was even a possibility, but she *did* admit to herself that she wanted to keep him around as long as she could. She liked him. She and her young son had made a friend. Maybe being a friend was even more important.

She finished the dishes, swept the cabin, made the beds, then picked up a basket of things she'd long intended to darn, but had never had the time to do before Jed showed up; there had always been things outside that Tommy needed help in doing. She smiled. It was nice to have time to do the things a woman was good at doing.

The sunbeam shining through the side window slanted toward the middle of the floor and became longer. Late afternoon. She'd better get supper started. She stood, stopped, and cocked her head. The sounds of a horse loping toward the cabin came to her.

She stood there a moment wondering where Tommy and Jed might be. Mobley had made sure she knew about the possible threat that was coming down on them. She didn't know whether to answer the door when the rider came to it.

She took the Henry rifle from the gun rack over the fireplace, jacked a shell into the chamber, and waited. The rider reined his horse to a stop; then she heard the squeak of his saddle when he shifted weight to dismount. He hailed the cabin.

"Yes. What is it you want?"

"Lookin' for Jed Mobley, ma'am, an' you an' your little boy. I come from over at Tuttle's place. Mobley knows me. Is he close by?"

"He should be down at the barn with Tommy. What is your name?"

"Cord Fain, ma'am. Don't blame you for bein' cautious. I'll look round out here for Mobley. While I'm lookin', it'd be a good idea for you to start packin' a few days' clothes for you an' Tommy. I'll find Jed, an' we'll be right back."

Fain found Jed and a young boy in the barn forking hay down to the two milk cows. "Mobley, time to get outta here. I brought in sixteen men. They're at Tuttle's place now. Dealy had a run-in with a couple o' Taggart's men, shot one, the other got away."

"Hey, slow down, Cord. What makes you think it's Taggart?"

"There're a few trail-branded longhorns beginnin' to sift onto Lazy T land." Fain ground-hitched his horse, then climbed the ladder to the loft. "Didn't see any o' those drovers we rode with on the way over here, but you can bet they'll be here right soon, if this is the place Taggart figures to take over. Fact is, if he goes after the Lazy T, this place would be a prime target for 'im."

Mobley frowned, then pulled Tommy to his side. "Tommy, I'd like you to meet a friend o' mine. We rode together on the same trail drive. Meet Mr. Fain."

Tommy stuck out his hand. "Glad to meet ya, sir. Mr. Mobley an' me's right good friends too."

Fain tried to smother a smile, and failed. This boy was what he thought he'd like as a son; polite, and had been taught how to meet people. He gripped Tommy's hand. "C'mon, I got your mother already packin' some clothes for the next few days. C'mon, Mobley, let's get movin'."

"We got time for supper 'fore we leave here?"

"Might have, but I'd rather play it safe for the lady an' young Tommy here. Let's get goin'."

They climbed from the ladder. For some reason, before leaving the barn, Fain pulled his rifle and saddlebags from his horse, pulled the saddle off, and turned the dun into a stall. Mobley frowned, jerked his head in a nod, and picked his rifle up from where he'd left it when he last took his gear from his horse. His rifle shells were in his saddlebags. He took them also.

They were about halfway between the stable and the cabin when a shot, with a simultaneous tug at Fain's shirt, caused him to pick Tommy up and run for the open door of the cabin. Mobley ran on his heels.

Jed slammed the door as soon as they were inside. "Close the shutters, Fain." Pam was already busy pulling them closed.

Cord pulled the last shutter closed, glad to see that they had rifle slots in them. "Wish one o' us had stayed outside; might figure how many o' them're out there an' be able to divide their attention."

"You figger what they is o' them're still out front, one o' you can get out the back," said Pam. She shuffled her feet, staring at Mobley. Her face flushed. "Jed, if you don't mind, I surely would like you to stay in here with me."

Fain took the hint. He didn't blame her. She didn't know him. She knew Mobley, and apparently trusted him to take care of her son and her. Cord, his face sober, nodded. "See y'all when we take care o' whoever we got out there." He slipped out the only back window.

When his feet hit the ground, he looked for the nearest cover. Stunted juniper stood about fifty feet from the cabin. He glanced to each side, then, hoping there was no one in the trees, raced for them, expecting with every step to feel a slug plow into his body. He got there without a shot being fired.

He dug his way into the thick juniper boughs, squatted, studied the cabin and what lay around it. He wished he'd paid more attention to the layout when he rode in.

Out beyond the cabin, to the left of the stable, a pile of boulders reared about fifteen feet toward the sky. That was where he figured the shot had come from.

He glanced at the sun. They'd better get rid of their problem soon. If dark set in, their troubles would multiply. He thought to throw a shot toward the boulders, frowned, and considered whether he'd be worth more out here as long as they didn't know there was someone on the outside. They'd seen both men go into the cabin, and apparently had not seen anyone come out. He decided to keep his rifle quiet until one of the attackers fired. Then he'd have something at which to aim. He hunkered in the scrub brush and waited.

The sun had already sunk behind the mountains, so he didn't look for a reflection off a gun barrel. He waited for a shot, and maybe smoke to indicate where the land-stealer might be. He had not long to wait.

A rifle slid from the rocks—he could see it plainly, aimed toward the cabin—then whoever held the rifle apparently changed his mind, and stood to maybe see better. Fain's sights were on him before the man could pull the trigger. Fain squeezed off a shot, and from where he hunkered, his eyes took in a blossom of red on the man's shirt-front. It wasn't large, but the red would spread.

The man, knocked backward, lost his rifle. It slipped down outside the rocks. Fain waited, expecting a shot in his direction. It didn't come. Instead, the sharp drum of hooves broke the silence. A horse, being spurred hell-for-leather, appeared from behind the boulders, its rider leaning forward over the saddlehorn, desperately spurring the horse to a faster gait.

Fain leveled his rifle, centered the sights between the man's shoulders, squeezed off a shot, watched the man slam forward over the pommel, then grab the horn.

Cord figured the man wouldn't ride far before he turned the horn loose and fell from the animal. Cord sat there in the needle-like leaves a few moments, then thought there were no more of them.

He stood. No shots came his way. He walked slowly to the front of the cabin, realizing only then how much the short fight had taken out of him; too, he'd been in the saddle since daylight, and hadn't eaten. Maybe they could take time for Mrs. Henders to fix some supper.

Back in the cabin, Cord glanced at Mobley and young Tommy. They looked to be taking everything in stride. He looked at Pam. "Mrs. Henders, you reckon you have anything for us to eat, something you can throw together kinda quick-like?"

"You reckon we got time?"

He nodded. "I figure that rider I shot was one that Taggart sent out to scout the land; see if maybe there were line shacks and about how many cattle were already on the land."

While Fain talked, Pam busied herself putting a haunch of venison on the stove to heat; she'd cooked it the day before, and heating it wouldn't take long. Since Jed had arrived, she'd learned that he'd often stop work briefly for a cup of coffee, so the coffee already sat on the stove, ready to drink.

Mobley took cups from a shelf on the wall and poured the three of them a cup, then poured Tommy a glass of milk. He looked up from filling the glass. "You think we might be safer if we stay here till dark, then try to make it to Tuttle's? I think probably all the drovers'll be wherever they have the chuck wagon."

Fain thought on Mobley's words a moment, a deep furrow between his eyes; then he let a slow smile break the corners of his mouth. "B'lieve you're right, Jed; fact is, I b'lieve it so strongly, I think I'll take four or five o' the boys I brought in an' pay them a visit while they lay in their blankets."

"You gonna let me go?"

Fain shook his head. "From what I've seen, Mrs. Henders will feel a lot safer if you stay close by for a while."

"No, Mr. Fain, you men have work to do, work a whole lot more dangerous than what we'll have sittin' there in the ranch house. If Jed thinks there's a place in your crew for him, an' you got it figgered you can use him, an' he wants to go"—she nodded—"so be it."

Mobley smiled. "Reckon that's settled. Let's eat, then help Pam put whatever she thinks she'll need in some tow sacks, an' wait for dark to settle in." He took a swallow of his coffee, cocked an eyebrow at the two of them, and said, "Seems to me we've met during circumstances that drew us together pretty well, so why don't the two of you stop the missusing an' mistering? Call each other by first names."

Pam and Cord both nodded. Fain looked at Tommy. "Son, is there anything you want to take with you? We might be there a while."

"Yes, sir, I'd like mighty well to take that there Henry rifle an' some shells fer it. Figger to help y'all do some fightin'."

Fain looked questioningly at Pam. She nodded. "He's helped us before, Cord." Her face sober, she shook her head. "We'd hurt 'is feelin's if we dealt 'im outta this fight."

Mobley looked at the little boy, pride lighting his face. "Cord, you've not had a chance to observe this young'un, but I'll tell you right now, I'd rather have him sidin' me than many a man I've seen."

With a slight smile, Cord nodded, but his thoughts were on the man and woman in the room with him. They might not know it yet, but he figured Tommy had found a man to help raise him, and Pam had found her a man to love. He had no doubts about how Jed Mobley felt; his feelings shone through every word and action.

Before long, Pam had the table set, and food in the middle of it. Fain marveled at how she moved about, never wasting a motion, and almost effortlessly fed them and got ready to leave. She wouldn't let Cord help. She said her two men could help, and when she said *two men*, her face flushed a beautiful pink, but she didn't go back and try to cover up what she'd said. Mobley looked almighty pleased.

They finished dinner, washed the dishes, took the things Pam had packed, along with Jed's bedroll, saddlebags, and rifle, and left.

They rode slowly, the horses' hooves making little noise in the soft dust. Every few minutes Fain stopped, cautioned them to keep quiet, then listened. He picked up only the customary night sounds, those of small nocturnal animals scurrying out of their way, and the sounds of a few birds.

They arrived at the ranch house to see no lights showing through the windows. Fain nodded to himself. These people knew what to do when in jeopardy. He stopped his party and told them to stay out a hundred yards or so from the house.

He dismounted and silently moved toward the darkened headquarters. When he got to the back door, he tapped lightly on it, then said, "It's me, Fain. I got Pam, Tommy, an' Mobley with me." The door opened to a dark room.

"Bring 'em on in."

In only a few minutes, Fain had the three in the house, the door had closed, and a lamp had been lighted. The shutters kept most of the light from showing, but Mrs. Tuttle or someone had draped blankets over the windows. He looked around the room. Five of his men were there. "Where you got the rest?"

Tuttle looked for Dealy to answer. The foreman, using his fingers to count, said, "Five here, three along with the ranch hands're in the bunkhouse, an' seven're in the stable."

Cord nodded. "Good. I'm gonna take 'bout four with me. Figure to pay Taggart a visit tonight, if I can find where he's parked the chuck wagon."

Tuttle frowned. "What you gonna do that for?"

Fain shrugged. "Figure if I can catch 'em in their blankets, we can cut the odds a little." He looked at the floor a moment, then pinned Tuttle with a hard look. He made his look and words fit the way his face felt—like old, sun-dried leather. "Don't like doin' it that way, Tuttle, but they outnumber us, figure we gotta take advantage o' every edge we can get."

His eyes swept the room looking for Ruth. She sat back in a corner, looking as though she wanted to disappear. He held his eyes on her for only a second, but long enough for his look to tell her he thought her a brat. He tipped his hat. "Ladies."

He snuffed the lantern, and he and Mobley slipped out the same way they'd entered. He glanced over his shoulder to where he knew Mobley walked. "I'll take men from the bunkhouse; that won't cut them too short. Tuttle's men're there."

He took four men, Pedro Menendez and Gene Shelton being two of them. "Bring your rifles an' a pocketful of cartridges. We're gonna do somethin' you may not like, but we need to cut their numbers the easiest way we can. Don't want any o' you gettin' hurt. If you can figure where their legs are, shoot at them. They got a hole in their legs, they won't be much use to Taggart."

While they saddled their horses, he explained what they were going to do. "Don't know where they've made camp, but we'll find it, fire no more than three shots each, then we'll get outta there. Meet on the north side of their camp and ride toward Denver. Don't want to lead them to the ranch house. We can circle back and get to headquarters in time for breakfast."

Pablo was the first to see the glowing embers of Taggart's campfire. "*Señor*, I think we found that for which we looked."

"B'lieve you're right. All right, men, ride in slowly to keep the noise down. I'll fire first. Remember, three shots only, then head north of their camp. Don't take any chances. If you run into a sentry, shoot 'im. We'll take it from there."

Mobley rode to Fain's side. "I think Taggart'll not have sentries. He's probably spread the herd and pulled all the drovers in close to him. We oughta shoot up the camp a little." He chuckled. "Like maybe put some holes in the coffeepot. You know there'll be a pot hangin' over those coals."

Fain answered Jed's chuckle with one of his own. "That'll make 'em madder'n hell. Yeah, good idea."

Being downwind, they'd not ridden much farther when Fain picked up the aroma of coffee, strong coffee. "Mobley, I figure we'll be doin' those drovers a big favor by puttin' holes in that pot. Bet they haven't had a *fresh* cup o' Arbuckle's since you an' I left 'em the other side of Raton."

He twisted in his saddle and waved his hand in a circling motion. The men broke away to take stations around the camp. He rode close enough to the chuck wagon that he could hear snoring from some of those in their blankets.

He slipped his Winchester from its scabbard, aimed at the big pot hanging from a bar across the embers, squeezed off a shot low on the pot so that if it were retrieved, it couldn't be made to hold water. About the time his shot hit the pot, it swung wildly, jumped from the hook it hung on, and bounced across the camp.

He shifted his aim, and shot into a blanket looking like it might have a man under it. He hoped he'd shot at the end where the man's legs were. Before he could draw a bead on another blanket lump, the blankets came alive. Wild-looking forms, looking like demons from hell, waved their arms, jumped around as though some one had thrown a hornet's nest into their middle. Some stood with their bedding still clinging to their shoulders, all had six-shooters in fists, all firing into the dark. Fain regretted his order about only three shots; he would have liked to sit his horse in the dark and throw shots into the bunch until he ran out of cartridges, but he urged his horse toward the north. At the moment he reined his horse to go around the camp, a streak of fire burned along his side. Maybe three shots had not been such a dumb idea after all.

He sniffled the sharp smell of gun smoke from his nose, tried to clear his throat, coughed, then spat. He leaned into the fire that ran along his side, tried to ease the pain, and at the same time, every muscle in his back tightened trying to ward off another expected bullet. A warm, wet feeling spread along his belt. He stripped his bandanna from around his neck and pushed it inside his shirt over the area that burned so fiercely.

About a quarter of a mile north of Taggart's camp, he pulled rein. Out of the dark, two riders came toward him, one from either side. They were his men. Then another joined them. Where was Menendez? He waited, and the longer he waited, the larger the lump in his throat grew.

Another few seconds that seemed like hours, and then the soft, slow hoofbeats of a horse approached from his left. "That you, Menendez?"

"*Sí, señor.* I have a little trouble gettin' here; I take the lead in my leg, an' I think something hit my side. Think maybe it hit my gunbelt. Hope so."

"You make it till we get far enough away from here?"

"*Sí.* I'll make it. *Vamanos.*"

Fain led his small group of fighting men about another mile to the north, then kneed his horse to the left.

True to his estimate, they rode into the stable a little before sunup. Fain told one of the men to take Pablo to the bunkhouse, check his leg and dress it, his side too if it needed it, and that he and the other men would take care of the horses.

He took a couple of lanterns from nails on the wall, and put fire to the wicks. They stripped the gear from their horses, and turned toward the door. "Go on up to the house, Jed. From the look in your eyes when you left Pam, if she feels the same way you do, she's gonna want to know you're all right."

"Don't know what you're talkin' 'bout, Fain. Hell, I just like . . ." He took hold of Cord's shoulders and turned him toward the light. "You're hit, man. Why the hell didn't you say somethin'?"

Fain shook his head. "Not bad. Figure I got a pretty deep crease. I'll take a look soon's I get to the bunkhouse."

"Bunkhouse? You're not goin' to any bunkhouse. You're gonna come up to the house with me an' we'll get it dressed."

Fain shook his head. "Not by a damned sight. I won't ever again give that poison tongued daughter o' Tuttle's a chance to give me a full load of her venom."

Mobley frowned. "Don't know whatever got into 'er. The boys, Pam, even Dealy said they never knew 'er to act like that." He again looked at Fain's bloody shirt. "I'll see if Mrs. Tuttle has any clean cloths to wrap your side in."

He looked into Cord's eyes. "You sure you're all right, pardner?"

Fain nodded. "Haven't taken a look at it yet; it's sore as the devil, but don't b'lieve it broke any ribs. It had, an' I figure I wouldn't be able to breathe as good as I can. Now go on up there an' let that pretty widow woman know you didn't get a scratch."

Mobely's face turned as red as a dust-laden sunset. He grinned sort of a silly grin and looked into Fain's eyes. "She *is mighty pretty*, isn't she?"

"Yep, mighty with a capital M, an' I'm gonna tell you, if you haven't noticed, she's got the same look in her eyes when she's around you that you have."

"Aw, hell, Cord, I'm only tryin' to help 'er. Her an' that little boy." His face brightened. "You ever see a boy like 'im? Why, man, it wouldn't surprise me to see 'im get elected president of this whole country."

Cord chuckled, then laughed outright, and grabbed his side, moaned, and looked accusingly at Mobley. "Oh, damn, Mobley, don't ever make a man laugh who's got a gouge outta his side, hurts like sin."

"C'mon, gonna walk you to the bunkhouse, make sure you're all right."

"No. Get yourself on up to the house. I'm okay. 'Sides, one o' these men who're gonna set up to defend the stable can get me up there if I figure I can't make it. Now get on up there."

Although seeming to be torn between seeing to it that Cord got proper care and going to the house to see Pam, Mobley again looked at Cord, then walked toward the house.

As soon as Fain got in the bunkhouse, he swept the area with a glance, wanting to find Dealy, and found him lying in his bunk. "Jim, we stirred up a hornet's nest over yonder. Better see to it the men're ready for a fight. I'll help soon's I get this scratch taken care of."

Dealy tried to argue Cord into letting him take care of

his wound, but Cord wouldn't hear of it. "Get the men ready for a fight, Dealy. I don't think it'll be long before we hear from Taggart."

The trail boss stared at the shambles left by the night riders. Coffeepot shot to hell, five men hit in the legs, two in the chest, and the chuck wagon had holes all over it. He had no doubt that some of the provisions were ruined. He cursed a blue streak. Finally he wore down. "Who the hell was that?"

"Don't know, Boss. Don't figger them what owns this here ranch has 'nuff men this time o' year to pull a raid on a outfit big as ours."

"Barnes, I ain't gonna tell you agin. Don't nobody own this ranch but me. Get use to talkin' 'bout me as the owner. Want people hereabouts to git used to it too." Taggart walked to the ruined coffeepot and kicked it beyond the firelight. He cursed again. "You notice that Lazy T on some o' them cattle we seen yesterday? Uh-huh? Well that T is for Taggart. You got that?"

Barnes looked at his boss squinty-eyed. Blood surged behind Taggart's eyes, his neck muscles tightened. Barnes wondered what he and the rest of the crew would get out of this land grab. The most he could figure was drover's wages on the trail, and here on the ranch they'd probably all get thirty dollars a month and found. Thirty a month, rotten grub, and a cold line shack to sleep the winter away in. He'd have to talk to the rest, or at least some of the rest of the crew. He'd have to be careful. Taggart had a terrible temper, and would shoot a man just for the hell of it. But yeah, he'd sound out the right ones and see if they were happy with the short end of the stick.

Taggart would not consider that he was being anything but fair with the men; giving them a steady job was all a cowboy needed. Barnes figured to bring it up when he had enough backing.

And Taggart, in his warped sense of fairness, thought

exactly the way Barnes figured he would. Hell, they'd rounded up those maverick cattle down yonder in the Big Bend of Texas. He, Taggart, had been the one who'd gotten the crew together and choused those longhorns out of the chaparral. He'd been the boss then, and he figured to remain in charge.

At first he'd thought to take the herd to Montana, as he'd been ordered to do. Then he got to looking at the hair-brand, and thought once that hair grew out, nobody would know who the cattle belonged to. With that thought he began to think of driving them to Dodge City. Abilene had outlawed Texas herds coming that far east. They said ticks was the reason.

For a time he locked in on selling the entire herd; then the idea hit him to keep the herd and steal only the land they'd graze. Yes. These were his cattle, and this land his. He never considered he was doing anything wrong. If you were big enough, to hell with the little man. If they couldn't hold the land and cattle, that was just too damned bad. Most of them didn't own the land they ran cattle on; they'd either leased it from the railroads, or had gotten there early enough that they claimed right of ownership by putting their cattle on the grass, taking out homestead rights on the available water, and then defending it against all comers.

Taggart again surveyed the ruined camp. Each time his eyes swept across the fire, the wagon, the ruined meal and coffee, blood built more pressure behind his eyes. His head felt like it would explode. Thinking back over the last few weeks, he tried to think of anyone who'd pull a raid on him. He figured the same as Barnes had. This raid wasn't one that a rancher would pull; ranchers just flat didn't have enough men this time of year.

First he thought of Fain. No. That milksop wouldn't try anything like this; hell, he didn't even have enough guts to wear a side gun. He thought of Cookie; no, he was too stove-up. Then he thought of Mobley, and nodded; that was one man who had the guts, and probably knew how to carry a grudge. But where had he gotten the men to ride with him? He thought on that a moment.

There were many punchers riding the grub line who most likely would be glad to join up with a man like the tall quiet Southerner. He nodded to himself. Yes, Mobley was the one. He'd kill him the first time their trails crossed again. Then he thought of Mobley's reputation as a gun-fighter. Maybe he should try thinking of another way to get rid of him.

He looked at his crew gathered around him. "Soon's it comes daylight, want you to trail them who attacked us, find 'em, then kill ever' damned one of 'em. Got that?"

"Yeah, Boss, but by sunup, I figger the way the wind blows here on these Colorado plains, they ain't gonna be no tracks to follow." The man who'd answered had so far done as the trail boss had directed. Taggart stared at him a moment, wanting to give him a butt chewing. He decided against it. He needed these men more than ever. "Check it out anyway, okay?"

The man nodded. Then Taggart looked at the rest of the men. "All right, the rest o' you get started on cleanin' this mess up." He looked at another of his drovers. "You, find another pot, pan, any damned thing, an' put on another pot o' water to boil. Want a cup o' coffee."

His glance swept the rest of his crew. "Come daylight, we gonna ride toward them hills; gonna find headquarters for this here ranch, gonna go in an' tell the man what runs it that he's outta business, that I'm the new owner. Got it?"

"Yeah, Boss." They said it in unison.

Fain stripped his shirt off, and twisted to look at the deep gouge in his side. Gonna be sore as a boil for a while, he thought, then looked at his shirt. It had two holes in it. He stuck a finger through each of them, and wondered when he'd have a chance to patch them.

He put water on to boil. He had to clean the raw flesh;

then he'd pour whiskey on it, then when Dealy got back with some clean rags, he'd bandage it. He'd only that minute decided on how to handle the bandaging when a voice sounded from outside the door. "Mr. Fain, are the men dressed? I want to come in and take a look at your side." It was Ruth who asked the question. He wanted nothing to do with her.

Cord glanced around the bunkhouse. All the men were dressed; most were cleaning and oiling their weapons. "No, ma'am, they're not dressed, an' you're not gonna take care o' my side. I'm doin' right well with that task myself."

"Don't be stubborn, Mr. Fain. Jim told me you had a right nasty wound. Please let me help you."

"Like I said, ma'am, I'll take care of it myself. Good night, ma'am."

An almost inaudible "Ooooh, damn a stubborn man" came to his ears; then footsteps withdrew from the door. He grinned.

"Reckon that's one you didn't win, brat."

While waiting for Dealy to get back with some clean rags, Fain looked at the men. "Think maybe soon's you men get your weapons clean, you better crawl in your bunks an' get some sleep. Don't figure any o' that bunch's gonna be able to track us back here till daylight." He glanced at his rifle lying on the bunk. "Reckon I better take care o' my Winchester soon's I take care o' me."

Dealy brought strips of sheets, and insisted on bandaging Fain's side. Every so often he'd glance at Cord, looking as though he wanted to say something. Finally, Fain gave him a tight-lipped smile. "All right, spit it out. You been itchin' to say somethin' ever' since you got back with those bandages."

Dealy nodded. "Yep, I been wantin' to say you're jest as hardheaded as that girl you sent away from here." He shook his head. "You ask me, she wuz jest tryin' to make up for treatin' you like she did."

Fain's face stiffened, then hardened. "Don't figure to give her another chance to scald me with that tongue o' hers." He shook his head. "Not ever again."

As soon as he had his side cared for, Cord went back to the stable to make sure the men there knew when he expected the ranch to be attacked. One of the men Fain had borrowed from his pa, a man named Bentley, scratched his head and looked at him. "Cord, you reckon that man figgers he's gonna run into trouble when he gets here?"

Fain shook his head. "Way I got it figured, he'll think this ranch, like all others this time o' year, will have only a small crew. He'll think he can ride in here an' take over."

"How you figger to handle it?"

Cord frowned, stared at the ground a moment, then pinned Bentley with a hard look. "We gonna let 'im ride in, make 'is demands, then I'll take it from there. *But,* if I start shootin', I want you men to start emptyin' saddles. Okay?"

Every man there, all only five to seven years older than Fain, answered with a resounding yes.

When Cord got back to the bunkhouse, he told Dealy how he planned to play the hand, and asked him to make sure Tuttle knew what he planned, and not to open the ball until he talked to Taggart. He figured to walk out to meet the land-grabber and let him know what he faced.

Dealy left to tell his boss, and Fain crawled between his blankets, sore, hurting, and hoping a fever didn't set in before he could face the land-stealer.

The morning, dark, dreary, with rain threatening, slowly pushed its dull, murky light into the room where the old timers and three of Fain's men still slept.

Cord rolled to his "good" side, as he thought of it, groaned, lay still for a moment to let the stiffness and pain wash through him, clamped his jaws tight, and sat. He jammed his hat on his head, then pulled on his boots and stood. He'd had every man sleep in his clothes, ready to meet whatever threat Taggart brought to them. He smelled food. Cookie had beat him up.

"All right, men, roll out," he called. "We got work to do today."

Groans, curses, both at him and about him, came from most of the bunks. He'd heard the same sounds and same words in every bunkhouse he'd slept in. "Get washed up. From the smells o' that bacon fryin', Cookie's got breakfast 'bout ready."

And like every other bunkhouse he'd been in, the mention of food squelched the bitching, and brought on grunts of approval. "Soon's you men eat, grab your rifles, jack a shell in the chamber, and park yourself by one o' these windows. I'll go out and do the talkin'."

Pablo Menendez stared at him a moment. "*Señor*, you ain't goin' out yonder alone, are you?"

A slight smile broke the corners of Fain's lips. "That's what I figure to do, Pablo, but I'm gonna let that bunch know there're rifles pointing at them from every window; here, the ranch house, an' the stable. Don't think any o' them're big enough fools to start shootin', not knowin' how many guns they're facin'. Even a few guns with them bein' out there in the open could cut more o' them down than they could get of us, not knowin' where to fire their bullets."

He picked up his gunbelt from the head of his bunk, buckled it, tied the holster to his leg, and eased the .44 in its holster. Pablo shook his head. "Any o' them *hombres* see you draw that six-gun, I think they'd still be runnin' next week, *Señor*."

Fain gave Menendez a long look. "Pablo, I'd appreciate you forgettin' you ever saw me drag a gun from my holster. I'm not lookin' to build a reputation."

Menendez stared at him a moment, an amused frown telling Fain that his wishes were in vain, the word had already spread from Taos. Pablo smiled without much humor. "*Señor*, I will do as you say, but I think it's already too late to think about that." He shrugged. "They was many who watched you give Dutch Gruder the chance, then you killed 'im." He shook his head. "Too late, *mi amigo.*"

Fain knew Pablo told the truth. As large as the West was, and despite the few people in it, the word would still spread like wildfire. Mentally he acknowledged Menendez's words, but he thought by the time he might be forced to again prove his gun skills, he'd be in Coyote, New Mexico Territory, among friends and family.

He ate and took up his station to watch for Taggart's approach.

FAIN STOOD BY the window, listening for the sound of hoofbeats or the sight of Taggart. He heard the horses first.

With his back muscles pulled tight as a bowstring, a hollow feeling in his chest, and his mouth dry as desert sand, he bent, again checked the tightness of the thong holding his holster to his thigh, slipped his Colt up in its holster and eased it softly down to eliminate binding, then looked at the crew. He grinned, not feeling any humor. "You men got your rifles loaded and a cartridge in the chamber?" They nodded. "Good. Don't want any o' you to pull trigger 'less they start the ball. They do, I want you to empty every saddle out there."

His side hurting like it would tear in two, he pulled the door open and stepped outside. His mouth was even drier now; he couldn't work up enough saliva to spit. He'd done a lot of dumb things, but this might take its place among the leaders. He shrugged mentally; he trusted those men in each of the buildings. Besides, he might stop a lot of killing later—if his plan worked.

The fifty or so yards to the front of the ranch house took

on miles of distance in his mind. Finally in front of it, he faced in the direction of the approaching horses. He heard a door open behind him. He twisted to look over his shoulder; Mobley stood there. "What the hell're you doin' out here?" Fain said. "Get back inside. Tell those people in there to not fire unless they see Taggart's bunch won't listen to reason. Now get, Mobley. Promise you I won't need any help."

Mobley stared at him a moment. "What the hell makes you think you won't need help? You only strapped on that handgun a few days ago."

"Believe me, I know how to handle a six-gun. Now get. Taggart sees more'n one man out here, he might ride in shootin'. Want to avoid that if I can."

Mobely stared at him a moment, shook his head, spun, and walked back inside.

Fain had never felt more alone in his life; even knowing there were about twenty rifles backing him up, if Taggart made a fight of it, he, Cord Fain, would be the first to go down. He waited.

In only a few moments Taggart's crew topped the rise in front of him, rode close enough to be well within six-shooter range, then pulled rein. "Well, well, if it ain't the milksop. Figgered I might see Mobley, a real man, standin' there. What the hell you think you gonna do standin' out here all alone?"

While Taggart talked, Fain felt the tightness leave his back and shoulders; the dryness left his mouth. A strange calm settled over him, a confidence that he alone could handle this situation. "Tell you somethin', Taggart. You and your men got at least twenty rifles pointed at you from every window in the house, bunkhouse, an' stable. Any o' your men make a motion for your weapons an' there won't be a one o' you ride outta here."

He squinted into the fine mist blowing on the wind. "Gonna tell you somethin' else if you're wonderin' where we got the men; Blackjack Slade offered me twice this many, but I figured only fifteen would be enough to handle your crew."

He'd not lied. Slade *had* offered him men, but he'd declined. He'd put the outlaw's name in the pot because he knew that Taggart knew him, and knew he had a salty crew. He'd probably respect that more than if he'd used his pa's name.

The trail boss's face turned red; veins stood out on his forehead and down his neck. He glanced toward the three buildings, then turned his look back to Fain. "You ain't asked me what I come here for." His head looked as though it pulled down into his bull neck; his face reddened even more. "This here ranch, soon's I spread my cows on it, became mine. I'm takin' it 'cause that's the way this here owner got it in the first place. He don't own but maybe a few acres. Now I got that herd on it, it's mine. Ain't no law gonna back you up. I done checked."

"You notice, Taggart, I haven't said anything 'bout the law. I got enough men here to back me up. We figure to use gun-law. An' I'm gonna tell you somethin' else; you try to ride north an' take over somebody else's land, we gonna follow you, stop you there—wherever. You hearin' me plain-like?" He smiled, knowing it was not a warm smile. "That two months' pay you tried to beat me outta is gonna cost you so damned much, you'll still be bitchin' 'bout it when you slither through the doors o' hell." He nodded. "Reckon you understand me now."

If possible, Taggart's face turned even redder; his hands trembled holding his horse's reins. "Y-you done strapped on a gun. Think I'll see can you use it."

"That would be the biggest mistake you made yet, Taggart. Even if you beat me, you an' your men'd die right here in this ranch yard. Gonna prove it to you so you don't cost your men their lives." He turned his head a bit, and yelled, "All you folks got a rifle in your hands, poke 'em through the gun slots. Let this garbage see I'm not bluffin'."

Before he finished speaking, rifle barrels poked out so

all could see. Taggart's eyes widened. The muscles at the back of his jaws knotted. He stared at Fain. "You an' me, milksop, we gonna meet someday when you ain't got a bunch o' people to protect you."

"You pile o' cow dung, you better hope that day never comes. Now get outta here. Remember, the only reason we haven't blown y'all to hell today is 'cause you gonna be the ones to start the dance, an' when you do—we finish it. Now get."

Taggart jerked the reins of his horse, spun him on his back legs, and dug spurs into the poor beast. Fain stood there, watched him until he disappeared over the brow of the hill, then turned his steps toward the bunkhouse. His knees felt limp as a dishrag, his back ached, his head hurt, fatigue gripped him as it had never done before, *but* he'd gotten away with his foolhardy stunt. Footsteps pounded behind him. Wash and Mobley pulled alongside. "Tuttle wants to see you. Come on up to the house."

He shook his head. "Not goin' in that house ever again. He wants to see me, he can come to the bunkhouse. He isn't payin' me. I don't work for 'im. I don't take his orders."

"What foah you gotta act like that, Cord? Mistuh Tuttle ain't nevah done nothin' to you."

"Wash, you an' Mobley both are my friends. Fact, is we might be partners when we ride outta here unless Mobley wakes up an' realizes what that widow woman means to 'im." He shook his head. "*But* I'm tellin' you right now, Tuttle's daughter's not gonna get another chance to tongue-lash me. Hell, a man talk to me the way she does, I'd beat the livin' hell outta 'im."

"Don't reckon ah'd blame you, pahdnuh. Reckon ah'd feel the same way. But why don't you give 'er 'nother chance."

Mobley gave Wash a "don't talk 'bout it anymore" look, then turned his steps toward the ranch house. Matthew "Wash" Black followed reluctantly.

Ruth Tuttle watched the two men coming back to the house—without Fain. Anger pushed bitter bile to the back of her throat. Why did that man act like he did? She was ready to tell him how sorry she felt that she'd acted as she did, but no, he was too stubborn to swallow his pride and acknowledge that a person could be sorry, could even be ready to apologize.

She swallowed the lump in her throat. Why should she care how a grub-line rider thought? Then her shoulders slumped. *That* was the problem; she *did* care. She told herself that she would have cared had it been anyone. That she would truly be sorry she'd treated anyone like she'd treated the quiet, gentle man who had only tried to do her family a favor.

Why had she acted the way she had? That question baffled her. She had never treated anyone the way she had treated Cord Fain, and she couldn't think of any reason why. Maybe it was because he'd come into their home and turned their, her, peaceful world into one of blood and bullets—again. *But* everything he'd said was true. She met Mobley and Wash at the door.

"He wouldn't come?"

Mobley shook his head. "No, ma'am, he allowed as how he would never come into your home again." He pushed his hat to the back of his head. "Reckon, Miss Ruth, you hurt that man more'n I can figure." He shrugged. "Don't figure I'd let a sharp tongue hurt me like he seems to hurt."

Ruth lowered her eyes, stared at the floor a moment, then looked into his eyes. "You sayin' I got a sharp tongue, Jed?"

He nodded. "Yes, ma'am, reckon that's exactly what I'm sayin'. Cord Fain's a proud man, an' I'm gonna add right now, ma'am, he *is* a man, one helluva man. He can stack up with any I've ever seen."

He walked to the coffeepot and poured himself a cupful, then walked to stand in front of her. "Miss Ruth, I don't know whether he can use that Colt he so recently strapped on, but I have a hunch he might be better at usin' it than most."

He frowned and shook his head. "Don't know why I feel

that way, reckon it's the cool confidence he has when he faces a man; 'course it wouldn't require a gun to give a man that kind of feelin' 'bout himself; seems to me it's somethin' inside a man."

Ruth stared at Mobley a moment, fought to hold back the tears, blinked to clear her eyes. "Jed, those men Fain sent here to the house"—she shrugged—"well, I overheard them talkin' among themselves." She shook her head. "I wasn't eavesdroppin', but I heard 'em, an' they all seem to have the same opinion of him that you do. Y'all must have seen him do things that I haven't, but I'll tell you honestly, I've never seen a braver, or more foolhardy, stunt than he pulled out in front of the house when Taggart rode in."

Tuttle came from another room, looked at Mobley, then looked about the room. "Where's Fain?"

"Wouldn't come. Said if you wanted to see 'im to come to the bunkhouse. Fact is, I reckon he'll want to talk to you anyway. Maybe to sketch out how he figures we ought to fight Taggart." Mobley pushed a slight smile past his lips. "Seems he's taken charge of this fight, an' if I were you, I'd leave 'im in charge. I think he knows what he's doin'."

Tuttle frowned. "You figger Taggart'll be back soon?"

"Nope, but if you're askin' do I think he *will be back*, the answer is absolutely. I think he'll come back because he hates Fain enough that he's willin' to jeopardize all his plans to get even."

"Why does he hate that boy so much?"

Mobley studied the floor a moment, then looked straight on into Tuttle's eyes. "You gotta understand that some people can't stand to have anyone stand up to them; Taggart's one o' those people."

Bob Tuttle gave a nod. "All right." He gave Jed an amused smile. "Let's go see how 'the man in charge' wants to fight your ex–trail boss."

Mobley glanced at Ruth. Her eyes had widened, her mouth hung slack. Jed thought she looked dumbfounded that her father would turn the reins loose so easily.

He stepped toward the door. "Let's see what he thinks,

an' don't figure for a minute he's gonna not ask for our opinion." He nodded. "I b'lieve that's why men are so ready to follow 'im." He frowned. "I figure he'll sort out what we suggest, then decide which way he wants to do it and go from there."

On the way to the bunkhouse, Tuttle asked Mobley if they were good friends, partners. Jed shook his head. "Can't say we are. Both of us are the kind o' men who sort o' stay to themselves, don't get too close to others. I have my reasons, an' I'm sure he has his."

At the bunkhouse, he opened the door. Cord met them there. "Saw you comin'. Let's sit over yonder at the table an' talk."

He looked around the room. "C'mon, men, want to hear what you got to say. First off, I'll tell you how I figure to fight Taggart, then I want to hear any better ideas any o' you have."

After they'd dragged up the various chairs and benches in the room, Cord glanced at them, then turned his look to Tuttle. "How many men you got up at the house?"

"Countin' the five you sent up there, I have seven; not countin' me."

Fain nodded. "An' there's five o' my men down yonder in the stable, and we got nine men here, countin' yours and mine." He frowned, then nodded. "I b'lieve we need to take some men from each place; maybe two or three." He looked at Cookie. "You got any fresh Arbuckle made?"

Cookie nodded. "Made it at noontime."

"Good, bring the pot over here an' sit it on the table. We can help ourselves when we get to wantin' a cup."

Cookie pulled away, his face flushed. "Ain't gonna do a dag-nabbed thing 'less'n you tell me you figger to use me to help fight Taggart."

Wanting to smile, but holding it back, Cord nodded. "Never had it figured any other way, old-timer. Drag your chair up to this parley."

When they were settled around Fain, and had coffee in front of them, he pulled his mouth to one side, frowned, then nodded. "B'lieve I got Taggart figured right. He wants this land; would like to take over the entire ranch, buildings and all. *But* make no mistake about it, he'll burn every building here to get the land if he has to do it."

He took a swallow of his coffee, blew through pursed lips, looked at Cookie, and said, "Hot." He sat forward to the edge of his chair. "Men, if we stay like we are in each building, we'll make it easy for that bastard to sneak up in the dark and set every building here on fire.

"I figure to pick me 'bout five or six o' you, an' we'll stay out in the brush, well within rifle range, where we can see the outside of every place where we got men an' women inside."

He turned to Tuttle and Mobley. "Want you to keep everybody you already got in the main house. We gotta protect the womenfolk up there no matter what happens."

He frowned and scooted to the back of his chair, wondering how many of the stable crew he could have without crippling their effort. He decided he'd better take only one. "Carl, I b'lieve you're in the bunch down at the barn, right?"

At Carl's nod, Fain told him that he'd be the one to stay with him in the brush. "And from in the bunkhouse, I want Frog Ballew and . . ." He twisted to see Menendez off to his right. "Was gonna name you, Pablo, but reckon those gunshots you got would be askin' too much for you to sneak around in the brush playin' Apache." Pablo opened his mouth as though to protest. Before he could say anything, Fain shook his head. "Nope, not gonna hear of it. You stay here." He grinned and looked at Cookie. "You reckon that stove-up old body o' yours can stand a day or two out yonder, sleepin' on the ground, bein' quiet when you have to, an' maybe crawlin' round on your hands and knees?"

"W-w-why, gosh-ding it, you young whippersnapper, I kin out-Injun you five ways from Sunday. Danged tootin' I kin stand it."

Cord thought he'd never seen a man who glowed, who exuded pride and pleasure, more than the old cook did at that moment. He'd given the old man a knowledge that he had faith in him, that he trusted him to do a very dangerous job.

Counting himself, there were three men for the outside. He looked at Dealy, and knowing he'd fought the Kiowa several times, thought he might make the fourth man. "How you feel 'bout goin' with me?"

Dealy looked at Tuttle, who smiled. "Don't look at me, Jim. Looks like Fain's runnin' this show. If you want to go with 'im, say so."

Dealy nodded. "Reckon that makes four of us, Fain. You think maybe that's enough?"

Cord smiled. "Any more an' I figure we'd be stumbling over each other. Yeah, we do it right, we got enough." He swept the men with a questioning glance. "Any o' you got a better idea, or any suggestions as to what each of you're gonna be doin'?" No one spoke up, so Cord stood. "You men who're gonna go with me, roll your bedding such that you can carry it over your shoulders, pack your pockets with cartridges, an' let's get ready to go." He looked at Cookie. "You got a good supply o' jerky? We won't be eatin' any hot meals, maybe till this is over."

Cookie grinned. "Dang tootin' I got jerky; 'nuff fer all us here." His grin widened. "Bein's I ain't gonna be cookin' fer a while, reckon these here tenderfeet who stay here ain't gonna know how to cook nothin'. They gotta eat jerky too."

"All right, get your gear ready; we'll be leavin' soon's you say you got it done."

Fain looked at the man who owned the ranch. "Mr. Tuttle, you never said a word. You got any exceptions to what I'm doin'?"

Tuttle shook his head, then apparently changed his mind. "Well, yes, I do." He stared right into Fain's eyes. "I wish you'd come up to the house when this is all over. See can't you an' Ruth find a middle ground where you can get along maybe a little bit."

"Sir, I don't know as how I can give you an answer to that right now; figure we got a lot more important things to worry 'bout."

Tuttle nodded. "Reckon you're right."

Fain glanced around the bunch and saw that those he'd chosen were ready. "All right, men, let's go. We'll squat out behind the bunkhouse an' powwow."

In the brush behind the bunkhouse, Fain hunkered down and looked at the four men. "Figure those in the buildin's can cover the front an' sides; our job's gonna be to keep Taggart's men from hittin' 'em from the back."

His gaze swept the brush, the backs of the buildings, and gauged rifle range across the cleared ground to where he intended to station each man. "Don't want any of you to get too far away so's you can't hit a man gettin' too close to where our people are. If you move around, an' I figure you're gonna have to, to keep from gettin' your head blown off, be damned careful not to show yourself." He assigned each of the four men a spot from which to cover the backside of a structure. "All right, men, don't take any unecessary chances. Let's go."

Inside the house, Mobley took young Tommy by the shoulders, looked him in the eye, and said, "Young man, when that man comes back who wants to hurt us, I want you to stay on the floor behind the heaviest piece of furniture in here."

Tommy squared his shoulders, and stared back. "Sir, I know you want to take care o' me, but I done fought Indians with my ma an' pa. I can shoot 'bout good as any man here."

A lump formed in Jed's throat. He was so proud of this little boy, he felt like he could burst wide open. "Son, I wanta tell you somethin'. If anything should happen to you, your ma an' I would feel like we'd lost the whole world, an' there wouldn't be anything I could do to keep your ma from cryin' all day an' night, day after day. We wouldn't want to see tears in her pretty eyes, would we?"

Tommy stood a little straighter. "No, sir. Don't figger neither me or you would want that." He squinted and held Mobley with his eyes. "Sir, you jest said as how you thought Ma's eyes were pretty. Well, I think so too. Fact is, I b'lieve she's pretty all over. I b'lieve she's the prettiest lady I ever seen."

Jed wanted to pull the little boy to his chest and hug him, but was fearful he'd embarrass him. He nodded. "Tommy, I don't b'lieve I've ever seen a woman, anywhere, anytime, I thought was as pretty as your mom."

Tommy's eyes grew large, widened. "You've done seen a awful lot o' ladies, ain't yuh? An you think Ma's got 'em all beat? Wow! That's some sort o' pretty. I gotta tell Ma what you said."

Mobley shook his head. "No, I figure that's somethin' a grown man's gotta tell a woman. Want you to promise me you won't say anything 'bout this little talk we've had."

Tommy frowned, then nodded. "If that's the way it's gotta be, sir."

Jed squeezed the boy's shoulders, and was about to stand when Pam walked up. "What are you two men talkin' about?"

Heat pushed its way into Jed's face. "Just tellin Tommy I don't want 'im to be standin' up when Taggart comes back. Told 'im it'd cause you to cry if he got hurt." He smiled. "Reckon it'd cause both o' us to do that."

Pam stared at him a moment. "You think a awful lot 'bout that boy o' mine, don't you, Jed?"

Mobley stared at the floor a moment, then nodded. "Yes'm, reckon if I ever have a son, I want 'im to be exactly like Tommy." He cleared his throat, wanting the lump in it to disappear. "But I'm sayin' right now, I don't want 'im where a bullet might catch 'im." He glanced at Tommy. "Now you stay down. Okay?"

Tommy nodded.

Mobley took Pam's elbow and pushed her toward one of

the inner rooms. "Want you to stay in here safe too." He grinned. "Fain seems to think I'm takin' an unusual interest in you an' your boy." He shook his head and muttered to himself, "Didn't know I was that easy to read."

"Land sakes, what're you talkin' to yourself 'bout?"

He jerked his head to look at her over his shoulder. "Didn't say anythin'. Nothin'. Maybe I was just sayin' I want Tommy to stay where I put 'im."

A slight smile creased the corners of Pam's lips. "Yes, Jed, I reckon that's what I heard."

He broke away from her and walked around the room. He checked every window where every man stood. Ruth and her mother also stood at a window, rifles in hand. "Miss Ruth, what you women figure you're doin'?"

"You men fight—we fight." The look in Ruth's eyes said she'd brook no argument.

"Why don't y'all take a safe position. Then if it looks like we can't do the job without you, come on into the fight."

She shook her head. "Nope. A whole bunch o' you who don't have a stake in this little war o' ours done sliced out a chunk o' the fightin' for yourselves. If you fight, we fight."

He looked over his shoulder to see Pam take up station by one of the other windows. His shoulder muscles tightened. His head hurt, but he'd not be the one to take Pam's pride from her. Let her do her part.

Back at the chuck wagon, Taggart stared at his men with a look that would have pierced steel. He walked from one end of the line his men made to the other, then back again. "Ain't gonna stand still an' watch a damned milksop buck me in this here deal."

He stopped at about the middle of the line and stared. "We gonna ride in there after dark an' set fire to every buildin' they got. Then when they come out coughin' an spittin' smoke, we gonna drop 'em where they stand. Ain't none o' 'em gonna get away, man, woman, or child. Y'all got that?"

Trig Barnes watched the bull-like man try to walk and talk his frustration away. He had talked with most of the men and knew where they stood. He stepped forward. "Taggart, you done talked 'bout what you gonna get outta this. Now what I want to know is, what're we gonna get outta it? I ain't stickin' my butt out fer no damned thirty an' found. We gonna share in that land, an' the calf crop what comes in the spring when the grass greens up."

Taggart's shoulders hunched, his neck pulled down into them, his fists clenched, and his face looked like it would burst every blood vessel in it. "What the hell you say to me, Barnes? You buckin' me? You are, an' I'll blow that ugly head off'n yore shoulders."

Trig went quiet inside. He hadn't thought Taggart would refuse to talk about their sharing in the land steal. But hell, he'd outdrawn and outshot better men with a gun than his trail boss. "Taggart, I ain't carryin' the name o' Trig around for nothin'. You figger to fight 'bout this, turn loose your wolf."

The trail boss stared at Barnes, then grinned. "Reckon I knowed I had a salty crew. Hell, no, I don't figger we gotta fight 'bout how we gonna split things. We can talk 'bout it after we take on the milksop an' that bunch he done pulled around 'im."

Barnes had not figured on Taggart backing down, and he knew he hadn't. He thought Bane Taggart wanted to hold the crew together long enough to get rid of the rancher's claim to any of the land or cattle. Then, Trig figured, Taggart would get rid of them—some way. But for now, Trig didn't want a fight either. They had to keep every man they had if there was any chance they could beat that bunch back at the ranch headquarters. He relaxed, but at the same time thought he'd not let Taggart get behind him.

"All right for now, Boss, but don't forget we gonna talk when we get things runnin' our way." He took a deep breath. "Now, what we gonna do 'bout them gunnies back there where they done holed up?"

The blood receded from Taggart's face, the hunch went

out of his shoulders, his fists opened. "We gonna do like I said, only we gonna ride partway; then I'll leave one o' you to stay with the horses while the rest o' us go in on foot." He looked around the crew. "Noticed a whole bunch o' hay stacked to the side o' the barn. I want every man here to grab a armload o' that hay, then sneak up to the side of one o' them buildin's, strike a lucifer under it so's it won't flare up till we get back in the brush, then we sit back an watch it burn, buildin's, people, ever'thin'. Y'all got it?" At their nods, he said, "Let's go."

They rode through the dark, misty night. No one talked; the only noise was that of saddles creaking, and an occasional cough. While riding, Taggart mulled over the opposition he'd gotten from Barnes, and had a hunch there were others who felt the same way, along with a few who would balk at shooting women and children. He shrugged mentally. Hell, nothing ever went smoothly.

He gave a thought to rounding up the herd and finding another place to take over; then hot blood pushed up behind his eyes. This place, along with the brand, fit his plans exactly, and he'd be damned if he'd let that milksop Fain spoil everything.

The longer he thought of Cord Fain, the madder he got. The goody-goody trailhand he'd hired had strapped on a gun and figured it made him a man. He hoped the mama's boy came through this fight alive. He wanted to stand in front of him and make him show yellow before he shot him.

Unconsciously, Taggart shook his head. Fain wouldn't back down or show yellow. He'd stood there east of Cimarron, without a gun, and bucked him. No. He'd have to kill him. But what was he going to do about Barnes and the men he'd apparently gathered around him?

Taggart pulled his bull-like shoulders down farther into his slicker. He'd have to take one thing at a time. First, he had to get this ranch firmly in his grasp. He'd thought at this time of year, before any of the ranches started hiring for fall roundup, that it would be just a matter of riding in and taking over. Of course he'd have to get rid of those who had called it home, but that wasn't anything to worry about.

After another thirty minutes, he pulled rein. "Gather round, men. We walk from here. Spread out, we'll circle the buildings, then dig under that haystack for dry grass. Use all the cover you can find getting to the sides of those buildings. The stable'll be the easiest to get to, don't figger they's anybody in it. Set yore fires an' back off into the brush, then wait fer 'em to come out." He laughed. "It'll be like shootin' ducks on the water."

As soon as Fain told the men to take their stations, he stopped, frowned, held his hand out for them to stand fast. "Just now thought o'somethin'. Once we know they're close to the buildin's, they're gonna be hard to see. Fact is, in this light I doubt we'll seen 'em till they're all round us—or round the buildin's. If they figure to set everything on fire, they'll be able to do it and get gone before we can stop 'em."

Frog Ballew hopped closer to Cord. "What you figger to do 'bout that, Fain?"

Cord frowned, wiped the toe of his boot across a tuft of grass, then looked up. "Got an idea if you think you can cover me."

Carl shouldered in close to him. Carl was the only name the man had ever given anyone when he came to work for Cord's pa fifteen years before. He said, "Let's hear what you figger can be done, an' I don't want to hear any damn fool stunt like you pulled when Taggart rode in with his bunch this afternoon."

Fain chuckled. "I gotta tell you, old friend, it's just 'bout that dumb, but I can't think o' anything else."

"Let's hear it."

While Cord studied how to lay it out for the four men, his mouth watered. He sniffed. The women in the ranch house were cooking supper. He could smell the aroma of fresh-boiled coffee—and stew, he believed. He swept his men with a glance. "Once we're sure they're in the yard, I think if I'm right careful, I can get to the haystack, grab an armful, pick up a few pieces o' firewood along the way, set it out yonder in that space in front o' the stable, bunkhouse, an' ranch house, stick a lucifer under it, an' get back in these cedar breaks 'fore they realize what I've done." He nodded. "That oughta work. It'll light up the yard an' we can shoot 'em while they're tryin' to get outta sight."

Cookie had his say. "Fain, that there ain't just 'bout as dumb. It outstretches what you done this afternoon by one helluva long way." He looked hopefully at Cord. "Don't reckon as how you'd let me do it—would ya?"

Fain grasped the old man's shoulder. "No, partner. I told y'all I wouldn't ask anybody to do anything that I wouldn't do. Well, this is one o' those things I gotta do myself."

9

NIGHT SETTLED IN. The mist had turned to a steady, gentle rain. Ruth stood at her station, staring into the darkness. She wondered if Taggart's men were out there in the cedar breaks close to Cord's men, close enough to pick them out of the darkness and shoot them. She shivered.

Why hadn't she made the tall man listen to her, stand still and hear her apology?

Everything she'd thought a man should be, Fain had measured up to any standard she'd ever set for the kind of man she thought she could be attracted to. Not attracted to as a man, but as a friend. Her shoulders slumped, her chest felt as though it was caught in a vise, cold pushed between her shoulders, *shame* flooded her. She'd never treated anyone so shoddily. Why had she acted the way she had? She admitted to herself that she liked Cord Fain.

A shadowy movement out in the yard drew her attention. She lost it while still swinging her rifle for a shot. Then she caught another shadow out of the corner of her eye. While she was trying to get her rifle pointed at it, a flicker of light—a match maybe?—flared, then looked as though it burned out, and abruptly there was a large flare.

She swung her rifle in the direction of the man running from the fire. *Fain!* She released the pressure on her trigger finger. Another foolish, brave, unbelievably stupid thing. Didn't he think anyone could kill him? And how had she ever thought he came up short when *men* were being made?

Then she remembered the other shadow, or shadows, she'd seen from the corners of her eyes. Taggart's men were out there too. They were where they could see him, shoot him, hurt him. She frantically searched for a target, saw a man raising his rifle to point at the hunched-over, running Fain.

Ruth swung her rifle, squeezed the trigger, and watched the other shadowy form stumble and fall. Other rifles within the confines of the ranch house were firing. Flashes of fire came from what she could see of the bunkhouse and stable. Two more men fell to the withering fire.

It sounded like every gun in Colorado fired, trying to outdo the others—then, abruptly, an ear-splitting silence. Nothing moved outside. Ruth snorted the acrid smell of gun smoke from her nostrils. Her gaze shifted over the lighted expanse of the yard, trying to penetrate the darker areas, looking for a target, but mostly trying to remember what Cord had been wearing, and seeking any hint that he could have escaped being shot by Taggart's men—or his own.

Three men lay out in the yard, none of them Fain as far as she could determine. She sucked in a ragged, deep breath, wanting to believe he'd gotten back into the scrubby cedar before being hit.

Then, from the window next to her, Mobley cursed. "That damned Fain, when I see 'im again I'm gonna knock the hell outta him. He thinks the bullet hasn't been made with his name on it." Then, almost as in a prayer, he said, "God, please let 'im be all right. He's the most magnificent bastard I've ever seen."

Ruth heard every word, and silently agreed with everything he'd said. Then she added her prayer to his. She began to wonder how strongly the feeling of friendship had hold of her.

She glanced around the room. "Didn't notice any o' those attackin' us doin' much shootin'. After Fain set that hay an' stuff afire, all they seemed to care 'bout wuz findin' some place away from here. Everybody in here all right?"

Her father grunted, and nodded. "Somebody light a lamp. I checked all them I could see. Didn't see nobody bleedin'." He leaned his rifle against the wall and went looking for Tommy; found him standing at a window with his mother. "Thought you promised Mr. Mobley you'd stay down."

Tommy nodded. "Did, sir, but soon's the shootin' stopped, I come over to check on Ma. From where I wuz, I seen Mr. Mobley wuz all right."

Ruth looked from Pam to her son to Mobley. A slight smile broke the corners of her mouth. She liked Pam Henders, and had worried many times how she would make it since her husband got killed. She swept the three again. Unless she was sorely mistaken, she wouldn't have that worry anymore. If those two didn't realize what they'd found, she'd just have to tell them.

As soon as he put a lucifer to the underside of the hay, Fain dug heels into the muddy earth, twisted, got his feet under him, and ran like he'd never run before. A shadowy form loomed out of the darkness. In one fluid motion, Cord drew, fired, and sprinted past the man, who buckled at the waist and fell. Something tugged at his shirt, then another tug, burn, and sledgehammer blow hit his right thigh. His leg went out from under him. He fell, skidded in the slick mud, got his feet under him, felt a fiery streak across his shoulder, dragged his right leg trailing behind him, and stumbled through the first scrubby cedar.

Two pairs of arms grabbed him and pulled him to the ground. "You hit bad, boy?" He recognized Dealy's voice.

"Don't b'lieve so, Jim. My right leg's numb right now;

got no pain in it. Soon's I figure that bunch has set sail for new pasture, we'll go back to the bunkhouse an' take a look at it. You men out here get any o' that bunch?"

Frog moved in close to him. "I got one. He's a-lyin' out yonder just outside o' these here cedar breaks."

Cookie, busy slitting Fain's jeans off his leg, looked up. "I got one too. He's out yonder 'bout twenty feet. Don't know whether he's dead, but I hit 'im with a load from this here Sharps. If he ain't dead, I guaran-damn-tee yuh he's tore all to hell."

Carl told them that nobody had come his way.

Feeling eased back into Fain's leg, and with it came gut-wrenching pain. He tried, but couldn't hold it back. A moan pushed through his lips.

"Here now, partner. I done got yore jeans cut away, so hold still till I git my bandanna tied round yore leg. From what I could see in the dark an' feel with my fingers, it ain't bad; went through nothin' but meat. Didn't hit the bone." Cookie tied a knot in the bandanna he'd placed around Cord's leg, patted it, and looked up at the other three. "It ain't gonna be easy, but the way I got it figgered, we better stay out here a little while till we make sure that bunch has done left for the night."

Fain knotted his jaws together as another stab of pain laced through him, then nodded. "B'lieve you're right, Cookie. Y'all got two of 'em, I got one, an' I think I saw another one or two of 'em go down while I was tryin' to get my mama's little boy away from there 'fore he got 'is damned fool self killed." He nodded even though he thought they couldn't see him. "We put a whole bunch o' hurt on that trail crew tonight. Really don't think they'll be back tonight. Don't know what they'll figure to do next. When we get back to the bunkhouse, we'll talk 'bout it."

They held their places for another thirty or more minutes. Finally, Cord said he thought the ranch would be safe for the rest of the night. "Let's go to the bunkhouse."

He tried walking, but his leg gave way. Dealy pulled Fain's right arm over his shoulder and supported him to the door, then helped him to his bunk. "Goin' up to the house an' git some more rags to clean an' bandage yore laig, Fain. If I bring Ruth back with me, don't want no fuss outta you, an' you gonna be nice, you heah?"

Right then, Fain wouldn't have argued if Dealy had said he would bring Taggart.

If Taggart *had* been brought into the bunkhouse at that minute, he'd have busted every blood vessel in his head. Soaked, bedraggled, he glanced at what remained of the seven men he'd brought with him; only one man sat his horse alongside.

That mama's boy had whittled the trail crew down. Mentally, Bane Taggart shook his head. He'd never been so wrong in judging a man. Where had Fain learned how to fight so quickly? He'd never impressed anyone that he knew anything about guns, or much of anything else. He'd always stayed to himself, didn't wear a handgun, didn't join in the drinking or cardplaying around the fire at night—but he did know cattle. And the trail boss remembered that no one crossed Cord Fain. Had they seen something in him that he'd missed?

Taggart frowned into the night, tried to swallow past the tightness in his throat, rolled his shoulders to relieve the stiff muscles between them, tried to squelch the hot blood pounding at his temples, and thought to go back and finish the job he'd set out to do. He shook his head. No. If he went back now, that bunch at the ranch would be ready for him. He'd wait until he thought to take them by surprise.

Who the hell would figure anyone would be stupid enough to stay out there where he could get shot and light off a fire that exposed every man Taggart had brought with him? By his estimate, he'd lost the advantage of numbers over the crew he had to fight. His jaws knotted. He'd fight down to his last man if he had to. He'd not let a milksop beat him.

When he rode to the chuck wagon, Trig Barnes met him. "Where's them others you took with ya?"

Taggart wasn't in any mood to take anything from any man. He swallowed the knot in his throat. "They're layin' back yonder in the mud in front o' the ranch house. They wuz ready fer us. Lit a fire out in the middle o' the yard an' could see every one o' us."

He stepped from the saddle and pinned Barnes with a gaze. "Don't want a damned thing outta you either, ya heah?" He walked to the fire, looked for the coffeepot, remembered it had gotten shot to bits, and felt blood push harder at his temples.

He went to the wagon, crawled under it to get out of as much rain as possible, stared into the fire, and figured he'd better take all but one or two men into Trinidad, buy provisions, and replace the things that got shot up. Who had pulled the raid on his trail camp?

Taggart scanned those men who huddled under the wagon with him. "A few o' us is gonna go buy what we got shot up. Want you to remember we don't want no trouble with the law. We gonna build ourselves a reputation what'll stand up after we take over that there ranch, one that'll make us respectable folks. Soon's daylight comes we leave."

Fain tried once to get off his bunk after Dealy went to the ranch house, but gave it up. His leg shot pain throughout his body. Footsteps approached the door, and he heard Ruth's voice telling the ranch foreman something he couldn't hear from where he lay. He sighed. Looked like he'd have to suffer through listening to that woman browbeat him again. To hell with it; he'd bite his tongue and keep quiet.

Dealy led the way to Cord's bunk. He held a bundle of rags in his hands. Ruth stood beside him holding a large jar of something that looked like axle grease. Fain stared at Dealy. "You find a bottle o' whiskey somewhere in this bunkhouse. I want a drink, and some of it poured on this scratch I got out yonder."

Dealy leaned over, untied Cookie's bandanna from Cord's leg. Ruth gasped. Dealy twisted his head to the side to look at her. "All that blood makes it look worse than I figger it is." He nodded. "Course it prob'ly hurts like Satan."

Ruth pierced Fain with a look, a look he'd learned to expect from her. "You know, Mr. Fain, that what you did out yonder tonight was 'bout the dumbest, but one o' the bravest, most magnificent things I've ever seen. Why'd you take such a chance? After all, standin' out there this afternoon and bracin' Taggart's crew alone 'bout took the cake. Didn't think I'd live to see the day you could top that stupid act."

Angry bile boiled under Fain's tongue, his face heated, his jaws knotted. "Ma'am, knowin' what you thought o' me, I figured to give you something else to give me hell about." He turned his face to the wall. "Get on with fixin' my leg, Dealy, then go get Tuttle an' Jed Mobley. We gotta have a powwow—decide what we're gonna do next, or maybe what we figure Taggart's gonna do."

"You're not gonna do anything," said Ruth. "You're comin' up to the house with me. I'll get you in bed so Mama an' me can take care o' you."

He turned his head from looking at the wall. "Ma'am, I'm not goin' anywhere with you. Fact is, I've had 'bout all the poison you spit at me every time I see you to last me a lifetime." He moved his eyes to look at Dealy. "Get on with the doctorin'; we got things to talk 'bout."

Before Dealy could respond, Ruth placed her hand on Cord's shoulder. "Oh, Cord, I'm so sorry. I don't know why I've treated you like I have. Please forgive me, let me try to make amends."

He again looked at her. "Ma'am, don't know as how I can do that. Don't know which o' you is gonna show up each time we meet. Reckon since most o' what you've said to me is pure-dee rattlesnake—fangs included, I'll play it safe an' stay clear o' your tongue. Now get on with fixin' my leg." She said something else, but he had already closed her out.

When Dealy finished bandaging his wound, Fain swung his left leg over the side of the bunk, grasped the thigh of his right leg, picked it up and carefully moved it to hang over, and lowered it to the floor.

"Where do you think you're goin', Cord? You're not able to stand." Ruth's voice showed genuine concern and caring.

A thread of what she was all about began to penetrate the pain in Fain's head. Could it be that when she was worried, or doubted one's ability to do what needed doing, she responded with anger? He mentally shrugged. Why should he care? Most everything he'd seen about her indicated she'd not be very pleasant to be around. He'd just stay away from her.

He looked into her eyes. Damn, but she *was* one pretty woman. If he could gag her, she'd be right nice to be around—just to look at.

Dealy had gone to the house to get Tuttle and Mobley. Ruth had made no move to leave. "Reckon you're gonna sit in on the meetin'," Cord said.

She nodded. "Since the women in that house up yonder fight right alongside o' the men, I reckon we got a right to be represented at any meetin' y'all have."

There was that stubborn streak again. He nodded. "Reckon as how you've said it like it oughta be." He tried to stand, stumbled, and as quick as scat she had ducked under his arm, pulled it around her shoulder, and helped him to the table. Fain had to admit to himself that she felt mighty good that close to him. She slowly lowered him to a chair, then stood back, her face flushed a pretty pink. Fain figured it best to not say anything even though he wanted to thank her.

He looked over his shoulder, spotted Cookie, and motioned toward the stove. "If that's fresh coffee you brewed since we got back here, reckon the lady and I could stand a cup of it."

In only a moment or two, Ruth and Cord sat sipping the

hot liquid. A few moments later, Dealy came in with Mobley and Tuttle.

He sat there through a chewing out by both the ranch owner and Jed before Tuttle asked what he wanted to see them about. "Figure we better decide what we gonna do now," said Fain. "Settin' 'nother fire out there won't work." He grinned ruefully. "'Sides that, don't think there's another damned fool in this bunch. I've had 'bout all I can stand of gettin' shot at up close for a while."

Tuttle glanced at Mobley, then turned his gaze on Ruth as though daring her to object to what he was going to say. "Well, young man, you have come in here an' taken over runnin' things." He nodded. "Yeah, you've done right well, so I'm gonna ask what you got in mind."

Ignoring Tuttle's sarcasm, Fain frowned, thinking. "You got a line shack where the women can get outta this weather?"

Tuttle nodded. "Got two; fact is, Mrs. Tuttle an' me lived in one o' 'em till we could build our house. Why?"

Cord frowned. "What I'm gonna say won't go down very well with Mrs. Tuttle, but it's gotta be said. We can't defend these buildin's anymore. They'll burn us out sooner or later; then we'll be easy targets they can shoot when we try to escape the flames. They'd kill all o' us—includin' the women." He drank the rest of his coffee and signaled Cookie to pour more.

No one said anything while Cookie poured; then Fain sat forward. "My idea is to leave here, take the women, Tommy, the crew, and set up in one or both o' the line shacks. Then we can make strikes on Taggart from there."

Ruth stared at the table a moment. "Cord, you're sayin', 'Let 'em burn our home'?"

He took a deep breath, expecting an argument, then nodded. "Yes'm, reckon that's what I'm sayin'. If they do, I'll keep my crew here an' help build y'all a new one." He shook his head. "Know it won't be the same as the one you grew up in, but figure it's better'n dyin'."

Then she surprised him. She looked around the table,

squared her shoulders, and looked each man there in the
eye. "Well, you've heard 'im. Reckon we better gather the
things we think most of, an' get outta here tonight while
they can't see to shoot us."

She swung her glance to her father. "Papa, we'd better
take the wagon, pack beddin' an' stuff like that so as to
make Mama as comfortable as possible." Then, as an after-
thought, she said, "Better pack cookin' things too—an'
provisions." She motioned to Cookie. "Know you heard
ever'thin' that's been said, so you an' me'll make sure we
got enough food an' things to cook with." She stood.
"Come on, y'all, we better get movin'."

Fain sat there looking at her as if at a different person. A
lot of his previous prejudices against her melted away. He
clamped his teeth together to keep his jaw from hanging
slack. "Okay, the young lady has said it." He turned to
Mobley. "Tell the men who've been protectin' the stable
what we're about, then figure out what animals we gonna
need to take with us, an' drive the rest of 'em into that shallow valley behind the house. We'll collect 'em after this's
over."

"Cord, you'll ride in the wagon with Mama an' me," said
Ruth. "I'll drive. You ain't fit to do nothin' yet; 'sides that,
I figger you're hurtin' too bad to take on that job right
now."

Fain figured he'd quit while he was ahead. The only
thing he said was, "Yes'm."

A couple of hours later, the wagon packed, the men with
their bedrolls behind saddles, rifles loaded, Ruth led them
from ranch headquarters.

She glanced at Fain to see if he looked at her, then
glanced back to look, perhaps a last time, at the only home
she'd ever known. She wiped her eyes.

"Know it's hard, ma'am," said Fain. "Reckon I'd cry too
if the same thing happened to me. Sorry it has to be this
way."

She snapped her head to the side to look at him. "Didn't

figger to let anybody see me act like one o' them soft town-livin' women. Reckon you're disappointed in me." As soon as she said that, she was sorry. What difference did it make whether he felt disappointment in anything she did? But the germ of knowing that it did make a difference already grew in her chest. What was wrong with her?

Cord smiled to himself. That woman wasn't as tough as she made out to be. For some reason he was pleased with the thought.

With the brightening of the eastern sky, the little caravan rode well out of sight of the ranch buildings. Land swells and piney woods stood between them and the house they thought destined to be burned.

Fain looked at the side of Ruth's face. "Glad you're gonna be this far from harm, ma'am. Gonna give this leg a good two days to get to feelin' better, then I'm ridin' in to Trinidad."

"It won't be that well by then, Cord. You're gonna give it more time than that."

He snorted. "No, ma'am, I'm not. When that bunch I took outta here, an' me, shot up Taggart's camp, we wrecked some stuff he's gonna have to replace. I figure he's gonna be in town."

"An' you're gonna go in there to face 'im?" Disbelief showed in her every word.

"Don't figure on a showdown, ma'am. Just want to show 'im we ain't whipped in any way. It'll work on his thinkin' till he won't know how to figure things."

"You ever give that pea-sized brain o' yours a chance to figger you only been wearin' a gun a couple o' weeks at the most? You ever figger he'll shoot you deader'n last summer's brown, dry grass?"

"Ma'am, I've taken a couple o' bullets the last few days. B'lieve me, I don't hanker to take any more any time soon." He frowned, then grinned. "'Sides that, I been prac-ticin' my draw, an' figure I might get to be pretty good with a handgun."

She shook her head. "I don't think you understand, cowboy. It takes a mite longer than a few days to get good with a handgun."

He kept quiet. Only the men he'd brought with him, men he'd grown up with, knew how good he was with his draw, as well as his accuracy. He might as well keep all that to himself until the time came that he might have to let others know. Then he answered her. "Miss Ruth, this is somethin' I b'lieve I gotta do in order to keep Taggart guessin'."

Ruth flicked her whip over the backs of the team, then again looked at him. "Somethin's still botherin' me, Fain. You ain't got a stake in anythin' goin on round here. Far's I can see, they ain't nothin' you can gain, so why're you helpin' us?"

He frowned, trying to think how to answer her. He'd wondered about that very thing himself. Why *was* he sticking his neck out for people he barely knew, people he probably would never see once he'd crushed Taggart? He cocked his head to look up at her from where he lay. "Miss Ruth, tell you straight out, if I had to come up with an answer that would make sense, I don't b'lieve I'd stand a chance of doin' it."

"Is it 'cause you hate Taggart?"

"Ma'am, I don't hate 'im; fact is, I don't hate anybody." He shrugged, knowing she couldn't see him. "Closest I can come to why I'm doin' it is 'cause he tried to cheat Wash, Cookie, an' me outta a couple months' wages." He chuckled. "Not that he succeeded in keepin' our money, we got it back in spades, but reckon just the idea he figured to cheat us made me madder'n a hornet."

He tried to move his leg to a more comfortable position, and regretted it with the stab of pain that shot from his groin to his foot. He moaned. "Too, ma'am, I was raised to treat others like I wanted to be treated. I just flat couldn't stand still an' let 'im take from people who had worked for everythin' they had. Reckon I'm just not cut out that way." He chuckled, then laughed. "'Sides that, I'm beginnin' to get an idea how we can all get somethin' outta this. Tell you 'bout it soon's I figure it'll work."

Throughout the conversation, Ruth's mother had kept quiet. Then, from the other side of where he lay, she said, "Line shack's just around the next bend."

Fain looked up at her outlined against the night sky. "Miss Eve—hope you don't mind me callin' you that—did we follow a trail in here, or is there a trail from the ranch house to here?"

"No. It's grown up with bunchgrass since we built the house years ago."

"Good. Now if this rain'll wash out our tracks, Taggart and his men won't be able to track us."

When Ruth drew rein in front of the line shack, the men were busy taking care of their horses. Cord was glad to see a shed where they could get in out of the rain. The animals would have to stay outside this night.

Taggart glanced at the steadily falling rain and changed his mind about leaving for Trinidad the next morning. He had a couple of men stretch a tarpaulin, held up by a couple of poles, from the chuck wagon. They'd stay as dry as the weather permitted for a couple of days—then he'd head for town. In the meantime, he might figure how to fight the Lazy T and the men Fain had brought in. It never entered his head that he might lose every man he had; the fact was, he didn't care. His sole thought now was getting even with Cord Fain.

It had been the milksop who'd set the fire and exposed his men to fire; he'd seen him plainly. But the chance the same trick would work twice was slim to none. So the option of burning them out was still there. He thought about that a few moments; suppose he could make things miserable enough for them that they'd vacate the buildings.

He thought about that a while. If they'd leave, then he'd have a ready-made headquarters. He'd be set up without having to turn a hand. He liked the idea. Now he'd have to think of some way to get them out of the buildings; then, when they came out, he and his men could shoot them. There would be no one to dispute his claim. He pondered how to get them out of the house for a few minutes, then gave it up, pulled his blankets up, and went to sleep.

As soon as Fain made certain the women were comfortable in the cabin, for that's what it was, he had Dealy help him to the shed, where a couple of the crew spread his bedroll and helped him to it.

While the men were setting themselves up in as much comfort as they could expect, the women made bunks, built a fire in the potbellied stove, and put on a pot of coffee. Mobley and Bob Tuttle elected to stay in the cabin with the women. Jed told them it would be best if there were at least a couple of men in there to help protect them if Taggart by some chance managed to track them.

When Ruth had a cup of steaming coffee in front of her, she felt her mother staring at her. She turned to look at her. "What you lookin' at me for, Mama?"

Miss Eve only shook her head. "Ruth, I do believe you've changed your mind about Mr. Fain. You were almost nice to him while we were ridin' in the wagon. You seemed to like him a bit."

Ruth nodded. "Do, Mama, ain't never disliked 'im. Why you say that?"

"Well, up till now, you've stung 'im with a mighty sharp tongue; then on the way over here you seemed more mellow, even right nice to 'im." She shook her head. "That man ain't changed one whit from the first time we seen 'im. Don't know why you treated 'im like you did, but I'm beginnin' to get a idea."

"Well, I declare, Mama, you're a puzzle. Don't know what you could be thinkin', but I'm right anxious to find out." Abruptly, she stood. "Speakin' 'bout Mr. Fain, I'll bet he'd feel a lot better if I took 'im a cup o' this hot coffee." She put actions to words, poured a cup, and went out the door.

Pam stared at the door a moment, shook her head, and looked at Jed. "Well, if I hadn't seen it with my own eyes, I wouldn't of believed it. What you reckon changed?"

Mobley frowned, then shook his head. "B'lieve she's only now beginning to see that she's had one helluva man right in front o' her all along." He smiled through his frown. "Huh, you reckon that's what's been botherin' 'er? You reckon she hates to think there's a man that strong; a man who could take charge of everything she is, thinks, and acts?"

Pam chuckled deep in her throat. "If she'd only looked around, she'd have seen two men who fit that bill."

Mobley thought about Pam's words a moment. "Who else is like that around here?" Then his face heated; blood rushed to his head. "Aw, now, Pam, you don't mean me, I'm not half the man Fain is."

In a very soft voice, Pam said, "I think so, an' Tommy would fight anyone who said different."

Mobley sipped at the coffee he'd poured a few minutes earlier, then looked into her eyes. "Pam, this isn't the time to talk 'bout this, but I ask you to let me say a few things when we get outta this mess we're in. All right?"

She smiled. "Jed Mobley, if you don't bring the subject up, I promise you, I will."

Outside the shed, Ruth stopped. "Ever'body in yonder decent? If y'all are, I'm bringin' Cord a cup o' hot coffee. Figgered a cup might make 'im hurt a little bit less."

Dealy chuckled. "Come on in, Ruth. I reckon he can pour that whiskey I jest now poured 'im into that there coffee. Make it taste mighty good."

About to take a swallow of whiskey, Cord dropped his hand from his mouth. To what in the name of hell did he owe this? Why had she suddenly started treating him like he figured a human being should be treated until he proved differently? He looked at her when she walked to his bunk. Hmmm, she surely was a nice-looking filly.

"Don't know what I ever did to deserve this, ma'am, but I appreciate it." He tilted the drink Dealy had poured him over the cup, then took a sip. He blew through his pursed lips, licked them, and nodded. "Mighty good. Thanks, Miss Tuttle."

She squatted, knelt on her knees beside him. "Mr. Fain, since you seem to be in charge of this fight, what you got planned to do next?"

Fain wondered again about her change in attitude; she'd as much as said she accepted his leadership. He decided to give her an answer, risk having her criticize what he planned. "I figure to lie here a day or so, then ride in to Trinidad, see if maybe Taggart's gone in to replace the things we shot up the other night."

She frowned. "You goin' in there to see if you cain't pick a fight with 'im?"

"Not unless he's lookin' for one." He chuckled. "Reckon if I was him, I'd sure be lookin' to tangle with anybody from here. Bet he's mad enough to spit."

"You takin' anybody with you?"

"Don't figure on it." He shook his head. "No sense in gettin' any o' the men shot all to hell, just because I got an enormous curiosity; want to know how mad we've made 'im."

"Well, Mr. Fain, I'm here to tell you, if you figger to go in alone, it ain't gonna happen that way. I'm goin' with you, an' I'm gonna take Papa's men with me."

He shook his head, and wondered if she could see him. "No, ma'am, you *ain't* goin' anywhere, especially into Trinidad with me."

"Wh-wh-who are you to tell me what I'm gonna do? I'll go anywhere I want to."

Fain chuckled, then laughed. "Now I know I been talkin' to Miss Ruth Tuttle, the woman with a tongue that could scald an iceberg. Know, 'cause I got the scars to prove it."

The dim light showed her shoulders droop, then slump. "Mr. Fain, know you ain't got any reason to think different 'bout me, know I done treated you mighty bad, but maybe someday I'll figger out why I've done it. I'll tell you then." She shook her head. "Jest don't want you goin' in there alone an' gettin' shot when there ain't nobody to cover your back."

"My back'll be covered. I've made friends with the U.S. marshal in there. Don't b'lieve he's gonna let anybody get behind me once he knows I'm in town—an' that Taggart's there too. I've told 'im 'bout my ex–trail boss."

"Who's gonna tell the men what to do while you're gone?"

"I'll tell 'em what I want 'em to do, then I figure Mobley can see they do it."

Fain turned his cup up and drained it. "Thanks again, ma'am; that was mighty good."

She reached for his cup. "I'll run get you another."

He swung his cup out of reach. "No, thank you, ma'am, reckon I've had enough. Gonna pull this blanket up an' get some sleep. Figure these scratches in my body'll heal a lot better if I give 'em a chance."

She stared at him a moment. "You ain't gonna let me do nothin' for you, are you, Mr. Fain?"

"Miss Tuttle, if there's ever a chance I'll know which one o' you is gonna show up, an' if it's the nice carin' woman you've shown me, only briefly"—he nodded—"then yes, I can't think of anything I'd like better."

He turned to his side. "Now, ma'am, if you won't think me rude, I'm gonna let these bullet holes in me stop hurtin'."

She gasped. "Oh, Mr. Fain, I'm sorry. Reckon I was jest likin' talkin' 'bout what you was gonna do." She rocked back off her knees and stood. "You sure they ain't nothin' I can do to make you feel better?"

He wanted to tell her to just go, but held the words. She'd tried to be nice, and he knew it had cost her a lot of pride. "Yes, ma'am, I'm sure. Now really, I gotta get some sleep an' rest. Thanks for the coffee."

As soon as Ruth left, Fain turned to his back and called Dealy to him. Dealy stared at Ruth's retreating back. "Wonder what the hell brought that on? That girl wuz jest 'bout the same sweet li'l ole girl I helped raise."

Cord grunted in disbelief. "She was right nice to me, but I can't believe she was ever nice most o' the time." He held his now-empty cup out. "If that coffee's ready I figure Cookie put on to boil soon's we got here, I'll have a cup. Then, if you don't mind, go get Mobley an' the three of us'll figure what to do next."

By the time Dealy brought him some more coffee, and brought Jed back with him, Fain had settled his mind on what to do next.

Dealy and Jed walked to the side of his bedding, squatted, and looked ready to listen. He took a swallow of the coffee Dealy had brought, nodded, and looked at them. "Think I got it figured. I reckon Taggart isn't a total damned fool, so I b'lieve he won't burn the buildin's 'less we try to keep 'im out."

"You sayin' fer us to jest let 'im an' his crew move in?" Dealy looked like he'd choke.

"Wait a minute, Jim; let's hear what Cord's got on his mind."

Fain took another swallow of his coffee, frowned, and said, "See what you think o' this. We let 'em all move in, that way we'll know where they are, then when they try to come out, one by one, or two, three at a time, we can have men set up in the cedar breaks an' pick 'em off a few at a time."

"You sayin' we gonna bushwhack 'em?"

Fain's voice came out like chips of granite. "That's what they figure to do to us, Jim. Damn right, that's what I think we oughta do, *and we might be able to save the ranch buildings*."

Dealy shook his head, his mouth a thin slit. "Ain't never cottoned to shootin' a man what wasn't lookin' at me."

Cookie's fire threw out enough light for Fain to see both men plainly. Mobley squinted at the foreman. "Tell you how it is, Dealy. Those men're hard cases. They figure to kill every one of us if they find a way to do it." He nodded. "I think Cord's got the right idea. None of us likes to think of shootin' a man from ambush, but we give 'em a break an' we'll be the ones buryin' our own."

Dealy frowned, pulled his shoulders up, then dropped them straight; an exaggerated shrug, Fain thought.

Then Jim glanced at them both. "Since you put it that way, reckon you're right. Pa use to say you gotta fight fire with fire."

"All right, we'll do it that way. Now I'm gonna sleep."

10

Taggart lay around the chuck wagon for three days, then the weather cleared. He saddled his horse, told the men to place a few of themselves around the ranch buildings, shoot anyone who came out, but not to burn the buildings until he came back from Trinidad.

He'd thought about what he intended to do all the while the weather dripped on the countryside and his temper. He had Trig Barnes figured as a troublemaker, and didn't want to leave him behind to stir the men up. He took him with him, and promised the crew he'd bring back a few bottles of whiskey, along with a coffeepot.

Two days later the two men rode into Trinidad, stabled their horses, and went to the nearest saloon. Taggart had taken several double eagles from his money belt and put them in his pocket while alone in camp. He dug down in his pocket and withdrew a coin. "Here, Trig, git yoreself a woman, a bottle, an' meet me in the mornin' 'bout ten o'clock at that there cafe I seen across the street. I'm gonna do the same, startin' right now."

Barnes glanced at the double eagle, then pierced Taggart with a look. "You gonna take this outta the pay I got comin'?"

Bane wanted to say, yeah, it would come out of Trig's pay, then thought it would be a good idea to be nice to the slim gunman, maybe get him on his side. Taggart shook his head. "Naw, figger we owe it to ourselves. We'll have a good time while we're in here."

Barnes stared at the trail boss a moment, raised an eyebrow, then dropped the coin into his pocket.

Bane had a couple more drinks, went to the hotel, got a room, and from there went to the general store. He bought replacements for the things Fain had made useless, along with coffee, flour, bacon, beans, and tobacco. He took his purchases to his room, glad to have that chore out of the way, then went back to the saloon. Barnes had either already taken a woman upstairs, or had gone to another saloon.

He had another couple of drinks, thought to go see the marshal, changed his mind, and decided to choose the woman he wanted to spend time with until he headed back to the herd.

To see the marshal now might be too early. He wanted to get things firmly under his control before he made the law aware that he now owned the Lazy T. Once he got rid of every living soul at the ranch, it would be easy to cover his actions. He could say he'd bought the ranch, and that the previous owner had packed his family up and headed farther west. They might not believe him, but they couldn't prove he'd lied. No one could dispute his word.

The fourth day after moving into the cabin, and leaving the men in the shed, Fain still felt weak, but figured to try the ride to Trinidad. His wounds still gave him trouble—in fact, they hurt like the devil stood there and poked his fork into him—but he had to make Marshal Worley aware of what had happened at the ranch and how they were faring in the fight. If he rode carefully, maybe he could keep from opening his wounds and starting to bleed again.

He went to the cabin to tell them his intentions. "Gonna head for town, see the marshal, an' let 'im know what's goin' on out here."

Ruth stood to the side, her eyes never leaving his. "You ain't fit to ride, let alone go in there, maybe meet some o' Taggart's crew, have a fight, an' get yourself killed."

Fain shook his head. "Know I'm not ready for a fight, gonna do all I can to avoid one, but Worley has to know what's happened."

"Let somebody else do it."

He shook his head. "Ma'am, there isn't anyone can do what I have to do. 'Sides, if it comes down to a gunfight, I'd rather it be me. In fact, if I meet Taggart in town, I won't be able to fight 'im any other way. Right now, a knuckle-an'-skull, or a knife fight, is out of the question. I couldn't handle it."

"An' you think you could handle a gunfight?" She shook her head. "Know you done a whole bunch o' dumb things that could've got you killed since you got back here, b-b-but I want you back here without gettin' hurt agin."

"Ma'am, I'm goin', an' I'm going soon's I can saddle my horse." He looked at Mobley. "Jed, want you to see that the men handle it like I said the other night, okay?" At Jed's nod, Fain said he'd see them in about a week, then left.

As soon as he'd gone out the door, Ruth turned to Mobley. "Send somebody to shadow 'im."

Jed shook his head. "Won't work. He's a good woodsman; he'd know it. Besides, we need every man right here. We still have a fight on our hands."

She looked at Dealy. "You do it, Jim."

He slowly moved his head from side to side. "Nope, we done put Fain in charge an' we gonna play the hand the way he's dealed the cards."

She looked to her father. "Papa?" He too shook his head. She spun toward the door, trying to keep her tears from being seen by those in there. When she got to her room, she sobbed, and told herself she cried because she was angry. But she didn't fool herself. By the time she'd regained her composure, Cord had saddled and ridden from the cabin.

He sat the saddle like he had a board tied to his back. He tried to keep the rough gait of his horse from racking his entire body. He managed to keep from pulling on his wounds, but could do nothing about the pain. Sweat poured from every pore, soaking his clothes. After a few miles, some of the stiffness went out of him.

He rode a wide circle around where he thought he might come on any of Taggart's men. Afternoon of the second day, he rode into town, got a room, shaved, bathed, wrapped fresh bandages on his wounds, then went to Worley's office.

When he walked in, the marshal stared at him a moment. "What in the name of heaven you been into, boy? You look mighty pale. You sick?"

"Long story, Marshal. Let me sit while I tell you."

Worley reached in his bottom drawer, pulled out a bottle with the seal intact, took two cups from pegs on the wall, poured the cups full of bourbon, handed one to Fain, then sat. "Okay, tell me."

Cord started at the beginning and told Worley about Taggart choosing the Lazy T as the ranch he'd take over. Then he told him what he and his crew had done and that he'd convinced Tuttle to take his family, and Pam Henders and her boy, and continue the fight from one of the line shacks. Then he told him about how he planned to fight the land-grabbing trail boss.

Worley nodded. "Sounds good, but the condition you're in, you better steer clear of your friend Taggart. He's here in town."

"Figured he might be." Fain chuckled. "He's probably tired of not havin' coffee for breakfast." He nodded. "But, yeah, I'm not in any shape to fight 'im, gotta get healed, an' some o' my strength back, before I attempt any kind o' fight." Fain let a cold smile break the corners of his lips.

"When I figure I'm ready, Marshal, I'm gonna force a fight on 'im wherever I find 'im. You gonna look the other way?"

Worley grinned. "That'll be kinda hard to do if I'm around to cover your back."

Fain nodded. "Thanks, Worley. Hoped it'd be that way." He packed his pipe, smoked, drank another drink with the marshal, then went to the hotel.

The next morning he stood looking out the window of his room, and saw Trig Barnes and Taggart ride out of town. He figured the fighting would now get rougher. He was damned sure it would if he had anything to do with it.

Before leaving the chuck wagon, Taggart had put his *segundo*, Pete Lambrey, in charge. As soon as the trail boss left, Lambrey sent four men to sit out in the cedar breaks. They were not to let anyone leave or enter the ranch house. He went with them, with instructions to the rest of the crew to come out, four at a time, every six hours to relieve the men on station.

"Ride careful, men. We ain't been showin' them ranch hands proper respect; they're fightin' men; let's treat 'em that way. Taggart's got 'is dander up. Right now all he wants to do is make Fain suffer for turnin' on us. He ain't thinkin' right."

In about an hour, the ranch buildings stood in front of them, stark and silent in the bright sunlight. "All right, you know what to do. Let's spread out, circle the buildin's such that we can cover every side. Ain't nobody gonna leave them buildin's alive. Got it?"

Each of them nodded. "All right, let's get at it."

Lambrey picked himself a place behind a stunted cedar, raked up some needles, and sat. The morning, bright, sunny, and sultry after the three days of rain, warmed quickly. By noon the sun sent its full hellish heat onto the backs of the men watching the ranch buildings. Every few minutes, Lambrey pulled his old railroad watch from his vest pocket, glanced at it, cursed, and slipped it back in his pocket. Time dragged. Each time he figured at least an hour had passed, his watch put the lie to that thought. Every time, the hands had moved only fifteen or twenty minutes, and every time, he'd shake it, put it to his ear, and listen for its ticking.

He squinted against the bright sunlight, stared at the house. Strange. There had not been movement of any kind since they'd gotten here. Smoke didn't stream from what he reckoned was the kitchen chimney. Didn't those folks cook? Didn't they even boil a pot of coffee?

At the thought of coffee, his mouth watered, but in a couple of days, maybe three or four, Taggart would be back with a new coffeepot. Then he figured to drink a whole potful. He sat there and sweated. Finally, four men circled in behind him. They were the ones to relieve him and the first bunch he'd taken from the chuck wagon.

The first man to him asked, "Anything happenin'? Seen anybody?"

"Not a thing. Don't even look like they's anybody there."

"Don't let that fool ya, Lambrey. 'Member the fight they put up the other night." The rider pushed his hat to the back of his head. "Tell ya, I ain't stickin' my neck out even one little bit. I'll sit here, shoot if I see anybody, an' wait'll the next bunch o' us comes out to relieve us."

Lambrey shot the man a crooked grin. "You might sit here, but I guarantee you, you'll prob'ly crawl under that grubby little tree for any shade you can find. Thought I'd flat out bake 'fore you all got here." He rolled to his knees. "See ya back at the chuck wagon."

Mobley made sure the womenfolk were as comfortable as could be under the circumstances, then went to talk to the men. At the shed, he gathered the men around him. "Tell you how Fain explained it to me, an' that's the way we gonna fight that bunch. He's been right so far, an' I'm not gonna change it."

He poured himself a cup of coffee, then walked back to them. "I figure to keep about three men out there to watch the ranch buildin's. Don't want any of you to let yourself be seen. Approach the area as though Taggart's men were there. Don't know if they'll be, but I want you to be careful. Okay?"

Frog Ballew blew a cloud of smoke toward him. The pipe smelled good; made Mobley pull his tobacco out and tamp his pipe. After lighting it, he looked at Frog. "Take two men with you, Frog. Soon's you clear these pine trees, tie your horses to a snag, an' go through the cedar breaks on your belly if that looks like the safest thing to do."

Frog grinned. "Reckon I can tell you right now, it's gonna be the safest thing to do. What you want us to do if we see any o' Taggart's men?"

"If you're not outnumbered, shoot 'em. If you are outmanned, or if you're not in a relatively safe place to fire from, just lie still and check on what they're doin'." He took a drag off his pipe, blew the smoke out, studied a clump of grass at his feet, then looked at Frog. "Just wonderin' how to get you an' your men relieved." He nodded. "Think if you all drift back to the pines an' wait by your horses in three hours, the next bunch'll find you." He took a swallow of his coffee. "All right. Get gone an' be downright careful."

Frog gave him a crooked smile. "Bet yore bottom dollar on that, Mobley." Ballew looked at Cookie. "Wanta go with me?"

Cookie grinned, pulled his rifle to him, and stood. "Let's get at it."

"You too, Slim?"

Slim Weathers, never one to waste words, simply stood, jacked a shell into the magazine of his Winchester, and went to his horse.

While riding, Frog told them the way he thought best to handle watching the buildings. "Figger if we stay together, maybe ten, twelve yards apart, slip to within a couple hundred yards of the buildin's, ain't a one o' us cain't hit 'em from that distance."

Slim nodded. Cookie smiled, then patted the stock of his rifle. "Frog, this here Sharps .50'll reach out git 'em a mile away, an' with me lookin' down the bar'l, I kin git 'em farther'n that."

They rode in silence until the edge of the pine copse showed bright sunlight ahead of them. Frog reined in, stepped from the saddle, tied his horse to a sapling, pulled his rifle from the scabbard, and looked at the others, who had aped his actions down to a T.

"No talkin' from here on. We'll use hand signals." With those words, Frog hopped silently to the edge of the trees. He held his hands to the side, palms facing back, then in little above a whisper said, "We stay here till we done checked ever' bit o' scrub brush out yonder. Look at the bottom o' stubby little trees from here to the cleared space around the buildin's. Now don't do nothin' dumb. Want you both to go back with me ridin' yore hoss. Don't want neither o' you slung crost yore saddle."

They stood there, checking the scrub. In the first hour, Slim held up his hand, pointed to a spot about fifty yards from the back of the house. Frog followed his point, squinted, and spotted a man lying prone, facing the back of the house. Frog placed his finger over his lips, and shook his head. In the next two or three hours, they picked out spots where two more men lay.

Frog had lifted his rifle to sight in on one of the men when dust rose from the other side of the buildings. Four horsemen circled the ranch house, then homed in on those Frog and his men had spotted. They all gathered in a bunch. That was when Frog nodded, lifted his rifle, and sighted on the man nearest to him. He squeezed the trigger. That man lurched to the side and fell from his saddle. Before he could fire again, Slim and Cookie fired. Two more men fell to the ground.

Taggart's men quickly spread and fired wildly toward where Frog and his men stood. Their shots, apparently aimed only at sound, clipped twigs from trees, thunked into tree trunks, or whined harmlessly by.

Frog snorted the acrid smell of gun smoke from his nostrils, jacked a shell into the chamber of his rifle, and fired again. Another man dropped, then two more.

With the first shot, every Taggart man ran for his horse. By the time Frog could draw a bead on another man, the remaining three were riding their horses belly-to-the-ground away from ranch headquarters.

Frog looked at Slim and Cookie. "Reckon that takes care o' that bunch. Don't know how many Taggart's got left, but I'm damned sure we got 'em outnumbered now. What'd we get, six, maybe seven?"

Slim only nodded and said, "Counted six."

Cookie stroked the barrel of his long gun. He frowned and shook his head. "Kinda hate what we jest done did. Sarah here's gonna git right upset with me if I keep shootin' from in this close. She likes to reach out an' git 'em from a distance that makes 'er work fer it."

Frog chuckled. "Well, you tell *Sarah* we gonna take 'em from whatever distance we kin git 'em." He glanced toward headquarters. "Reckon bein's they done rid off, we oughta git out there an' see if them men're in the next world. Don't want none o' 'em lyin' out yonder hurtin'."

Slim ran a patch down the barrel of his Winchester, sighted down the bore, grunted, then nodded. "Better wait a while, see if any come back."

They hunkered down in the shade of the pines. About an hour passed. Frog stood. "Let's go check 'em. Don't jest walk up on 'em. They ain't dead, they might be able to shoot."

Frog squinted toward where the shot men lay. "Don't reckon we better walk in." He sighed. "On yore bellies, men. We gonna crawl in."

Every few seconds, Frog slowed enough to make certain the two men with him were as quiet as he was. He didn't hear anything that would alert him if he was one of those lying out there. After covering the couple of hundred yards in about an hour, he came on the first man, who lay on his stomach. Frog slid his hand under the man's shoulder and flipped him to his back. Blood, already congealed, laid a path from the corner of his mouth and down his chin. Frog crawled on, came to another man. This one lay on his back. Frog flipped him and saw a huge hole in his back. He could have doubled both fists and fitted them into the cavity the bullet made when it came out. He muttered, "That Sharps o' Cookie's shore opens a hole in a man."

A noise a few feet to his side pulled his attention—and his rifle barrel—in that direction. Slim held up two fingers, then flicked his thumb to the side. That accounted for four of those they'd shot. Before that idea settled in his mind, the dull sound of a pistol shot caused him and Slim to flatten out on the ground. Then Cookie's voice, little above a whisper, sounded about ten yards to their left. "Wan't dead, is now. This'n is the second I done found. How many y'all find?"

"Come on over, Cookie. Reckon we got six o' them."

Frog frowned, then looked at Cookie. "You b'longed to that bunch. How many men you reckon they got left?"

Cookie looked toward the sky, looking as though he studied a vagrant cloud, then squinted toward the distant horizon to the east. "Wal, now, don't know how many we got when we raided the chuck wagon, but lookin' at what we got the night they came at us to set fire to the house, an' what we got here, I'd say they ain't got more'n maybe fourteen left."

Slim shook his head, his face sober. "Shore hope we don't have to kill 'em all 'fore they quit an' leave."

Cookie went to his horse, slipped his Sharps into its saddle scabbard, and shrugged. "Depends on what Taggart's done promised 'em whether they leave or stick."

Cookie looked at Frog. "You figger us to stay out here till Mobley sends somebody out to relieve us?"

Frog shook his head. "Naw. Y'all go on back to the shed. I'm gonna stay; see if any o' them jaspers come back. They do, I'll hightail it back an' get some help."

Cookie cocked his head to the side, squinted at Frog, chomped on his tobacco, and asked, "You ain't gonna be foolish nuff to tackle 'em by yoreself, are you?"

"Nope. Jest gonna make sure they ain't none o' 'em comes back to do any mischief. Now y'all go on—git."

About an hour later Slim and Cookie rode to the front of the cabin. Mobley watched them ride in without Frog, and his throat tightened. He liked the crippled, wiry little puncher. If he was hurt, shot, surely they would have brought him back, even if across his saddle. He stepped out the door. "Where's Frog?"

"Stayed to see if what we left of 'em come back. Don't think they gonna want more o' what we dished out." Cookie slipped from his saddle. "Better git over there an' fix us some dinner 'fore one o' them punchers messes up a bunch o' my provisions." He stopped, cocked his head to the side, twisted a little, then said, "Rider comin'."

Before he could say more, Fain rode in. To Mobley's thinking, he looked better than when he'd left. He didn't lean into the side he'd caught the bullet in; he rode looser, not stiff, not like he had a board holding him erect. "Howdy, Fain, how'd things go in Trinidad?"

Fain shrugged. "Nothin' happened I didn't figure on. Taggart was in town; I saw 'im but stayed clear; didn't feel like a fight of any kind." He grinned. "Ain't up to that yet." He looked toward the shed. "Let's get outta this sun, 'bout to bake, then I'll tell you what I told Worley."

Before he and Mobley could pour a cup of coffee and find a place on the ground to sit and be comfortable, Dealy and Ruth came up at a pace he would have described as almost running.

Ruth stopped, scanned Fain from head to toe, then pinned him with a look. "You all right, Cord?"

He nodded. "Yep, didn't get a scratch, no fight, nothin' but what I figured to do when I left here."

Her breasts rose slowly; then she let her breath out in a great sigh. "Thanks, God, you let him get away with another dumb stunt." Then her eyes slitted, still holding him with her look. "An' what wuz it you figgered important enough to try to get yourself killed?"

"Didn't ever figure on tryin' to get myself killed." He shrugged. "Only wanted to make sure the U.S. marshal knew what we were doin' an' intended to do, so we'd not be in any sort o' trouble legally with the gov'ment."

He took a swallow of his coffee. "We ain't in any trouble"—he shook his head—"an' not gonna be. Fact is, Worley, without me askin', said as how he figgered to cover my back when the time comes that I brace Taggart."

A deep crease showed between her eyes; her lips quivered. "You didn't tell 'im you figgered to fight Taggart, did you?"

Fain studied her a moment. Why did she suddenly seem to care what happened to him? Why, when he'd made up his mind to stay away from her and her acid tongue, did he now want to be around her? Mentally he shrugged. Maybe he was just one of those people he'd heard about who liked to be browbeaten. He decided he'd better answer her question.

"Well, yes, ma'am, I figure to get some o' my strength back, then give my ex-trail boss a choice: fists, knives, or guns. Gonna get 'im outta our hair once an' for all."

Her eyes widened in mock astonishment. "Oooh, he outweighs you by maybe fifty pounds, has prob'ly had a whole bunch o' knife or gunfights, an' I bet you'll take him down a notch or two real easy. An'-an' I'll bet he's gonna just stand there an' let you do it without raisin' a hand."

"Ma'am, gonna tell ya, know you got a pretty low opinion o' me an' the things I'm capable of, but I'm tellin' you right now; I'm a whole helluva lot more man than you think." He swallowed a couple of times to let the anger seep from him. He turned his attention to Mobley.

"Cord Fain, I-I-I . . ."

He ignored her. "What's been happenin' here since I left?"

Mobley glanced at Cookie, who had been rattling pans and trying to get supper started. "Cookie, you can tell Fain what's been goin' on better'n I can. Tell 'im."

Cookie pushed a pot close to the fire and came over. He told Fain about the gunfight they'd had, how many men they'd killed, and that he'd left Frog out there to watch.

Fain frowned, thought a minute, then shook his head. "Don't know whether we want to keep 'em outta the ranch-house." At Cookie's slumped shoulders and dejected look, Fain knew the old man had hoped for praise. "Aw, hell, Cookie, y'all did good, real good. You got rid o' some o' them we'd have had to fight; now we don't."

Cookie's face lighted such that it reminded Cord of a kid who'd just been handed a piece of peppermint candy.

Fain looked at Slim. "You know where Frog's holed up, so reckon I'm gonna ask you to ride out yonder an' tell 'im to come on in. We ain't gonna try to keep 'em outta the ranch house now that y'all thinned 'em down some."

He threw the dregs from his cup, and before he could stand to pour himself another cupful, Ruth leaned over, took the cup from his hand, poured it full, and handed it to him. He looked at her, thanked her, and turned his attention back to Mobley and Dealy.

"Way I got it figured, if we let 'em into the house, they won't burn it, and"—he smiled—"if we keep enough men around in the brush, we can seal 'em off in there. We'll have 'em trapped."

"What you figger to do, shoot 'em if they try to come out?"

Fain looked straight on at Dealy. "You got any better idea?"

Dealy shook his head. "Nope. I jest hate shootin' a man from ambush."

Fain, his face feeling stiff as a new pair of jeans, lifted his shoulders, then let them drop. "So do I, Dealy, but I don't know of any other way to do it without gettin' some o' our men killed. I won't swap *one* o' ours for *all* o' theirs."

Slim had thrown the kak onto his horse, and looked to be about to climb aboard when Fain stopped him. "Tell one o' the other men 'bout where Frog's hunkered down; let whoever goes out there stay an' watch what goes on. We need to know if Taggart takes his men into the house. Don't want any shootin'—just want to know if they go in; then we'll use all our men to circle the house an' keep 'em inside."

11

Taggart stepped from the saddle, looked at his men, then slapped the pile of stuff he had on the packsaddle. "We gonna drink coffee tonight, boys." He swept them with a glance. "Where's the rest o' the men?"

Lambrey, his face hard as granite, stared at Taggart a moment. "This's all we got left. That ranch bunch wuz waitin' in the brush when we got there to see what wuz goin' on at the ranch house. They shot hell outta us 'fore we could get gone."

Taggart cursed, using every word he knew, then looked at Lambrey straight on. "You say they shot from the brush. You see anybody movin' round them buildin's?"

"Nope, fact is, them buildin's looked to be empty. Wan't no smoke comin' from the chimney like they mighta been fixin' supper." He shook his head. "Same story at the bunkhouse, an' nothin' happenin' at the barn. Shore looked like they done left 'em to us."

Taggart gave a nod. "Good. We'll wait'll after dark, then take over them buildin's. Figure they stand on land Tuttle owns, an' if they leave, we can claim they abandoned 'em."

His face hardened. "Ain't nobody can say we took 'em against what the law allows."

Lambrey gazed at the trail boss a moment, looked as though he wanted to say something, then clamped his mouth closed. He nodded. "Reckon if you gonna play it that way we'll side ya—for now."

Taggart stood there, staring at his *segundo*. He wondered if Lambrey was going to buck him on the way he was running things. His neck muscles tightened. First Barnes, now maybe the one man he thought he could count on to side him in any kind of trouble.

He swallowed a couple of times. He didn't give a damn if the whole bunch quit; he figured to get Cord Fain, kill him, and he'd do it if he had to do it alone. Fain had been the one who'd started all the trouble. Then, to break the tension that stretched between him and his men, he grinned and pulled the packsaddle from the horse. "Let's boil a pot o' coffee, men. I got a couple bottles o' pretty good whiskey here too." He handed the new coffeepot to Barnes. "We take over the ranch soon's it darkens 'nuff for us to git in them buildin's without bein' seen."

Barnes filled the pot with water from the barrel strapped to the side of the chuck wagon, glanced at his boss, and wondered if Taggart's proposed plan of going in the ranch house was very smart. Hell, he'd rather be out where he could move around, find out what the people he was fighting were doing. Then he thought of what he might get out of this fight. He shrugged mentally. It was worth the chance. He'd play along . . . for now.

Fain had talked with Miss Eve—he'd taken to calling her that when he heard Jim Dealy address her as such—and they decided that it made sense for Cookie to cook for the entire crew until they could again take over the headquarters. Scattered about the grounds close to the shed, they filled their plates and ate supper.

Mobley squatted next to Fain, and Tommy sat as close to

Jed as he dared without crowding him. Mobley saw Cord wince when he shifted positions to hold his plate more comfortably. "You still hurtin' pretty bad, Fain?"

"No, reckon I moved wrong. I'm feelin' a lot better'n I felt a couple days ago."

They ate, not talking for a few minutes; then Cord looked at Mobley. "Wish I knew how many men Taggart's got left. Think we got 'em pretty well accounted for 'cept those we shot up around their camp." He forked beans into his mouth, chewed, frowned, then nodded. "We might not have killed any of 'em—most o' us shot at their legs that night, prob'ly put some of 'em outta the fight—but wish I knew how many we still got to face."

Jed thought a moment, then stared at Cord. "Reckon soon's it gets good dark, I'll ride over yonder an' take a peek; then we'll know."

Fain chuckled. "Jed, I know you're mighty good with that handgun you wear, but don't know what kind o' woodsman you are. You any good in the woods; any good at movin' 'bout so nobody can see or hear you?"

Mobley looked Fain square in the eyes. "Cord, I grew up in the South; spent most of my boyhood huntin' an' fishin'. One o' the few friends I had back then, a grown Chicasaw Indian, taught me how to get around in the woods." He nodded. "I figure I'm as good as the best; better'n the rest."

"All right. You be mighty careful." Fain's eyes moved to the little boy huddled next to the man he seemed to think mighty highly of. "Know you've already figured it out, so I ain't tellin' you anythin' new; there're a couple o' people round here who think you hung the moon. You get hurt, it'll hurt others maybe as much as it will you."

Mobley put his arm around Tommy's shoulders and pulled him close to him. The little boy came closer. He looked up at Jed. "Sir, you gonna do what you said? You gonna be right careful an' come back to Ma an' me?"

Mobley's throat tightened. He swallowed at the lump that had swelled there. He tightened his arm about the boy. "Son, I'll tell you right now, I don't think there is anything that could stop me from comin' back to you and your ma."

Tommy took Jed's now empty plate from him and stood. "Reckon as how I might's well make myself useful. Ain't been much good for nobody in this here war. I'll clean yore plate for you." Mobley thought he detected a break in the boy's voice. The lump in his throat grew larger.

As soon as Tommy went to clean their plates, Cord looked at Jed. "Gonna tell you, Mobley, that boy's taken to you like a mama bear does to her cubs. You be almighty careful out there. It looks like you got any kind o' trouble, hightail it back here, you heah?"

Jed stared into his friend's eyes. "Cord, there isn't anything I wouldn't do for that boy—or his mother. Know this doesn't come as any surprise to you. Figured I might as well level with you." He stood. "Better saddle up. I'll get back here soon's I find out what we need to know."

In only a few minutes he rode from the people who'd in only a few days had grown from strangers to fast friends. He felt Pam's eyes follow him until he disappeared into the trees. He wondered what she'd think of him if he said what had been inside of him since the second day he'd stopped at her homestead.

He had nothing to offer her and Tommy. About a year's wages nestled in his money belt. He shook his head; that wasn't much to bring to any woman. He'd seen Pam sit by the fire at night and darn sox, patch dresses and jeans, and sew a sunbonnet for herself from clothes too worn out to salvage. He mentally shook his head. He'd try to make up to them for any shortcomings he had in the way of money. He'd just have to work hard.

Abruptly he frowned. What was he doing? He was thinking as though he'd already said the things he still must say and gotten the right answers from Pam. He turned his attention to getting his horse through the heavy tree growth.

A couple of hours later, when it was now black dark, he reined his horse in and listened. He thought he heard the rattle of trace chains. About to nudge his horse ahead, he held fast; the noise he heard rattled again. Yep, he'd bet his bottom dollar the noise was made by a wagon pulled into the ranch yard.

He climbed from the saddle to keep from silhouetting himself against the night sky. He listened a few moments longer to determine the line of travel of those he heard, slowly led his horse to the side so as to be out of their line of travel, then stopped, hardly daring to breath. There was not only the sound of a wagon being pulled, but the soft sound of many hooves.

He waited until they were well past him, then toed the stirrup and followed. The riders and wagon tracked straight toward ranch headquarters. Taggart and his outlaws were on the move. Mobley now thought of Taggart as an outlaw; no decent person would do the things he did.

He followed them to the house, watched them take over the stable, bunkhouse, and ranch house. He stayed until lantern light painted the windows a golden glow; then he climbed to his saddle and headed for the cabin. He'd not been able to determine how many men the trail boss still had with him.

When he was still a quarter of a mile from the cabin, a voice spoke from the dark. "Hold steady an' I won't empty yore saddle." He recognized Slim's voice.

"Me, Slim. Mobley. Anybody still awake at the cabin?"

"Nope."

"Well, I gotta get Fain up, an' when I do, I figure he'll get the rest of 'em up. We got things to do."

"How many men they got left?"

"Couldn't get a count of 'em; too dark."

Slim rolled a quirly, lit it, then said, "Ride on in. I'll stay out here in case they got anybody scoutin' round to see what we're doin'."

Only a few minutes after leaving Slim, Mobley climbed from his horse, and in the faint glow of the cooking fire found where Fain had bedded down. He squatted by his side. "Cord, wake up. Tell you 'bout what Taggart's up to."

Fain groaned, rolled from his blankets, put on his hat, then his boots, and poured himself a cup of coffee. He squatted by the glowing embers, then looked at Mobley. "Okay, tell me."

It took Jed only a few minutes to lay it out for Fain. "What you figure to do now that they've taken over headquarters?"

Cord grinned into the faint light. "Reckon we're gonna make 'em sorry they ever went in those buildin's. They gonna find it's a lot harder to get outta them than it was for them to get in."

"Yeah, that's the way I'd play the hand too. I'll wake some o' the men an' we'll ride out."

"No. You're not ridin' with the men. You been up a mighty long time now. Get some sleep. I'll ride with 'em."

"You've not healed enough to do that, Cord."

"Ain't gonna heal, get strong, if I keep lettin' this wound slow me down like I been doin'. I'm ridin'. Get some sleep."

Fain pulled his watch from his pocket and held it close to the slight glow of the embers. Twelve-thirty. "Gonna take three men. Send out four to relieve us when the sun breaks the horizon."

Cord wakened Dealy, Wash, and Frog. In an hour he had them posted around the ranch buildings with instructions to shoot any who tried to leave. "We'll keep 'em bottled up inside; maybe they'll get enough to make 'em throw in the towel.

"Figure those men'll take only so much before they decide they have enough. There'll be some who quit—if Taggart'll let 'em. He's mean enough, an' I figure mad enough at me, to kill any who try to leave."

Dealy glanced at the sky. "Shore wish they wuz a moon. We ain't gonna see much 'bout what they doin'. Hell, they could all ride out an' we'd never know it."

Wash rolled a quirly, licked the paper, and sealed it,

then stepped from the saddle, hunkered behind a juniper, and put fire to the limp cigarette. "Tell you what I b'lieve. I reckon they gonna stay right where they is. They got what they want. They got them there buildin's without gittin' shot, an' they ain't gonna know we done got 'em sewed up in there till they staht tryin' to move round come daylight."

Fain frowned, thinking about what Wash had said. He nodded. "B'lieve you're right, Wash. Two men might even be able to keep 'em penned up in there, but if they decide to send anybody out despite the losses they'd take, two men would be in deep trouble tryin' to keep 'em there. My aim is to get this thing done without losin' a man. So far we've been lucky."

Wash chuckled. "Mistuh Cord, long's that man what don't git shot is me, reckon I done made up mah mind to do whatevuh you say."

"Kinda figured that's the way you'd play it, partner." Fain gathered the reins in his left hand. "Well, let's get at it. One man to each side o' the ranch house."

About to urge his horse into a walk, Fain stopped, frowned, and swept the men with a glance. "Jest thought o' somethin'. Know how I can find out how many men they still got."

"Aw, now, pahdnuh, you ain't gonna go down there an' count 'em, are yuh?"

"Naw, nothin' that dumb. While it's still dark, I'm figurin' to slip down to the barn an' count the saddles they used to get here."

Dealy spoke up. "Fain, you ain't got a gut in yore head. That's jest as dumb as countin' the men. S'pose they left a man in the stable, or several men; you wouldn't stand a chance."

"Gonna do it anyway. Y'all hear shootin', you'll know I bit off a large chunk o' hell." He shook his head, not knowing whether any of them could see him. "You hear shootin', stay right where you are. No need for any more o' us to git shot."

Wash shook his head. "Mah partner already done got hisself shot somethin' awful, now he gonna try to do it all ovah agin."

Fain had listened to all that he thought he could stand. "Each o' you take a side o' that house and watch it good. I'll be back in 'bout thirty minutes." Without giving them a chance to do any more talking about it, he handed Wash the reins to his horse and drifted into the night.

Careful where he put his feet, he walked silently toward the dark bulk of the stable, and not knowing whether Taggart had posted sentries, he stopped every few feet to listen. If a man stood anywhere close, he thought he might hear him breathing, or if he was lucky, find him smoking, or if the man hadn't bathed in a while, he might even *smell* him.

When still about fifty yards from the back wall of the stable, he stopped and tried to draw a picture in his mind of the layout of the barn. Finally, thinking he had it right, he thought there were enough stalls to hold the horses Taggart's men rode in on, and he had a hunch the saddle for each horse would be slung across the stall wall.

He eased toward the back, more careful now than ever. It seemed to take him forever, but finally he felt the rough wood under his hand. He moved over to where he remembered the back door to be.

He felt along the splintery sides of the door, letting his hands do what his eyes couldn't do, and hoped the door was hung by leather straps rather than squeaky iron hinges. He got lucky.

He lifted the latch, then lifted the weight of the door so that it didn't rest on the straps, and slowly pulled the door toward him. He'd moved only a couple of steps into the dark maw of the stable after easing the door shut when a voice several feet ahead of him said, "That you, Miles?"

A sleepy voice off to Fain's left side answered. "Me what? What the hell you talkin' 'bout?"

"Nothin', jest thought I heered somethin' back there.

Prob'ly a rat. 'Fore it got black dark I seen three or four o' them. Bigger'n cats they wuz."

"Wish to hell you hadn't said that. I done heered 'bout them big'uns bitin' men, chewin on 'em. Now I bet I don't sleep 'nother wink 'fore daylight."

Fain stood frozen, not daring to move. He couldn't guess how long he stood in the same place, but after a while he heard the drover off to his left snoring, despite saying that he wouldn't sleep a wink.

Fain ran his thumb down the hammer of his Colt to make sure the thong was off. It was. Then he pulled his bowie, and placed one foot carefully in front of the other toward the snoring man. He took another step—and his boot toe raked down the side of the man. The man cursed and rolled away from Fain.

As soon as his boot touched the man and the curse came simultaneously, Fain stepped to the side, his shoulder rubbing the barn wall. He shifted his knife to his left hand and pulled his handgun.

"What the hell's wrong with you? One o' them rats git ya?"

"Don't know. Somethin' rubbed down my side. Know damned well I ain't gonna git any sleep now. You might's well bed down."

Fain had always hated rats, but with the words the two exchanged in the black dark, his hate lessened a little. Then the one who had apparently stayed awake said, "You reckon the boss'd mind if we lit a lantern—if we could find one? I ain't stayin' out here in this here dark."

"Don't give a damn whether he minds or not. He ain't paid us a dime since we left the Big Bend. You got a lucifer, light it."

With their words, Fain knew the next thing they would do would be to strike a light to see if there was a lantern handy. He'd be hung out to dry.

He hoped his memory served him well now. He needed to get inside a stall, out of sight. He tried to picture the inside of the barn from the back door. He thought he remembered an open place at the end of the last stall. He moved into the area he thought might give him a chance to hunker down and stay out of sight. He squatted.

He'd not gotten his head below the top rail before a flame flared only a few feet from him, but on the other side of the railings. He sucked in shallow, quiet breaths. Then the man he'd stepped on apparently saw what he looked for.

"Hey, Slats, ain't that a lantern hangin' from that peg at the end—down there by the front door?" Then he cursed, dropped the match, and stepped on the flame. "Held that lucifer till it burned right up to my fingers."

"Stand still. I got one right here 'tween my fingers. I'll see if what you seen wuz a lantern."

Fain still hadn't seen where they hung their saddles, but if he could get out without being seen, shot, or dead, he figured to forgo that bit of information. He thought to try to leave while still in the dark, but the man he'd stepped on hadn't moved. He stood only a few feet from where Cord held his gun and knife, one in each hand. Then it came to him how he would play the hand. He had no other choice.

In only a moment, a match flared, then a brighter light as the flame took hold of the wick. Fain was sure now that the two men were the only ones in the stable. No one else had entered the conversation.

He waited until Slats hung the lantern to a peg, then stepped into the runway. "Hold it right there an' I won't shoot you."

Miles, the other man Cord now recognized, twisted as though to go for his gun. "Don't be a fool, Miles. My gun's already clear of its holster." Miles froze. "Now both of you turn your backs to me. Don't make a move to look at me; I might mistake it an' think you're gonna draw."

"Fain, you already got Taggart mad 'nuff to bust a gut. He's gonna come after you if he loses ever' one o' us; the cattle too. He don't give a damn 'bout nothin' now 'cept to git even."

"How much has he paid any o' you since we started on this drive?" Then, without waiting for an answer, Fain jabbed them with more. "He ain't paid none o' you any-thing—an' he won't. If you got any sense at all, you'll sad-dle your broncs an' cut outta here soon's I leave. Head for Texas fast as your horses'll get you there 'fore cold weather sets in."

"You ain't gonna tie us up?"

"Nope. Figure all I gotta do is step out this back door an' be gone 'fore y'all could get outside to try to find me, but don't reckon I gotta worry 'bout that 'cause I figure you're gonna slope outta here."

"I ain't never seen ya pack a side gun 'fore. You better practice up with it 'fore Taggart finds you; he's s'posed to be right handy with that hawgleg o' his'n."

Fain chuckled. "Don't seem to me he's gotta look too hard, I been doggin' 'im ever since I left the drive." He frowned. "How many men has Taggart got stationed in the bunkhouse?"

"Ain't got none there. We ain't got 'nuff men left to watch everythin'." Slats pushed his hat back. "You done raised hell with the whole crew. They's three o' us cain't do no fightin' noway; y'all shot hell outta us at the chuck wagon. Them three's shot in their laigs. They ain't gonna be botherin' nobody."

Cord nodded, slipped his bowie back in its sheath, ghosted to the back door, slipped through into the dark, listened a moment, heard one of the men say something muffled to him, then faded into the cedar breaks, but only far enough to wait and see what the two men de-cided to do.

After only a couple of minutes, he knew they were going to take his advice, or they would have already raised the alarm. He found what he'd come here for. While their backs were turned to him, he'd swept the walls and counted eight saddles hanging there. Now he had it figured there would be only six, and three of them unable to do much fighting.

Another couple of minutes and the slit of light shining through a crack in the wall went dark, and a moment later two riders left through the back door. Yep, he'd figured right.

He stood there listening. When the soft hoofbeats faded into the distance, he turned and made his way back to the men he'd left.

When still several yards from where he thought they'd be, he stopped, listened a moment, then whispered, "Don't shoot. It's me, Fain."

Wash's soft words floated out to him. "Come on in, Cord. Wuz beginnin' to worry 'bout you."

Cord chuckled. "Nothin' to worry 'bout, partner. I'm back."

"Wuz you able to find out what you went out yonder to find out?"

He nodded, though knowing Wash couldn't see him. "Yep. We got 'em whittled down to size. Reckon I better get Frog and Dealy over here. Tell y'all all at once."

Wash laughed down deep in his chest. "Reckon we could walk to them faster'n it take fer one o' us to bring 'em back heah."

"All right, Wash, let's go tell 'em."

In no more than fifteen minutes, Fain had the three men briefed. Then they spread around the ranch house again, waiting for the next watch to come relieve them.

About two hours later, Taggart rolled to his side. Thin light filtered through the windows. He sniffed, didn't smell bacon frying, and bellowed at the top of his voice. "Who the hell's s'posed to cook grub? It's almost full daylight. I'm hongrey. Barnes, you fix somethin' to eat *now*, an' Lambrey can git somebody to cook the next meal."

"What the hell you gonna be doin' all that time, Taggart? You ain't paid us since leavin' the Big Bend. Fact is, you ain't done nothin' but give orders. You want grub— you fix it."

Taggart rolled to his feet, picked up his belt and holster,

buckled it on, and stared through the early morning light to where he remembered seeing the drover bed down. "You buckin' me, Barnes? You been awful mouthy lately; you figger on takin' over this operation? I hear any more mouth outta you, I'll blow six holes in you."

"Taggart, if'n they wuz more light in here, an' you looked real close at me, you'd see I already got my Colt pointed right at yore gut. Don't you never tell me what you gonna do to me 'less'n you're ready to back it up right then. You heah?"

Abruptly, Taggart forgot his stomach. Blood pushed to his head. He swallowed. The huge knot in his throat remained there, and his anger threatened to enlarge it even more; but a .44 pointed at his gut was no time to push his luck. "Aw, hell, Barnes, reckon that damned Fain's got me so riled up I ain't thinkin' straight. I'll start the coffee, then one o' the other hands kin git the bacon an' beans to cookin'."

Barnes said nothing, just sat there atop his blankets and stared at him, but his handgun still pointed at Taggart's stomach. Taggart stood, went to the coffeepot, filled it, and set it close to the coals still glowing from last night's fire. He had to wait until the water boiled to spill grounds into it.

He didn't want to anger the slim, dangerous cowboy further. Hell, he'd already lost too many men, and three of those he had left weren't in any shape to fight, what with their shot-up legs. He'd better calm down until he got Fain out of the way; then he'd take care of any who bucked him. He thought over who he had left: two in the stable, six here in the house, of which only three could fight. He shook his head. He needed every man he had.

He thought to take some of the money the company had advanced him before he left Texas and pay those men he had with him a few dollars. No. To hell with them. He'd wait until he knew who would stick; then he would let go a few of the bucks in his money belt.

• • •

While Taggart struggled to find a way to get out of the confrontation with Barnes, Fain watched the sky to the east lighten, then grow still brighter through the thin, wispy clouds. He cocked his head, hearing the soft hoofbeats of approaching horses. Although knowing it was time for their relief, he thought to play it safe. He hunkered behind a stubby cedar and waited. When they came into sight, he nodded to himself, stood, and motioned them over. He pointed to where he thought Frog, Dealy, and Wash to be, and told their relief to tie their horses close by where they stood and to walk to the places where they were to stand watch.

When Wash walked to stand by him, Fain grinned. "You bored standin' out yonder with nothin' goin' on, Wash?"

Wash's grin was bigger than his own. It showed every snow-white tooth in his mouth. "Cord, you give me a choice o' bein' bored or bein' shot at, reckon I'll take a whole bunch o' that bored stuff." He looked over his shoulder. "Soon's Dealy an' Frog gits here, reckon we bettuh git goin' 'fore I stahve to death."

Fain laughed. "Sounds like you almost hungry as I am. Shore do wish we had some o' those eggs from down at the house. Figure I could eat 'bout a dozen of 'em 'fore I really got down to satisfyin' my growlin' stomach."

"Whooooeee, reckon I don't wanta git in yore way when you push up to the grub Cookie's done cooked."

Dealy walked up, Frog right on his heels.

"C'mon, men, let's head for the feed trough," said Fain.

An hour later, Fain and the crew, except for those standing watch at the ranch house, sat eating one of Cookie's better meals. He'd cooked an entire shoulder of venison, potatoes with wild onions, beans that Mrs. Tuttle—or Miss Eve, as Cord was now calling her—told Cord Ruth had canned, along with the peaches they had for dessert.

Cord looked at Cookie. "Gonna tell you somethin'. You cook like this an' I figure Bob'll take you up to the ranch house to cook for the family. Reckon Miss Eve can cook

good as you, but she would likely let you take over; give
'er a little rest that way."

"I can cook too, Cord."

Fain looked at Ruth, and a smile threatened to break the
corners of his mouth. "Ah now, young'un. It takes a whole
bunch o' years for a person to learn to cook this good. You
only now gettin' to be a woman, just ain't had the time to
learn yet." He got the response he wanted.

Fire built behind Ruth's eyes; then the blue in them
chilled to pure ice. "Gonna tell you right now, Cord Fain,
I ain't just now gittin' to be a woman. I been a woman
long 'nuff to learn to cook an' do 'bout everthing any
other woman can do. I—I . . ." Abruptly the ice went from
her eyes. They softened; then she smiled. " 'Nother thing
I learned is to know when a man delights in teasin' me,
makin' me madder'n Hades." She shook her head. "Don't
know, though, why you always like to put a burr under my
saddle. Reckon you just like me to be mad at you."

Fain stared at her a moment, then slowly shook his head
from side to side. "Ma'am, I don't like to have you mad at
me. Most o' the time I don't know why you've got your
dander up, so if I tease you an' you get mad, then I got a
good idea what you're spittin' mad 'bout."

Ruth clasped her hands tightly in her lap, stared at them
a moment, then looked into Fain's eyes. "You reckon you
an' me could go off somewhere alone sometime an' let me
tell you why I been gettin' so mad at you?"

Cord was now fully aware that not only had Bob and
Miss Eve heard the whole conversation, but the entire crew
had, and they all seemed to be hanging onto every word.
He felt his face warm, then turn hot. "Yes'm, reckon we
could do that."

He took another bite, chewed slowly, swallowed, then
glanced around at the men and three women. He wanted to
talk with them, but before he could say anything, Bob Tuttle caught his eye, then nodded, apparently wanting to say
something.

"All right, Bob, you look like you're 'bout to explode with words bottled up in you, so spit 'em out."

Tuttle took a bite, chewed, nodded, pulled his shoulders up in an exaggerated shrug, then stood. "I got a question, Cord. Been worryin' it round in my mind for some time now." He glanced around at the men, mostly those Fain had brought in. "Gotta admit you got me worried. You got me, my family, an' my crew in a position where we'd have to do whatever you say. You brought in a right salty bunch o' riders, so I gotta ask, 'What you an' yore men figger to get outta all this?' "

Cord studied the food on his plate, frowned, then put his plate on the ground beside him. He pulled his mouth to the side in a grimace, then shrugged. "Gonna try to answer you, Tuttle. At first when I come in here, I was mad, madder'n hell to think a man like Taggart would take somethin' somebody else worked for, fought for; then when I got here, got to know y'all, liked you, I got to wonderin' how to stop my ex–trail boss.

"Hell, I didn't have any men, had nothin' but me, Wash, an' Cookie. There was no way we could stop 'im with us an' the men you had.

"But after thinkin' 'bout it a while, I figured I knew where to get men who would stick—but I needed to pay 'em fightin' wages. That would take every cent I'd saved." He nodded. "Yeah, I been savin' up to start me a ranch for some amount o' years now; figure I got enough now."

He picked up his plate, took another bite, then shook his head. "Nope, they wouldn't have asked me to pay 'em a damned nickel, but I wouldn't ask any man to put his life on the line without pay. So I got to wonderin', tryin' to figure out where to get more money so's I'd still have 'nuff left to eat on when I left here.

"Well, I come up with a idea; don't know how you folks gonna take to the way I got it figured; don't reckon I'll ever know 'less'n I tell you 'bout it."

He toyed with the food left on his plate a moment, took

his last bite, then packed his pipe. "Gotta tell you, what I come up with ain't entirely unselfish. Don't feel right good 'bout that."

Tuttle, obviously having hung on every word to now, didn't seem to be able to hold his curiosity. He walked to Fain, stood over him a moment, then exploded. "Well, dammit, boy, you gonna tell us what you got in that there hard head o' yores? You gonna leave us hangin' out here without knowin' nothin'?"

Cord, his head bent back to stare up at the rancher, tried to keep from smiling. This was no laughing matter, but he couldn't contain the smile, let alone the laughter that pushed itself through his teeth. He laughed until he had to hold his sides.

Tuttle still stood over him. "Wh-what's so damned funny?"

"Y-you, Bob. You standin' there lookin' down at me like you're 'bout to jump right straddle me, spittin' an' sputterin'." He pulled his mouth into a straight line, and made his face as somber as he could make it, hoping it looked serious enough to quiet Tuttle's concern. "All right. Gonna tell y'all what I got in mind. You don't like the idea, now's the time to say so."

He stood, went to the coffeepot, poured himself a full cup of the thick liquid, came back to his previous place, and sat. He lighted his pipe, took a swallow of coffee, looked up into Bob Tuttle's eyes again, almost broke into laughter again, sobered, and nodded. "All right, here it is; we gonna pay these men I brought with me fightin' wages an' a little bit more, purely 'cause they're friends o' mine, then we gonna stock your ranch with as many cattle as it'll feed without overgrazin', then we gonna see how many head o' beef Mobley an' Pam's gonna need to get things on a payin' basis along with a bit o' money to buy the things they need to get goin' good."

Tuttle stood back a few steps, then pinned Cord with a look that could penetrate a four-foot adobe wall. "First off, I'm askin' you where the hell you gonna get all them cows an' money—then I'm gonna ask you the same thing I started off with. What you gonna git outta all this?"

Fain took a couple of deep drags on his pipe, bracing himself for an argument from most who sat around him. "Well, gonna tell ya. Gonna answer your first question first." He sniffed, thinking the food still simmering over the fire smelled too good to not have another helping. Wanting to put off the objections he figured to get, he stood, filled his plate again, then sat.

He swept all around the fire with a glance. "You got right close to three thousand head o' longhorns grazin' your range that will soon eat what grass you got right down to the roots. Those're the cattle I'm talkin' 'bout. I figure you, Pam, an' Mobley will want to keep some o' those cattle. The rest, we'll make a trail drive to Dodge City an' sell 'em.

"We might get there ahead o' most o' the big outfits an' maybe get a pretty good price. I'm thinkin' maybe twenty-seven dollars a head." He shrugged. "Course we'd take a little less."

The only sounds were those of the crackle of the fire, the heavy breathing of those around him—and the sound of a horse coming at little more than a gallop, by Cord's reckoning.

Thinking the rider would be one of their own, Cord hesitated, then to be safe, pulled his .44 and held it in his lap. A few moments later he recognized the rider as one of the men his father had loaned him, Ben St. John.

As soon as the ranny pulled his horse to a stop and slid from the saddle, Fain slipped his Colt back in its holster and eyed the rider. "What's happened?"

A grin stretching from ear to ear, the cowboy shook his head. "Ain't nothin' *bad* happened. Jest had to come in an' tell you what's goin' on at the house."

Fain motioned toward the fire. "All right, grab a cup o' coffee, set, an' tell us."

Tuttle spoke up. "While he's drawin' his coffee, gonna tell ya, I still wanta hear what you gonna get outta all this. You gotta be gettin' somethin'."

Cord only nodded, his attention locked on the rider.

St. John squatted to the side of them, still grinning. "Gotta tell you folks, Taggart only a little while ago found out he ain't in no part of control over what's goin' on." He took a sip of his coffee. "'Bout full daylight, a couple o' his men come outta the house, headin' for the woodpile." He looked at Fain. "We done like you said, Boss. Didn't shoot to kill either one o' 'em, but planted a couple o' shots at their feet." His grin turned into a full-blown laugh. "Whoooee, y'all ain't never seen nobody jump as high as them two rannies did, an' when their feet hit the ground they wuz diggin' dirt. I had to look twice to be sure they'd been there at all.

"They disappeared back inside the ranch house a whole bunch faster'n they come outta it." He sobered, then nodded. "Course if they hadn't hightailed it back inside, we'd of put our lead where it counted."

Fain's smile showed no humor, to his thinking. He didn't feel any. "Good, grab yourself some grub. I'll send the relief crew out to spell those out there."

He stood, poured himself another cup of coffee, looked a question at those still seated to see if they wanted more coffee. They shook their heads.

"Okay, Cord, I been standin' here waitin' to hear what you got in mind for yoreself," said Tuttle. "Let's hear it."

Fain stayed on his feet this time. He stared at his boot toe, worked it around in the dirt a moment, then glanced around the circle of people he'd grown to consider friends. "Okay, but I'll tell you right up front, if y'all think I'm not bein' fair, I won't take anything.

"Anyway, I got to thinkin', thinkin' 'bout wantin' to start myself a ranch, maybe get married if I could find a woman who'd have me; never really had enough money to think seriously on the idea, but when I came up with this idea, I figured I might not ever have another chance, so I counted myself in on the divvy of the herd. When I say herd, I'm talkin' 'bout the one Taggart spread out on your range, Tuttle."

He took a swallow of coffee. "Like I said right from the start, y'all think I'm not bein' fair, reckon I won't take anything."

Before anyone could respond to his words, Ruth stood. "Cord Fain, gonna say it like it is. You thinkin' to not take anything makes me know you gotta have somebody, maybe a woman, take charge o' any business dealin's you gonna make. You're jest too danged fair—wanta make ever'body happy but yoreself.

"To my thinkin', ain't nobody got a claim on nothin' you done figured out 'cept them men you brought in here. They need to be paid fightin' money."

Before Cord could respond to Ruth's latest outburst, Tuttle said. "I agree with Ruth. You got it figgered out what the divvy'll be—an' a even bigger question, is all this within the law?"

Fain nodded. "The only brand any o' those cattle have on 'em is a trail brand. Mobley there can tell you we choused those cows outta the chapparal down in the Big Bend o' Texas. Taggart has no claim on 'em. The cattle company what paid Taggart money to pay us? Well, we never got any pay. If anybody owes anybody anything, Taggart owes the company he works for. Those cattle b'long to us as much as they do to anybody." His voice hardened. "I'm gonna take 'em."

He took a couple of quick steps toward the fire, turned, and came back. "Yep, I got the divvy all figured out. Ain't a soul here gonna be unhappy with what I got figured."

"What we gonna do 'bout Taggart?"

Cord looked at Wash, who had asked the question. "Partner, I figure we'll play that hand when the cards're dealt."

"You know he ain't gonna let it rest till he can get you in front of his gun, don't you?" Ruth's words came out in a breathless whisper—almost scared.

Cord, surprised at her obvious concern, frowned, then looked her in the eye. "Ma'am, I been practicin' with my Colt; figure I might be able to take 'im on when the time comes." He felt no guilt in letting her think he was a neo-

phyte where guns were concerned. She'd given him too
much grief to consider her feelings now.

"Cord, a few days' practice isn't enough to get you
ready to face a man like Taggart. From what I done
heered 'bout that man, he ain't only dangerous—he's
ruthless."

Still puzzled that she seemed to care, he stared at her a
moment. "Ma'am, I'm not relyin' on a few days of practice; believe me when I tell you I think I can handle 'im. If
you don't believe me, there's some in the crew I brought
with me who will tell you I'm not bein' a fool. They'll tell
you that maybe I got more'n a good chance." He straightened his shoulders. "Now, ma'am, that's all I'm gonna tell
you."

He took a swallow of his coffee. It had gotten cold. He
threw out the dregs and poured himself a fresh cupful. Pam
walked over to look into his eyes. "Mr. Fain, would you
walk outside the firelight with me? I have a few questions I
need answered."

Cord stared at her a moment. "Yes, ma'am, why not let's
do it right now?"

He held his arm for her to take hold of, and led her
from the firelight. Once out of hearing of those about the
fire, she turned to face him. "Mr. Fain, you seem to have
lumped Mr. Mobley, Tommy, an' me into the same bunch
who's gonna share in the cattle. That ain't fair. Whatever
Jed deserves is his. Tommy an' me figure we owe *him*.
He's done work around our cabin, taught Tommy things
his pa mighta taught 'im if he'd lived, fought for us." Her
voice came out as though trying to pass a heavy lump.
"Mr. Fain, he's even give my Tommy love." She shook
her head. "No, sir, he don't need to split anything with me
an' Tommy." She cocked her head to the side, apparently
studying him, and looking like she wanted to ask something else.

"All right, ma'am, go ahead; ask what you really brought
me out here for."

"Oh, Mr. Fain, you're not gonna leave me with a shred of pride, are you? You're gonna make me say what I wouldn't say to anybody." She squared her shoulders. "Okay, I'll ask. Has Mr. Mobley said anything to lead you to figger he an' I might mean somethin' to each other? If not, then I'm here to tell you, you ain't splittin' nothin' of his with me an' Tommy."

If Pam hadn't been so pitifully courageous—and obvious, Cord might have laughed; instead, he gripped her shoulders in his big hands. "Mrs. Henders, I'll not say the things, or ask things that are none o' my business. I figure when the time comes—you know, when all this shootin' an' fightin's over—you an' Mr. Mobley're gonna have a lot o' talkin' to do." He chuckled. "Ma'am, Jed Mobley is a right smart man in my opinion. I don't reckon he's gonna let you get away from 'im."

He twisted as though to head back to the fire, then turned back. "Ma'am, gonna say this knowin' it ain't none o' my business, but yeah, Jed's given Tommy his love, an' if you ain't noticed, Tommy's latched onto him like a cockle burr. That boy o' yours jest 'bout figures the sun rises an' sets right inside o' Jed Mobley." He let a slight smile break the corners of his mouth. "I figure you an' Mobley gonna have to figure out whether the boy an' the man's feelin's are enough, or should there be more."

Pam took his elbow in her rough, work-hardened hand and turned him toward the bunch gathered around the fire. "Mr. Fain, I reckon the questions I asked wasn't fair to you. I asked you things that any self-respectin' woman wouldn't have asked anybody, an' I'll have to say you answered them without strippin' all my pride from me." She looked up at him. "Gonna ask you one more thing. If you will, please don't say nothin' 'bout what we talked about."

Fain chuckled. "Mrs. Henders, the only thing I remember of our conversation is that you told me you weren't gonna take any part of the divvy of the herd; that the whole kit an' kaboodle b'longed to Mr. Mobley."

She squeezed his elbow. That was the only thanks he needed. Now if Jed Mobley didn't take over from here, he'd have to revise his opinion of the man's intelligence.

12

Taggart's two men scrambled back through the front door. They were the only two the trail boss had left in the house who could get around; the other three were stretched out on the floor, in their blankets.

The trail boss stared at them; he'd apparently not heard the rifle fire while they tried to reach the woodpile. "Where's the damned wood you went out yonder for?"

Barnes and Lambrey stared at him a moment; then Lambrey flicked his thumb toward the door. "You want wood, git the hell out yonder an' git it yore self."

"What's that mean? What's the matter with you?"

The two men stared at him a moment; then Lambrey answered. "Tell you what it means, Taggart. Fain's got us boxed. He's got us in this here house where we cain't git out without gittin' killed. He's outfoxed you."

"You wanted it all, Taggart: cows, money, land," Barnes said. He shrugged. "Now you know what you got left? Two men who *can* fight, but ain't gonna fight for *you*. I figger them two you sent to the stable to keep watch sloped outta here durin' the night."

He grinned, and to Taggart's thinking there wasn't an

ounce of humor in it. "Where you gonna spend all that money the company give you to pay us with? You ain't give us a dime, so I reckon you got jest 'bout all of it left."

"I figgered to pay y'all when we got the cattle on good grass and set up to ranch."

"You did like hell." Barnes rolled a smoke, lit it, blew the smoke toward the ceiling, then glanced at Lambrey. "Know what, Lambrey? When we get outta here, I ain't takin' none o' that money 'cept three months' pay what's owed me. Know why? Well, I'm gonna go to the closest law, make damned sure he knows I ain't got a cent, 'cept 'bout that three months' pay, plus fifteen bucks what I left the Big Bend with, an' if you're smart as I think, you'll do the same. That way, when the company sends out notices for Taggart's capture, we ain't gonna be in the same stew pot with 'im."

Barnes stared at the floor a long moment, then pinned Lambrey with a look that went right through his soul. "Know what, partner? You an' me, well, don't reckon neither one o' us has been lily-white durin' our lives, figger we done some right rotten things, but don't figger we ever stole nothin' but a few head o' cows now an' then."

He shrugged. "Know damned well I never stole nothin' from folks who worked like hell for what little they had. You an' me? Well, we strung along with the *colonel* here—don't know what he ever wuz colonel over—but we strung 'long with 'im hopin' to git our pay one o' these days." He nodded. "An' yeah, I reckon we both thought of a big payoff if this here thing worked, but I'm here to tell ya I been givin' this thing Taggart's got cooked up a lot more thought"—he shook his head—"an' I don't figger neither one o' us has sunk low enough to go along with *the colonel*."

Lambrey nodded. "B'lieve you right, partner. I ain't wanted by no law nowhere; don't b'lieve you are either." A cold smile flitted across the corners of his lips. He pinned Taggart with a hard, chilly look. "Know where that leaves you, Taggart?"

"Damn you! Damn you both to hell. Ain't neither one o' you outta this house yet. If Fain don't kill you, I will."

Barnes shook his head. "No, now, don't you see, *Boss*? You done made another big mistake. You're thinkin' you're still in charge. You ain't. Fain's in charge. An' you're thinkin' you can beat us to the draw. I don't figger you can take either one o' us—but I'm shore willin' to find out."

A shiver ran up Taggart's back. He stared at Barnes. He'd always thought the slim drover might be a dangerous man to cross. And now that he'd crossed him, he knew he'd been right.

The man who surprised him was Lambrey. He'd figured he could control his *segundo*, but looking at him now, he knew he'd made a big mistake. Lambrey might be even more dangerous than Barnes—and Taggart realized he didn't want to find out. He knew fear for the first time in his life. He wasn't only afraid of the two men facing him. Now he might have to face the law, and he had no defense. But if he had a choice, he wanted to live to get even with Cord Fain; if he never did another thing in his life, he wanted Fain. He'd been the one who'd started his game to unravel.

Cord and Pam walked back to the fire. Cord felt every eye of the group stabbing him. He didn't know why he felt guilty, but he did, and felt obligated to tell them why he and Pam had gone out there, with much of the conversation left out. He returned everyone's stares. "Mrs. Henders wanted to make it plain to me that she had no claim to any of those cattle; I told her we'd talk 'bout it later."

He walked to the fire, poured himself a cup of coffee, then swept the group with a glance. "Now, if you folks agree with what I told you I figured to do, we got a roundup ahead o' us. Don't figure to brand those cows we gonna drive to Dodge—or maybe Denver, but we gotta separate the trail herd from those we figure to keep, then we'll brand the ones we're gonna put on our own grass." He grinned. "Reckon Pa's gonna help me find some good land close to where he has his ranch."

He took a swallow of his coffee, threw out the rest, and picked up his saddle. "Saddle up, men, we got cattle to gather. We're gonna keep a couple men watchin' the ranch house to keep Taggart an' his men inside; the rest o' us'll divide up to close-herd them cows we're gonna sell. The rest'll get branded."

He looked at Tuttle. "How many you figure you can stand to add to your herd without overgrazin'?"

Tuttle shook his head. "Fain, way I got it figured, you an' yore men done 'nuff jest by savin' my ranch fer me. You make sure y'all got what you need for your own goals. I wuz gittin' long mighty well till Taggart come 'long. Figger now that you 'bout got him neutralized, me an' Eve kin make out fine." He hunched his shoulders. "Our needs ain't very much noway. We got 'bout all a man an' woman could ask fer; we got each other." He grinned. "An' a mighty fine daughter when she ain't got 'er dander up."

Tuttle's words sank in; Fain realized for the first time that a man was damned little in the great plan of things if he didn't have a woman to share with. For some reason, he looked at Ruth. Her eyes locked on his; then her lids drooped to shut out what she might have been thinking. He was in trouble.

He wanted to know what she wanted to talk to him about when she got him alone, but dodged even the thought to ask her when she wanted to talk. Besides, he and his men had some cowboying to do. He swept the crew with a glance. "All right, men, let's get after it. Gonna be a long day. Check your gear, don't want any broken ropes causin' y'all to get hurt. Ain't none o' this gonna be new to you. While we ride I'll tell you 'bout how many we want to sell. We'll separate that many. A couple o' you can hold 'em, an' we gonna brand the rest."

Marshal Worley watched the stage come in, off-load some mail sacks and passengers, and then unhitch the tired team that had pulled it from the last stop. He drank a couple cups of coffee, then walked to the general store. The post

office was located in the rear. They should have the mail
sorted by now. The postmaster handed him a bundle of
mail tied with a string. He tipped his hat and went directly
to his office.

When seated with another cup of coffee in front of him,
he untied the cord from the bundle, sorted it, then picked
up the notices of wanted men, leafed through them, pushed
them aside, and picked up a bulky letter from headquarters.
It had a wax seal on it.

He broke the seal, pulled a sheaf of papers from the envelope, and from the first page a picture of Taggart stared
at him. A letter followed. It described Taggart in detail,
stated he was wanted for absconding with funds from the
Philadelphia Land and Cattle Company, 4200 dollars, and
three thousand head of cattle. Their Denver office had ad-
vised them the herd had not come through there.

In his mind he separated the money from the cattle and
mulled the problem over. He came up with the answer in
his own mind, but would have to wait until he talked with
some of Taggart's crew to determine whether the law could
get him for both offenses. He sighed and wondered
whether the company money had ever been paid to the
crew. He nodded, then wondered where Taggart had set up
shop and where he might find his crew.

When Fain and his crew drew rein where he figured to have
the branding fire, he motioned Mobley to his side. "You
been over Pam's homestead. How many head o' these cattle you figure it'll graze along with what she's already got
runnin' on her grass?"

Jed pushed his hat back, swabbed sweat from his brow,
and squinted as though thinking. After a moment he nodded, then looked into Cord's eyes. "Reckon with the few
head she's already runnin', another four hundred head'd
do it."

Fain pulled a stubby pencil from his shirt pocket, felt in
his shirt, grunted, then pushed his hand down into his saddlebag, raked it around, and pulled a dog-eared sheet of pa-

per from it. "Y'all gonna need money for things I figure she's been in need of for some time." He licked the end of the pencil, nodded, and mumbled, "Nine hundred head."

"Aw, hell, Cord, looks like you already got me an' Pam married. I haven't said a word to her 'bout how I feel. She might not even want me hangin' round."

Cord pinned him with a straight-on look. "You love that girl, Jed? Know it ain't none o' my business, but I wanta know." At Mobley's blush and nod, he continued. "Gonna tell you, cowboy, if you don't say somethin' to her 'bout your feelin's, I reckon I'll jest have to do it for you."

"Aw, hell, now, Fain, you wouldn't do that, would you?"

"As sure as I'm sittin' here in this saddle. Now when we get these cattle separated, an' get those branded that I figure on not sellin', I want you to ride back to the cabin, take that girl for a walk, an' tell 'er you want to marry her. All right?"

Mobley stared at Cord, slowly shook his head, and frowned. "Damned if I ever saw how bossy you were when we were workin' that big herd. Seems you've taken charge of everything."

Cord grinned. "Somebody had to do it; seemed like I was the one."

"What you spike out nine hundred head for? That's too many."

Cord heard him, but wrote down nine hundred head anyway. When he looked up from the piece of paper, the boys had the branding fire going, and were already herding cattle into a closer bunch. He'd have to tell them how many they figured to sell. He rode to where Frog sat his horse. "Put Mrs. Henders' Slash H on four hundred head. 'Fore we get through brandin' them, I'll see how many we gonna make Bob Tuttle take; then I'll have to decide how many I'm gonna keep. It'll depend on how much money I figure it's gonna take to get my own herd started."

The branding went slowly. Using a running iron made it hard and tedious work to keep the iron hot and trace the brand into the hide of the cattle.

Fain thought he'd better ride back to the cabin and see if

Tuttle and Pam had irons where he could get to them without getting shot. He figured Tuttle's stable would have branding irons hung on the wall by the forge, and Pam's should be where he could put his hands on them easily.

He broke into his thoughts and yelled at one of his men. "Make sure you get mostly heifers an' a few bulls in that mix. Mrs. Henders is gonna need breedin' stock."

By the end of that first day, every man looked like he wore more dirt than the surrounding ground. Sweat caked the dirt so much that Fain figured it'd take an hour to wash it all off, and there wasn't water enough out here to clean up one man, let alone his entire crew. It was black dark when the men came to the fire, poured themselves cups of coffee, and slouched tiredly to the ground.

Fain had brought Cookie with him. The ladies back at the cabin once again did the family cooking.

Cord looked across the fire at Menendez. "Pablo, want you to take charge out here. I'm gonna go back to the cabin, see if Mrs. Henders knows where she stowed her branding irons. Then I'm gonna go get 'em, an' Tuttle's, an' bring 'em back here. Oughta be back by daylight."

Tuttle cut in, "Mine's hangin' on the side o' the forge."

Fain nodded. "Good. I'll bring 'em back with me."

He threw the dregs from his cup, knocked the dottle from his pipe, and stood. "I'll grab somethin' to eat when I get to the cabin. Cookie's got grub fixed for y'all soon's you get enough git-up-an'-go to walk to the fire an' get it. I'm gonna head out now."

"Cord, you go gittin' yoreself shot agin, yore *padre*'s gonna skin me alive for not takin' better care o' you. You be careful messin' round the Tuttle ranch yard, ya heah?"

"Pablo, you an' the men took care o' me when you taught me how to use guns. Pa ain't gonna hold you responsible for keepin' my hide in one piece this late in the day."

He'd not stripped the gear from his horse when he rode in. Now he toed the stirrup and headed for the cabin.

As soon as he rode beyond earshot, Tuttle looked at

Menendez. "What Cord mean when he said you learned 'im how to use guns?"

Pablo stared at him. "Gonna tell you somethin'; don't want you tellin' nobody, not even your family. All right?"

Bob nodded.

Menendez looked in the direction Cord had ridden, then turned his look on Tuttle. "That boy who just now rode outta here may be the fastest gun in this part o' the world. We taught him till he wuz 'bout sixteen years old; by then they wuzn't nothin' else we could teach 'im. Fact is, he coulda learned us a lot by then. An' I'm gonna tell you the truth: He ain't only fast, I ain't seen 'im miss what he wuz wantin' to hit since he wuz fourteen."

He shook his head. "Ain't nobody gotta worry 'bout him. Only thing we gotta worry 'bout is somebody shootin' 'im from behind." He laughed. "But that ain't likely to happen 'cause he usually keeps his back to a wall."

"B-b-but, hell, he wasn't even wearin' a gun when we first seen 'im there at the ranch. Fact is, Ruth figgered 'im for some sort o' pilgim—maybe even scared to pack a iron."

Pablo laughed. "Scared, that boy scared? Naw, I don't figger they's anythin' that boy's scared of. He didn't pack a side iron when he left home 'cause he promised his pa he wouldn't. His pa didn't want 'im to get a reputation, an' knew he would as fast as he wuz. He promised, an' that boy never broke his word to no one fur's I know."

Pablo leaned against his saddle and stared into the fire. Then, so soft as to hardly be heard, he said, "If I'd ever got hitched an' had a son, reckon I'd want 'im to be just like Cord Fain."

Tuttle looked at Pablo; a deep frown creased his forehead. "Why for is he packin' now? You say he always keeps 'is word."

Menendez nodded. "Jest gonna tell you that. When he rode into his pa's ranch figurin' to borrow us to help 'im fight Taggart, he told his pa what he figgered to do, then asked 'im if he'd release 'im from his promise. His pa give 'im permission to tie one to his leg." He squinted at Tuttle a moment. "Now don't you ferget an' let it slip that he's right handy with any kind o' weapon."

Tuttle stared at the fire a moment, then nodded. "Give you my word, didn't I? Well, I'm one to keep my word right along with the best." He grinned. "Eve's gonna be right happy 'bout what you told me, soon's she finds out." He pushed his hat to the back of his head and ran his fingers through the sweat-wet strands. "She done stood up for that boy agin Ruth an' me both." He chuckled. "I kin hear her now, tellin' me, 'I told you so.' "

Menendez stood and took his dish to the fire. "C'mon, boys, Cookie ain't gonna hold this grub fer us much longer 'fore he throws it out."

Cord rode to the cabin, stepped from the saddle, and while going to the pump to wash up, sniffed. "Danged if that grub don't smell good as Cookie's been fixin'." He glanced at Ruth. "You oughta be ashamed lettin' your ma work so hard. You shoulda helped 'er fix supper."

"Cord Fain, what makes you think I didn't help 'er?"

Tongue in cheek, he stared at her a moment. "Fact is, I thought you mighta, but changed my mind. It smelled too good."

Ruth clenched her fists, stood there, and glared at him a moment; then her fists unclenched, she visibly relaxed, then grinned. "Still pushin' yore luck, ain't ya, cowboy? Figgered to git me mad agin." She nodded, her grin softened to a smile. "Didn't work this time, maybe not ever agin."

"Aw, now, young'un, don't know what I'll do if you ain't scaldin' me with your tongue at least once a day. Gonna feel downright neglected."

"Soon's you scrub half o' Pa's ranch off'n you, come on to the fire. We got supper ready. Notice, Cord Fain, I said 'we.' " His answer was a smile.

They sat around the fire eating. They stayed outside because there wasn't enough room in the cabin for the two old punchers of the Tuttles and them. Fain asked Pam where she kept her branding irons. She told him. Then he said he thought to get hers and Tuttle's to take back to the branding crew. He chuckled. "Usin' them runnin' irons are makin' hard work even harder." He shook his head. "Too, usin' a runnin' iron makes me feel like we're rustlin' those cows." He chuckled again. "Reckon my feelin's aren't too far wrong at that."

He became aware that while he talked, Ruth had pinned him with a questioning look. He glanced over the rim of his coffee cup at her. "What you worried 'bout, young'un?"

"Ain't worried. Jest wonderin' why you don't pull that big iron you done started wearin' an' blow yore brains out. Save all the trouble you been goin' to to have somebody else do it." She took a deep breath. "You figger to ride into the ranch where Taggart's holed up and pick up our brandin' irons without nobody shootin' at you?"

"Well, yes'm. It'll be dark, don't figure they'll see me." He took another bite of the food Ruth, her mother, and Pam had prepared, mentally compared it with Cookie's cooking, and thought he wouldn't mind eating any of it for the rest of his life.

He chewed a moment, swallowed, frowned, and said, "Might take a peek into the family room to see if I can get a count of how many o' Taggart's men are wounded." Abruptly, he saw a side of Ruth he'd not thought existed.

"Oh, Cord, please don't do that. Please. You're gonna get yourself all shot up agin. I don't think I can stand any more of that kind o' thing where you're concerned."

He frowned, looked at her, really studied her, then being very careful to not have any levity in his voice, he shrugged. "Young'un, I ain't gonna put myself in a bad situation, guarantee you I won't." He took a swallow of coffee, then stared straight into her eyes. "Gonna tell you, girl, that talk you wanted to have with me? Well, I figure soon's we got these cattle branded, those we gonna sell sold, then the money divided up, well, that talk you wanted to have with me alone—we gonna have it."

"That's what I'll be waitin' for, Cord. Ain't gonna let you forget it neither."

For some reason Fain glanced at Eve, only to see a slight smile trying to break the corners of her lips.

Several minutes later, Cord finished eating, washed his mess gear, toed the stirrup, tipped his hat, and rode out. He felt Ruth's eyes follow him when he rode away.

When he came close to Pam's cabin, he climbed from his horse, tied him to a stunted cedar, and slipped in afoot. He didn't think Taggart had enough men left to have taken over the Henders homestead, but had no intention of getting shot because of carelessness.

As soon as he had the cabin and its outbuildings in sight, he studied them; the cabin was dark, no smoke trailing from the chimney, no sign of life, or that anyone had been there in days. But he sat there another hour, then, satisfied the place was deserted, slipped to the back side of the barn.

He found a knothole a couple feet from the door and stuck his eye to it. He studied the darkened interior for a long ten minutes. No movement.

From past experience he thought the back door would be hung with leather straps. He was right. He swung it open only enough to slip through, moved to the side, and stood there, listening, testing the air for smells of fresh droppings and trying to penetrate the darkness with his eyes. He depended a lot on feeling. His muscles were not very tight, his back didn't ache. His muscles relaxed. He had the place to himself.

Cord thought to grope for a lantern, light it, then search for the branding irons where Pam had told him they'd be. He decided to trust his sense of feel instead.

Despite having come in from the dark, his eyes further adjusted such that he could define shapes. He thought he could pick out the squatty shape of the forge, and on searching feet worked his way to its side. He moved his hands around the iron bowl feeling for tools of any kind. He felt the tongs and other tools, but nothing that felt like a branding iron.

From the forge he moved to the closest wall, and found what he looked for as soon as he moved his hands along its rough surface. He took the two irons from the nails upon which they hung and moved to the back door.

Another few hours' ride, and he came to the area where he hoped to find his own men on watch. After he identified himself and told them what he figured to do, and to be damned careful not to shoot him, he ghosted to the back of the Tuttle stable.

Remembering where most things were located, and trusting that his men had kept his ex–trail boss pinned in the ranch house, he used less care in getting into the barn.

Here, he found what he wanted within only moments. When he'd identified one branding iron, he groped along the wall for another, didn't find it, shrugged, and took the one from the side of the forge, then slipped to the back side of the stable.

He figured to have less cattle to brand for Tuttle than for Mobley. Ruth's pa had indicated that he wanted nothing but control of his ranch back. Now Fain wanted to see what and who Taggart had with him. He didn't feel too good about trying to get across the open space between the stable and the house.

His stomach muscles tight, his scalp feeling as though his hair stuck straight out from his head, he moved to the front of the barn, then carefully placed Tuttle's iron on the ground. He didn't want to hit it against something and have it ring like a church bell.

He gauged the distance to the bunkhouse, then looked from it to the house and figured the distance to be considerably closer. He ran to the corner of the crew's lodging, then stood there and stared at the house.

He wondered if Taggart had men looking out the windows with rifles or scatterguns primed to fire at any movement in the yard. If he could have known that Menendez had told Tuttle Fain wasn't afraid of *anything*, he would have put the lie to his friend's words.

From the corner of the bunkhouse, he studied every window, giving each window about fifteen minutes close look. Then his eyes moved along the sides of the house that were in his view. He moved his eyes only a foot at a time along the base of each wall, looked for darker, or lighter, shapes that might break the the night's pattern. He didn't find any.

He thought to run to the house, stop, and listen for any sounds other than those he expected to hear on a quiet night. He changed his mind, dropped to the ground, and pulled himself along with his elbows, his rifle cradled in their crooks. It took almost an hour to cross the seventy-five or so feet to the base of the wall, and with each inch of it his eyes continued to try to pick out movement, sound, or even smells that he didn't expect.

Finally, his hands touched the walls of the house. He stood, then bypassed the darkened windows, thinking that whatever men Taggart had left would be in the room from which lantern light showed. He searched the ground with his feet, each step a challenge to keep quiet. Finally, bent almost to the ground, he stooped under the window he remembered as being one that looked in on the family room.

He pulled his hat from his head, folded it into a flat bundle, and stuck it inside his waistband. Keeping his eyes on the windowsill, he inched his head up to bring his eyes level with the glass. The first person he saw was Trig Barnes; then his look took in Pete Lambrey several feet from Barnes. They both stared in the same direction.

Fain moved his eyes to look in the direction the two men stared. Across the room from them Taggart sat in what Cord guessed was the chair Bob Tuttle used when in possession of his home. Cord smiled to himself. It was obvious the two men had separated themselves from each other and Taggart. Fain wondered if they were all distrustful of each other, or if they didn't trust their trail boss. He hadn't long to wait for that bit of information. The evening was warm. The windows were raised. The talk within came to him clearly.

Barnes stared at Taggart. "Know what, *Mr. Boss*, I figure Fain's got us right where he wants us, an' he ain't gonna turn loose till we give up. But I'm tellin' you right now, when he walks in here to take us, they's gonna only be five o' us alive—me, Lambrey, an' them three wounded punchers. Gonna call you, *boss man,* gonna make you draw on me first—then I'm gonna put a couple .44 slugs in your gut." He shook his head. "We wuz dumb to stick with you long's we did, but reckon I kept hopin' you'd pay us what wuz rightfully ours. You ain't paid us, but 'fore we give in to Fain, me an' Pete's gonna take what's our'n, not a penny more, then tie yore money belt back on you an' then surrender." He rolled a quirly, lit it, and looked at Lambrey. "You figger we might talk Fain into lettin' us go?"

From where he stood, Cord saw Lambrey's brow crease; then he shrugged. "Don't know, Trig. I always figgered Fain for a square shooter." He grinned. "An' I'll tell you, I never thought he was a pilgrim. Somehow I always figgered that young man could handle himself in 'bout any situation he found 'imself. Fact is, I sort o' cottoned to that cowboy."

Barnes chuckled. "Yeah, me too, but a helluva lot o' good that's gonna do us now." He laughed. "Don't think he's gonna ask us our opinion of 'im 'fore he blows us to hell—an' for some reason I figger he's got what it takes to take us on, guns, knives, or fists."

Lambrey nodded. "Way I got 'im figgered."

Fain, standing outside the window, hearing himself receive such praise, smiled to himself. Hell, they didn't know that at that very moment he sweated bullets, pure fear that he'd be caught this close and wouldn't be able to get away.

He frowned. Those two cowboys in the room with Taggart were what he'd figured them to be: tough, hardworking, first-class cowmen, and dangerous as a rattlesnake to cross. He wished he could think of some way to cut them loose and keep Taggart until he got ready to face the trail boss.

When he faced Taggart, he wanted it to be an even break. He mentally shrugged. Right now, he had branding to get done, and a trail herd to round up. Before slipping from the window, he swept the room with a glance to see if any more men were there. He'd done that earlier, but had been more intent on seeing what the three men he could see plainly were doing. This time he saw the bottom half of three men stretched out on the floor, bloody bandages around their legs, knees, and feet.

He slipped from the window and the ranch yard, retrieved the branding iron, then went to the two men he had guarding the house, told them what he'd heard, and headed for the camp he and his men had set up for the roundup.

Eve studied her daughter, whose eyes still followed the path Fain had taken from the cabin, even though he'd been gone from sight for several minutes. She walked to Ruth, put her arm around her shoulders, and looked in the direction Ruth looked. "My daughter, often when a woman feels herself threatened by a man, her freedom or way of life threatened, or even when she has seen a man who might attract her and he doesn't quite measure up to what she expected him to be, she gets mighty testy, and shows it to the world in an unreasonable show of anger."

Ruth twisted to look at her mother. "Mama, I've been a real shrew. I've treated Cord like pure dirt, an' he's taken everything I could throw at 'im, an'-an' teased me instead of gitten mad at me." She brushed at her eyes. "Aw, hell, Ma, I got reason to be ashamed o' callin' myself a *real* woman."

Eve chuckled. "No, my daughter, you're actin' eggzackly like a real woman would act." Her chuckle changed to an outright laugh. "We're an unreasonable breed. No man can figure us out, an' most o' the time we can't figger ourselves out. If *we* could, it might make it easier for our men to do so, an' pshaw, we surely couldn't stand to have 'em do that, could we?"

Ruth swiped at her eyes again, then came into her

mother's arms. "Oh, Mama, I wish I had been nicer to him, he's such a strong man. I reckon if I wuz thinkin' 'bout gittin' real serious 'bout a man, I'd be lookin' at Cord Fain mighty close."

Eve, with those words of Ruth's, burst out in a laugh that would have done honor to a deep-chested man. "Honey, I reckon you've done been lookin' at that man—closer'n you'll admit."

13

BACK AT THE roundup camp, Fain asked Tuttle and Mobley to come sit with him. He wanted to talk. They each poured a cup of coffee and sat close to the fire.

"Gonna tell y'all how I figure to divide the herd, see if you both agree." He frowned. Menendez should sit in on this. Cord figured to have him in charge of cutting out the trail herd; the one they were going to sell. He looked over his shoulder. "Pablo, you better sit in on this so I won't have to say it twice." He thought a moment, then yelled for the whole crew to gather around.

Tuttle, as soon as Menendez came to the fire, pinned Fain with a no-nonsense look. "Son, I done told you, I figger you already done enough for me an' my family. All I want is to git them cattle off my land, git Taggart an' his bunch outta here, an' git back in my home an' start livin' normally agin."

Cord looked straight on into his eyes. "Cain't talk you into takin' some o' them cows, maybe a hundred head?"

Tuttle shook his head. "Nary a one. Gonna be jest like I told you."

Fain nodded. "Okay, it'll be like you say." He twisted to

look at Mobley. "Gonna give you those four hundred head you say Pam can handle on her land; then gonna sell off five hundred head an' give you the money from the sale." He wrote down under a column he'd listed as "Sell" five hundred, and four hundred under "Keep."

He studied on how many to sell in order to pay the men he'd borrowed from his pa. He thought 750 would be about right. That would allow each of them 1250 dollars, if he got twenty-five dollars a head. He looked at Menendez, told him what he thought to pay each of his pa's men, which would leave about 1250 head.

"I think to keep 'bout twelve hundred fifty for myself if y'all don't think I'm bein' selfish. Gonna sell five hundred of them, an' drive the seven hundred fifty to where I figure to set up ranchin'." He took a swallow of his coffee. "That means we gotta cut out seventeen hundred fifty head to drive."

Mobley eyed Cord a long moment. "You said you intended to set up to ranch. You aren't keepin' many for yourself."

Cord nodded. "Yeah, I am. If I cain't make a go of it with that start, I figure I ain't much of a cattleman. I want to keep mostly heifers, maybe 'bout five bulls, an' hope like the very devil I get a good calf crop in the spring. Too, I got a little money, an' with what I sell, I figure to have enough to buy me some land, an' a couple o' purebred Hereford or Durham bulls."

Mobley nodded. "Pam'll need 'bout three bulls, the rest heifers."

"Okay, men, we know how many we gonna drive outta here. Start in the mornin' to puttin' the trail herd together. We can divide up them cattle we gonna keep when we get back.

"Oh, hell." He twisted to look at Tuttle. "Bob, you reckon them cattle I figure to keep till I can drive 'em off will overgraze your land?"

Tuttle shook his head. "Naw, I can handle 'em, but I figger we better brand Pam's cows an' I'll have the boys drive 'em to her range. Reckon we better brand yore's too while we at it."

Fain swept them with a questioning look. "Any o' y'all figure I took too much for myself?"

Tuttle spoke up. "Cord, if it hadn't been for you an' yore boys, they wouldn't of been nothin' to keep." He shook his head. "Nope, I figger you done been more than fair." He looked at the others around the fire. "How 'bout y'all?"

Frog Ballew grinned. "I guaran-damn-tee you I'm happy. I come along for the chance to have a good fight. Didn't never figger to get no pay outta it. Reckon the boys Fain brought with 'im come along for the ride jest like I did."

A chuckle, seeming to come from the entire crew, hit Cord's ears. Then from the middle of those gathered about, Wash spoke up. "Ah reckon all's I figuhed to git outta this wuz a trail pahdnuh. Now since he gonna be a big rancher, first thing I want is foah him to give me a job."

Fain stared at him a moment, then shook his head. "Nope, no job for you, Wash."

Wash's face literally fell to his chest. His Adam's apple bobbed up and down a couple of times. He looked like he might cry. Then, obviously with a great effort, he shrugged. "Well, Cord, reckon I had to hope."

Cord continued. "We figured to be partners when we broke loose from Taggart—an' that's what we gonna be, ranch an' all."

Wash's face shone all the way through the black, but he argued a moment that all he wanted was a job. Fain vetoed the idea. He looked at those gathered about him. "All right, men, we got a lot o' work to do. Let's crawl in our blankets an' hit the ground runnin' come daylight."

Taggart's trail herd had not had time to scatter and find the ravines, thickets, or shallow valleys to hide in, so the roundup, hot, dirty, dangerous, went smoothly, and while the crew pulled the gather together in the bunches they needed to keep separate, the branding went a lot faster now that they had irons to do it with, all except Fain's cattle.

He pulled Wash from the crew. "Wash, want you to go to Mrs. Henders' place. She's got a forge there. Beat us out a iron for you an' me. Make us a F-B, F-bar-B, Fain an' Black, 'less'n o' course you want to make it F-W, W for Wash."

The big black man laughed, then shook his head. "No, suh, reckon B for my last name'll be right nice." He frowned. "Cord, what you reckon Miss Ruth's gonna say 'bout you makin' me a pahdnuh?"

"What's she got to do with *who* I make my partner?"

"Well, suh, ah done seed the way she been lookin' at you, an' I gotta tell you, ah ain't seed you lookin' no different at her."

Fain stared at his partner. Had he been looking at Ruth in any way than he had thought of her all along? He decided he'd have to give that question more thought, a lot more. With that in mind, he mulled over Wash's question. After a few moments, he decided that whatever he figured about Ruth, she wasn't going to make a decision as to who he chose for friends—or partners, and Wash was both.

He realized he still stared at Wash. He shrugged. "Gonna tell you right now, partner, nobody's gonna tell me who I can befriend." He nodded. "That's the way it is."

Wash's smile showed every tooth in his head.

"Okay, now get on over to Mrs. Henders' place an' make us a brandin' iron, better make it two irons."

Wash toed the stirrup and rode off. Fain saw a heifer with Taggart's trail brand quit the herd, and rode after it.

Back at the cabin, about the time Fain rode after the heifer, Pam took a tin of biscuits from the oven and glanced toward the door. She had hoped Jed would have had some reason to come back to the cabin. Tommy had been underfoot ever since Mobley rode off.

She knew her son missed the big man. He'd practically fastened himself to Jed since the second day he'd ridden into their lives. Now she was fearful that if Jed left, it would be more than the boy could stand, especially since losing his father.

She switched from thinking about Tommy and Mobley to thinking about herself and the quiet man. What were *her* feelings for him? She didn't bother pondering that question very long. She knew the answer. He was a gentle man—with her and Tommy, but, she suspected, a very dangerous man to cross, especially if it involved someone he thought a lot of, and she knew from watching him that she and Tommy were among those he thought a lot of.

She knew from what Fain had said the last time he came to the cabin that he thought to give Mobley some sort of split with the cattle. She didn't care whether Jed got anything. He'd helped to rid the range of the land-grabbers; that was enough.

She and Tommy had been making do before he rode into their lives. She smiled to herself. If she had anything to say about it, she'd not let him just ride out after this was all over. It wasn't that the few days he'd been at her homestead he'd taken Tommy, and together they'd gotten things running smoothly, along with repairing fences, the corral, the barn, and even a few minor things in her cabin. The main thing was that *she* wanted him to stay, she *needed* him, and when a woman needed a man, not just any man, but a specific one, she should do something about it—and in her thinking, Jed Mobley was *her* specific one.

When Wash got back to the roundup camp with the branding irons, things went much faster. After burning the F-B onto about five heifers, Cord frowned, studying the ones wearing *his* brand. As soon as he got back home, he'd have to ride down to Santa Fe and register that as his and Wash's.

While he worked, mopped sweat from his face and neck, and threw another loop around another animal, he pondered the two men he'd heard talking to Taggart, then wondered about the men he'd seen lying on the floor. They needed to see a doctor. He shook his head. How could he spring the two he'd heard, and the wounded three? How could he make certain he kept Taggart around until he was ready to take him on in a stand-up gunfight? He'd made up his mind to not let the trail boss go without paying for what he'd tried to do.

Fain's mind shifted to what they'd already accomplished. Taggart's scheme to take over land that others had fought for had already been derailed. Wasn't that enough? Would the big, brutal man just ride off and leave things alone?

He thought about that a few moments, shook his head, and knew that this would not be over until the trail boss was dead, or in prison; he'd just gather another group of hard cases and try to recoup what had been taken from him.

That night, sitting around the fire, dirty, tired, and sweating, the crew drank coffee as hot as they could brew it.

Fain wanted to ride in to Trinidad and buy a few bottles of whiskey. The men would like that, but he thought he would be shirking the job at hand if he left for any reason.

Dealy stared across the fire at him. "This coffee sure would taste a lot better if we had somethin' to sweeten it with, Cord."

Fain grinned. "Was just thinkin' that very thing, but then I figured y'all needed me here more'n you needed a drink."

"Aw, hell, boy, why you makin' up our minds for us? To my thinkin', they ain't a one o' us who would mind takin' on a little extra work while you ride in there." Dealy swung his gaze around the group. "What you say men, we gonna do Cord's work for 'im?"

From the response, Fain doubted that a man there disagreed with Jim Dealy's assessment. He nodded. "All right. I want to talk to Worley anyway. Tell y'all the truth, I cain't figure what to do 'bout Taggart." He nodded. "Yeah, we got 'im trapped there in the house. I can't let Barnes an' Lambrey take those three men outta there without doin' somethin' 'bout that damned trail boss." He shrugged. "I'd like to let those men go. I trust 'em to head on back to Texas, or wherever they want to go, but that leaves the one I want to take down a notch.

"Cain't just take 'im out an' shoot 'im." He shook his head. "Ain't legal. 'Sides, I don't figure to act the same way I figure he'd act. That'd make me no better'n him. I sure hope I'm a better man than that."

Frog cut in. "Why not keep 'im penned up in there till we get through with sellin' them cows we gonna drive outta here, then take 'im to Trinidad. Let Marshal Worley handle 'im."

Cord studied the bottom of his empty cup a moment, then looked up. "Reckon I'll head for Trinidad in the mornin', get our whiskey, then see if the marshal's got any ideas." He stood, went to his blankets, and crawled between them. He looked at Cookie. "Get me up when you start the fire for breakfast. I'll leave then."

With the blankets pulled over him, he said, "Leave everything at the ranch house as it is till I get back. Just keep a close watch on it."

The next morning, long before the time he'd told Cookie to call him, Fain was in the saddle and headed for town. He rode down its main street just as the sun slipped behind the peaks at the edge of town.

He figured to get a bath and a shave before he did anything else. He'd brought a change of clothes with him; then, after getting clean and changing to clean clothes, he'd buy the bottles he promised the men, stash them in his gear, then get some supper.

After an hour or more in town, clean from the skin out, he went to the cafe, ate supper, then headed for the U.S. marshal's office.

Worley looked up, stood, and held out his hand. "Just thinkin' 'bout you, boy. How you doin'?"

Cord gripped the lawman's hand, grinned, and shook his head. "Sure hope your thinkin' kept me on the law side of things."

Worley nodded. "No question 'bout that." He frowned. "But Fain, I got a problem an' it's named Taggart."

Cord chuckled. "Reckon you an' me's got the same problem. Tell me 'bout yours, then I'll tell you mine."

Worley pulled a thick envelope from the top drawer of his desk, stuck his finger into it, and removed several folded pages. He tossed them to the top of the scratched and marred surface. "Wouldn't ordinarily share such as this with anyone, but I figger you can help me with it." He nodded. "Go ahead, read it."

Fain spent a few minutes reading every page, then read them again. He looked up and stared across the desk at the lawman. "Gotta tell ya, Marshal, you an' me's got the same puzzle."

He then told Worley about having Taggart trapped inside Bob Tuttle's ranch house, about wanting to let the men inside with him go free, and about wanting to know what to do with the trail boss.

Worley stared at him a moment. "You had a drink since you hit town?"

Cord shook his head. Worley stood, put on his hat, and waved his hand toward the door. "C'mon, let's take care o' that right now." He smiled. "'Sides that, I figger you an' me's got some serious thinkin' to do." He pulled his mouth down to one side in a grimace. "It ain't gonna be easy to take care o' what we wanta do, an' keep it legal right down the line."

"That's why I come to you, Worley. I don't want to end up wanted by the law, an' I sure as hell don't wanta get you in no trouble." He nodded. "Yep, we got us a reeeal problem." They pushed through the batwings. The stench of stale whiskey, stale sweaty bodies, and tobacco smoke hit Fain like something physical. He sucked in a shallow breath, then breathed normally, marveling at how quickly he got accustomed to smells—much quicker than switching one's eyes from light to dark.

After they'd gotten a bottle from the bar and gone to a back table, each putting his back to the wall, Worley poured them a full glass of whiskey, then turned a troubled look on Fain, his brow deeply creased. "You say you wanta turn those punchers loose?" He shook his head. "An' you wanta git the money outta Taggart's money belt an' get 'em paid?"

At Fain's nod, he continued. "Way I got it figgered, that'd make 'em guilty o' helpin' to steal them cattle from the cattle company."

Cord shook his head. "Don't see it that way at all, Worley. Way I see it is that they drew some money for work they done, work they done *before* Taggart said anything 'bout takin' those cattle, an' somebody else's land. Thing that bothers me is, once they took company money for bein' drovers on that drive, does that make them cattle legally the property o' the cattle company?"

Worley knocked back the rest of his drink and poured another, looked at Fain's glass, and topped it off. "Why you ask that?"

Cord gave him a straight-on look, a hard look. "'Cause, Marshal, I'm figurin' to take those cattle, every damned head of 'em. They's people who've been put outta their homes, people who've suffered the pain of worryin' 'bout their loved ones, an' men who've had their pretty pink hides punctured by lead thrown from that bunch." He nodded. "Me bein' one o' them. I figure to take them cows, distribute 'em 'mongst them people, includin' myself, maybe kill Taggart—if I'm faster'n him, then figure the slate's wiped clean."

Worley frowned, shook his head, and grunted. "Damn, boy, you ain't brung me one problem, you done brought me a whole bunch o' problems, mostly all legal ones." He shrugged. "I ain't a lawyer. Some o' them things you've proposed sound downright wrong to me—wrong in a legal sense, but right in a justice sense."

Fain shot the marshal a cold smile. "Didn't figure you to be hired to serve the law. Figured justice would be your goal."

Worley stared at Fain a long moment, his eyes hard as

agates, his face a frozen leather mask. "Boy, you ain't cuttin' me any slack at all, are you?"

Fain returned Worley's look, hoping it was as hard and
unrelenting as the marshal's. "Didn't figure to, Worley.
They's right, they's wrong, an' they's what the law says.
I'm interested in right an' wrong." He shrugged. "Got you
figured that way too." He packed his pipe, lighted it,
knocked back his drink, and sat there pinning Worley with
a searching look.

The marshal followed Fain's actions, then after getting
his pipe going, poured them another drink. He grinned.
"Well, boy, you done throwed 'nuff on the table to take
care o' this whole bottle while we study on it."

Fain felt his face soften; then the corners of his lips crinkled. "Hoped you'd see it that way, leastwise where the
bottle was concerned." He pulled his shoulders up around
his neck, then let them drop. "Just figured to give you
somethin' to study on. Now let's get serious 'bout that bottle."

He shook his head. "Gonna leave come daylight.
Promised the boys a couple o' drinks. Time I see you
again, I'll be in a whole bunch o' trouble—legally, or I'll
be ridin' high—where justice is considered." He swallowed the rest of his drink and held his glass out for the
marshal to fill.

Taggart stared across the room at his hirelings, men who he
distrusted, men who had bucked him in his plans. He swept
the room with an unbelieving look: five men, and three of
them cripples. How the hell did everything go wrong?

As soon as he asked the question of himself he knew the
answer: Fain—that damned milksop Fain, a man who
didn't have the guts to tie a .44 to his leg and force a decision, force a showdown.

Mentally, he shook his head, and glared at the two men
facing him across the room. Maybe with the promise of
money, more than they would have made with regular

drover's pay, he could buy them off. If he had to pay them, he would, but he'd avoid that chance if he could. "S'pose I say I'll pay you twice what you wuz gonna draw if you help me git back at Fain, what'd you say to that?"

Lambrey, his face devoid of expression, then a slight smile breaking the corners of his lips, shook his head. "Taggart, you're a crooked sombitch, an' you cain't separate bein' hard from bein' a damned crook. Me an' Barnes're salty punchers, ones who don't stand to be crossed. That's one helluva long way from being crooks.

"You could pay me ever'thin' you got in that money belt an' I wouldn't go along with you."

He shook his head. "'Bout three or four in the mornin', me an' Barnes're gonna slip outta here *with* what we got comin' in rightful wages, an' leave you to face Fain alone."

He chuckled. "Figger you gonna be right surprised when you look across a gun barrel at that cowboy. Figger he's gonna give you the break, grin at you, then blow yore worthless brains out. Think on that a while, Taggart. You ain't never faced a shore-'nuff salty gent afore. You got it to do now."

A cold finger traced its way up Taggart's spine. He'd heard that a feeling like this was because someone had stepped on your grave. He shivered, pushed the thought of his, or anyone else's, grave from his mind. He had to get these two men to go along with him—as long as he needed them—and to hell with the three lying there on the floor shot all to hell; he couldn't use them.

Lambrey, never changing expression, said, "Think I'll get a drink o' water." He stood, and while straightening from his chair, pulled his Colt. He pointed it at Taggart. "Gonna tell you once, *boss man*, you make a motion o' any kind toward that iron on yore laig, an' I'm gonna make yore kinfolk what done passed away mighty unhappy they gotta look at yore ugly face agin. You unnerstan' what I'm tellin' you?"

Without looking at Barnes, he said, "Stay clear o'

walkin' 'tween me an him, Barnes, go git 'is money belt, count out three months' pay to the dime for each o' us, give me mine, stick yore's in yore pocket, then tie his money belt back in place. We gonna leave here with what's ours an' nothin' more."

"C'mon, man, y'all kin take one third o' what I got on me, share an' share alike," said Taggart. "We kin skip outta here a whole helluva lot better off than we come into this here game." Taggart's voice, now a lot less than the commanding one he had used on the trail, sounded more like that of a squealing rat.

Barnes laughed. "Jest keep yore hands where I kin see 'em while I walk over there. Don't wanta kill ya; want Fain to do that."

He walked to his ex-boss' side, leaned over, unbuckled his gunbelt, dropped it on the floor, unbuttoned his trousers, felt around his waist, untied his money belt, pulled it from him and counted out six months' wages, separated the pile into two three-month ones, plus the extra money Lambrey would have drawn as *segundo*, then tied the belt back around Taggart's waist. "Now gonna tie you up so's you won't mess up me an Lambrey gittin' outta here alive." He kicked Taggart's gunbelt over toward Lambrey.

Lambrey, not wanting to use rawhide pigging string, looked in the kitchen for something that would not stretch with moisture, perhaps even sweat. He slit some flour sacks, which had been washed to use for dish towels, into strips, tried to tear them by pulling lengthwise on them to be sure Taggart, by straining, couldn't tear them, then tied his ex-boss securely to the chair in which he sat.

While looking through the kitchen for something with which to tie Taggart, he'd seen an almost full bottle of whiskey on a shelf behind some canned foods, some apparently canned by Mrs. Tuttle and some in the airtights now sold in the general store. He took the bottle, left two cartwheels on the counter, and went back to his seat in the parlor.

He had brought two glasses with him. While he poured

himself and Barnes drinks, he told him he'd left a couple of bucks on the counter to pay Tuttle for it. "'Fore we leave, gonna take some money outta *the boss's* pockets to pay fer what we done et while we been here."

Barnes took a swallow of the raw whiskey, coughed, rolled a quirly, took another swallow, and grinned. "Now all we gotta do is sit here, have a few drinks, an' wait fer 'bout three o'clock to come—then hope like hell Fain don't kill us when we try to git clear o' this here ranch."

Lambrey cocked a quizzical eyebrow at the man he now thought of as his partner. "You notice whether they's a moon?"

Barnes nodded. "Yeah, they is one, only a sliver. It'll be long gone by the time we try to ride out."

Lambrey only nodded, but gave a deep sigh.

After a couple of drinks, Barnes dozed. Lambrey, after one of his infrequent glances at his partner, went to the kitchen and poured some water in his drink. No point in letting the whiskey cut the edge off his alertness.

He let Barnes sleep until one o'clock by his big silver Waltham railroad watch. He wakened him, told him to stay awake, and said he would catch a few winks.

At exactly three o'clock, Barnes touched Lambrey's shoulder. "Time to test our luck, partner. Sunup'll be in 'bout three hours an' a half. We oughta be long gone by then."

Lambrey nodded, stood, looked at Taggart, then cast his partner a cold smile. "You check them rags we got 'im tied with lately?"

"Yep, jest 'fore I woke you up."

Barnes took another look at his ex-boss, frowned, then grimaced. "Well, reckon it's time for one o' us to see if we got any luck left. I'll see can I git outta here an' down to the stable without gittin' shot. I'll saddle our horses."

Getting the horses saddled and to the house would be the most ticklish part of the escape to Barnes's figuring. When he turned down the lantern and stepped out the door, Lambrey wished him luck.

Just before going out the door, he'd told his partner to be ready to grab for a stirrup as soon as he rode to the front of the house. He figured from that point it would be a horse race to get away.

He moved to the side of the house closest to the barn, stood there for several minutes waiting for his eyes to adjust to the dark, then stood there another fifteen or more minutes. During that time he searched every shadow, every inch of ground that came under his eyes. Finally satisfied he had the area to himself, he thought the riflemen out in the brush would have to have the eyesight of a cat, and the luck of the Irish, to hit him with any kind of shot. He sprinted for the stable.

He slowed to a walk before he could be brought up hard against the wooden side, then circled the rough wooden building to the back door, found it open, and smiled to himself with the thought that the two drovers who had been there had cut out. He slipped inside, stood still a few minutes, listening for deep breaths, cloth scraping along the rough boards, any sound that might indicate he didn't have the stable to himself. The scurrying of rats and the sighing of wind through the cracks were the only sounds that came to his ears.

He wished he dared light a lantern, but that would be pushing his luck too far. He'd have to trust his sense of touch, hope he could identify his and Lambrey's saddles in the dark, then get the horses saddled and to the front door of the house without being discovered.

He frowned into the darkness. The sounds, what was wrong with the sounds? His breath shortened. He listened, his ears searching, then knew what was missing. He should have heard the breathing, shifting of weight from one hoof to another, maybe a snuffle from the horses. Those were the sounds missing. Damn! Were they going to have to walk out of here? Trinidad was one helluva long way to walk.

To make sure the horses were only unusually quiet, he

moved to each stall, went in, hoping to feel the warmth of a big hairy body. After a complete search, he knew he and Lambrey would have a long walk. He thought about that a moment. Would it be better to wait until some of Fain's men came to take them? He thought about that, thought they'd be taking a big chance on getting killed no matter how Fain decided to try to capture them.

He decided to tell his partner what kind of fix they were in. He took as much time getting back to the house as it had taken him to get to the stable.

When he came up against the side of the house, he worked his way to the front door, tapped on it with his fingernails, and waited.

"Come on in, it's open."

"Don't shoot, partner. It's me, Barnes."

"Wait'll I douse the light, then come on in."

With Barnes still sliding through the doorway, Lambrey growled, "Where the hell's the horses?"

Barnes slipped into the darkened room. "Ain't no horses. Fain's done had 'em taken somewhere else." He waited a moment for that to sink in. "We either gonna have to walk outta here, an' it's a long way to Trinidad, or wait fer them men o' Cord's to come take us, or kill us. I'm for the long walk."

Silence reined for a long moment, then an explosive "Damn" came from Lambrey. Then he said, "Wait a minute, I'll light the lamp. We gotta talk 'bout this."

The sound of a lucifer scraped along cloth, light flared, then took hold on the wick, and they stared at each other. Barnes felt his lips crinkle at the corners; then he laughed. "Partner, if I wuzn't feelin' so damned dumb, I think I'd cry." He shrugged. "Fain's done out-figgered us at every corner."

Lambrey stared at his partner a moment, shook his head, obviously thinking he looked at a crazy man, then he too laughed. Maybe he was also a little on the short-brained side. "Wish to hell Fain had been in charge o' the herd we left the Big Bend with. I figger that cowboy would've gotten us to Montana without no trouble a-tall."

"Any o' that bottle left?" At Lambrey's nod, Barnes continued. "Let's pour us a *big* drink, then figger what we gonna do." He felt his shirt pocket, ran his fingers into it, and shook his head. "You got any smokin' tobacco left?"

His partner tossed him a half-empty sack of Bull Durham. "Keep it, I got another." While Barnes rolled his smoke, Lambrey poured them each a water glass full of Bob Tuttle's whiskey.

They sat there occasionally glancing at Taggart, who sat there gloating, a hard grin breaking the corners of his mouth. Barnes wanted to stand, walk to him, and slap his bullish looking face, but that wasn't his way—besides, he thought the bull of a man would whip him if he turned him loose so they could have a fair fight. His mama didn't raise any fools, so he ignored the trail boss.

They finished that drink, and were halfway through another, a lot of whiskey to Barnes's thinking, when Lambrey gave him a silly grin. "Know what, partner?" He shook his head. "I done got a mighty fine idear." His grin widened. "Sometimes outta a bottle o' whiskey comes some mighty damn smart thinkin'."

Barnes chuckled. "Somehow I figger this ain't one o' them times, after lookin' at that there dumb-ass grin you got plastered on yore ugly face." He shot Lambrey an exaggerated sigh. "All right, let's hear it."

Lambrey stared at his partner a long moment, then nodded. "Think you an' me both got Fain figgered for a fair gent. Right?" At Barnes' nod, he again grinned. "Know what I figger'll work?" Without waiting for Barnes' response, he nodded.

"I figger we can leave outta here right now, walk to where we figger Fain's set up camp. Course daylight's gonna catch us out there on wide open grass where we kin git shot right easy, but I don't b'lieve none o' that bunch he's got ridin' fer 'im would shoot a man without gittin' shot at first." He took a deep breath, then continued. "I think maybe you an' me can walk right into their camp, tell 'em what we done with Taggart, tell 'em we done made up our minds to head fer Texas, but they done took our horses, an if'n they'd give 'em back we'd be mighty happy." He shrugged. "Fact is, reckon I'd jest as soon they shoot me as to have to walk to town." He shook his head, knocked back the rest of his drink, poured them each another, and stared at his partner, obviously waiting for an answer, then apparently not being able to stand the suspense any longer, leaned forward. "Well, what you think?"

Barnes frowned into the now-full glass, set it on the floor at his feet, rolled a smoke, lit it, then let a smile spread across his face. "Damned if I don't think it'd work. Only reason I think that is, I figger Cord Fain's 'bout as decent a cow nurse as I ever seen." He nodded, wondering if maybe they weren't both a little more than drunk. Then he made a decision on that too. Yep, they were both drunker'n skunks.

Lambrey stood. "Reckon we better git goin'. We wait'll mornin' two things gonna happen. First off, we might git killed gittin' outta here; second, reckon if we waited till mornin', we'd be so damned sick from all this here whiskey we done drank, we'd jest flat sit here and let the time go away without makin' a try at gittin' outta here." He looked at Taggart. "Better check; see if that piece o' cow dung's still tied good's we had 'im."

Barnes stood, weaved a little, then went to Taggart's chair. He reached for the rags with which they'd tied the trail boss. Just as he was about to test them, the bull of a man came out of the chair swinging. His first punch dropped the slim puncher like a paddy from a tall cow. He turned toward Lambrey, and stared into the maw of his *segundo*'s Colt. He stopped, his face a shade paler.

"All right, now sit down. You step toward me an' I'll scatter yore brains all over this here room." He glanced at his partner. "You hurt, boy?"

Barnes shook his head. "Jest my feelin's. Now reckon I'm gonna find somethin' better to tie that garbage with."

With those words, he went to the storage cabinet and pulled things from the shelf. After rummaging through the contents of two shelves, he found a roll of sturdy cord, about a quarter of an inch thick.

He held it for Lambrey to look at. "Figger this here'll hold 'im." He grinned. "Course if he tugs agin it, it'll cut off blood goin' to 'is hands." He shook his head in mock sympathy. "Tch-tch. Now that'd be a shame. He might even lose them hands from lack o' blood."

14

AFTER TYING TAGGART securely, the two men searched the house for weapons and any ammunition. They found none. Then, with the trail boss's weapons slung across their shoulders, they stepped out the door together.

The two men slipped through the dark, and after maybe a hundred yards, Lambrey whispered, "Hope to hell we ain't walkin' right toward one o' Fain's men."

"Jest thinkin' 'bout that. We better hold down any noise we might make fer maybe 'nother quarter o' a mile. We both done fought Indians, so that might not be a problem."

After about an hour, with the eastern horizon promising a rising sun in the next half an hour or so, Lambrey straightened and looked at his partner. He smiled. "So far, so good. Don't think I coulda stayed stooped over much longer. I got a kink in my back that'll take one o' them saloon girls, a gallon o' whiskey, an' a long week to work its way out."

"Damn, me too, partner." They continued walking toward the northeast. "Shore hope we done picked the right direction; we ain't, an' we could be walkin' till next month."

Lambrey swung his gaze from north to south, then looked almost straight east. "Reckon if that there's a fire out yonder, we'll be comin' up on their camp a little after sunup." He shook his head. "You reckon they'll feed us, or jest tie us up an' let us starve?"

They turned their steps toward the faint flicker of firelight. Barnes shrugged. "If Fain or Cookie is in camp, they ain't gonna let us go hungry. They might not give us our horses, but they ain't gonna torture us neither."

Lambrey nodded. "Think you're right. That is, if Cookie hooked up with Fain."

Another hour and the two men were close to the fire. They held their hands high when they came within hailing distance. "Hello the camp," they yelled in unison.

"Come on in. We've had you in our sights for some few minutes now." Jed Mobley chuckled. "You can drop your hands; don't b'lieve either one o' you are dumb enough to pull iron in our camp."

"Don't figger to try shootin' none o' you anyway." Barnes, always hungry, glanced at Cookie. "You gonna let us eat, Cookie?"

"Don't see no reason to keep you away from the feed trough." Cookie frowned, studied them a moment. "You ain't got no eatin' gear so you gonna have to wait'll one o' the crew gits done eatin'." He grinned. "What y'all doin' walkin' round out yonder in the dark with no hosses?"

Lambrey shrugged. "Reckon y'all kin answer that better'n we can. Figger you folks done took our hosses. Too, I don't give a damn 'bout waitin' fer eatin' gear long's I know you ain't gonna starve us."

Lambrey glanced around the circle of riders, then realized he knew only Cookie and Mobley. "Fain anywhere around?"

The slim man, Mobley, who most of Taggart's crew had figured as a gunfighter, nodded. "Yeah, he's around, went into town yesterday, should be back 'bout noon. What you want with 'im?"

Lambrey looked at Mobley. "Figgerd to ask 'im fer our

horses, then head outta the country, if he wuz of a mind to let us."

Mobley gave the man who had been the *segundo* of the trail crew a hard look. "What makes you think Fain's in charge o' this bunch?"

Lambrey shot Mobley a thin, cold smile, then swung a glance at the circle of men about him. "Well, tell you how it is; I don't recognize none o' these men here, but Fain knowed Blackjack Slade there outside o' Cimarron, an' if he knowed *him*, I figger he could round up a right salty crew. This here crew you got round you is, from first look, a right hard bunch."

Even though the night had cooled the morning air, the *segundo* sweated, and it wasn't all caused from the long walk. He pushed his hat to the back of his head. "Way I got it figgered, Fain's in charge o' these here men."

The slim gunfighter chuckled. "You got 'im pegged right to a T." He nodded. "Yep, he's in charge, so you gonna have to wait for your answer. Menendez over yonder's runnin' things till he gets back."

The weathered Mexican nodded. "You men leave yore guns here in camp. I'm gonna put you to work till we see what Cord says. He's a right notional waddy." He chuckled. "Hell, he might even decide to shoot you—or give you a job." He shook his head sadly. "Cain't never tell 'bout that boy."

Barnes cut in. "I never figgered Fain as one to shoot a man without givin' 'im a chance, so what makes you think he could beat either one o' us?"

"Tell you what, young'un. Cord Fain could face both o' you at the same time, give you the draw, an' still beat you."

Barnes looked at Lambrey. "What'd I tell you? I figgered he wuz a right handy man with a gun even though he never wore one."

The trail *segundo* nodded. "Way I had 'im figgered."

Frog Ballew scrubbed out his eating gear with sand, and handed it to Lambrey. "Jest set it over yonder when you git through. I'm gonna git me a cup o' coffee right now, then

I'll rope you a horse so's you kin hep us git these cows branded. Fain should oughta be here when we come in for our noonin'."

Through the morning, they sweated, cursed, gathered layers of dust into the sweat, and branded as many as forty heifers and bulls.

When the sun stood straight overhead, Menendez motioned them toward the chuck wagon. "Let's eat." Then he looked at the two latest escapees from Taggart's crew. He shot them a hard grin. "Figgered you two as bein' top hands." He shook his head. "Ain't never been wrong."

When they rode to the wagon, Fain sat in its shade. While the men filled their tin plates and started eating, Cord pinned his look on Lambrey and Barnes. "Cookie told me 'bout y'all. What took you so long to break loose?"

Barnes gave Cord a straight-on look. "Had to wait fer a chance to get a gun on 'im without one o' us gittin' a dose o' lead." He shrugged. "Soon's we had a chance, we done it." He grimaced. "Too, I reckon we figgered to git our pay 'fore we left. We got it right down to the cent what wuz owed us, no more, 'fore we cut outta there."

Fain nodded. "Never had either one o' you figured for a crook. Glad to hear you took only what was owed you."

"You gonna let us have our horses, Fain?"

"They're right there in the cavvy. Figure the men been usin' 'em since they didn't have y'all to ride 'em." He grinned. "Done wore 'em down a bit." He nodded. "Good cow ponies."

Lambrey glanced at Barnes, who gave him a slight nod. "You let us have 'em back, Cord, an' we'll work a few days fer you for nothin' 'cept grub."

Fain studied the fire a few moments, then looked up. "Gonna be a couple o' days 'fore I can leave here. Gotta take those two men an' their rifles away from the ranch house 'fore I let y'all ride in there to get your gear; they might take a few shots at you. I figger saddles, bridles, sad-

dle scabbards, even yore bedrolls are still there. No point
in wastin' men watchin' over Taggart."

He thought a moment, shook his head, and looked at
Lambrey. "You say you took his weapons 'fore you left,
an' left 'im tied tight enough to cause 'im to really suffer?"

The *segundo* nodded.

"Gonna let 'im go 'fore 'is hands rot off," said Fain.
"Ain't gonna give 'im a horse, though. Maybe he'll head
for Texas soon's he can find a horse."

Barnes shook his head. "Fain, that man, ever time yore
name is said round 'im, he gits so mad he looks like he's
gonna choke. He hates you worse'n poison. He ain't gonna
leave without he faces you."

Cord let a cold smile break the corners of his lips. "Way
I had *that* figured too. That's really the only reason I'd let
'im go."

Lambrey's eyes never left Fain's. "Cord, I kinda got you
figgered as pretty good with that gun I ain't never seen you
wear before. Now I'm gonna lay it out barefaced. The men
say you're right good with it; now I'm askin', you any
good with it?"

Before Cord could answer, Frog Ballew cut in. "He ain't
gonna tell you, he ain't one to brag, but I will; he's good,
damned good. Menendez done told y'all how good. You
can b'lieve 'im."

The trail herd *segundo* frowned, studied Fain a moment,
shook his head. "Why for you gonna let 'im go?"

Cord chuckled. "Not 'cause I feel sorry for 'im. Nothin'
like that. It's only because keepin' 'im will be more trouble
than lettin' 'im go. I'd have to have somebody watchin' 'im
round the clock; have to feed 'im." He shook his head.
"Yeah, be a lot easier to head 'im out.

"I got an idea he won't leave here without facin' me, so I
won't be takin' much of a gamble he'll keep goin'." He
shrugged. "Figure by the time he gets to Trinidad he's
gonna be so damned mad at me, he'd wait'll hell froze over
'fore he'd cut out without tryin' to shoot me."

Lambrey chuckled. "You can bet yore saddle on that." He frowned. "Sounded while ago like you gonna drive some o' these cows to Dodge, that right?"

Fain nodded, shrugged, and said, "Either there or Denver. Why?"

"Well—two reasons. First one is, I don't want to run into Taggart agin; we'd have a gunfight an' I don't cotton to havin' to kill nobody else. Second, if you go to Dodge, let us ride with you. We might be able to hook on with one o' them south Texas trail crews till we got back to Texas.

"Wouldn't figger on gittin' no job with 'em, but crossin' Comanche land with a bunch like that would be a lot safer'n tryin' it alone." A slight smile broke the corners of his lips. "You gonna take Cookie with you?"

"Figured on it."

Lambrey chuckled. "Well, that brings on a third reason. You let us ride with you, I know we gonna eat mighty good on the way. Don't figger on no pay from you, jest wanta ride along."

Fain frowned. "Tell you what, you an' Barnes go with us I'll pay you drover's pay till we get there, buck a day and found." He thought a moment, then added, "That way I can leave a couple more men here to help Bob Tuttle git things back to normal."

Lambrey glanced at Barnes, then back to Cord. "You done hired yoreself a couple of drovers."

Fain glanced at Menendez. "Soon's yore noonin's over y'all get back with the cattle. I'm gonna go to the ranch house, send those two standin' watch back to you, an' turn Taggart loose."

He shook his head. "Not gonna give 'im a horse, so I'll ride alongside of 'im till we get mighty near to Trinidad, then I'll leave 'im." He toed the stirrup, and looked down at Menendez. "Lambrey and Barnes won't either one be much worth a damn workin' those cows without their saddles an' lariats, so I'll take 'em with me. They oughta be back by mid-afternoon."

Another hour and Fain, Barnes, and Lambrey were

halfway to the house. Trig rode up alongside Cord. "Hope he ain't got away. He's mean 'nuff he'd burn the house 'fore he left."

Fain slanted him a look. "Even if he gets outta the ropes you tied 'im with, he ain't gonna go outside without gettin' shot all to hell." He shook his head. "Nope, he hasn't gone anywhere. Gonna let y'all get your gear an' ride away 'fore I bring Taggart out, so soon's we get there get on into the stable, throw your kak on your horses, and get gone."

He rode with the two men until they slanted off toward the stable, then held an arm above his head and signaled the two men on watch to come to him.

It took them a few minutes to get to their horses; while he waited, Fain packed his pipe and lighted it. As soon as they rode up, he grinned at them. "See those two men that rode in with me?"

They both nodded, but Shelton frowned when he did. "Yeah, we seen 'em. They wuzn't none o' our men. Who were they?"

"Well, one was Taggart's *segundo*, the other was Trig Barnes, also one o' my ex–trail boss's men. They just simply walked outta that house 'bout three o'clock this mornin'. I let 'em go to the stable to get their bedrolls an' such. They gonna ride for me till we get to Dodge City."

He nodded toward the house. "Taggart should still be in the house. They didn't leave 'im with any weapons, so I'm goin' in there.

"Shelton, want you to ride to the cabin an' bring those folks back here. Reckon Miss Eve can set up housekeepin' again. You, Slim, get on out to the chuck wagon, they need you."

He told them he would escort Taggart to within a mile or two of town, turn him loose, then head back to the herd. "Tell the folks back at the cabin we'll see 'em 'fore we head for Dodge."

He watched them split, one going to the cabin, the other for the grueling work at the roundup. He walked his horse to the front of the house, tied him to the hitching post, and walked to the door.

He pulled his Colt before pushing into the big family room. If Taggart had managed to get loose, Cord knew he couldn't fight him as weak as he was. The time would come when he would be strong again, but he couldn't stand a fist fight or knife fight now.

The door swung wide, and the first thing he saw was the trail boss, tied tight to the chair. If the poison Taggart stared at him could kill, Fain knew he'd be dead meat.

He glanced at the three wounded men lying on the floor, looked from them to Taggart, then swung his eyes back to the man in the middle of those lying there, a man Cord had known as Bennett. His eyes stared at the ceiling, eyes that would never see again. Fain looked at Taggart. "How long's Bennett been dead?"

The bull of a man only stared at him. "Okay, Trail Boss, you don't need to talk. Soon's Tuttle's crew gets here, I'll have them take 'im outta here 'fore the ladies get here." He looked at the grandfather clock sitting against the wall: four o'clock. Too late to start walking Taggart back to town.

"Gonna cut you loose from that chair, leave your hands tied behind you, take you to the barn an' tie you to whatever I figure'll hold you till daylight, then you an' me gonna head for Trinidad—me ridin', you walkin'."

"You think I'm gonna walk to town, you're crazy as hell."

Cord chuckled. "You'll walk, or I'll drag you at the end o' my rope. Your choice."

The blood that had been threatening to pump right through Taggart's skin receded. His face paled, then paled even more. His lids closed to slits over his eyes. "Gonna kill you, Fain. Gonna gutshoot you, then cut yore laigs out from under you an' stand there an' watch you die slow-like. Gonna do it right there in the middle o' town where everybody can see I give you a even break."

"Been kinda hopin' you'd see it that way, boss man. That way I know you'll still be there when I get back."

"Get back? Where you goin'?"

Fain stared at him a long moment. "Tell you that when I get back—just before I kill you. Right now, shut the hell up. Gonna sit here an' wait'll Bob Tuttle's men get here." He went to a chair, spun it around, and straddled it. He didn't dare get too comfortable; he felt like he'd never known a bed, never relaxed, and if he did now he'd go to sleep and sleep forever. Those bullets had taken a lot out of him, and he'd had some long days since then.

Finally, the drum of hooves broke the stillness of the hot late summer day. He stood, hoping the womenfolk had ridden the wagon. He needed time to get Bennett out of the house and away from the buildings. He got lucky. Four of Tuttle's riders rode up.

He told them to take the body out of the house, get it buried, then to drag, or carry Taggart, chair and all, to the stable. That he'd take it from there. He stood in the yard thinking to see the wagon in only a few minutes. For some reason he wanted to see Ruth. He shook his head, then chuckled; he must be a brute for punishment. He puffed on his pipe and waited.

When the wagon came into sight, Fain saw that Ruth held the reins. In only a few minutes, she drew the team to a stop alongside him. She raked her eyes from his boots to his head, then pinned him with a hard look. "See you ain't managed to get any more holes in you."

He nodded. "Good to see you too, ma'am, don't know what I'd do without a cheery greetin' ever' time I see you."

Still giving him a hard look, she nodded. "You earn them greetin's the hard way, Cord Fain; it ain't as though I wouldn't like to look at you an' not have the question in my mind are you all right."

He shrugged, then glanced toward the house. "Y'all got a couple o' guests in the family room. They're lyin' on the floor, need some bandagin' done to their legs. Soon's they're able to ride I'll send 'em on their way."

He twisted to turn his steps toward the stable, then turned back. "Those men who need care are the ones we shot up at their camp the first night. They been hurtin' a mighty long time without anybody takin' care of 'em. They're not bad, just took a slight bend in the trail that wasn't right." Not waiting for her reply, he headed for the barn.

Inside, he checked the ropes around Taggart, found them secure, then pulled some hay into a pile and sat. He only sat there a few minutes before his eyelids got so heavy, he knew it would be only a short time before he gave in and went to sleep. He stood, walked to the door, and hailed one of Tuttle's hands. "Come on in the barn. Got a job for you."

As soon as the rider came in the stable, Cord pointed to Taggart. "Want you to keep watch on that man. He's the one who caused us all the trouble." He walked to the hay he'd pulled into a pile only a few moments before, sat, then lay down. "I gotta sleep a little while. You begin to feel sleepy, get one o' the other men out here. Don't want that man to get away till I walk 'im outta here." He pulled his hat over his face and went to sleep before his hands fell to the dirt floor.

He came awake with a soft touch on his shoulder. "Hated to wake you, Cord, but figgered you wouldn't want to miss supper." Fain pushed his hat off his face, stared up into Ruth's eyes, and smiled. "Mighty nice way to wake up, ma'am, seein' you lookin' down at me."

He'd expected a sharp-tongued retort. Instead, she stared at him a moment, gave him a soft look, and said, "We gonna talk 'bout that soon's we take that walk together." Without further words, she spun and left the stable.

He stared at her departing figure. Despite the fact that she sometimes acted more like a cowboy than a girl, the beautiful sway of her hips was utterly feminine. He wished that talk she'd mentioned at least a couple of time could be now—but he had more work to do, and something to settle in Trinidad as soon as he got back from the trail drive.

He rolled to his side, flinched with pain, stood, and went to the pump.

After washing most of the dust from his face, he ran his fingers through wet hair, looked toward the house, then hesitated. He'd vowed to himself that he'd never set foot in that place as long as Tuttle's sharp-tongued daughter was there. He shrugged. Hell, sometimes a man lied to himself. He headed for the house.

Tuttle met him at the door. "Come on in, boy. We'll have a drink 'fore supper. I had a bottle in the cupboard, but some o' Taggart's crew drank it, left me a couple o' dollars in payment, but I had one hid outside." He gave a nod. "Reckon the womenfolk gonna have one with us seein' as how this's sort o' a celebration gittin' back in our home. The boys're gonna eat in here with us since you took Cookie to the chuck wagon. Eve an' Ruth cooked supper fer us."

From the kitchen door, Ruth spoke up. "Notice Pa included me when he said who cooked supper."

Cord looked toward her, then trying to hold a straight face, shook his head. "Yes'm, I heard 'im, came danged nigh to headin' back to the barn an' fixin' my own grub—but figured that would be downright impolite." He shook his head. "Sure is a puzzle what a man'll put 'imself through for the sake o' bein' nice."

She didn't clench her fists. Her face didn't flush. Her mouth didn't press into a straight-lipped line. She just stood there, a smile softening and lighting her face, then turned back into the kitchen and a moment later came out, a water glass in her hand with what looked to be straight whiskey filling it. "Thought you might need this to ease the disappointment of you not being able to get my goat."

Fain let a slight smile crinkle the corners of his eyes. "Yes'm, reckon it'll help some, but it might even take two like that to do the trick." She laughed and handed him his drink.

After a couple of drinks, in which the ladies joined the men, they sat to eat. After eating, sitting with full coffee cups in front of them, Tuttle looked at Fain.

"Reckon since you're still runnin' things round here, you might tell me what you got on your mind to do next?"

"Well, first thing, Bob, I'm gonna *walk* Taggart to just this side o' town an' cut 'im loose; then I'm gonna drive the herd to Dodge, come back, an' wrap things up round here." He shrugged. "Figure I'll have done what I came here to do, so I'll head for home, buy me some land, an' settle down to a life of sheer boredom."

"You walk Taggart to Trinidad, he's gonna be waitin' for you when you get back," Ruth said, she took a sip of her coffee, then gave him a straight-on look. "Meetin' him is part o' what you mean when you say you gonna wrap things up around here, ain't it?"

"Ruth, that man hates me enough right now that you couldn't drive 'im toward Texas without he meets me first." He shook his head. "It's somethin' I gotta do, ma'am."

Her face turned a few shades whiter. She didn't argue about it. She only nodded, then looked into her cup. Cord would have sworn her eyes flooded with tears. He turned to look at Tuttle.

"Bob, since Taggart's gonna be roamin' round loose, reckon it would be a good idea to keep one o' your boys on watch every night till I can get back an' get all the loose ends tied together." He drank the last of his coffee and stood. All the "guests" had left except Pam and Tommy. He moved his eyes to Mrs. Tuttle.

"Sure enjoyed the meal, Miss Eve." He grinned. "Even that part that Ruth cooked. Reckon I won't be seein' y'all till I get back from Dodge."

Abruptly, Ruth pushed her chair back and stood. "You gonna let me walk to the barn with you?" Her eyes begged him.

"Ma'am, I surely will if you promise to let me steer the conversation. There's things you an' I need to talk 'bout, but this isn't the time."

Without breaking her gaze, she nodded. "If that's the way it's gotta be, Cord Fain, we won't even say nothin' if you say so."

He put his hat on, settled it in place, and held his arm out for her to take. At the same time, he noticed Tuttle frowned deeply—but Miss Eve had a slight smile breaking the corners of her lips. Her face glowed.

True to her word, Ruth and Cord said nothing until they stopped short of the barn door. He swallowed, finding it hard to let her go back to the house. "Ruth, wanta tell ya, I got a lot to say to you when I get back, but now just flat isn't the time."

"I know, Cord. When you get back, maybe you'll take a long walk with me an' we'll talk—just long's you want; or maybe long's I tell you it's gotta be 'fore I let you go." She turned from him and, almost running, headed for the house. He stood there and watched until she opened the door and disappeared inside.

As soon as she closed the door behind her, her mother said, "Mighty short walk." There was disappointment in her voice.

Her father cut in. "Jest 'bout long enough. I wuz 'bout ready to come lookin' fer you."

Ruth stopped and pinned her father with a don't-argue-with-me look. "Pa, next time Cord an' me take a walk together, you ain't gonna come lookin' for me. We gonna take a long walk, jest long's Cord wants it to be, an' maybe till I let 'im leave me if that's the way he wants it."

"G-g-girl, don't you talk to me like . . ."

"Bob Tuttle, that's enough. Our daughter's a grown woman. We've raised her right. I ain't worried 'bout her one ounce. If she wants to take a walk with a young man, especially *that* young man, we ain't gonna say one word 'bout it. Know what I'm tellin' you?"

About the same time, they all seemed to remember that Pam and Tommy were in the room. The little boy sat huddled close to his mother, his eyes as round as saucers. With an embarrassed chuckle, Pam took a swallow of coffee, then looked at Ruth. "Sounds like you an' me's got the same sort o' problem."

Ruth shook her head. "Nope, we ain't. You ever take a close look at the way yore man looks at you? If you ain't, you better start payin' closer attention to 'im." She grinned. "I guarantee you they's one member o' your family who's already made up *his* mind."

Pam put her arm around Tommy and pulled him closer to her. She chuckled. "His ma's done made up her mind too, but she's gotta wait an' see if any nice words get said. Ain't rightly proper fer her to say anythin' till then."

Ruth looked at her, an intent look that speared right into her friend's soul. "Gonna tell you somethin', Pam. Nice words be damned. If he don't say 'em, you say 'em." She stood back and looked defiantly at her father, as though daring him to say otherwise. "That's what I'm gonna do, an I don't care who don't like it."

Her father sank back in his chair; her mother beamed like the sun had only then broken through clouds on a rainy day. Pam stared at her friend as though she'd never seen her before, then broke into a deep-throated laugh. She laughed until tears streamed down her cheeks. "Sounds like them men got no chance at all."

Not knowing his fate was being sealed inside the ranch house, Cord told the man watching Taggart to go to the bunkhouse and roust out his relief; then he pulled the pile of hay into a more comfortable-looking pile, checked the trail boss's bindings, and lay down to wait until the next guard came in.

The next morning before daylight, Cord saddled his horse, untied the rope that held Taggart in the chair, put his lariat around the beefy man's waist, and led him from the stable.

Before leaving the barn, Fain filled a canteen and hung it from the trail boss's belt. "That's all you gonna get, so make it last. I ride, you walk."

It took two days for Fain to get Taggart close enough to Trinidad to cut him loose. In those two days Fain's ex-boss cursed him with every name Fain had ever heard, and many he thought he'd never hear again. Cord only gave him a cold smile each time the man started a new tirade, and reminded him that all that talking would make his throat drier—and that he wasn't going to get more water. By the time they were about three miles outside of town, Taggart's voice sounded like a frog's croak to Fain.

He reined in, stepped from the saddle, and when close to the man, ordered him to turn his back to him. He loosened the lariat from Taggart's waist, and allowed it to drop to the ground around his feet. "Step outta the loop, keep your back to me, and I'll cut your wrists loose. You even make like you gonna turn to look at me, I'll slam this .44 against that thick skull you been carryin' round for some few years."

With Taggart walking free, Fain toed the stirrup, and rode a wide loop around him. "See ya in 'bout a month, or a little more. I'll be in Trinidad when you're ready."

Cord thought to head back to the herd, changed his mind, and reined toward Trinidad. He wanted to see Worley.

Less than an hour later, he walked into Worley's office. After the routine greetings, and with a cup of coffee in front of each of them, Fain told the marshal all that had happened in only the few days since he'd seen him last, then took a sip of coffee and stared at his friend. "Worley, know you got the paperwork in your drawer there to arrest Taggart, but I'm askin' you to not take any action on it. I'm askin' you to wait'll I get back—be 'bout a month, maybe a little more, then I'll be in town an' we'll talk 'bout it. All right?"

"Done made up my mind to play it your way, Cord. If I'm *reeeeal* wrong, I'll turn in my badge." He grinned across the scarred old oaken desk. "Notice I said *reeeal* wrong?"

Fain shot him a slight smile. "Noticed you sortta stressed the word, Tom. 'Preciate you givin' me a shot at settlin' this my way." He stood. "Gotta get goin'. My men figure I'm sittin' out here loafin' till they get all the work done. There's some mighty fine men in that bunch, men I want to think well o' me. Not gonna do anythin' to change their opinion."

Only half of the sun was still above the western mountains, and Fain lusted for a good bath and a soft hotel bed, but he didn't want to be in town after Taggart had a chance to buy a gun, and Taggart would be walking into town in short order. Fain walked to his horse and left town.

He thought to ride to the chuck wagon, crawl into the back of it, and get some sleep, but it would be morning before he got to camp. There wouldn't be a chance to sleep then; he'd work with the crew. A couple of hours out of town he made camp, careful to be far enough out that Taggart wouldn't cross his trail.

15

BACK AT THE herd the days melded into a couple of weeks. The men came to the chuck wagon every night bone-tired, dirty, and getting leaner and meaner every day. Finally, Fain called Mobley to him. "Not takin' you on the drive, Jed. Figure you gonna be mighty busy gettin' yours and Pam's cattle back to her range; they're all branded an' ready to fatten up a little 'fore winter sets in."

Fain chuckled. "If you haven't said anythin' to her 'bout y'all ridin' in double harness by then, reckon I'll just have to say it for you."

"Aw, hell, Fain, you wouldn't do that—would you?"

Cord sobered. "Tell you for a fact, my friend, I damn sure would, so you better get the right words said."

Mobley's face, under all the dirt and dust, turned white as bread dough. "Cord, she might not take kindly to me sayin' those words to her." His shoulders slumped. "Hell, Cord, I'd jest as soon face three men in a gunfight, at the same time, as stand there an' have 'er tell me no."

Not giving Jed any slack, Fain stared at him steely-eyed. "I'll be gone 'bout a month. Git it done. Gonna check soon's I get back." He stood to get himself another cup of coffee, then looked at Jed. "Pick yourself a couple of men to help drive your herd, then keep 'em there to get things runnin' good till I show up."

The next morning, Cookie had left camp with the chuck wagon a couple of hours before Fain got the herd strung out and moving east. The old man would have their noon-ing ready by the time they caught up with him.

Mobley was headed for Pam's homestead. He'd taken three men to help drive that bunch of cattle, and the mixed herd Cord had kept for himself soon scattered on Tuttle's grass. Those cattle Fain figured to sell would bring much-needed money to them all.

Cord made sure the cattle were moving well, then leaving Menendez in charge, rode out ahead of the herd and soon passed Cookie and the chuck wagon.

He'd never taken a herd over this route, but knew they'd be crossing Kiowa and Comanche hunting grounds. If the Indians they met were hunting parties, he had enough men to handle them if they wanted a fight, but a war party would cause him some discomfort. He chuckled to him-self; discomfort was a pretty mild word to define what he'd feel.

The smell of grass dried in the summer heat, mixed with dust, was a smell he knew well. Despite the unsea-sonal rain they'd had this year, the land dried quickly, and dust already boiled under the hooves of the slow-moving herd.

The feeling of again doing the things he liked lulled him into a false sense of security. He jerked his head impa-tiently, and centered in on the job at hand; all of the fight-ing might not be behind him.

He kept his eyes searching the long rolling plains. He looked for rising dust more than he did mounted warriors. Any hostiles in their path would not allow themselves to be seen, but keeping their ponies from raising dust clouds would be impossible.

He ranged out ahead of the herd as much as four or five miles by his best guess, held that distance until the sun positioned itself about an hour from straight overhead, then turned back.

The better-than-usual rainfall kept Fain from worrying much about the chance for grass fires. But despite the amount of rain, he still worried. He studied the grass, stepped from his saddle, pulled a few blades, and checked them for brittleness. He nodded. Good, they were not entirely dry. He toed the stirrup and rode westerly.

The chuck wagon's white canvas top showed long before the rest of it rose out of the distance. He drew alongside it at the same time he saw the point riders appear.

They let the cattle graze while they ate; then back in the saddle, they got the herd moving again. Fain wanted to let the cattle drift, snatch a mouthful of grass, and amble along. He thought to make about ten miles a day; that way he'd keep as much tallow on their bones as possible. Fat meant money at trail's end.

That night, after posting the night herders, Fain gathered the rest of the crew about him. "Gonna tell you men the rules in a town like Dodge. Gonna tell you 'cause most o' you came West with Pa right after the War 'Tween the States, an' haven't ever been to these towns with a large herd."

He packed his pipe, lighted it, then swept them with a look that said he didn't like the rules, but they were in place and had been for several years. He nodded. "The rules I'm talkin' 'bout were set up 'cause of the way most trail crews behave when they get to town after months of no whiskey, no women"—he grinned—"an' not many fights.

"I'm gonna ask y'all to stay south o' the tracks when we get to Dodge. All that stuff I'm talkin' 'bout is available if you don't cross the railroad tracks; an' the law won't interfere with you havin' a good time. But you get north o' the tracks an' you're gonna be in trouble. Don't know who's the town marshal now, but long's you don't break the rules he'll leave you alone."

Fain knew what the banty-legged little cowboy, Shelton, would say before he said anything. The sly smile he cast Cord said it all. "Boss, I got a question. If they's women an' whiskey on the south side o' the tracks, why the hell would any good cowboy in 'is right mind ever go north o' the tracks?"

Fain grinned. "Been wonderin' that myself, Gene." He shook his head. "But you never know what kinda twisted ideas some men'll get—'specially after they've had a woman an' a few drinks." He shrugged. "Reckon they just get to wonderin' what's over the next hill." He shook his head. "Or maybe if they got a mean streak runnin' through 'em, they just go lookin' for trouble." He frowned. "A streak like that'll get you killed deader'n last year's grass."

"Naw, Boss, you don't need to worry," Menendez said. "We gonna do jest like you spiked it out." He smiled. "Gonna see to it myself, 'specially since I done told the men you wuz gonna take us to Trinidad, pay all the bills, an' let us raise hell 'fore we get on the trail to Coyote."

Fain stared at his old friend. Pablo Menendez had been almost as much a father to him as had Pa. He let a thin smile break the corners of his eyes. "Good. Since I kind o' figured to pay y'all when we got back to Coyote, I can take that party outta your pay."

Pablo's grin widened. "Cord, we wuzn't 'spectin' to git no pay noway, so don't figger that's gonna eat at our gizzard much."

Satisfied that his men would do as he said, Fain beat them all to their blankets. He'd put in a long day's work, riding twice as far as his drovers.

In the days that followed, they crossed Apishap Creek, which still had a little water running in it due to the latest rains, then a couple more creeks with less water, then the Purgatoire River, where they watered the herd and let them graze a day before heading them out again.

At the Purgatoire, the men enjoyed the water as much as the cattle. They bathed, washed their clothes, most of them not bothering to take off anything but their boots and hats. They splashed water on each other, pushed some under the muddy stream, and all in all, acted like youngsters. Cord broke out a couple of bottles of good bourbon for the occasion. Then the next morning, back to the grind.

The herd tracked northeast, crossed the north fork of the Cimarron, then Crooked Creek, and Cord bedded them down a mile or so south of Dodge. He glanced at the sun. Almost high noon. He might get business taken care of before sundown.

It had taken them a little more than three weeks on the drive, but would take much less time heading home without the cattle to slow them down.

Fain dug in his money belt and gave his crew each thirty dollars to spend while he tried to find a buyer for the herd.

He washed most of his dust and dirt off with water from his canteen, rolled a change of clean clothes and tucked it under his arm, toed the stirrup, and headed for the hotel. He'd find a buyer there, and if not there, he was certain to find one in the Long Branch Saloon.

He didn't find what he wanted at the hotel. Before looking in the saloons, he stopped at the barbershop and bought the works: shave, shampoo, bath. Now clean enough that he figured the *decent* citizens of the town wouldn't smell him coming from a mile away, he headed for Front Street, where most of the saloons were.

As soon as he pushed through the batwing doors, he saw a buyer, Bubba Atkins. He'd tried to do business with the man before, and knew he'd be offered the lowest price per head for his cattle. He'd take them back to Colorado before he'd sell to the man—but at least he'd see what Atkins had to offer.

Atkins glanced his way, turned his head to look past him, then turned his look back to Cord. He knocked back his drink, put his glass on the bar, and walked toward Fain, his hand extended. "Fain, good to see you. You up here with a herd?"

Cord nodded. "Yep, an' from the looks of it we're the first ones up the trail." He grinned. "Reckon you'll offer best price, right?"

Atkins shook his head. "Fain, you know danged well, to get here first you probably ran most o' the tallow off those cows."

While the buyer still uttered his words of despair, Cord slowly shook his head. "Nope. Fact is, I'd say every head I bedded down out yonder is carryin' more weight than when we left home. If you're really interested, let's walk out yonder an' take a look at 'em." He wanted to see what Atkins offered so he'd have a starting price to begin negotiating with the buyers who weren't so stingy with a buck.

The buyer nodded. "Let's take a look."

It took only a few minutes for them to ride back to the herd. While Atkins studied the cattle, Fain studied Atkins. The buyer's eyes widened; then he closed his lids down to slits and looked at Fain. "How many head you bring in?"

"'Bout twenty-five hunnerd head, give or take a few."

The buyer frowned, studied his boot toe a moment, then pinned Fain with a look that said he'd make one offer. "Yeah, they're in a little better shape than I figgered 'em to be, an' you're the first herd up the trail; how's twenty-three a head sound?"

Cord stared at the man. His lips quivered, then he laughed, sucked it in, couldn't hold it back, and guffawed. He sobered. "Atkins, I knew when we rode out here I was wastin' my time. You're not even close to what I figure on gettin'."

Atkins' face flushed a bright red. "Fain, the Eastern market is down. We ain't payin' as much this year as we wuz last year when you wuz up here."

Fain sobered, nodded, and swept the herd with a glance. "Tell you how it is, Atkins. You may be right, but I think I'll talk to a couple more buyers. Figure if I don't get more'n you offered, I'll drive 'em back home. If Deak Talbert's in town, he'll treat me right." He reined his horse back toward town. "Gonna go cut some o' this dust outta my throat now."

Fain left the cattle buyer sitting there staring at his back.

Fain found Talbert and two other buyers in the cafe a couple of doors from the hotel. "What you city folk doin' sittin' here on your duffs? You oughta be out yonder lookin' at my cows, see which one o' you is gonna give me the best price."

After the greetings ceased, Talbert glanced at the other two buyers. "He always starts off like this to make sure he gets as deep in our pockets as his hand'll reach." He looked back at Cord. "What you doin' gettin' here this early? We thought it'd be maybe another week before herds started to show up."

"Long story, Deak. I'll tell you 'bout it after we get business taken care of. Buy you a drink then."

Fain looked at the other two buyers. "Why don't the three o' ya come on out; we can take a look together."

Talbert grimaced. "Know what he wants to do? He wants to get us to biddin' against each other."

"Nope, just tryin' to save goin' out yonder several times. You can give me your offer separately, okay?"

Talbert stood. "Let's go."

A few minutes later, the three buyers, standing shoulder to shoulder, their eyes ranging over the cattle, some grazing, others lying down chewing their cud, looked at each other, then at Fain. Cord could see the question in all their eyes, but Talbert put it into words. "How'd you get 'em here in this good a shape? Hell, they look like you jest now drove 'em in from the pasture."

Fain grinned. "That's part o' the story I'll tell y'all over a bottle o' good bourbon. You've seen 'em, now let's get back to the Long Branch while you think 'bout what kinda offer to make."

After a few drinks Talbert's two companions made Cord

an offer. Then Talbert, after they'd said they couldn't go higher, asked Fain if he had a couple of hands who'd be willing to ride the cars to Chicago with the cattle.

Cord frowned, then thought a moment, figured Frog Ballew and Gene Shelton would jump at the chance to see the bright lights for a change, then nodded. "Yeah, I figure most of 'em would. You'd have to make it worth their while, plus train fare back as far as end o' track."

Talbert laughed. "You don't miss a bet, do you, Cord?" Then, not waiting for an answer, he nodded. "Of course I'll take care of them. Don't dare to let you tie their expenses onto what my final offer is." He frowned, then gave a nod as though to say he agreed with what he was thinking, then gave Fain a straight-on look. "Twenty-eight a head."

The other two shook their heads, and one of them, Stumpy Jones, shrugged. "Can't beat that. I gave you the best offer I'm allowed to make. Tell you one thing, though. The shape those cows are in, they're worth every cent Talbert's payin' you." He cleared his throat. "Let's have another drink."

The next day, the count made, the herd in the holding pens, the money paid, and Ballew and Shelton having agreed to nursemaid the cattle to Chicago, with the promise they had a job when they got back to Coyote, Fain told the crew they'd spend one more night in town, then head back to Colorado.

After getting Pam's cattle to the homestead, and driven to the backside of her range, close to one of the shallow valleys in which he wanted them to winter, Jed Mobley killed all the time he could before going back to Tuttle's ranch to escort Pam and Tommy home.

He wanted, desperately, to be with Pam, but had to plan some way to get around to asking her the question Cord said he'd ask her if he, Mobley, didn't.

He sat by a lonely fire the second night after letting the small herd spread out on Pam's grass. He stared into the flames, something he would never do if he'd been out on the plains where the Kiowa, Comanche, and Apache roamed; or if they'd not settled with Taggart.

He ran every reason he could think of through his mind that might cause Pam to tell him no. Suppose she told him she didn't think of him the way he hoped she did. Suppose she told him thanks for what he'd done for her and Tommy, but she'd rather he saddled up and rode on. Suppose-suppose-suppose . . .

Finally, after taking as much time as he thought he could get away with, he rode toward the Lazy T to let the chips fall where they would. That was what he told himself he'd do, but he knew better.

He mentally shook his head. He thought of all the situations he'd been through without giving them a second thought. He'd been reared by a good family, and had been versed in the polished way of standing around a drawing room making idle conversation, he'd faced dangerous men in gunfights, he'd been through pure hell in the War Between the States, he'd fought Indians, been in stampedes, suffered through droughts, been in grass fires—hell, he'd been through it all, and here he was, terrified to say a few words to the one woman who meant more to him than all the world, and when he boiled it all down, what he feared most was a little two-letter word—"No."

His line-backed dun, without being reined in any direction, walked into the stable at the Lazy T before Jed became aware of where he was. He pulled the gear off his horse and swung it over one of the stall rails, then cocked his head to listen to the light patter of small feet running from the house. Then Tommy launched himself into Mobley's arms.

"Oh, Mr. Jed, I wuz so afeared you'd done rode on like Ma said you might have."

A knot, seeming to be the size of an apple, formed in Jed's throat. He hugged the little boy to him, wondering at the love he had for the small bundle of manhood; love as strong as that he had for the boy's mother, but different.

After a long moment of just holding the boy close to him, he squatted, settled Tommy on the ground, held him out from him, and looked him in the eye. "Tommy, I promise you something right now; I won't ever ride away from you an' your ma unless one o' you tell me you don't want me around anymore." He spun the little fellow around in his big hands, patted him on his rear, and said, "Now you get on back to the house. As soon's I clean up an' change clothes, I'll come up an' tell y'all what's goin' on. Okay?"

"W-well, all right, sir, if you're sure you ain't gonna jest ride out."

"Tommy, I've already promised, an' no one should ever make a promise unless he figures to keep it. Now you get on up to the house; I'll be there shortly."

Tommy, reluctantly, with several hesitant looks over his shoulder at Jed, went from the stable. Mobley watched him go out the door, the knot in his throat not having shrunk even a little bit. Hell, if Pam wouldn't marry him, maybe she'd let him stick around to take care of her little boy. That thought made him feel a bit better—just a bit.

After Tommy left, Jed searched through his bedroll for a change of clothes, went to the pump, drew a couple of buckets of water, then went to the bunkhouse to bathe, wishing he was cleaning up so he could hold Pam close to him.

Fain took payment for the cattle in cash. He wanted to be able to pay those who would share in the sale, then get on the trail to Coyote.

When he thought of the town in New Mexico Territory where he hoped to settle down, Ruth came to mind for some reason. Now why in the name of tarnation had he thought of that poison-tongued woman?

He mulled that question over a few moments. Well, hell. She wasn't always poison-tongued; fact was, she was soft as a windblown dandelion bloom when he wasn't getting himself in trouble. He mentally shook his head; he couldn't understand her.

But when he did get in trouble, she got upset. But why did that make a difference to her? Nope, he damned sure couldn't understand her. He frowned, and wondered if he understood any female, then realized he had no basis on which to draw a conclusion. The only females with whom he was acquainted were dance hall girls. He shook his head. Dammit anyway.

After supper he went to the saloon, had a couple of drinks, then went to the hotel. The next morning, he met the crew at the depot, checked that they had their gear and were ready to ride.

Before heading out, he frowned, swept them with a glance, and asked, "Y'all got plenty o' rifle cartridges? We might not be as lucky headin' back as we were comin' here." At their nods, he led them out for Tuttle's ranch.

He glanced at the sky, and figured they'd be riding in rain by evening. He shrugged mentally. He'd take the rain over the scorching sun, which was their only alternative. Close to three o'clock, a soft, gentle rain set in.

While shrugging into his slicker, he looked at his men. "Don't gripe, men. We could be gettin' one of those thunderstorms, along with hail, lightning, and twisters." He chuckled. "I'll take this every time." Getting his rain gear on, he toed the stirrup, pulled the slicker out over his saddle to keep it dry, then rode on. He frowned. If the rain didn't get heavier, it wouldn't wash out their horses' tracks, and he didn't have enough men with him to fight off a large party of Indians. He smiled grimly to himself. Hell, he'd fought off pretty good-sized bunches of them when he was alone.

The third day, now into Colorado—they were averaging about forty miles a day by Fain's reckoning—they crossed their first tracks of a band of horses. It was late afternoon. Cord estimated there to be about eight in the band. He

thought that that small a bunch wouldn't attack. Chances
were that his men were better armed than the Indians, if
they were Indians. The soggy earth gave up no clues
whether the tracks were made by shod or unshod ponies.
"Keep your eyes peeled, men. They might join up with another party—*that* could keep us busy, might even spoil our
supper." He was right.

About six o'clock, the clouds made it almost dark. Then,
without warning, a larger group than the eight he'd estimated came over the brow of a hill to their right. They
yelled like demons from hell.

"Stay close, men. Find a buffalo wallow—any kind of
ditch, rein in, pull your horses to the ground, and set up to
fight." It was then that he saw a ditch caused by runoff. His
gut muscles felt as though they'd pull themselves in two.
He headed for it, pulled his Winchester, slipped from the
saddle, jumped into the shallow water onto his stomach,
pulled his horse down beside him, and faced the yelling
demons. His first shot peeled a rider off the back of his
horse; his second dropped one off the side; by then his men
were firing, and two more dropped.

The warrior in the lead held up his hand, and kneed his
pony out of rifle range; the rest followed, then gathered
around him.

A couple of Fain's men got to their knees as if to stand.
"Stay the hell down, men. Look to our backs. They didn't
attack us with that small a band. There's more of 'em
close by."

With those words, Fain twisted, rolled to face the other
side of the ditch, and another party came at them. They appeared as though rising from out of the earth.

Two of his men faced the same direction as did Cord.
They jacked shells into their rifles, fired as fast as they
could pull trigger. Three warriors fell; another pulled his
horse to the side, then fell off the side of his horse into the
mud. Fain dropped one. That bunch also pulled their
horses out of range. "Stay down. They'll come at us again."
Cord yelled only loud enough to make those around him

hear. Then both groups of Indians kicked their horses into an all-out run toward the ditch. Every rifle in the ditch talked to the Indians; four in front of Fain dropped. He glanced over his shoulder to see two more drop from the other band. They all withdrew again.

Fain snorted to get the acrid stench of gun smoke from his nostrils. "They may give it up for today. They've lost a lot o' men. They lose stomach for fightin' when they aren't winnin', but stay down. Anybody hurt?"

He didn't get an answer, so he figured they were all okay. He squinted to see through the murky light. It would soon be black dark. What should they do then? He didn't want to stay in the ditch, but if they didn't, they'd give up what little protection it afforded.

He pondered that problem while watching each band knee their ponies around and ride off. "Don't let them lookin' like they gonna quit fool you, men. They might let it get darker, then come at us again."

As soon as he finished telling his men not to be fooled, he made up his mind. "Tell you what we gonna do. Soon's it gets black dark, get your horses on their feet, then stayin' bunched close to each other, we're gonna lead our horses away from here, bein' damned quiet-like. Now wait'll I give y'all the word. Keep your rifles in hand."

They lay there in the mud for another half hour. Then Fain whispered, "No talkin'. Let's get the horses up an' leave here. Stay close."

Twelve ghostly figures slipped from the ditch. Cord was now even happier that they hadn't had a gully-washer. It would have made their departure more dangerous. The rain having been light, the horses' hooves didn't make a sucking noise when they stepped from their poor fortification. They trekked silently through the darkness, one hour, two hours, then Fain, his voice little above a whisper, told them to climb aboard their horses, that he thought they were through fighting for the night.

"What you mean, 'for the night,' boy? You mean you think they might git after us agin come daylight?" Menendez sounded like he'd had a gut full of Indians to do him the rest of his life.

Cord, even though knowing they couldn't see him, nodded. "Yep, old friend, that's exactly what I mean."

"Damn, boy, when you give yore word, you really mean it."

"What you mean by that?"

"Well, you told yore pa you wouldn't wear a gun, an' I reckon you ain't, but the way you told us what to do when them Injuns hit us, you done fit 'em before—a lot."

"Yeah, reckon you could say that, old-timer, but remember, I told Pa I wouldn't strap on a side gun. Didn't say a thing 'bout not usin' a rifle."

Menendez chuckled. "That's a fact, son, damn if it ain't."

Still talking in little above a whisper, Fain told them they'd ride on through the night; it might put them far enough ahead of the war party that they wouldn't bother chasing them, "But just in case, men, I want every one o' you to keep an eye out for places to hole up. Do this all the while we ride. Pick places at all times close to us. We might not have a chance to make a run for it, 'specially as tired as our horses are."

Hours later, hours that seemed like weeks to Fain, the sky brightened only a little in the east. Rain still fell. The dawning day looked to be one that would stay dark and dreary. Cord sensed that it would fit the temperament of each of his men—but it was a lot better than not having your scalp still sitting firmly on your head.

During the day, he led them around any land swell that might be a place for horses to hide behind; then about noon, he thought they might be far enough from the Indians to look for a place to camp. He discarded the idea that they might be able to find a cutbank in a ravine; with the rain, the ordinarily dry beds would have water flowing in them. "Y'all see a jumble o' rocks, or an escarpment with a hole in the side where we might take the horses in an' hide 'em, we'll make camp. The horses an' all o' us are worn to a frazzle. We gotta get some rest." He chuckled. "Sure is good y'all are so tired; maybe you can sleep with an empty stomach 'cause we won't be able to find buffalo chips, an' sure as hell no wood we could get to burn. It'll all be soggy as a soup-dipped biscuit."

Cookie growled that he wished they hadn't sold the chuck wagon when back in Dodge.

Cord gave him a hard look. "What would you have done with it while the Comanche rode in on us?"

"Ain't give that much thought." He shook his head. "Nope. Reckon they wouldn't of been no place to park it while we fit off them devils."

Fain chuckled. "Now you know why I said we had to get rid of it. Glad we did too."

Another couple of hours, and one of the riders rode back to Cord. "Seen a heap o' rocks out yonder what looked like they'd been piled up by some giant storm. Wanta head fer 'em?"

Cord nodded. "Yeah. Lead the way."

It took them only a few minutes to ride into the jumble of boulders, spread groundsheets, then their blankets, pull slickers over them, and fall into an exhausted sleep. Cord took the first watch; he'd wake somebody to relieve him when he got too sleepy to stay awake.

Jed finished his bath, put on clean clothes, and headed for the ranch house. He'd decided he wouldn't say anything to Pam until after they got settled back into her cabin. He admitted to himself that he was putting off doing what he needed to do for his sake, Tommy's, and Cord Fain's. He shrugged. What the hell, he'd do it in his own sweet time.

When he stopped and raised his hand to knock on the screen door, it swung out almost in his face and Pam stood there. She raked him from head to toe in a searching gaze. "Glad you took time to wash the dirt and dust off a you. Tommy allowed as how he'd smelled wet dogs that smelled better."

Jed chuckled. "From the way that little critter met me, I don't believe he told you anything like that."

Pam came closer, obviously held herself back from stepping even closer, then against him. He struggled to keep from reaching out and pulling her into his arms. She stepped back, held the screen door for him to come on into the house.

When inside, he had no other chance to talk to her. The Tuttle family gathered around wanting to know what was going on at the camp. He grinned. "I'll try to answer y'all's questions one at a time." He took the drink Bob Tuttle held out to him, took a sip, then walked to a chair and sat. "Need to sit. Been kinda busy the last few days." He took another swallow of his drink. "I took Pam's cows over to her place, drove 'em on over to one o' those shallow valleys, an' turned 'em loose."

"Figured that's what you done, Jed Mobley. Tell us 'bout Cord an' his men. What they doin' now that I reckon the brandin's all done?" While Ruth asked the question, Mobley thought she sat there looking as though she wished he'd say Fain would be here in time for supper. He shook his head. "Ma'am, I reckon Cord's got the herd well on its way to Dodge City by now. He'll be back in a little over a month." He placed his glass on the floor at his feet, then turned his eyes to Tuttle. "Said to tell you he'd get back soon so's his cows wouldn't overgraze your range."

Ruth didn't wait for her father to answer. "He's gonna be gone a month?"

Mobley nodded. "Yes'm, it takes a while to drive a herd that far. They gonna make 'bout ten miles a day."

"He gonna come back to the house when he gets back? He better. It'd be downright impolite for him to jest gather his cows an' head 'em toward that New Mexico Territory."

"Ma'am, I reckon Cord Fain'll always do the right thing." He nodded. "Yes'm, he'll come by here, then down to Pam's place, settle up with all of us with the money he figures he's gonna split with us for what he got from the cattle, *then* he'll get along toward his home."

Jed looked at Pam. "I came to take you an' Tommy

home. Reckon Fain's made certain things're safe around
here." He looked at Miss Eve. "Ma'am, I think it'd be a
good idea to wait'll mornin' before I take Mrs. Henders
outta here. Be midnight before we got there if we left
now."

"Why, I should smile, young man. You need a night's
rest, an' Pam'll need to get her things together." She nodded. "'Sides that, I ain't never let nobody leave my home
hungry. Yep. Gonna feed y'all supper, then breakfast in the
mornin', then you can get 'em back to their home."

Jed sighed. That gave him another night, and maybe the
next day, before he had to figure out how to ask Pam to
marry him. He felt like he thought a man would feel if the
judge came up at the last moment and took his head out of
a noose. He stood. "Reckon I'll get on down to the bunkhouse. See y'all in time to leave in the mornin'."

"Sit down, young man. Bob, get the young'un another
drink." Miss Eve turned her gaze back to Jed. "I'm doin'
the cookin' till Mr. Fain brings our cook back. We'll all eat
here in the dinin' room."

Tuttle handed Jed another drink. While taking the drink
from Bob, Mobley became aware that Ruth still stared at
him, seeming to have more questions. He looked at her.
"Ma'am, you have something you want to say?"

She nodded. "Dang tootin' I do. Wantta ask you if you
ever been on any long cattle drives 'cept the one when you
an' Cord drove Taggart's cows up here?"

Mobley wondered what brought that question on. He
nodded. "Yes'm, I been on three drives, one to Abilene an'
two to Dodge City. Why?"

"Jest wonderin' if you figger they's much of a chance for
trouble 'tween here an' Dodge. I'm talkin' 'bout Comanche or Kiowa trouble."

Now Mobley knew why she'd asked; she was worried
about Fain. He'd seen the way she looked at him, and
there was something more than friendship in those looks.
He frowned, then shook his head. "Miss Ruth, I wish I
could tell you that everything out that way is safe. I can't

do that. I never made a drive but what we had Indian attacks."

She didn't say anything else. She shrank back into her chair, her face frozen into an expression of worry, deep lines creasing her forehead, her lips pulled tight against her teeth.

Miss Eve gripped the arms of her rocker, apparently making ready to stand. Pam placed her hand on Ruth's mother's forearm. "Let me. I know exactly what she's feelin' right now. B'lieve I can say the right words to 'er." She spoke softly so that Ruth's mother would be the only one to hear.

Miss Eve looked into her neighbor's eyes a moment, then nodded. "Bless you, Pam."

Pam went to Ruth, held out her hand, and when her friend gripped it, she gently pulled her to her feet. "Let's take a walk."

When they walked from the room, Miss Eve glanced at Jed. "Reckon you know how it is, son. I b'lieve we got two young women here who have found their man. Know it ain't none o' my business, but want you to notice I said *two young women*." She gave a quick nod. "An' from my reckoning, I gotta say them two young men don't know they got a chance with them girls." She sat straighter in her chair, and pinned him with a look that went right through his soul. "Gonna tell you right now, both you men need to get off'n the get go, take them girls for a long walk, an' tell 'em what you feel." She nodded. "Yep, I done also seen how y'all looked at *them*." She cleared her throat, leaned back in her chair, and smiled. "Reckon after them walks you take 'em on, they'll be four right happy young'uns round here."

She speared her husband with a look that defied him to say a word, then put her look into words. "Bob Tuttle, don't you say nothin'. We gonna let them young'uns find their own way."

All of this had taken place only a few days after Cord left to take the herd to Dodge City. Now, a little over a month later, he was almost home.

• • •

The morning after they'd holed up in the pile of boulders, they came awake slowly, crawled from soggy blankets, walked to their horses, threw wet saddle blankets over wet hairy backs, then saddled up.

Fain swept them with a glance. "Don't any o' you men say anythin' till we find some dry wood and make us a fire to fix coffee an' grub. Know none o' us is in any humor to be friendly this mornin', an' we don't need any trouble 'mongst ourselves. Indians or no Indians, the first creek we cross we gonna look for firewood." There wasn't a man there who didn't give him a sour look.

That day, Fain saw scouts watching them from the tops of knolls, buttes, and sometimes out on the relatively flat plains out beyond rifle range—but they didn't close in.

That night he made sure the camp afforded them protection from attack, and most importantly firewood. They'd found a deep cutbank along a creek that, even with the rain, had only a few inches of water in its bottom.

They had their first meal in a couple of days, and despite being worn to a frazzle, their spirits perked up. Cord had brought two bottles of good whiskey with him when they left Dodge; he thought this would be a good time to break them out and have a drink or two.

He figured it best to have a couple of men stand watch throughout the night. The Comanche knew where they were, so he made no effort to keep their fire from being seen. After he had spiked each man's coffee with whiskey, he stood and looked each man in the eye. "I'll stand the last watch before light. We'll have a watch set throughout the night. I figure if they're gonna hit us again, it'll be 'bout first light, an' they'll come at us outta the sun. Y'all be ready, an' if I fire, wait'll you see 'em plainly, then cut 'em down. Don't any o' you stick your neck out. We don't want any dead or hurt heroes."

Only minutes after they crawled into damp blankets, snores could be heard from every man in camp except the man standing watch. Some had draped their bedding over branches, hoping they'd dry out a little, and slept with nothing under or over them but their groundsheets.

About four o'clock, Wash touched Fain on the shoulder. "Time you wuz goin' on watch, pahdnuh. Ain't seen or heard nothing out yonder."

"Didn't figure you would. First we'll see of 'em will be when they come screechin' right at us." Fain tested the air and caught the aroma of fresh-brewed coffee.

Cookie already had the coffeepot on the coals. Wash pulled his cup from his possibles bag and poured himself a steaming cupful. Cord realized his friend would drink his coffee, then watch their backside.

Rather than try to see movement, Fain tuned his ears for the first rustlings of small animals, or birds moving about to start another day. After about an hour of silence, the underbrush came alive with the sounds he expected to hear. Then, with the sun peeking only a sliver above the horizon, the sounds ceased. Cord twisted to look at Wash. "Wake the men. Put half o' them coverin' our back, the other half facin' the way I am."

Without asking what had warned his partner, Wash went to each man and touched him. In only a few moments, the men lay on their stomachs; some had stopped to pour themselves a cup of coffee, and drank it while stretched out, peering over the edge of the creek into the murky light.

Abruptly, the silence became an earsplitting crescendo. Deafening yells, bloodcurdling screams, all melded into the sharp sounds of rifles firing. The Comanche made their attack on foot; something they seldom did—and they were paying a terrible price for it.

Fain's men fired, jacked shells into the chambers of their rifles, and fired again. Almost on the end of Fain's gun barrel, Indians threw up their hands and fell. Two ran over the lip of the stream's bank and fell at Cord's side. Without thinking, he pulled his bowie knife, slit their throats in case they were still alive, jacked another shell into the chamber of his rifle, twisted, and squeezed off another shot into the chest of a warrior who had launched himself over the stream's bank. The rifle fire slackened, almost like a receding thunderstorm; then a deafening quiet fell across the landscape. Now the fear and shakes would start, especially for those who'd never fought Indians before.

Fain rolled to his side, swept his eyes along the row of men on his side of the creek, then glanced at those on the other side. "All right, men. We hurt 'em bad this time. Don't figure they'll try us again. Cookie, go ahead an' fix breakfast. Anybody hurt?"

He got no answer, then fear grabbed him. Those hurt bad enough, or dead, wouldn't be able to answer. He pulled his legs under him and walked to each man, most of them still lying against the creek bank. He touched each man and asked the question. Then he came to Wash. Before touching his partner, he saw the gory mess alongside his head.

Fain dropped his Winchester and went to his knees. He worked his hands under the big man and turned him over gently. Wash still breathed.

Cord ran to his saddlebags, pulled the remains of one of the bottles of whiskey from where he'd stashed it, grabbed a spare shirt, tucked the bottle in his waist, and began tearing the shirt into strips.

He went back to Wash, poured whiskey on a strip of cloth, and sponged at the ragged tear along the side of his partner's head. He glanced over his shoulder, saw Menendez. "Pablo, go to each man, check them over. Wash's hurt. I'll take care of him."

It was then he heard a steady stream of cursing. He glanced to the side and saw Slim Weathers holding his thigh with both hands. They were red with blood. "Somebody take care o' Slim," Fain yelled. "He took one in his leg."

Fain worked on Wash for several minutes, cleaned the wound with whiskey, bandaged it, and made him as comfortable as possible, but the big man still hadn't moved. Fain stared down at his partner. His chest muscles pulled tight against a rib cage that felt like everything inside it was empty, just a big throbbing, hurting void.

He'd seen wounds like this before; there were times when the wounded person stayed unconscious for long periods, then came out of it all right, and there were times when they woke up that they didn't remember anything, not even how to button their shirts—and others never came out of it. Cord squeezed his eyes tight to rid himself of the tears that threatened to flood his eyes, then turned to Slim, who sat drinking a cup of coffee.

He glanced into Slim's eyes. "That slug hit a bone?"

"Naw. Went straight through. Hurts like hell, though."

Fain nodded. "Gonna hurt worse in the next day or two." He looked for and found Menendez. "Anybody else hurt?"

The old *vaquero* shook his head. "Nope. Just the two we done took care of. Figger we wuz lucky."

Cord nodded. "You can lay money on that, *mi amigo*."

Cookie, in a quiet voice, told them breakfast was ready. When all had food in their mess kits, Fain walked among them and told them how proud he was to be their friend. "Most o' you fought in the war, but this's 'bout the first time y'all fought Indians. 'Spect it's a little different."

Menendez growled, "A little different? Hell, Cord, we ain't never seen no screamin' bastards like these." He shook his head. "Shore don't want to ever again neither."

One of the men asked with a mouthful of food, "You fit these devils many times?"

Fain nodded. "More'n I like to think 'bout, cowboy, an' I guarantee you it never gets easier." He glanced over the edge of the creek's bank. The Comanche had not had a chance to carry off their dead, and there were a bunch of them. He estimated they'd lost at least thirty warriors. "Men, soon's we eat an' clean up our mess, we gonna make a couple o' travois to pull Slim an' Wash on, then we gonna get outta here. B'lieve if we give those red devils a chance to take their dead away, we won't have any more trouble."

He stood there a moment, listening to the loud talk, unnecessary, hollow laughter from some, and an eerie quiet from others. He shook his head. It never changed. Men vented their tightly strung nerves after a battle in different ways. His muscles, pulled tight as a bowstring across his back, would probably loosen some by supper time.

16

PAM HELD RUTH'S hand while they walked out past the bunkhouse and on into the cedar breaks a few yards. When finally it became apparent Ruth wasn't going to say anything, Pam stopped and faced her friend. "He's gonna be all right. That man o' yours is one tough *hombre*. I don't b'lieve every danged Comanche or Kiowa out yonder could whip 'im."

Ruth stared into Pam's eyes; then her own eyes flooded, tears spilled down her cheeks, and she threw herself into her friend's arms. "Oh, Pam, I've treated 'im so badly. He don't have no idea how much I think of 'im, a-an' if he gets hurt bad, he ain't never gonna know. I-I reckon I'm jest a mean danged woman who don't know how to treat 'er man. M-maybe if I get another chance, I can show 'im I ain't such a terrible woman after all."

Pam held her friend close to her breast and ran her hand down her back, down her long brown hair, clucking soothing, mostly meaningless words.

When finally Ruth's sobs subsided, Pam held her out at arm's length, and looked at her straight on. "You're not a terrible woman. You're jest filled with so much love you don't know what to do with it." She smiled. "But I'm tellin' you right now when that man says them good words to you, *then* you gonna know danged well what to do with that love, an' it's all gonna be aimed at him. You gonna be all over 'im like a chicken on a June bug."

"S'pose he don't never say them words."

Pam chuckled. "Now you know we done talked 'bout that. If they don't say nothin', *we* gonna say it. Know from watchin' 'em they both wanta tell us what we want to hear, but reckon they, brave as they are 'bout most things, jest ain't got themselves to the point where they figger they can stand the thought we might tell 'em no."

She pulled her apron up and wiped at Ruth's eyes. "Now we gonna go back by the pump, an' you gonna wash your face an' dry your eyes, then we gonna go in an' have a cup o' coffee an' visit some more 'fore Jed Mobley takes me an' Tommy home in the mornin'." She chuckled. "By the time I see you agin, an' Cord's done got home, I'll have told Jed I'm gonna be Mrs. Mobley." They walked a few steps, and Pam again chuckled. "Heck, we might be able to let the preacher man marry both o' us couples at the same time."

A few minutes later, Ruth's face washed, but her eyes red and swollen, they walked into the house. Miss Eve handed her daughter and Pam a drink. "It'll help y'all feel better."

Fain made sure the travois the two wounded men were on were each guided around ruts, holes, anything that would cause the men in them discomfort. Slim swore Cord looked for every prairie dog mound and ravine to drag them across just so they would hurt worse. Wash hadn't opened his eyes.

Cord rode beside his partner every moment, and looked down every few seconds to see if his eyes had opened. Then, late in the second day after the fight at the creek, he heard a groan, then noticed Wash's mouth working as though trying to say something; his eyes were still closed.

Fain stepped from the saddle and, leading his horse, leaned close to his partner. "Damn, Fain, what kinda pop-skull whiskey you feed us last night? Mah haid's bustin' wide open; ain't nevah had such a headache."

Cord's throat swelled, such that he had to swallow several times to try to rid himself of the knot in his throat. His chest felt like it couldn't hold his heart. "Aw, now, partner, your head's gonna get better now. Just don't try to talk. We'll make camp soon's we find a good place an' I'll tell you all that's happened."

"Don't need you tell me what's happened. Know all that. Need a few more hours sleep; get rid o' all that poison whiskey outta mah haid you done give me."

Fain looked across the travois into Cookie's eyes. "Comin' outta it. Find us a place to camp." He smiled. "Wash thinks his headache is from the whiskey he drank the other night." His smile widened to a grin. "We stop an' we can help him get things straight in his mind."

Less than an hour later, Cookie signaled he had a place to camp, and an hour after that he had supper ready. Wash still had not opened his eyes, so Cookie fixed him some broth from a prairie hen one of the men shot earlier in the day.

Fain had the crew make beds for the two wounded men; then he squatted next to the one Wash lay in. He told his partner what had happened, and that now he was on his way to getting well. "We should be to Tuttle's place by tomorrow noon. Get you into a real bunk, an' let you sleep till your headache goes away. That slug plowed a furrow alongside your skull such that I was mighty fearful you might take that long last sleep. Now that you've waked up, you're gonna be all right."

"You tellin' me them Comanche pahted mah hair?"

Fain chuckled. "Yeah, reckon they parted it such that you gonna always have a part where that bullet plowed along your thick skull. Sure glad your head's so hard."

Wash laughed, then groaned. "Ooooh, pahduh, don't make me laugh. Makes mah haid hurt worser."

"Cookie has fixed you some broth. Know you're probably hungry 'nuff to eat a bear, but we gotta see how the
broth rests on your stomach 'fore we feed you solid foods,
stuff that'll stick to your ribs."

"Figger it'll rest right good. Jest try it first."

Despite Wash pleading for *real* food, Cord made him
drink the broth, and while having it spooned to him, the big
black man went to sleep.

The rest ate, then crawled in their blankets. And despite
not having seen any more of the Comanche since the big
fight, Fain posted a watch that night.

They ate breakfast before daylight, and were well on
the way to the Lazy T when the sun eased above the horizon. Fain rode up between the two travois, then glanced
at both men. "Gonna tell you right now. When we get to
the ranch you men're gonna get put in a bunk, an' you
gonna stay there a couple o' days. I'll have the boys
pullin' our herd together, then we gonna head for home—
our own home."

Slim cut in. "Hell, Fain, I don't need no more rest. I'll
help the boys."

Cord shook his head. "Nope. I want you well an' ready
to do a day's work when we leave here."

Slim griped that Fain hadn't taken that kind of time
when he had worse holes in him, but he didn't win that
argument.

Another three hours, and the ranch buildings came in
sight. Fain held the men in a tight bunch while they closed
in on the house. Ruth must have been looking out the window, because when they were still a quarter of a mile away,
she ran from the front door and didn't slow down until
Cord reined in beside her. He held his hand out, she
grabbed it, and he pulled her up behind him.

"How'd them boys get hurt?"

Fain answered her with one word. "Comanche."

"Oh, dammit, I just knew y'all would find trouble—
knew it."

Cord felt her lean back from him and knew she was

checking him over. "No, I didn't take any lead," he said. "Wash did, though. Wish I could've taken it for 'im."

"Cord Fain, you've already taken more than your share. Want you to stay here now till them men get well."

He nodded. "Figured to do just that if my cows aren't eatin' your pa's grass down to the roots."

"Don't care, Cord. Anyway, it's gonna take y'all a few days to get your cattle together so's you can start for New Mexico Territory. You an' the boys can get rested up durin' that time."

Cord chuckled. "You figure roundin' up my herd is gonna be restful?"

She had her arms wrapped around his waist while riding; she tightened her hold on him. "We'll see. You know we still gotta have that talk you promised me."

"Figure to do that right soon if you'll promise not to take my hide off every day." Her hold on him only got tighter.

Mobley and Tommy worked from sunup to sundown every day, and Jed kept counting the days until he thought Fain must be getting mighty close to getting back. He knew he'd put off talking to Pam as long as he could. "'Sides," he muttered to himself, "I never asked anyone to do my talkin' for me, an' Fain sure sounded like he'd try to do just that." He sighed. "Reckon I better say somethin' to her."

That night after supper, sitting at the table drinking coffee, Mobley looked at Pam. "You reckon after we get Tommy to bed you an' I could take a walk? Weather's mighty nice this time o' year."

Pam stared at him a moment. "Yes, Jed, I think I'd enjoy a walk; get outta this cabin for a little bit."

An hour later, the dishes done, Tommy in bed, they stepped out the door. They'd not walked ten steps when Pam, walking as close to him as she could, placed her hand in his. He looked at her, and even in the twilight he thought her the most lovely woman he'd ever seen. "Pam, I have somethin' I need to say to you. Reckon you've noticed Tommy has taken a pretty strong likin' to me, an' I gotta say it isn't a one-sided thing. I love your little boy. He's gonna make one heckuva man." He cleared his throat, which for some reason had caused his voice to get husky. "Well, don't know how you feel 'bout it, but I'd kinda like to stick around an' help 'im to grow up into that kinda man." He stumbled over a small rock. "Well, thought I'd ask. I wouldn't cost you anything 'cept food."

Pam turned his hand loose and moved a few steps from him, then turned to face him. "Jed Mobley, don't see as how I can agree to what you done asked."

Everything was happening the way he thought it would, and now she'd told him no just as he'd feared. His voice now even huskier, he nodded and went on. "Figured you were gonna tell me no. Can't blame you. So don't reckon you'd take kindly to it when I tell you I love you more'n life, an' been so danged scared to even think 'bout it. I couldn't stand to have you tell me no to that too."

Pam stood still as though frozen in place. "What did you say, Jed? Tell me them words agin."

"Hard enough sayin' 'em once, but now that I've said 'em, I reckon I've already braced myself to hear you deny me." He took a deep breath. "I said I love you more than life, want to marry you, want to live the rest o' my life with you, lovin' you, holdin' you, kissin' you."

Pam stood there a moment, then so softly Jed had trouble hearing her, said, "Them's the words I was hopin' to hear. Them's the words I can say yes to, Jed Mobley. Reckon I been lovin' you ever since you first come into my an' Tommy's life." She stepped closer to him. "You reckon it'd be all right if I collected that first kiss you promised I could have so many of for the rest o' my life?"

Before she could say more, Jed pulled her into his arms.

Unashamed tears flowed down his cheeks—and he didn't know whether it was hers or his that made his face so wet. After a long moment, maybe minutes, they pulled apart, breathless. Then, after another few moments, Pam said, "Reckon now I can tell Tommy you ain't never gonna ride away from us."

"If there's anything you can tell 'em, then that'll be right at the top of it all."

Cord got his two wounded men settled into the bunkhouse, asked Bob Tuttle if his range could handle his cows a few more days, and got Tuttle's answer that due to the unseasonal rains the grass could, for several days, handle even more cattle than Fain had on his range. The next morning, after telling the ranch owner he'd come in in about a week and settle up with him before he headed for New Mexico, he rode to the makeshift camp his men had set up to start their gather.

Menendez rode alongside him until he drew rein and stepped from the saddle. "Pablo, want you to take charge of the gather. I gotta go into Trinidad. Got some business to take care of there, an' I'm gonna take Cookie with me. We gotta have another chuck wagon an' get it stocked for the drive to Coyote." He chuckled. "If things go right, I might even buy one o' those Conestoga or Studebaker wagons to drag along."

"Boy, if everythin' goes right', I reckon you're thinkin' o' asking that sharp-tongued filly to marry you?"

Fain looked at his old friend and nodded. "You just might be right. If she'll have me, what you think Ma an' Pa's gonna think o' that?"

Menendez chuckled. "Reckon you could bring home a rattlesnake an' if it meant you wuz gonna stay, they'd be happy as a hawg in slop."

"Well, I'm sure as hell gonna ask 'er. If she says yes, I might sleep in the bunkhouse with you men most o' the time, but the way I got it figured, the rest o' the time would make it worth it."

Menendez stared at him a moment, a slight smile crinkling the corners of his eyes. "Way I got it figgered, once you quit getting in situations where you git shot all to hell, I figger she's gonna quit scaldin' you. Don't figger they's gonna be no bunkhouse sleepin' fer you."

Fain only grunted.

He looked at the roundup area, saw Cookie, and motioned him over. "Want you to go in town with me in the mornin'. Need a new chuck wagon an' to get it stocked for the drive home. Reckon you gonna stay with Bob when I leave here?"

Cookie nodded. "Reckon I will, Cord. He an' Miss Eve seem to like me, even want me to cook for the family. Reckon they might keep me for good."

Cord nodded. "Think you're right, old-timer, but want you to help me with this. Okay?"

As soon as Fain walked away from Cookie with his agreeing to help him this one last time, Menendez pinned Cord with a hard look, one that would take the bark off an oak tree. "You goin' in there to find Taggart, ain't ya?"

Fain shook his head. "Nope, don't figure I'm gonna have to hunt 'im. Figure he's gonna find *me* bad as he hates me." He nodded. "But you're right, if he don't find me, I'm gonna go lookin' for 'im. Don't figure to be sweatin' a bullet in my back the rest o' my life. Think I'll end it right there—one way or the other."

"You ain't gonna let that young filly know you're goin' in alone?"

Cord shook his head, then chuckled. "Hell, no. I let 'er know an' she'd have the whole crew go in with me. We got work to do."

Menendez laughed. "Whoooee. I'd shore like to hear the butt-scaldin' she gives you when she finds out." He shook his head. "Naw, reckon I'd druther be in the next county. Don't never like to see a grown man git beat down to a nubbin by no woman." He shook his head. "Makes me feel downright ashamed to be a man."

Fain gave him a soft punch on the shoulder. "Not foolin'

me, old friend. If you'd found the right woman, you'd have gotten married years ago, butt-scaldin' or not."

Menendez grimaced. "Yeah, Cord, I shore would. Gits kinda lonely without one too." He shrugged. "Don't figger they's one left who'd have me now."

Cord studied his friend a long moment. "Don't bet on it, Pablo. There's a woman waitin' for you somewhere. I'd stake my life on it."

Menendez didn't say anything. He studied his saddle-horn, then looked at Fain. "Want me to go in there with you?"

Cord shook his head. "Nope. This problem is of my own makin'. I'll take care of it alone." He thought a moment. "If Ruth comes out here, just tell 'er I'm out in the cedar breaks."

"That ain't gonna work. She'll ask me which direction you went an' then go lookin' fer you."

Fain chuckled. "It's a big ranch, Pablo. She'll just have to mark it down as lookin' in the wrong places."

That night, Fain cleaned his weapons, oiled his holster, replaced the thong on its bottom, the one he'd tie to his leg if looking to get his Colt free of leather in a hurry. Then, the next morning after eating, he and Cookie rode toward Trinidad.

They rode in silence as men will do in the hours soon after daylight. Finally, Fain felt Cookie staring at him. "What's the matter, Cookie?"

"Well, figger you goin' in there to find Taggart, you gonna need somebody to cover yore back; want you to know I'll be there."

Fain shook his head. "Don't want a stray bullet to get to you. The marshal'll be there to see no one gets at me from that direction."

His voice low, sounding rejected, the old man asked, "You don't trust me to watch out fer you, or you think I'm too danged old to get the job done?"

Fain's head snapped to the side to gaze at the crippled-up

old puncher. He swallowed twice to get rid of the knot in his throat. He'd hurt Cookie's feelings, and he'd rather take a beating than have the old-timer think he was not wanted by the kinds of men he had for many years ridden along-side. "*Mi amigo*, want you to know I'd as soon have you there as any man I know, but you've done your part in fightin' *my* fight, as well as other men's fights on your back-trail." He shook his head. "Just don't want you gettin' hurt."

Fain's words seemed to satisfy Cookie. They rode a little farther before Cookie said, "Most men in our crew, trail crew that is, figgered Taggart as bein' a right fast man. The men what've knowed you most o' your life figger you as bein' one o' the best. Ain't you nervous?"

Fain frowned. "Reckon I oughta be, reckon I might be comes closer to time, but I found long ago that worry, about anything, doesn't get a man anywhere."

Cookie shrugged.

Fain thought about Ruth, then wondered if maybe he should buy enough provisions to set up housekeeping while in Trinidad, but decided against that. Even if Ruth said she'd marry him, there were towns closer to where he wanted to buy his ranch.

They didn't do much talking from then until they made camp that night. Sitting drinking coffee after eating, Cookie shook his head. "Shore wisht you didn't have to do this, Cord. Even when you win—you lose. Ain't good to ever kill a man."

Fain stared into the fire a moment, then looked at the old man. "Know what makes it worse?" Then, not waiting for his friend to answer, he nodded. "Yep, makes it worse 'cause I'm goin' in there knowin' I gotta shoot 'im dead. Never done that, but if I don't, I know I'll never know a moment's peace. Bad's that man hates me, I figure he'd follow me to hell in order to get even."

"You sorry you decided to ruin 'im, cost 'im everythin' he'd set out to do?"

Fain shook his head. "Nope, but I'd been right sorry if I

let 'im get away with what he figured to do." He shrugged. "Uh-uh, I couldn't a lived with myself if I let 'im take somebody's ranch."

They turned into their blankets soon after drinking the last of their coffee. Then the next afternoon, they rode into Trinidad about three o'clock.

Fain got them each a hotel room, gave Cookie a double eagle to buy himself a few drinks while *he* went to see Marshal Tom Worley.

Worley swung his feet off his desk when Cord came in. "Damn, boy, ain't seen ya in 'bout a month. Where you been?"

Fain grinned. "Told you last time I was in town I figured to make that trail drive over to Dodge City. That's been 'bout a month ago." He pulled his mouth down to the side in a crooked grin. "Takes a little time to push that many cows that far."

Worley poured them a cup of coffee. They talked until their first cup was about empty; then Worley pinned Fain with a straight-on look. "You come in here to face Taggart?"

Cord shook his head. "Nope. I came in to see if the man down at the wagon yard's got a used chuck wagon I can buy, an' maybe a Conestoga or Studebaker."

"What you need them for?"

Fain shrugged. "Gotta feed those men I brought in here to help fight Taggart. Gonna go home with 'em, a bunch o' longhorns—an' maybe a wife."

"So that's what you want that prairie schooner for. Who is it, Tuttle's girl?"

"Yeah. Haven't asked her yet, but figure she's gonna say she will. Hell, she has too much fun chewin' on me to let me get too far from 'er."

Worley chuckled. "Wordsworth wrote a poem once, somethin' 'bout what man does to man. He shoulda said what man'll do to himself. You ain't never gonna be able to relax."

Fain's face lost its smile. He looked into the marshal's eyes. "Now I'll answer your question. Reckon there's no way I can avoid facin' Taggart, an' when a man's got a job to do, reckon he just bends his back to it an' gets it done." He nodded. "Yeah, don't see any way to dodge it. If I could, I would."

Worley shook his head. "You're right, Cord. You cain't git outta it. He's been stompin' round town for almost a month now, tellin' anybody who'd listen that if you weren't a coward, he figured to shoot you, gutshoot you."

Fain raised his eyebrows and forced a smile, knowing it showed no humor. "Just goes to show you how a man's temper an' big mouth can get 'im into more trouble than he can get outta—alive."

Worley had been smoking his pipe, and the aroma of the smoke, and the strong coffee, made Fain reach for *his* pipe. The two men sat there smoking. Fain felt they were both enjoying the quiet, and the knowledge they each sat across the desk from a friend. He wondered that his nerves weren't strung tight as a fiddle string. Instead, he felt more relaxed than he had in months, since before Taggart had announced that he figured to take over someone else's land and ranch buildings. After several minutes, he glanced at Worley. "You know which saloon Taggart hangs out in?"

"Yeah. Trail's End, a couple doors down the street. Why?"

Fain raised his eyebrows and his shoulders at the same time, his gesture saying that he really didn't know. Then he decided the reason was that he wanted to have a drink in peace, eat supper, get a good night's sleep, and meet Taggart the next day. He told Worley his reason.

"I ain't never seen 'im in the Alpine. You sayin' you gonna buy me a drink?"

Cord smiled. "Yep, let's go."

The marshal and the cowboy had a couple of drinks, then before Worley went back to his office he extracted a promise from Fain that he'd come tell him before he met Taggart—he wanted to cover his back. He'd chuckled when he said it, saying that he didn't think the trail boss had a friend who would try to get at Cord's back. Then Fain headed for the cafe, a block down the street. He ate, then went to the hotel and to bed.

He lay there long into the night thinking about the coming gunfight. He'd never thought to deliberately face a man without anger prodding him on, or without having been attacked with the hostile one shooting at him. Killing Taggart, if Fain was the lucky one, was not something he wanted to do, but a man did what he had to.

Then his thoughts turned to Ruth. He thought of the times she'd scalded him, and the times she'd been so tender he had to wonder that she was the same girl. Then he wondered how it would be to hold her close to him, feel her body press against him, and her lips on his. He swung his legs over the side of the bed, put a lucifer to the lamp, packed his pipe, and sat on the bed's edge smoking, hardly tasting the smoke he pulled from his pipe. Hell, he had to somehow get his mind off the girl he'd discovered he wanted to live his life with.

He smiled into the room. Bet she'd give me hell if she knew what I been thinking 'bout us. His smile developed into a chuckle. He finished his pipe, lay down, and went to sleep.

The next morning he and Cookie went to the wagon yard, which was located in back of the livery stable a block off the main street.

The liveryman greeted them at the gate. Fain told him the kinds of wagons he looked for, not new ones, but ones that had been well used. "Can't afford to buy either one o' 'em new, but I don't wanta buy any junk heaps either. You got anythin' like what I just told you?"

"Chuck wagon's gonna be harder to find in that bunch I got parked here than the kinda wagon you're lookin' for to put yore family in." The livery man made a sweep with his hand to take in the wagons parked there. "A few folks got this far, set up a business, an' sold, or give me, their wagons. Too, not many trail herds come through here, an' those that do keep right on a-goin' up the trail. I got only one chuck wagon."

Fain looked out over the lot, and thought he could do business with the man without getting robbed; fact was, he, his bride, and his crew would make do without either kind of wagon if it looked like the man wouldn't talk turkey.

A half hour later, Cord owned both a chuck wagon and a Studebaker. The Studebaker needed new canvas on its hoops; the chuck wagon was in good shape except for a split axle. The liveryman promised to have a new axle installed, as well as new canvas on the Studebaker. Then, Fain bought one four-hitch team and one two-hitch team of mules to pull the wagons.

That business taken care of, he went with Cookie to the general store, told the proprietor to stack whatever Cookie bought, that he'd come by later, pay for it, then load it and take it away. He looked at Cookie. "Gonna go see Worley, I'll see ya when you get through shoppin'." He grinned. "Be sure to put some canned peaches in those things you buy. Might have to feed Ruth some as a peace offerin'." He frowned, shook his head, and grinned. "Then too, I might wear one o' those cans 'longside o' my head."

Cookie laughed and slapped his thigh. "You takin' bets on that, I'll bet on the side o' yore haid."

"Ain't takin' bets either way." He turned to walk away, then turned back. "Better buy some chewin' an' smokin' tobacco for the crew. Get plenty, don't know how they're fixed for either one. They haven't been in town for a while."

When Fain walked from Cookie, he felt worried eyes on his back.

He went from Cookie to Worley's office. Inside, he poured

himself a cup of two-day-old coffee, looked at his friend, and nodded. "This's it, Tom. Don't wanta drag you into this, but if you insist, reckon we better get at it."

Worley nodded.

17

Worley eased his Colt in its holster to make certain it came out smoothly, then went to the gun rack and took down a twelve-gauge Greener, broke the action, and shoved in two fresh shells. A scattergun was never wasted insurance when he might have to control more than a couple of people.

While the marshal made sure he had the proper weapons, Fain pulled his Colt .44, removed the cartridges, and slipped in fresh ones, then gently dropped the handgun into its holster, and made a couple of practice draws. Worley had finished his task and stood watching.

"Do-diddly-damn, boy, ain't nobody ever told me you wuz fast. They couldn't of told me you wuz *that* fast noway; I jest flat wouldn't of b'lieved 'em."

"It's not anything I'm proud of, Tom. It's a skill I developed as a boy; then Pa made me promise to not ever wear a gun unless I couldn't get outta whatever trouble I was in. Reckon the time's come when I can't get outta it."

"Yeah, Cord, I'd say this's the one time you gotta buckle it on. Taggart's been makin' 'is brag for over a month now. He ain't gonna let it go without facin' you."

Fain lifted his Colt once again, and let it into its holster real easy. He looked at Worley. "Well, let's go see if he can back up his brag."

It was then that he became aware that his stomach felt like an empty void, his neck and shoulder muscles tightened to the point of pushing pain into his head. He studied on his feelings a moment. Was he afraid? Was the possibility that he'd never see Ruth again sitting at the back of his mind and giving him this feeling, a feeling he'd never experienced?

He thought back to his Indian fights, and couldn't remember feeling like this. He mentally shook his head. This wouldn't do. He had to relax. He took several deep breaths, let them out slowly, forced Ruth from his mind, then centered his thoughts on the big brute of a man he would face.

He wondered what weapon his ex–trail boss would choose: fists, knives, or guns? He allowed himself a slight smile. Taggart would choose guns, if for no other reason than he thought Cord to be a neophyte where weapons were concerned, thought he would have a distinct advantage if he chose handguns. Fain took another couple of deep breaths before stepping out the door with Worley.

The marshal slanted him a worried look. "You nervous, boy?" At Cord's nod, he shook his head. "Relax. Ain't gonna do fer you to go into nothin' like this with your nerves *an'* muscles tied up in knots."

Fain cast him a slight smile. "B'lieve I'm not 'fraid o' dyin'." He shrugged. "Reckon what I'm nervous 'bout is losin'. Don't reckon I ever lost at anythin' before, anythin', that is, that I made up my mind I had to win." He shook his head. "Don't reckon I ever been in any game where the stakes were so high."

While they walked to the saloon, Worley reached up and squeezed Cord's shoulder. "Just concentrate on Taggart, nothin' else. I'll have the rest o' the room under my scattergun."

They'd reached the boardwalk. When they stepped up on the splintery surface, Worley turned loose of Fain's shoulder. "Wait a couple o' minutes. I'm goin' round to the back. I'll be in there when you come in."

Fain nodded, and stepped to the side of the doors to wait for the marshal to get to the back and inside. He waited for what he thought would be long enough, then pushed the batwings open, stepped inside, and slipped to the wall to wait for his eyes to adjust to the dim light of the room.

He stood there for several minutes; then, when he could plainly see Worley standing at the back of the room, he sucked in another deep breath. When he let it out, a cold calm came over him. His nerves and muscles relaxed at the same time. His senses sharpened. He could separate the smells of stale beer from the stench of cheap cigars. His hearing picked up the sounds of poker chips at the back of the room.

He swept the room with a glance, and at first failed to see Taggart; then he looked again. The trail boss sat at a back table, hunched over, looking into an empty glass. Then, apparently looking for a girl to bring him another drink, he looked up, straight into Fain's eyes. He carefully placed his glass back on the table and stood. He took a couple of steps farther into the room toward Cord.

"Well, well, the milksop's done made a mistake. Bet you wouldn't of come in here if you'd knowed I wuz here." His head pulled down into his shoulders and he took another step toward Fain. "What'd you do with my cattle?"

The tall cowboy shot Taggart a slight smile, only the corners of his eyes crinkling. "Didn't know *you* had any cattle, Trail Boss. Me an' my men *found* some: a whole bunch o' cows, steers, bulls grazin' on a man's grass. That man denied any claim to 'em.

"We searched around other close-by ranches, an' none o' them had any claim to those cows, so we rounded 'em up, drove 'em to Dodge City, an' sold 'em for a right nice chunk o' change."

Taggart's face reddened such that Fain thought he'd burst a blood vessel. Veins stood out at his temples and on his forehead. A vein in his neck thickened until it stood out as big as Fain's little finger. "Them wuz my cows. You stole 'em."

Cord shook his head. "Naw, now. You must be mistaken. The owner of the ranch we found 'em on told us we could use his trail brand, a Lazy T. We used it, an' got no contest outta them buyers in Dodge."

Fain stood there, surprised that he enjoyed this cat-and-mouse game he played with the bull of a man. His voice hardened. "Now I'm gonna tell ya somethin' you should a known bein' here in the West. What I'm gonna tell ya is, you just accused me o' stealin' cows. Figure I got every right to blow your brains out, what little brains you got, that is, but I'm gonna give you a chance to see if you can whip me with your fists, or with knives, or with handguns. You make the choice."

A canny gleam showed in Taggart's eyes. Fain knew he'd put the right idea into the bully's head. He'd choose guns, primarily because he'd never seen the tall cowboy wear a gun until recently, and probably thought it would be a cinch to kill him.

"You give me my choice? Hell, I been figgerin' all along to shoot you when I seen ya. So, I notice the milksop's done buckled on a side gun." His right hand splayed close to his holster. "Anytime you ready, milksop."

Fain shook his head. "No. I don't want any question about whether it's self-defense. Go ahead." Then wanting to make Taggart even angrier: "After I kill you, I'm gonna live high on the hog spendin' all that money I made on those cattle."

Taggart's hand swept for his pistol. He was fast—very fast. Fain waited until the man facing him had his gun on the way out of leather, then almost lazily pulled, fired into the big man's chest, thumbed back the hammer, fired again, and a second little black hole appeared next to the first one. They both leaked red.

Taggart, his eyes wide with surprise, disbelief, and even more, anger, took a step backward with each slug's force, then stepped toward Fain, trying to get off a shot. No lead spewed from his handgun. He took both hands and squeezed the grips. His thumb slipped weakly on the gun's hammer. Two fingers inside the trigger guard tried to pull the trigger, but obviously couldn't muster the strength. Fain stared into the beefy man's eyes, eyes that at first showed disbelief, then terror, then a fading awareness of what had happened to him.

Fain squeezed the trigger of his Colt again. This time his shot centered into Taggart's gut. "You crooked bastard, you learned your lesson too late. You shoulda learned long ago if you want anythin' worth havin', you gotta *work* for it."

Taggart bent at the waist, his handgun rolled around his trigger finger, then slowly he fell. His gun hit the floor first, then his face plowed sawdust, spit, spilled beer, and dirt ahead of it when it hit the floor. His face pushed the filth ahead of his body. His hand groped to try to again grasp his gun, but he jerked once, then again, and lay still.

Fain swept the room with a glance. "He got any friends in here?" Dead silence answered his question. He nodded. "Then I reckon I'll have a drink." He looked at the bartender. "Pour two; one of 'em's goin' to my friend the marshal back yonder." It was only then that the men in the room came out of their shock at what they'd seen. The room exploded with noise.

Worley walked up to claim his drink. He had a strange look crinkling his forehead, his eyes squinted, his mouth pulled down at the corners. "Why didn't you tell me how good you were?" His eyes still squinted, he shook his head. "Hell, you didn't need me here, you coulda took on the whole room."

Fain still gripped his Colt in his right hand. He picked up his drink with his left, tilted the glass, and knocked the raw whiskey back. He held his glass out for another. "Tell you how it is, Tom. A man's gun-quick isn't somethin' he brags about." The bartender put his drink in his hand. Cord shook his head. "'Sides, I been told by more'n a few men how fast Taggart was." He shrugged. "I didn't know whether I could beat 'im."

Worley knocked his drink back, and Fain motioned the bartender to fill it. "Son, I'm gonna tell ya. I never seen a man who I thought could beat the draw—an' shootin'—I seen a few minutes ago."

Men throughout the room talked of the draw they'd only a few minutes ago seen—but none came close to Fain to slap him on the back or offer him a drink. That didn't surprise Cord; right now they'd be worried about getting close to him, leery of accidentally offending him. Besides, he knew none of them. "Marshal, let's go over to your office and talk 'bout whether what I've done, not only killin' Taggart, but the cattle problem, as well as the Eastern company what might claim 'em, is within the law."

"Got somethin' to do first." Worley walked to Taggart's side, squatted, stripped his trousers back, and removed the money belt from his waist, then went through his pockets, pulled out a Bull Durham sack, tossed it aside along with roll-your-own papers, pulled a pocket knife and change from another pocket, stood, looked at the bartender, and said, "Get 'im buried. I'll pay for it outta what he had in on 'im."

Worley turned toward the door. On the way, the grim look slid from his face, only to be replaced by a smile. "We don't have a problem. I sent a letter soon after I figgered you taken off for Dodge with the herd. Told 'em Taggart figgered to steal the herd, but most o' his men deserted 'im without bein' paid, an' the cattle scattered over all this part o' Colorado. That them cows b'longed to anybody who rounded 'em up an' drove 'em to market. Done got a letter back on it. What you done"—he grinned— "an what I done is jest flat out legal. So ferget it. I'll send 'em what's left o' the money they sent Taggart."

Fain took one of the bottles he'd bought for the crew to Worley's office; they had a couple drinks out of it, then Cord headed for his room.

He thought to take a nap. He felt empty, numb, drained

of all emotion, all feeling. On the way, while crossing the dusty street, he unbuckled his gunbelt, wrapped it around his holster, and carried it with him like that.

When in his room, he stuck gun and gunbelt in his saddlebag. He decided he'd not wear it again unless he or his loved ones were threatened. Wearing a gun invited toughs and white trash to pick fights with you. He figured he could find enough trouble without inviting it to his doorstep—especially if Ruth said yes—then he'd have all the trouble he could handle. Now he better see what she thought of the idea.

He decided he'd better tell Cookie they'd head for the ranch the next morning. Too, maybe the people at the general store hadn't gotten the chuck wagon loaded, and he could help.

He found the old puncher behind the store, almost through with getting things arranged in the wagon so whoever cooked for Fain's outfit on the way to Coyote would be able to find things easily.

After he'd checked on whether Cookie needed help, he noticed the old man staring at him. "You done it, boy?" He shook his head. "Never figgered you wouldn't git the job done. Knowed all the time from what the boys what work fer yore pa told me you could take care o' 'bout any gun-totin' bully."

Fain nodded. "Yeah, old-timer, I took care of it—but it's not somethin' I'm proud of. He just flat wouldn't have it any other way. Gonna go to the room now an' take a *siesta*. See ya in the mornin'."

The liveryman had not yet finished getting the Studebaker canvas replaced. Cord told him that he'd be around to hitch the team about noon the next day. The man nodded. "Good. I'll have 'er finished by then, an' if I got time I'll hitch the team for you."

The next day, Fain and Cookie ate lunch at the cafe across the street from the hotel, then went to the livery. The Studebaker was ready to travel. Cookie had left the chuck wagon there for the man to watch until he and Cord came for the ones they would drive. They tied their horses to the tailgate of the prairie schooner and pulled out of town.

Before leaving town, Cord had told Cookie they would drive late that night so they could reach the ranch by sundown of the third day. He allowed them that much time because the wagons would be a lot slower than horseback.

Ruth had been out to the herd and found that Fain wasn't there. Menendez had given her an evasive answer as to Cord's whereabouts. She had ridden back to the ranch with the feeling that the *vaquero* had been a little less than truthful, but she couldn't call him a liar, because she was certain he really *didn't* know where Cord was. Every evening about sundown, she'd listened for the sound of a horse approaching, but by the sixth day since he'd headed out to round up his cattle, she'd not seen him.

She knew he was a man of his word from the weeks she'd gotten to know him; and they'd still not had their talk. He'd come to the ranch, he'd said, and he'd settle up with those he figured had a slice of what he'd gotten for the herd. Too, they *would* have their talk. She decided she'd talk to him if she had to do it right in front of her family and his crew.

That night after dark, the clank of trace chains and the creak of wagon wheels came to her from down by the stable. She frowned. That couldn't be Cord; he didn't have a wagon, and besides, it sounded like more than one. She stood to see what the sounds might mean.

"Sit, girl. You don't know who that might be. I'll check on it an' see what it is." Her father stood, pulled a Winchester from the gun rack, and headed for the door. Despite her father's words, she followed him to the porch. Before either of them could step to the ground, Fain walked to stand at the bottom of the steps, the lamplight from the doorway bathing him in its soft glow.

"Drove my wagons to the stable, Bob. Hope it's all right. Cookie's gonna un-hitch the teams for me." He held a bottle in his right hand. "Figured we might have a drink while I tell ya all that's happened."

"You been to Trinidad, ain't ya?" Ruth knew her voice sounded scared, and weak, and didn't care. Anger at the thought of what must have happened in the town, and that Cord hadn't had anyone with him, drew her eyes to study his tall frame. She couldn't see him plainly. "Come on in the house, Cord, an' tell us what damn fool thing you went an' done now." Her voice came out a little breathless.

"Reckon I can tell y'all better if I got a drink in my hand." He chuckled. "Figure I'm set up to get scalded again. Seems there isn't any way I can ever have a talk with you without already bein' in the fryin' pan."

"Come on in," Ruth and her father said at the same time.

Inside, a drink in his hand, Fain looked at Miss Eve. "Ma'am, I brought your cook back. Know you'll be pleased for 'im to give you a bit o' rest outta the kitchen."

Then, tongue in cheek, a slight smile crinkling the corners of his eyes, he shifted his eyes to Ruth. "Know it won't make much difference to Ruth; she probably doesn't spend much time in the kitchen anyway, probably tryin' to dodge her ma tryin to teach 'er how to cook."

"Changin' the subject ain't gonna work, Cord Fain," Ruth said. "Know you've went an' done some dumb thing, an' I want to hear 'bout it right now."

Ignoring her statement, Cord looked at Tuttle. "I figure the roundup's 'bout finished. My cattle hadn't scattered very far from where we left 'em after the brandin', what with the grass greenin' up like it is, so if you'll give me a couple more days on your grass, I'll drive outta here." He knocked his drink back and stood to pour another; after all, it was his whiskey, so he felt free to drink whatever he wanted of it.

Before her father could answer about the couple of more days, Ruth's eyes squinted toward Cord's waist. "You ain't wearin' your six-shooter. You figger Taggart's not gonna attack you here?"

Fain, feeling the blood surge to his head, held the sting-
ing reply he was about to make and again looked at Tuttle.
"About the extra days, Bob, you figure your range can
stand them?"

Tuttle nodded. "With all the rain we've had, the grass is
putting on new growth." He shook his head. "Heck, no.
Even a week more wouldn't hurt anything."

Fain nodded. "Good. Now if you'll lend me a puncher to
ride over to Mrs. Henders' place an' bring her, Tommy, an'
Mobley over here, I figure to settle up with all o' you at the
same time; then I can get outta your way."

"Ain't in my way, son, never have been." Tuttle took a
swallow of his drink, then nodded. "'Sides that, I done told
you that whatever you got in mind 'bout givin' me, ferget
it. Jest havin' my ranch back, an' bein' able to live a normal
life, is worth more than any money."

Fain smiled. "We'll talk 'bout that in the mornin'." He
looked at Ruth. "Now I'll answer your question." He nodded. "Yep. I figure Taggart won't attack me here."

She opened her mouth as though to say something about
his comment. Before she could say anything, Cord continued. "I went to Trinidad. Didn't want any o' my men, or
yours, Bob, to back me. Tom Worley was the man I wanted
at my back, and he was there." His voice hardened, his face
felt like dried mud. He swept them all with a glance. "I
shot—killed Taggart three days ago. Didn't want to, but he
wouldn't let it go. Reckon he hated me bad enough he
didn't give a damn 'bout anythin' else." He gave them a
hard grin. "Too, reckon he figured he had me at a disadvantage; figured he was a lot better'n me with a handgun
since he never saw me wear one long's I rode for 'im.
Shows how wrong a man"—he looked directly into Ruth's
eyes—"or a *woman* can be." He took another swallow of
his drink, chuckled, then shrugged. "What you see isn't always what you get."

Ruth's mouth pulled into a straight slit; her eyes sparked
blue fire. "Knowed it all the time. Knowed you wuz gonna
do some fool thing alone. You don't never want help with

anythin', seem to think ain't nothin' you cain't do better'n anybody. It ever enter yore hard head he mighta killed *you*?"

Fain nodded. "Yes'm, reckon that did figure in it, but it was somethin' I had to do, an' didn't want anybody else gettin' hurt on my accord."

The fire went from her eyes; her shoulders slumped. "Glad you come through it, Cord." She shook her head. "Don't know what I'm ever gonna do with you."

He chuckled. "Well, I got some ideas 'bout that." He stood, then pinned her with a gaze. "Reckon it's time you an' me took that walk we been talkin' 'bout for some time now."

Her eyes opened wide. Her lips trembled. She stood. "Been waitin' for you to say it wuz time, Cord Fain. I been ready longer'n you'd believe."

Tuttle gripped the arms of his chair, looked ready to stand, but Miss Eve shot him a stare that could penetrate granite. "Sit still. Don't say nothin', Mr. Tuttle."

He sat back, his jaws clamped tight as a vise, if the knots at the back of them showed any indication of the effort it took for him to obey his wife.

Ruth walked to Cord's side. He took her arm and walked toward the door.

Outside, she reached for his hand and held it while they walked a distance from the house; then she turned to face him. "What you gotta talk to me 'bout, Cord? If we ain't gonna talk 'bout the same thing, reckon I got things to say too."

"Well, Ruth, reckon I gotta find out somethin'; you reckon it'll ever get so's you won't bite my head off every time I see you?"

By now his eyes had gotten used to the dark, and he saw her shake her head. "Don't reckon I can stop long's you keep puttin' yoreself in places where you might get hurt.

"It ain't like I'm ever mad at you; it's that I get so scared, worried, I reckon my feelin's just come out in sharp words—words I don't mean like they sound." She lowered her head, and so softly Fain had to lean closer to hear, she said, "Reckon I care so much, I'd rather get hurt myself than to have you hurt."

"How much carin' is that, Ruth?"

She stood back, and even though he couldn't see the fire in her eyes, he knew it was there. "Oh, damn you, Cord Fain, you gonna make me say it 'fore you ever say a word, ain't ya?"

He reached for her shoulders, pulled her toward him, and she came willingly. Then, his face close to hers, he murmured, "No, my sweetheart, I'm gonna say it first. I love you. Then I'm gonna ask if you care that much for me."

"Oh, Cord, you know you didn't have to ask that. I been showin' you ever' which way I knowed how without jest flat throwin' myself at yore feet an' beggin' you to show me, even a little bit, that you could maybe put up with me—for life."

"You sayin' I gotta borrow another one o' your pa's hands to go to Trinidad an' bring back a preacher man? You sayin' you gonna marry me?"

She pulled back from him. "Reckon I gotta be asked right proper 'fore I say yes, an' I'm tellin' you right now I'm sure gonna say yes." He pulled her to him. After a kiss that was as wild and giving as he'd thought it would be, she laughed, as happy a sound as he'd thought it would be. "Man, Cord, I ain't had no practice doin' that, but it seems we did right good at it. You think so too, Cord?"

He chuckled. "I can't say I've had any practice at it myself"—he nodded—"but I will say this. If it gets any better than that, I don't think I could stand it."

She laughed, hugged his arm to her breast, and shook her head. "Ooooeee, this's gonna be one helluva marriage. Let's go tell the folks."

"Better let me ask your pa if he'll say I can ask you. Reckon that's the way it's s'posed to be done."

"Nope. We'll let Ma take care o' him."

Miss Eve *did* take care of the situation—while Bob Tuttle drank the rest of Fain's bottle.

Two days later, Fain had given Jed and Pam the money from their share of the cattle sale, tried to get Tuttle to take a share and been refused; the preacher had tied the knot between Fain and Ruth, and Jed and Pam, then almost as soon as they'd been allowed to kiss the brides, Ruth raked Fain from head to foot. "You ever gonna buckle on yore Colt agin?"

Cord laughed, then swallowed it and shook his head. "Only to protect me from you, honey, an' from what I've seen, it won't only be 'cause you're mad at me." He frowned, then shook his head. "Don't reckon I want to be protected from you if you're not mad at me, maybe if you're just gonna attack me from wantin'." He nodded. "Reckon we both gonna need protectin' in that case."

TIN STAR
Edited by Robert Randisi

New tales of the West by...
Elmer Kelton • Loren D. Estleman
Frank Roderus • Ed Gorman • and others...

In the Old West, men from all walks of life
wore the fabled "Tin Star"—the badge of a
lawman. From legendary sheriffs and
marshals, to ever-vigilant Pinkertons and
railroad detectives, each story in this unique
anthology revolves around the badges
those men wore—and the bravery
behind them.

0-425-17405-0